The
ROSE
VILLA

LEAH FLEMING found her true
calling as a storyteller after careers in
teaching, catering, running a market
stall and stress management courses
in the NHS, as well as being a mother
of four. She lives in the beautiful
Yorkshire Dales but spends part of the
year marinating her next tale on her
favourite island of Crete.

leahfleming.co.uk
@LeahleFleming

LEAH FLEMING

The
ROSE
VILLA

An Aria Book

First published in the UK in 2022 by Head of Zeus Ltd,
part of Bloomsbury Publishing Plc

9 7 5 3 2 4 6 8

A catalogue record for this book is available from
the British Library.

ISBN (HB): 9781801108799
ISBN (XTPB): 9781801108805
ISBN (E): 9781801108775

Typeset by Divaddict Publishing Solutions Ltd

Printed and bound in Great Britain by
CPI Group (UK) Ltd, Croydon CR0 4YY

Head of Zeus Ltd
5–8 Hardwick Street
London EC1R 4RG
WWW.HEADOFZEUS.COM

With thanks to
the HOPE FOR TOMORROW FOUNDATION
Bringing Cancer Treatment Close to Home

Chapter 1

Riviera, France
December 1918

Flora Garvie stood on the cliff top gazing down at the Mediterranean, glimmering like frayed silk. The daylight was fading now as the sun set over the horizon.

'For heaven's sake, Flo, don't stand so close to the edge,' warned Maudie Wallace, hovering behind her. Her friend meant well by visiting so soon, but Flora needed space to be alone with her grief.

'I'm fine, don't fuss,' Flora snapped. 'Isn't it beautiful? So blue, so calm, and the sun is like a golden ball.' The lightness and colours soothed her dry eyes but she felt thirsty. The stash of sedatives she had hoarded gave her dreamless sleep, helping to calm her spirit, but they also dried her mouth.

Maudie strode ahead along the path to the beautiful villa with its pink sugar-almond stucco walls and pretty terrace draped with foliage, now a convalescent home for sick nurses and other medical staff.

I must be getting better, Flora thought as they walked back to the villa. Colours were brightening, no longer dull and grey. Even at this time of year, the villa was full of sunlight, with its open windows, lush oriental carpets and the kind of antique furniture seen only in the best houses in Glasgow. Her bedroom was palatial, with an en-suite bathroom with a roll-top bath. The December warmth was comforting to the invalids. It was as if the war had touched nothing here; only the odd sightings of crippled men with sticks staggering out on their constitutional and a posse of basket chairs catching the last rays of daylight served as a reminder. As she sat amongst the last of the bougainvillea, her former life seemed like a far-off dream. It filled her with guilt to think that other nurses must be taking her place while she was surrounded by such luxury. She must return north so some other worn-out VAD could experience this, too. The worst cases stayed here for weeks or months and sometimes their next posting would be a suitable asylum or discreet home for broken nurses whose hold on reality slipped away into a nightmare of hallucination or self-harm.

That could have been me, she sighed, but for the eagle eyes of Sister and the MO. Exhaustion from night and day duty on the ambulance trains takes many forms. In her case the inability of her septic finger to heal had weakened her very core. Now from her balcony she stared out over the bay, empty of all feeling. Where was the girl who had been so full of hope and energy? She slouched against the cushions of her lounger. *I feel like a sick war horse.* The memory of those deserted beasts, left to rot or shot by the sides of the railway tracks, haunted her. Why am I feeling so useless?

Flora lay back in the chair, the walk back along the cliff path had exhausted her. She must fight this sloth and find the fighting spirit lost somewhere in the hospital tents of Flanders.

An hour later she was woken by a knock. 'Only me!' Maudie shouted. 'Time for afternoon tea.'

It was good of Maudie to give up some of her precious leave to come here to chivvy her up. She'd found a smart *pension* close by and was in no hurry to head home. 'Had a letter from my chum, Olive. She's coming down to join us. Won't that be fun?'

Flora nodded more out of duty than enthusiasm. Trust Olive Buckle to barge in on their reunion but it would be mean to deny Maudie's chum some Riviera sunshine.

'And talking of fun, there's a notice downstairs inviting you to a musical soirée at the officers' hotel up the road tonight. We are their guests, sounds rather jolly. All the nurses were deciding what to wear, until Matron announced it was strict uniform code. Come along, they've got some super pastries in the Conservatory.'

'I need a bath,' Flora replied, knowing she was not ready to join the others yet.

Sinking into the warm tub, sprinkled with perfumed bath salts, was one of the most luxurious ways to relax. After years of hospital stink, washing in freezing tents, never feeling clean, this was a time to shut out the world and soak away the glums. She loved the privacy, the scents of vanilla, rose and lavender. She dunked her hair, rinsing it with a cold tea and rosemary concoction, drying it as best she could. Now it was cut shorter it dried quicker but still must be hidden under her cap.

Maudie had made herself at home. Being a senior nurse now, she knew just how hard their lives had been. Flora dressed quickly and went to join Maudie, finding her scoffing some nibbles laid out on the drawing room table.

Flora had found eating difficult when she first arrived, used as she was to skipping meals and snacking on the run. Now she was tasting flavours again, feeling the sensations at the back of her throat without gagging. She was looking forward to a large glass of Bordeaux with their evening dinner. Her appetite was returning at last; the sea air, the view, the rest calming her troubled spirit.

Chapter 2

The concert party consisted of a violinist, an accordion player and a pianist playing some ragtime music, thumping out the rhythm on a grand piano. Toes were tapping, as it was music for dancing, but rules were strict. No fraternising with nurses in uniform, and Matron was keeping a wary eye on her girls.

There was a festive air because it would soon be the first Christmas since the Armistice. Flora searched the room for familiar faces from ambulance trains, but most of her former patients had been too sick and had returned to Blighty.

The usual smoky fug was wafting like mist and there was still a tinge of hospital in the hotel corridors. This was a convalescent home, like the Rose Villa, with a sense of weariness, masked by false jollity, too-loud laughter. The pianist stood up to let someone else tinkle the ivories and then a lone voice croaked a rendition of 'Loch Lomond'.

By yon bonnie braes and by yon bonnie banks
Where the sun shines bright on Loch Lomond.

Where me and my true love will ever wont to gae…

They all joined in the chorus:

Ye'll tak the high road and I'll tak the low road…

The singer was slightly out of tune but emotion swelled up in Flora as she thought of home outside Glasgow. She couldn't see the soloist. He must be from one of the Scots regiments. When he finished, they all cheered. 'Well done, Padre.'

The crowd parted to reveal a tall man with a crop of auburn hair who now turned away, embarrassed at this attention.

'Good Lord, look who it is!' Maudie made to rush to greet him, but Flora held her back.

'Not now.'

'Why ever not?' Maudie shook off her hand. 'Kit Carlyle, how good to see you!'

'Miss Wallace, what are you doing here?'

'Visiting Flora Garvie in the nurses' villa… Where she's got to now…'

Flora was already disappearing into the crowd in the dining room surrounded by nurses filling their plates. She didn't want to see Kit, not yet. He was too close a reminder. He was Fergus's friend not hers. He was a ghost from the past. But there was no hiding place and Maudie was pushing Kit forward to follow her. 'Isn't this wonderful; a "kent face". Of all the places to greet one of our very own. How are you?' Maudie laughed.

He was staring at Flora with those piercing blue-grey eyes she recalled so well.

'Maud says you have been unwell,' he said, with that concerned padre look she recognised so well from innumerable hospital visits.

'Fine now, and you?'

'Oh, just a bout of this influenza, left a bit of muck on my chest. They think the sea air will straighten it out.' The schoolboy who had thrashed them all at tennis at Kildowie House was gone. In his place was a man with sunken cheeks, a scar on his cheek, hair greying at the temples and heavy-looking eyes. 'Glasgow seems a long way away. I did get back once. Did you? Are your family well?' he said.

Flora sensed the effort to be polite. 'I had no chance to get back.' That was a blatant lie. How could she face her family after her brother was killed?

'It was unsettling to see life going on as normal,' Kit added. 'Where are you both stationed?'

'I was in a base hospital but Flora was on the trains, weren't you?' Maudie replied. 'Must grab some grub before it vanishes,' she said, determined to leave them alone.

'I thought I saw you once on a train after the push at Amiens,' Kit whispered once they were alone.

'Yes, it was me and I recognised you on the platform trying your best to get a stretcher case on to the train.' Flora saw his eyes give a warning as Maudie began to advance back in their direction.

'Does she know it was her brother I was trying to help?'

'No, and she won't from me. She took comfort in your letter.'

7

'How hard it is to tell the real truth to relatives. Why have they sent you down here?'

'Like you, a bout of something nasty that wouldn't heal and I was able to escort some other sick nurses here.'

'How good to see someone from home.' His hand reached out to touch her, but she quickly stepped back, changing the subject. 'How is Muriel Armour-Brown?' She was the minister's daughter he had been walking out with.

'Fine, the last time I heard from her. She's busy in the church.' An officer barged in between them. 'I say, Padre, let's have another sing-song and get the girls to join in.'

Kit ignored him, his eyes never leaving her face. 'Are you here for long?'

'Not sure,' she replied.

'Come on, you two, if you talk any longer, Matron will be on to you. She's been hovering in the doorway. Come and join the feast.'

'Not hungry.' Flora paused to shake Kit's hand. 'Nice to meet you again. Glad you recovered when so many didn't.' Flora found herself retreating, pausing only to speak to Matron. 'The padre was one of my late brother's best friends. Only two of them have survived. There was so much to catch up on.'

Why was she making excuses for a casual conversation? Why was seeing him so unsettling? Kit was from the past, from those golden days before war tore everything apart. If only he were Fergus…

When the concert was over, Kit stood out on a balcony smoking his last cigarette while dawn crept slowly into the darkness and the first orange light rose from the sea. He hadn't slept; too much booze, too many people. The singing had forced the last dregs of cheer from him. The songs of home brought only a sad nostalgia. He belonged on the battlefield among his men and now that, too, was gone. Seeing Flora and Maud had brought home how out of touch he was with women; even his own girl, Muriel, had not written for weeks and when her letters did come, they were filled with news of people he no longer cared about or knew.

Who would want this burnt-out shell of a priest who had lost the last shreds of belief down in the mud of the trenches? The lines of scared but battle-hardened men living daily with the putrid odour of death was the only world he had known for years. His dreams were filled with the bodies of young men rotting under grey blankets, piled high for burial like dead cattle. How could it not have left him numb? His only wish now was to crawl into a hole to find some peace.

Flora Garvie's unexpected presence unnerved him. Here was a girl who knew him as he once was. The shipbuilder's daughter had changed too, the innocence of her youth long lost. She looked so like her brother, Fergus, square-jawed, with glossy dark hair, and those deep dark eyes. Her eyes looked as if she could see right into his soul, full of pity and warmth.

Pull yourself together, Carlyle, life goes on. It was just a chance meeting, he told himself. Yet, deep down, he knew he would see her again. He sensed she, of all people, would understand how much he had changed. Her company might cheer his troubled spirit.

Chapter 3

The note from Kit, inviting them to take tea somewhere in town, was a surprise. Flora was not sure how to respond, knowing Matron must inspect it before giving approval. There were strict rules about visiting officers unless they were relatives. Maudie would chaperone, of course. The fact he was a family friend and a chaplain would surely persuade Matron their virtue would be safe.

Matron gave her consent on the understanding it must be for a short time only and in daylight. Flora sent a reply saying they would be shopping and suggested a hotel close to where Maudie was staying.

'I say, he didn't waste much time. He looks as if he could do with a hearty meal, never mind afternoon tea. I never thought of Kit as skinny. He does look very distinguished though. I want to buy some presents. Olive will be arriving soon and I want to show her the sights. You won't mind being alone with him. I know you never liked him that much.'

Why should Maudie make such a comment? Flora found

herself defending her brother's friend. 'He's changed from the boy we once knew. I think he needs cheering up.'

'Flo, you're wasted as a mere VAD, you have such a knack of seeing right into people. I noticed you in the villa, talking with those nervous invalids and listening to their woes.'

Flora was surprised. 'We all do it, it's part of our work.' How many hours had they both spent holding the hands of young lads who would never see their loved ones again? Sometimes those faces merged in her dreams, into a man in pain calling to his mother, clinging to her fingers until the worst was over.

'Meet you by the *parfumerie* to buy some bits and pieces to take home,' Maudie suggested.

'Don't you be long, I daren't go unchaperoned. Someone is bound to see me alone with a man in uniform.' For some reason Flora was feeling nervous.

He was waiting outside the hotel and guided Flora to a terrace facing the sea. 'Maudie won't be long,' she said, suddenly feeling exposed in daylight. How pale he looked now. His eyes sunken and his cheek twitching. The stitches had barely been taken from his scar. He was dressed in full uniform with a dog collar. She, in turn, had made the effort to coil her hair loosely under her boater, which she wore to shade her face from the winter sunlight.

'Miss Garvie, thank you for coming.'

'Flora, please, we've known each other since I was in pigtails. We're off duty…'

'Why did you need to run away last night?'

'I didn't,' she said, shocked by his directness. 'I was tired and it was a surprise to see you again after all this time.'

'We never seemed to hit it off, did we?' Kit replied.

Flora smiled, recalling how she had teased him and called him bookish. She had been jealous of his friendship with her brother. 'Seeing you like that reminded me of Bertie and Hector thumping balls on our tennis court. How you all came to the house and took over and we girls didn't get a chance to play. I don't suppose you ever noticed.'

'I do recall you scowling at me a time or two.' Kit smiled and his face lit up.

'Silly the things we remember, and it's all so far away now.' Flora sighed. 'At least the war is over.'

'Is it? The war is only over for the dead. I fear for many of us it's just beginning.' He turned away from her to stare out at the view.

'What do you mean?'

'Coming to terms with all we have lost, returning home where we will be expected to pick up where we left off and move forward...'

'I see what you mean but at least you have Muriel who will surely be anxious to see you again?'

'I'm not sure she'll want the man I've become – a smoker, an imbiber who prefers the company of unbelievers to Holy Joes.'

Flora could hear the bitterness in his words. 'I'm sure Muriel will understand after all you've been through.'

Kit turned back to Flora. 'I gather from your father you were a witness to the terrible Quintinshill train disaster where your brother...' Kit shook his head, unable to continue, but Flora nodded.

'I was lucky, my carriage was at the rear, we walked off the train unharmed but others were not so fortunate. I had no idea until… We did what we could… It was such a comfort to my family to know you were there for Fergus.' How could she forget the carnage, the flames and the cries of wounded soldiers? She had done what little she could to help them. How strange they were both at the scene.

'He died bravely trying to help others. But why are we talking of such sad things?' Kit took her gloved hand and this time she let it stay within a tender grip that shook her with its power. 'You have such kind eyes for someone who's witnessed so much. To go into that hell and back, survive when so many good men didn't, well, it leaves its mark.'

'Surely your fellow chaplains have some comfort to offer on this matter?' Flora could see his despair and it frightened her. His defences were so weakened, revealing an exhaustion of the nervous system that was oh, so familiar. In some ways it was like looking in a mirror. 'I'm not sure I'm qualified to talk on spiritual matters or anything much.'

'They sent you down from the front line to rest but it's hard to leave it behind. I feel it like a sack of stones on my shoulders.'

This intimate talk was not right and Flora got up to leave but then sat down again. How could she walk away? Fergus would never forgive her. 'I will be leaving here soon. There's so much work to do before we have a true peace. There are still months to go on my contract.'

'We chaplains are free agents, in some ways,' Kit replied. 'I know there's a congregation in Kelvinside waiting for this hero to return… if I return.'

Flora was shocked at this honesty. 'They will be grateful to see you safely back in the fold, especially Muriel.'

'Sorry to prattle on like this. I think only of myself these days. Forgive me for speaking out of turn. You will have a loving family to greet you. The Garvies always made us so welcome at Kildowie House.'

Suddenly Maudie appeared, striding towards their table. 'Look who's turned up early. This is my chum, Olive, from Dumbarton, no less… the Reverend Kit Carlyle, friend of Bertie and Flora's brother. Sorry we're late. I went to the station to check some times and there she was…'

Olive was wearing thick tweeds and carrying a portmanteau. She looked as if she was here for the duration. Flora found her uninvited presence intrusive but she was Maudie's friend not hers. 'Do sit down,' she said, smiling.

'Yes, do join us,' said Kit. 'Look, I've had an idea. Why don't I borrow a chap's roadster and drive you all round the coastline to see the scenery? The views are spectacular. We can find a beach for a picnic if it's not too cold. It will be like old times.'

No, it won't, Flora thought, but she was relieved by this sudden change of mood. 'Sounds jolly but Matron will have to approve. Perhaps next week, in case I'm sent north and another sick nurse needs my bed.'

'Super-duper,' Maudie added. 'You mustn't go before Christmas, Flo…'

They chatted for a while before Kit stood to take his leave, claiming a pressing engagement. Maudie turned to Olive. 'He is rather splendid, isn't he?'

Olive shrugged. 'Can't stand some of these padres, a waste of space in my book, getting in the way, preaching platitudes.'

Flora wanted to protest. Olive didn't know Kit at all and he was being so kind. In his uniform, with a battle scar, he did look rather splendid but she was no longer sure she could see him in a black gown with white tabs, behind a pulpit.

Chapter 4

A week later Kit dreamt a familiar haunting dream. He could hear the screams of a drowning man, a man he couldn't reach, however hard he crawled across the mud to find him.

'Hold on, lad, I'm coming for you!' he was shouting but the gunfire obliterated his words. He woke screaming and cursing. Why could he not find the boy? His nightmares were like hangovers that lingered all day. No amount of whisky could blot them out.

He rose early for a morning stroll along the beach where his feet took him towards the steps of the rose-pink villa. He was searching for a glimpse of Flora.

He had caught a brief sight of her at a choir rehearsal but with no opportunity to talk. He could not get her out of his mind. She had such soulful dark eyes, as she listened intently to all his nonsense. He was the one who ought to be listening, comforting, an example of good faith. Somehow her presence calmed his restlessness. He tried to be a cheery chappie in the mess but he was tired of the act. When he was with Flora, he could be more himself.

Kit turned towards the grey water with its hard metallic sheen and found himself staring into the waves. He could see his friends kicking a ball, rested, laughing, free now from any pain or the stench of death. They didn't notice him as he sniffed the salt air and waved, only the lap of the waves on his boots made any sound. 'You are one of the lucky ones,' they seemed to say and for that he must be grateful. Had he been of any use with his Bibles, medical bags and cigarettes? The countless dead were the lucky ones, he thought, over there on that far distant shore.

True, he had a comfortable billet, three good meals a day and plenty of company to while away the hours. The other men seemed intent on getting themselves fit to go home to wives and children. They were lucky, too.

He had no one in particular except his senior kirk minister, Andrew, with a daughter who they all thought would make him a good manse wife. He couldn't even recall Muriel's face.

'You're a padre with nothing to give, a burnt-out shell,' he whispered to himself. The band of brothers he once knew was gone, left behind him years ago in that first flush of gallantry and derring-do. They were the unlucky ones, schoolboys thrown into the furnace of war.

Kit felt the water soaking into his boots and stepped back. A voice was calling him back. He turned to see Flora racing down the steps, hair flying.

'What on earth are you doing?'

'Just testing the water to see if I dare take a dip,' he lied.

'It's freezing, even in the Med. You gave me a fright. I opened my curtains to see you walking into the waves.'

'You have a fine view from the villa, very picturesque.' Kit tried to change the subject but Flora was having none of it.

'Look at the state of you – soaking, and your boots are sodden,' she chided.

'Walk with me,' he said.

'You know the rules, I can't.'

'But you will, won't you?' he said, drinking in her wild hair and scarlet cheeks.

Flora smiled. 'Just for a few minutes.'

'Talking to you has made me think. If this war was fought for anything, it was for the freedom to live useful, fruitful lives without fear of being subjected to the domination of others. We know there must never be another war like this and yet it has accelerated so many scientific inventions, machines, ways of treating the sick. There's a new era coming and I've realised that preaching has only a small place in a padre's toolbox. For example, one night there were no rations and I went out to forage and found a pig. Don't ask me how,' Kit laughed. 'There was a butcher in our ranks so he did the necessary and we roasted it over a fire, the best meal for weeks. The men listened to me after that. It's what you do that counts, not what you say.'

'"Deeds not Words!" our Suffrage motto.'

'Ah yes, you, Rose Murray and Maudie screamed that in our faces often enough on the tennis court. We laughed at you and you at us... Flora, you're such wonderful company. You chase the black thoughts away.' Kit clutched her hand but she shook it away.

'Not now, not here...'

'Then where? We never got a chance to talk when I took you all on the scenic tour. That Olive never stopped butting in... Now that we've found each other after all these years, there's so much to discuss, don't you think?'

'I'm sorry, Kit, it's just not possible. People might see us together. There are rules. We never got to thank you for giving us such a wonderful afternoon. I'm sorry. You must think me ungrateful.

It will be Christmas soon. You will be busy taking services and I have Maudie and Olive to entertain, as well as visiting my sick nurses. There'll be a party and you'll all be invited. We can be friends, of course, but no more, not here.' Flora hesitated. 'I have a reputation to guard.'

'Why are you being so sensible?'

Flora paused turning back towards the villa. 'No more walking into the sea nonsense. Pull yourself together, shape up and forget any of these soppy conversations or I'll ask to be transferred.' Flora gave him one of her stern 'Votes for Women' looks.

Kit grinned. 'You're a cruel woman but you'd make a good wife, guarding the manse door...'

Flora stormed off, laughing. 'No, I would not!'

Chapter 5

The Christmas party was in full swing in the large drawing room of Rose Villa. All the nurses were laughing at each other's makeshift costumes; girls dressed as tommies, footballers, Christmas fairies with tinsel wings, wise men and shepherds. Even Matron had made an effort to disguise herself. The proposed afternoon tea had grown into a full-scale party so there had been a flurry of sewing and borrowing. 'Olive will come as a pirate,' Maudie had announced. 'I'm going as an Egyptian mummy wrapped in bandages.'

'All I've got is a silk dressing gown,' said Flora.

'If you pile up your hair, put a knitting needle through it and whiten your face with powder, wrap a scarf like a sash with a bow, you can go as a Japanese geisha,' Maudie suggested.

Earlier in the day the nurses had been busy making presents for each other: Dorothy bags full of soaps and chocolates, embroidered handkerchiefs sent from England, little bits of home to give cheer and hope. In town, Flora found a beautifully shaped bottle of perfume for Maudie, who adored the scent of roses, and lace-edged hankies for the others in the group. She even bought a fine cigar to give to Kit Carlyle. It was going to be a memorable evening and she wanted to thank him for taking the trouble to escort them around the coast.

It was strange how she kept coming back to the sight of Kit walking into the waves, knowing she just had to chase after him. He was so much more interesting than she recalled back home. She had snuck into the service where he was preaching and found his sermon thought provoking, by no means dull. She was hoping he would come to their gathering tonight. Would he ever wear the kilt again? She hoped so.

I shouldn't be thinking about Kit in this way, she reflected. It was making her cheeks blush. Now it was time to return to her tasks.

The sickest nurses were still confined to barracks, busy making paper chains. Flora felt a fraud as her poisonous finger was healing well, her weight had increased and her appetite was almost back to normal. The camaraderie made her sad at the thought of leaving to return to Scotland. Would there ever be such a time in her life again?

Christmas in this lovely villa felt like a special gift – to be waited on hand and foot was such a luxury that most of the nurses would never forget it. There wouldn't be snow or ice skating on the lake, or a winter in the hills, but they would create their own special time.

The villa was decorated with greenery and berries and a Christmas tree bedecked with little gifts. Cook made mincemeat for the pies which sent a wonderful smell of spices up the stairs. This will be the first Christmas of peace, Flora thought, sewing up the sashes of lavender into little pouches to pin on the tree. She was going to stay until after Christmas. She had seen nothing more of Kit since that episode on the beach. She hoped he would enter into the spirit of the Christmas celebrations – it was an important part of a padre's duty – but he wasn't your usual run-of-the-mill chaplain and his uncertainties worried her. He was no longer the young man full of firm convictions she recalled in Glasgow but then neither was she so sure of her beliefs.

The officer contingent arrived in good spirits with bottles of wine and Christmas cheer. Flora searched for Kit but he wasn't among them. Maudie and Olive, dressed to the nines, mingled happily but Flora felt flat. Why hadn't he come? Was he avoiding her?

'Come on, Flo, it's time to sing carols,' Maudie shouted. 'You look like you lost a bob and found a tanner... Cheer up, might never happen!'

Then, to her relief, she saw him in the doorway and her heart leapt with excitement. He was staggering under an enormous box wrapped in festive paper.

'The padre's here at last... Bring it over,' said a young captain leaning on a stick.

Kit put the box on to the table. 'This is from us to you, with compliments of the season. Matron Burke, will you do the honours?'

Matron tore off the wrapping to reveal a basket of fruit and nuts, chocolates, a fancy card and bottles of champagne. Everybody clapped and cheered and Miss Burke blushed. 'We thank you most heartily,' she said. 'But we must share it with you.'

'Nonsense,' said Kit. 'Many of us would not be here but for all your good work.'

'So now let the party commence,' added the young captain.

'Can we have a reel?' the officers begged Matron.

Miss Burke hesitated. 'Oh, just this once. It's not usual but it is Christmas,' she replied.

As if anticipated, someone produced a wax record to put on the gramophone, the carpet rug was lifted, furniture shifted and the music began. It was Strip the Willow, girls on one side, men on the other as they skipped arm in arm then under the arches of arms.

Flora found herself smiling with Kit as they danced. His eyes never left her face and her heart thumped in her chest. As their hands clasped together something strange was happening in her body. She did not want the dancing to end, but end it must. The buffet was ready in the dining room and then the piano lid was raised so singing could begin.

It was later, when the men were ushered out into the starlit night, that Kit hung back whispering, 'I'll be walking back on the beach. Can you meet me there?'

Flora shook her head. 'You know I can't. It's not allowed.'

'Please find an excuse. I'd like to talk more.'

'What about?'

'Can't you guess?' He touched her hand briefly as if by accident. 'I'll be waiting for you down by the steps.'

'But I can't,' Flora said, without conviction. She saw again that war-weary look in his eyes and knew she must find a way. It was Olive and Maudie who gave her an excuse as they strolled hand-in-hand into the darkness.

'Wait, wait… I think my friend's left her bag… I'll just catch them up so don't lock the door,' she said to a nurse standing by the door. Flora made to follow them down the path, and then turned down the steps that led to the beach, knowing Kit would be waiting.

'You came!'

'I can't stay long. What is it you want?'

'Flora, why were we never friends in Glasgow?'

'That was ages ago, before… we were just young kids.' She paused. 'Before the train accident and Fergus and before we grew weary of war.' She looked into his face. How could she have ever thought Kit to be standoffish? His eyes were so sad, his once auburn hair sprinkled with white, his face etched with lines and marked by the scar where shrapnel had hit him. Suddenly a surge of love and pity for this brave man, aged before his time, flooded over her. Her hand went to his cheek and she touched the scar tissue. In that brief gesture, something burst within her, warmth flooded her heart as his hand covered hers.

'Dear, dear Flora,' he said, holding her so tight she could feel the beat of his heart, the scent of his carbolic soap, the tobacco on his uniform and the whisky on his breath.

'What happened to you being teetotal?' she whispered.

'A man must warm his throat and numb his mind, to steady his nerves,' he replied. 'The laddies looked to me for courage and confidence even though I was often quaking in my boots, knowing any moment could be our last.'

'But you came through.'

'If you can call it that. What would my parish make of me now?'

'Muriel will understand.'

'Do you think so? I don't. She's a stranger to me now. I'm not who I was.'

'None of us are. We live with ghosts. None of it was our choosing,' Flora said.

Suddenly words were no longer enough as they walked arm in arm in the darkness, hearing the sea lapping on the shore. Flora was so very late now but nothing mattered as they clung to each other for comfort.

'We had some good times, friendships made and lost. Remember the tennis party in Kildowie when you didn't want to be my partner?' Kit said, his arm around her waist.

'We were young and sure of ourselves,' Flora sighed.

'What are we now?' Kit said, turning back towards the promenade.

'I don't know, just us, stripped of all pretensions, tired, lonely at times. You know, I really must go. If Matron Burke catches me...'

Kit held her tight. 'Would you mind if I kissed you?'

She smiled, putting a finger on his lips before leaning towards him in an embrace. They clung together, drawing strength from each other. Flora was shocked by the power of this sensation.

'Let me see you back safely.'

'No, we mustn't be seen together.'

'We must meet again... I have to see you again.'

'There's Muriel to consider. I can't do this.'

'Muriel's not here. Please, Flora.'

'There's another choir rehearsal, we can meet there,' she whispered before she fled back towards Rose Villa, her heart pounding with fear and excitement, his kiss still warm on her lips.

*

Kit strode back to the hotel in confusion. How had he ever thought Fergus's sister a spoilt brat? The woman before him was like an image of himself, wounded, exhausted, no longer sure of the world around her. Hers was a strange sort of beauty, her body was thin, yet strong from all her nursing. He had known nurses in the dressing stations and seen the strength and comfort they gave to men. Their courage and calm in the face of appalling mutilations was something he would never forget. In Flora's eyes he saw the sadness of losses she could not control, but when she reached out and touched him, it was as if she lit a fire within him.

Flora was a reminder of home, her accent reminding him of happier days, singing with Muriel round the piano, strolling in Kelvingrove, playing tennis on Kildowie House lawn; those never to be forgotten days of youthful innocence.

Flora had been tempered by the refining fire of suffering. She reminded him of something he had forgotten existed: a yearning for physical touch and for pleasure. He must see her again, to draw strength from her. She was bringing him back to life. Then he thought of Muriel waiting in the minister's parlour, full of plans for their future together. Oh, Muriel...

His euphoria burst like a punctured tyre. How the hell could he return to her now? She was no longer real to him. Her image had faded long ago. This place was real enough: the sea, the hills, the beauty, and here was Flora Garvie. She was all that mattered to him now.

Chapter 6

Christmas passed in a blur of celebrations, carol services and walks along the shore, and now it was New Year and another gathering with the officer contingent in the villa. Flora watched the door for Kit's arrival, her heart thumping. She wanted to see him more than anything, but it troubled her. Was it right to poach another girl's beau? Was Muriel waiting for his return, ready to plan a wedding? How could Kit dismiss that so lightly? It was all so confusing.

Perhaps there was something about the luxury of this villa, the scenery, the relief of being away from petty rules, uniforms and the misery of war that lifted her spirits? She could not forget that kiss, her first kiss, and the passion within it. The thought of living in his arms filled every vacant space in her mind. She was like a silly schoolgirl with her first pash. A door had opened into a world she never knew existed. This was a world that her doctor friend, Rose Murray, had found with Hector; her mother and father, too.

Now she was in thrall to a desire to be with Kit no matter the consequences, and this worried her deeply.

Then Kit appeared in his kilt, his hair flattened, his eyes searching the crowd for her, and Flora knew what they were feeling was mutual. She drifted towards him, trying not to draw attention to herself. Rules were rules and Matron must not see the flush on her cheeks or how her hands trembled. She must not show any partiality towards him and that was agony. They both circled round the chattering crowd trying to look casual and disinterested. Everyone was admiring the delicious spread of cake and pastries, waiting for the New Year chimes. In a few hours it would be 1919; a new beginning, without war. Into this bubble burst Maudie: 'I say… Can't wait to sing "Auld Lang Syne"… Are you all right, Flo? You look awfully hot.'

'It's the crush, I'm going for some air on the balcony,' she said, hoping it was loud enough for Kit to overhear.

'I'll come with you,' Maudie offered. 'Olive didn't feel up to coming tonight because she thought it was more my thing. We've made plans to leave soon, so she's busy looking up timetables.'

Flora wasn't listening. 'I'm fine, just need to cool down, so thanks. You go and find the buffet.'

'Oh, I can see Kit over there. I wonder how he's getting on? Oh, he's gone! Pity,' said Maudie. 'There's lots to catch up and I wanted to thank him for that excursion along the coast. It was such a jolly treat.'

Flora drifted towards the balcony. She fluttered her fan to indicate she was going to cool down, but nobody noticed. At the far end of the terrace, the silhouette of a lone figure stood smoking, half hidden in the darkness.

Kit turned and smiled. 'Glad you managed to get away from the squash in there. We have to talk. Why can't we just be alone?'

'I know, but you know the rules – no fraternising with the enemy. Matron is a stickler for propriety.'

'Then we must find time to be alone together. There's so much still to say.' Kit reached out for her hand. 'Now I've found you, I don't want to let you go.'

'I have to be chaperoned. You know how it is,' Flora said.

'Well, at least with Maudie and her chum, you can always get permission to visit them.'

'They're leaving soon.'

'All the more reason for a farewell visit. Matron wouldn't deny you a day out with them. Then we could meet up and make a day of it somewhere. What do you think?'

Flora nodded. 'It's risky, but worth a try. Where shall we go?'

'Leave that to me. A day out to ourselves. We deserve that.'

Suddenly bells were ringing in the New Year and it was time to re-join the celebrations in a sing-song. Together, they sang the old Scots' anthem, happy that it was easy to hold hands and join in the fray. Now there was a plan that might just work. 'Perhaps I should tell Maudie?' she whispered as they swayed back and forward.

'Better not... don't want to involve her. Best no one knows our plan,' Kit replied.

'When?'

'You ask for permission to visit and I'll do the rest. I'll send a thank you card with date and time. No one else must know.'

⋆

'I fancy a breath of mountain air,' said Kit. 'Anyone know a good place?' He was in the mess, hoping for some ideas.

'You should take the little railway line into the hills, if it's open, to Entrevaux up the Roya valley,' the major suggested. 'Splendid scenery. It's called the line of pines.'

'So where do I catch it?'

'At the railway station in Nice... It will take you high into the Southern Alps, but it will be snowy. I think there are a few stations where you can stop to hike.'

This sounded ideal but how to get to the station and not be spotted? Flora must not wear her uniform. Perhaps if she walked in the direction of her friends' *pension*, he could offer her a lift. They would let it be known they were both going to say farewell to their childhood friend, then, once out of sight, drive to the station for tickets. They could travel two or three stations, not too far, have lunch somewhere and then come back. Kit could not wait to have Flora all to himself. Somewhere to make plans for the future and settle things, once and for all.

Chapter 1

Flora watched the clock carefully because the timing needed to be perfect. She had asked Matron for one day's leave, explaining how important it was to bid Maudie and Olive farewell. It was possible that Captain Carlyle might accompany her because they were all close friends from childhood. How easy it is to lie when you are trusted, she thought.

Matron Burke gave her permission gladly. 'It's good to know you have such loyal and long-standing friends. Cherish them well.'

Wearing her two-piece tweed jacket and skirt, cape and jaunty tam-o'-shanter, Flora began her stroll down the hill towards the *pension*, just as a sleek French car slid alongside her.

'Can I give you a lift, Miss Garvie?' Kit said. Flora stepped up into the vehicle with a smile: so far, so good, she thought.

They drove into Nice and found the station, parking well

out of sight. Kit bought tickets for the little line while Flora stood waiting anxiously. This was going to be such a special day and nerves must not spoil it.

The railway journey took them up a beautiful wooded valley. It grew colder as they rose above the city's sprawl into a hilly outcrop of jutting rocks. There were pine trees tipped with snow, looking like something on a Christmas card. They held hands, gazing astonished at the magnificent vista before them, then alighted at the second halt. The air was crisp and frosty, but Kit hoped they would find the *auberge* serving piping hot soup, a *plat du jour* and a plate of cheese as the officer had promised.

He had forgotten to tell them that there was a winter timetable and the *auberge* was closed and shuttered. There was a small café where they sat patiently for the dour-faced woman to offer them an omelette and a glass of red wine.

'This reminds me of the *estaminet* in the rest areas,' Kit said. 'It's not quite what I had in mind... wait till I see the major.'

'It's perfect. Just look at the view,' Flora said.

'But I don't like the look of those dark clouds over there,' Kit replied.

'Don't be a grump. We'll be back long before they spill their load on the mountains,' Flora replied setting off briskly along a mountain path. Kit followed but paused reading the skies again. 'We really should turn back now.'

Wrong again. Silently, slowly at first and then swiftly, the snowflakes began to fall like feathers onto the village. Now the hills looked grey and menacing.

'I suppose we'd better get back to the station halt and take the first train back,' Kit suggested.

'But it's not due for an hour.' They found walking suddenly slippery. Flora clung onto his arm.

'This is not a good idea. I'm sorry,' Kit said as they slithered down the path to the station halt.

Everything was going wrong, but Flora refused to be downhearted. There was plenty of time to get back, she thought, as they made for the little *cabine* to sit out the snow storm. At first they waited patiently but the return train did not come. Hour after hour and no sign of it. Now darkness was creeping down the valley, and they huddled together to keep warm, hoping against hope for its arrival.

It was pitch dark when the station keeper arrived with a lantern. '*Monsieur*, there is no more train tonight. It will arrive in the morning,' he said in a thick dialect that was hard to understand.

'Is there somewhere to stay?' Kit asked in broken French. '*Une chambre, peut-être?*'

The old man shrugged his shoulders. 'Everything is closed, but there is the church. The priest is away... And there's a stove in the vestry... Come with me this way, *madame et monsieur...*'

The snow was deep and their boots sank into it but the church was not far away. The old man pushed open a side door. '*Voilà...* there is wood for the stove, a bench. I will bring something for your wife. She looks frozen.'

Flora blushed at her title. Thank goodness her gloves hid a bare ring finger. Panic flooded through her at being stranded so late. How would they explain her absence? After the man left, she turned to Kit, trying to stay calm. He took her hand reassuringly.

'I'm sorry, this is not what I planned. I should have checked the timetable, but at least we're dry and can get warm. We'll spend the night here and trust there will be a train in the morning. I never meant...' He paused, seeing the look of panic on her face.

Flora surveyed their surroundings. The vestry was damp and soulless, just a cupboard with vestments, empty vases, a picture of Our Lady and child on the wall, a crucifix and some papers. There was a little woodstove on a stone floor. At least it was dry and heat from the stove would keep them warm.

'Ah well, here we are.' Flora sighed, her mouth dry with tension. 'Better make the most of it. We wanted to be alone and now we really are. The old man is being very kind. We must offer him something in return.'

The old man lit the stove and found a thick tablecloth to act as a blanket. 'I will wake you in the morning. It will be clear by then.'

As the stove began to heat, they pulled the bench closer to its glow. There was silence inside, for the walls were thick. There was nothing to do but wait while the little stove came to life. 'That's better,' said Kit, pulling Flora towards him, settling her into his arms. Their kiss was long and deep and she sensed that this night would change everything. It seemed natural for Kit to spread his greatcoat on the floor and for Flora to shed her cape, so that lying together gave up a heat of a different kind.

Flora was no stranger to men's bodies, but she suddenly felt shy and vulnerable as she slid down her wet skirt and Kit loosened her jacket and blouse, kissing her breasts through her chemise.

'Flora... I don't want to do anything...'

'Don't stop,' Flora whispered. 'But I have no experience.'

'Neither have I,' he replied, nuzzling her ear.

'Then we'll learn together,' she said, allowing his hands to stroke her body. They lay entwined, feeling their way into a slow languid opening to this first act of love, after which they slept, locked in each other's arms.

Suddenly at first light, Kit sat up, turning to Flora. 'Marry me, Flora, right here, right now. Don't let's wait...'

Flora sat up, startled. 'You can't mean that. You're not free. There's Muriel to consider.'

'I don't love her. I don't think I ever did,' Kit replied.

'Then you should go back and tell her so. I won't be party to any deception.'

Kit lay back again. 'And say what? She must sense by now that we are not suited. With you it's so different.'

'This is madness and it's all too soon. You're not thinking straight.'

'I thought you felt the same, Flora.'

'I do, but this isn't right, not as it is... If we were found out...' Flora felt panic rising again.

'So what... this is between us alone. I found you and I love you,' said Kit.

'But I care that we do what is honest, even if you don't... I just can't be party to anything else.'

Kit grabbed her hand. 'You can't mean it. Don't you want to marry me?'

'Of course, when the time is right, but not like this. You must go home and sort things out properly. Perhaps time apart will give us time to reflect.'

'How can you say that after what we've just done?'

'There's no rush, we can have a lifetime to be together, but not like this.'

Kit stood up, impatient. 'Life is to be lived now. It's all we have. I have no desire to go back to my old life, so let's just elope.'

Flora jumped up, grabbing his hand. 'Don't be cross, you have your duties and I have mine. You are still a chaplain, don't forget.'

'I'm a sham, a rotten padre, and I don't believe half of what I am expected to do. There, does that shock you?'

'My dear Kit, you've not been well. This is all part of your confusion and despair. You need to calm down and think about it. All I'm asking is for you to sort out your private affairs. I can wait… It's not a lot to ask.' The atmosphere in the vestry was cooling. Flora was trying to be gentle as she let down his impetuous ideas.

Kit's face hardened. 'I'll write her a letter, then.'

'That's a coward's way and you know it. We've both lied enough to parents and wives, softening the blow of a son's death with lies… It's not fair on Muriel. She's waited all these years for you. I won't be privy to it. This demeans you.'

Kit pulled on his greatcoat. 'I'm not listening to this. I thought you wanted me and now you're backing out.'

'I'm doing no such thing. Just asking for time to do everything right.' Kit was being obstinate now.

'You don't know what you're asking, Flora, you just don't understand.'

'Please don't be angry. I'm trying to be sensible,' she pleaded.

'To hell with sensible. We met and fell in love. Now we're one body and soul – at least I thought so.'

Flora kissed him. 'Don't let's fall out. These past weeks have been wonderful. I never expected to have such feelings. Our love can wait a month or two, surely?'

'I suppose so,' Kit said.

'Now you're sulking,' Flora teased. 'We have all the time in the world, but first we must prepare for the troubles that will be waiting for us down there. Matron will want an explanation.'

'Does it matter? It's none of her business. I'm sick of hiding in corners, so let's come clean and take the consequences.'

'There you go again, making plans. Just be patient. It'll soon be morning.' They sat together in silence. Flora felt a chill between them. This was their first quarrel and probably not their last.

It was a relief when the old man returned. '*Monsieur,* the snow is melting a little. Come, the train won't be long,' he said.

Flora was already dressed and ready. Kit was still in his shirtsleeves, scrambling to tidy the floor, hiding evidence of the bed they had made. '*Merci, vous êtes très gentil. Et votre nom?*'

'Laurent. François Laurent, *monsieur.*'

'You are very kind,' Flora said, offering him something from her purse, but he stepped back, shaking his head. '*Non, madame.* It is our duty to welcome strangers just as the innkeeper welcomed Our Lady into his stable...' The old man smiled and guided them back down to the station. The sky was blue, without a single cloud. However, the frost between them was still in the air.

★

Kit sat on the train, staring out of the window, smiling to himself. What a perfect day, even if everything he planned had fallen apart. To have spent the night in Flora's arms was wonderful. Puritans would call this an act of reckless fornication. What a cold judgemental word that was to describe what had happened between them. He was glad he had not succumbed to his friend Dr O'Keeffe's tempting offer to visit a dubious dance hall in Paris when they were on leave. There was such a feeling of joy, he thought, in the act of love. It had been such a release and a pleasure to have shared it for the first time with Flora.

Now all that remained was to get her back safely to her billet, using the excuse that she stayed out longer than she meant to with her friends until it was too cold and dark to leave. This was the best he could think up. It was easier for him, officers had freedom to come and go. Some even went to casinos, bars and brothels around the city.

As for the other matter, he must write to his boss in Glasgow and to Muriel, make excuses for delaying his return home. He just couldn't face their inevitable disappointment in him. Aunt Jessie would feel shame that he'd let the side down somehow. It was too complicated and would spoil the joy he was feeling. Now the black cloud that sat above his head was lifting. Everything was possible with Flora by his side.

Together they would start a new life. He would start training as a serious artist. He had always suppressed his passion for painting until now. Perhaps they could both teach, not in Glasgow, of course, but somewhere far away. His plans had no boundaries, but he sensed it was too soon to share his thoughts with Flora. These lofty ambitions might worry her. She was noticeably cautious when discussing the future. Slowly, slowly, Carlyle, he muttered to himself. For the first time in years, he felt almost giddy with optimism.

Chapter 8

Kit left Flora a street away from the villa, so she could walk the rest of the way as if she were coming up from Maudie's *pension*. They had called there, but the concierge said the two ladies were out. There was now no time to explain to them how the snow had prevented their return.

When Flora climbed the steps to the villa, a nurse was standing in the doorway. 'There you are... we were so worried. Matron wants to see you. Where on earth have you been?'

'It's a long story,' Flora replied, sweeping past her. Taking a deep breath, she knocked on Miss Burke's door, hoping against hope her story would hold.

'Ah, Garvie, sit down. Thank goodness you are returned to us intact... An hour longer and we would have informed the *gendarmerie*. Where have you been?'

Flora could not look her in the face. The lies stuck in her throat as she coughed. 'As I told you...'

'Oh yes, a farewell visit to Miss Wallace and Miss Buckle. Let me stop you right there. Those two friends of yours came looking for you yesterday because they were leaving shortly for Monaco, unaware, it seems, that you had made plans with them. I'm afraid that little excuse won't suffice. Whereabouts exactly did you spend last night?' Her tone hardened.

'I went for the day into the hills for some fresh air and the views on the *train des pignes*, but the snow came down suddenly and there was no return train. The stationmaster took pity on me and gave me shelter.'

'So, you went alone, unchaperoned?' Matron eyed her with suspicion.

'Not exactly, Captain Carlyle chaperoned me. He was my brother's best friend.'

'You spent the night alone with him?'

'There was no option, as I said. The train was delayed, but Monsieur Laurent will vouch for us.'

'I'm sure he will. Did you tell him you were unmarried?'

Flora hesitated. 'He assumed we were man and wife.' Her cheeks flushed with embarrassment.

'And are you man and wife?'

'No, Matron,' Flora bowed her head. 'We have plans to marry.' This was the best she could offer.

'I see...' Matron took off her glasses with a sigh. 'I am very disappointed in you, Garvie. I did not expect such deception from one of my VADs. We look for high standards from all our staff and you have clearly let yours slip. An assignation with an officer is a serious misdemeanour and strictly against the rules, as you well know. I therefore have no alternative but to ask you to pack your bags immediately. You will be escorted to the next northern-bound train. From there you will go to HQ in London, where your contract will be terminated and you will be dismissed. What a waste of talent.'

'I'm so sorry,' Flora croaked, tears welling up.

'Sorry is not good enough, Garvie. You should have thought of that when you were making plans to deceive us all here. What a poor example you have shown to the other girls. You were sent here to convalesce and to help. You were in a position of trust. We cannot condone behaviour like yours, especially not with a man of the cloth. You are dismissed forthwith. Please leave your uniform behind. You are not fit to wear it.' Matron pointed to the door.

Flora fled to her room in tears of shame and frustration. Once there she folded her uniform and left it on the bed. Still wearing the clothes from last night, she shoved all the rest of her belongings into a valise. The only thing she did was pull out a postcard and a stamp so she could write to Kit. This, she would post at the station. The other nurses stood along the stairs, faces shocked at her dismissal. Someone touched her arm. 'We'll miss you, Flora. You were so kind to me.'

Flora couldn't speak, or look at her colleagues, for the shame she was feeling. Transport was waiting and the two nurses who were going back north escorted her to the station like wardresses. There wasn't even time to post Kit's card, no time for a backward glance as they mounted the train for Lyon and then onwards to Paris and the boat train to London.

Flora couldn't sleep or eat for embarrassment and anger. It wasn't fair. She loved a man and for that she must sacrifice everything. To be heading home in disgrace choked her. How could her life be turned upside down in just one day?

★

Kit couldn't wait to see Flora again, but thought better of seeking her out. He prayed that Matron had accepted the explanation of her absence but he would learn more at the Sunday church service. To his surprise, Flora was not in the congregation in the little Protestant chapel, but he tried to look for her just in case he'd missed her. At the end of the service, to his surprise, Miss Burke took him aside.

'I want a word with you, Padre.' Her tone was sharp. 'I think it's disgraceful that a man of the cloth should dishonour one of my nurses. What have you to say for yourself, Captain Carlyle?'

'I'm sorry, what is this about?' Kit felt the first stirrings of alarm.

'You put Miss Garvie in a very compromising position last week. I know what happened and it won't do. I've reported you to higher authorities. I can have no such behaviour on my watch.'

'Miss Garvie and I are to marry shortly,' he replied. 'We wanted to meet in private, to discuss our future. But you keep your charges on such a tight rein, it's not surprising we had to use subterfuge. We have known each other since childhood.' Kit shook his head, hoping this would calm her obvious fury.

'I'm sure you have, but that is no excuse for philandering behind my back. It is not honest. Attachments of this kind are not permitted. You have flouted the rules.'

'What does Miss Garvie have to say?' Kit was trying to stay calm.

'Garvie has been dismissed, of course. We have standards to uphold and she knowingly broke them.'

'I must speak to her. All this is my fault.' Kit felt sick.

'She is halfway back to Scotland by now. I doubt if she ever wants to see you again. You have ruined her promising career as a qualified nurse.'

'Is that so? Miss Garvie and I made plans for the future and they did not include nursing,' Kit replied, sensing worse was to follow.

'I doubt if the Church authorities will permit you to follow your vocation once they've been informed of your loose behaviour.'

'Who cares what they think? Flora is all I care for now. As far as you are all concerned, you can go to hell.' Kit stormed away, throwing off his clerical robe in disgust. Who were they to judge?

Back in his room he poured a large glass of whisky and wrote a rambling letter to Flora, but when he read it, he crushed it in his palm. It was a self-pitying rant.

Later, he went down to the mess. There was silence at the dining table. Pogo Latimer stood up, shouting across the table. 'I say, Padre, who's been a naughty boy? Got a poor nurse into trouble and here we all were thinking you the white hen that never laid away.'

'Go boil your head,' Kit snarled in broad Glaswegian.

'Oh dear, scratch a Scotsman and there's no gentleman underneath, only peasant stock,' Latimer continued.

Kit jumped up to thump him but his friend, Major Fox, held him back. 'Carlyle, calm yourself, you're drunk.' Kit left the dining room and stormed out of the hotel onto the promenade and down to the beach. What have I done?

What's wrong with me? Why do you get it so wrong? Fergus, Bertie and now Flora have gone. His mind was in turmoil as he tried to put his thoughts into some sort of order. How he had miscalculated everything. All that was beginning to be so wonderful in his life now lay in tatters at his feet. He had been impatient to secure Flora's love, desperate to be alone with her. She had risked her reputation to please him and now the poor girl had been sent home in disgrace. It was all his doing. He was supposed to set an example, but now the other officers were laughing at him.

He stared out over the gun-metal sea. I am no use to anyone. Flora must hate me, my church will disown me, Muriel and Andrew will despise me. Who cares if I live or die? Standing at the edge of the shore, searching the rolling waves for an answer, how easy it would be, he thought, how easy just to walk in there, to end it once and for all.

Then he recalled Sam O'Keeffe's words. 'There's one way out, Carlyle... over the top and out like a light... You're quite the martyr and death will release you from your obligations: to church, to the girl back home, the lot...' Kit sat on the wet sand, deep in thought.

Was it better to be a coward for a minute, than dead for the rest of your life? Where had he heard that? In his haze of whisky and confusion, he could see no future; his life was hurting those he loved the most. He must set them free, Flora and the others, free to forget him. He had shamed Flora, betrayed Muriel, let down his church and his calling. There had to be a doorway out of this mess, but where was the key to unlock it?

Chapter 9

The boat train disgorged its weary passengers onto a wet platform at Victoria station. Flora stood for a moment remembering wartime 'stand-tos', waiting for the ambulance trains to offload their sick patients, while onlookers were held back, lest the sight of the wounded lowered public morale.

Her escorts left her by the ferry port and now she was alone. The postcard to Kit was burning a hole in her pocket. It had the wrong stamp and must be rewritten.

She gave her address as the VADs' hostel in Upper Cavendish Street. Here there was time to collapse. If asked she would say she was back from France on sick leave. Taking an omnibus to the nearest Bank of Scotland, she withdrew enough money from her allowance to tide her over while she was in London. She wanted to buy fresh clothes, to rid herself of the smell of travelling grime. When Kit returned, she wanted to be looking her best for him.

For a few hours after making her way to Oxford Street, she lost herself in Mr Selfridge's store, browsing the latest fashion in gowns. Hemlines were above the ankles now, with looser-fitting dresses that looked comfortable but expensive. She must eke out her allowance and budget carefully for a while. There was enough for a pretty blouse, though. She sent a postcard to Kildowie, saying she was on leave and would return when her contract was terminated.

In her heart Flora knew she was not ready to return to the bosom of her family, to a life that, if she was honest, no longer held much appeal. Better to stay down south, and wait for Kit's letter. But after a week without a reply, she felt restless and concerned so she wrote again and again but there was still silence.

One night she wrote a long letter to her dear friend Rose in Glasgow, explaining the truth about her return and her relationship with Kit Carlyle. A letter came back to the hostel almost at once, containing a letter from Maudie Wallace and was full of apologies.

Dearest Flo

I didn't know where to send my letter when it was returned from the Rose Villa. I'm so sorry that you have been dismissed. If only you had confided in us, Olive and I would have covered for you willingly.

Kit has a lot to answer for, in putting you in such a position. I hope he's worth all the trouble he has brought to your door. I must say he has changed a lot since we first knew him, but then the war has done strange things to all of us.

Olive and I have decided to stay in Switzerland. There is a clinic specialising in those with mental scars from their war wounds and experiences. It is by a lake in

Lucerne and the views are wonderful and food delicious. We were hoping you would come to visit us but Rose tells me you are in London at the hostel.

Perhaps this enforced separation from Kit will give you both a chance to reflect on your future plans. Don't be downhearted. But a sisterly warning. If he has let down Muriel Armour-Brown, he could well do the same to you. I don't want to see you hurt. Men are so weak and unreliable, I find, the best of them being long gone from us now. I thank God I have such a chum in Olive, for she is now my companion. We are different in many ways, but we work and live amicably together. Do write to me to say all is well and again I apologise for letting you down, but perhaps it is for the best in the long run.

Cheery bye and best love

Maudie

Oh, Maudie, she sighed, putting down the letter. How little you know me, or what Kit means to me. We are two of a kind, though his silence is unnerving. What if he was sick again? What if he had been dismissed? *Write to me please*, she prayed, not able to settle in idleness. The days were long, waiting for the post to arrive, but still she refused to attend the headquarters for another dressing-down. VADs were volunteers, after all, and she no longer felt the loyalty she had so proudly embraced. When Kit returned, she would marry him quietly, with no fuss and no family. Then they could begin their new life together.

One morning a maid arrived, carrying a small package. 'For you, miss...' It had been posted from abroad but not in Kit's handwriting and she feared it was from Miss Burke, demanding to know why she had not gone to HQ. Flora left it unopened, until curiosity got the better of her. What did she care now for Matron's opinion? The address at the top was from the officers' hotel and dated nearly two weeks ago. Inside were her own letters.

Dear Miss Garvie

I do apologise for opening your letters, but I needed to find your address. There is no easy way to explain my action, except that I am afraid I have bad news regarding Captain Carlyle, who I know was a particular friend of yours.

Three weeks ago, Carlyle, who had a habit for sea bathing even in inclement weather, took himself off for his usual swim. When he did not return to the mess, a group of us went in search of him, thinking him perhaps unwell, for he has been much troubled of late.

We found his uniform folded on the beach, along with his towel and shoes, and the alarm was raised. We fear a terrible accident befell him in the chill water; cramp or fatigue while he was swimming. It has been a great shock to all of us, for he was a popular chap and an excellent padre, much decorated for bravery at the front.

His belongings, papers and effects were returned to his next of kin in Scotland, but I could not let you go on thinking he was still resident here. I am so sorry to be the bearer of such shocking news.

Please take comfort from knowing he would not have suffered for long in that cold water.

Yours Sincerely

Charles Fox (Major)

Flora sank to her knees in shock. Kit, no, no, Kit, why did you risk the chilly water? Or did you? She recalled him walking in a daydream into the sea, the first time they had talked alone. A terrible thought filled her with dread. Was this an accident or was it… She could not say the word.

You said I brought you back to life. Surely our love was enough to calm your fears? You stupid, stupid man, I loved you from the moment I saw you pleading for Bertie Wallace to be put on that ambulance train all those years ago. I loved your off-key singing. I loved every beat of your heart as we lay together. How could you risk your life when so many of our dearest lost the chance of life?

They had no choice, but you had life and the promise of the future and you let it go. It was no accident, of that I'm sure, and I hate you for it. I thought my loving gave your whole new life purpose and now you throw it back in my face like this. I can't believe you took the coward's way out. Did you give in to fears and weakness, or did you see it as a brave act of defiance?

Now you have brought grief to all who love you, Aunt Jessie, Andrew, Muriel, but most of all to me. I would have waited a lifetime, until you were free to be with me. How can I go back home, bearing such news? They must never know I lost my reputation because of you, and I gladly lost it. I was not ashamed of giving myself to you, but now I feel only shame to have loved such a coward.

Flora sobbed hot tears of anger into her pillow, a bitter bile burning in her throat. She cried until sleep overtook her wounded soul.

★

Kit pedalled like a man possessed, ever westward along the coastline. With each calf-aching mile on this old boneshaker, he felt himself releasing his past life. His mind was on fire with possibilities. What he was doing not only freed himself, but all the others in his life. This plan was the kindest of all. There would be no body to return, no military funeral, no inquest, no suspicion about his motives. Any doubts or shame stabbing within him were shoved from his mind. Thoughts of the consequences of his action were no longer important.

A burst of euphoria fuelled him with excitement. He was breaking free from his past life and setting everyone else free from his failures. Taking this flight from reality no longer worried him. He could not go on living a lie. He didn't love Muriel, or his vocation. The war had drained his faith. As for Flora, she was better off without him. He didn't deserve her. He had betrayed her trust and for that he hated himself. You are a weak waste of space in the world. How can anyone ever trust you again? These were his disordered thoughts, as he cycled on, until he lay exhausted in a barn, dead to the world.

He woke next morning and the euphoria of the night before was punctured like a blown tyre. Hungry and aching, he suddenly realised what he had done and felt sick. What had prompted such cowardice?

Now he lay, covered in straw, in the shabby workman's clothes he had cunningly bought in a flea market. The familiar itch of lice rubbed his skin. His head, shaved in a cheap barber shop, hid any evidence of his flame-red hair, making him look like a convict. He had a hunk of cheese and a stale crust of bread in his pocket. Now he rose in search of water to quench a raging thirst. What had he done? It was too late now to go back. His legs were aching, his chest was tight. You've made this bloody bed for yourself, now you lie on it, old boy. No looking back. It's too late for second thoughts. No one would recognise him wearing these old clothes and a beret. His French was basic, but he would soon learn. He bought a loaf and slice of *jambon*, a bottle of cheap wine and found a fountain in which to douse his face. He would sleep wherever there was shelter from the winter chill: in barns, church porches, washing in streams. He was travelling light, possessing only two clean shirts. As for his identity, he had figured it best to lose his real name in favour of something close but different.

Kristian was easily translated into Christophe. As for Carlyle, he thought of the moorland railway track north, stopping at Beattock and Carstairs en route to Glasgow. There was an asylum at Carstairs. What better reminder of this act of madness than to call himself Chris Carstairs? When he eventually reached Marseille, he would register his lost papers and claim a new identity. Then he could lose himself in the countryside and throw himself into a new life.

Only at night, under the stars, did his conscience torture him with thoughts of Flora. His death must be added to all her other losses. She was strong and deserved a better man than he had become. There would be no other women in his life. His desire was spent, but he would cherish that winter night of love-making for ever. The door to that sort of happiness was slammed shut. A wretched man like him was no longer worthy of joy or sympathy.

He had made this reckless plan one night when sleep eluded him. Once Flora had gone, it was as if some strange mania had taken hold of him. He made a list of what he must purchase and store away until the opportunity came to put his flight into practice. He stepped up his swims, so everyone knew his routine. Purchasing a bicycle came next. He told his fellow inmates he wanted to be fitter, making sure it was in its usual place when he left. The old boneshaker was hidden in a shed along with the flea market clothes. He took care that everything in his room looked as untidy as usual, even leaving a bottle of best malt whisky half drunk. Taking his bathers down to the beach as usual, he diverted along a path back to where he had hidden everything ready for departure when darkness fell. It was a devious plan and it worked.

Now there was no turning back. Bridges were burnt and a new life was opening up before him. He had no idea what he would do to earn a living, but chances came to those who went in search of them. One thing he would do, though, was observe people and places, sketch and perhaps paint. He tried not to think of Aunt Jessie in mourning, or Andrew advertising for a new assistant. It was only when Flora's dark eyes flashed before him that he knew this act of escape was unforgivable, cruel and cowardly, but it was too late now for second thoughts.

Chapter 10

In the summer of 1919, Flora signed up with an agency. She could not face returning to Kildowie. Better that they thought she was still under contract in London. With the epidemic of influenza at its height, there would be every reason for her to remain in service.

She wrote letters of condolence to the Armour-Brown family and was rewarded with a cutting from the Glasgow *Herald*, containing Kit's glowing obituary. If there had been enough witnesses, The Reverend Kristian Carlyle DSO would have been awarded a VC for his valiant attempt to save a soldier in the mud of Passchendaele. Flora could hardly bear to read the rest. What a waste of a good life, she cried in anger. She still couldn't believe he was dead.

There was only Hector Murray and his wife Rose left from their school days. Maudie remained in Switzerland. Flora felt isolated, sick of the smoky city, sick of living a lie, and took the first position offered to her, after Rose wrote her a glowing reference.

On the train from Paddington, Flora wondered if fleeing

to a strange county was the best decision, but it was too late to change her mind. As they left the suburbs, the landscape changed from grey to green in a soft golden light. At each station she peered out at unfamiliar names. By the time she reached Cheltenham, half asleep, she felt ready to face her new employer.

A sleek limousine, with a chauffeur and maid, was waiting to escort her to Bordley Court, home of the Pickford family. The maid stepped forward to greet her. 'Miss Garvie, welcome to Gloucestershire. We hope you will find your stay suits.'

'Thank you,' she replied. 'It would help to know what I am to expect and who I will be nursing? This dreadful flu takes no prisoners but I hope there have been few losses here.'

'No, miss, we are free of contagion. Miss Pickford does not require urgent nursing.'

'But I thought I was here...' Flora said.

'Nothing like that, miss. It's just that Miss Pickford needs constant care. She is an invalid confined to her room. The last nurse left under a cloud. Miss Pickford is very particular about her care.'

'I see.' Flora felt the first stirrings of unease as she peered out of the vehicle onto a picturesque scene of golden stone cottages, lush trees, fine churches with tall steeples, golden fields, horses pulling carts and quaint cobbled streets. It all looked so warm and inviting to eyes starved of sunshine and picture-postcard views.

They entered a long drive lined with oak trees and stopped outside a large stone manor house with mullioned windows, roses and borders full of flowers.

'First, I must show you to your room, Miss Garvie. I'm Minnie Carver. I'm afraid there is no housekeeper. Mrs Fisher left a while ago but we do manage.'

'Where are the rest of the Pickford family?'

'The Miss has a brother, Lionel, who lives abroad. Miss Pickford lives alone now, since her father died. There's Cook, Mr Barnes, the head gardener, the daily comes in from the village. There used to be lads to help but the war took them away and none came back, I'm afraid. My brother Bill was one of them.'

'I'm so sorry,' said Flora. 'The war has a lot to answer for.' She did not want to share her own sorrows but made her way behind Minnie up a grand oak staircase to a room at the back of the corridor looking out onto a walled kitchen garden.

Minnie saw her looking out of the window. 'I'm afraid it's a bit of a mess. It's a good job the Miss don't see how it has fallen away but Barnes can't get the help. He does his best. I hope this room suits.' Minnie smiled.

Flora took in the large four-poster bed, the washstand, the wardrobe and well-upholstered armchair. It was private and she felt she could be comfortable here.

'I put some flowers in a vase for you, but you mustn't bring them near the Miss. They makes her sneeze and she don't like the smell. I'll leave you now to unpack. We won't disturb Miss Pickford. She must have her afternoon rest. At four o'clock she has her tea, lots of sugar and fresh cake, being very partial to cake. Cook will send them up and you can meet her then. The Miss will give you her schedule. We keeps to a strict timetable, because she don't like to be kept waiting.'

Flora nodded, her heart sinking. 'What do I call her?'

'Miss Pickford.'

'But what's her full name?' Flora was curious.

'Don't rightly know, miss. It begins with a D, I think,' came the reply.

'Thank you.' Flora dismissed the cheery Minnie with a smile, but inside she felt sick. One invalid and a houseful of servants, a rambling mansion with empty rooms. What on earth was she doing here, miles from anywhere?

At four o'clock Minnie was waiting with the tray. Flora hovered by the door while the maid set the table. The thick lace curtains were half drawn so the room was dim, the fire in the grate blazed although it was full summer.

'Who is this?' came a faint voice from the bed.

'It's Miss Garvie, the new nurse. She arrived on the twelve forty-five from London.'

Flora stepped forward to peer down at the woman in the bed. Her hair was covered with a lace cap, face flushed with the heat, the cheeks full, her chin plump.

'Lift me up, girl. I can't see you, slumped like this,' came the first order.

Flora lifted her gently, plumping the pillows to form a back rest.

'That's enough, girl. I don't want to catch a chill.'

'Are there any notes to advise me of your condition?' Flora asked, seeing a collection of bottles and pill boxes on the bedside table and reading the labels.

'As you see, I must have my pills on the dot. I ring when I require my commode. The room must be kept warm, day and night. I require you to read to me before the light goes out. I will ring for bed-turning. My sheets are changed daily when I'm bathed. You will help me to sit on the daybed, where I take luncheon. I then walk round the room for a while before my afternoon rest.'

'When do I help dress you?'

'Never, I'm far too frail for that palaver. I do not entertain except for the vicar. Talking exhausts me. As you see, I'm resigned to my fate. I will not make old bones. Like my poor mama, I will fade into a shadow when the Good Lord calls me.'

Flora bit her tongue. 'You look a long way from such a fate.' She took her pulse. It was regular and strong. 'Your flesh is pink, if a little plump. I do not detect any symptoms of such a decline.'

'What gives you the right to question my diagnosis?'

'Just experience… I was a nurse in the war,' Flora replied. She was not going to take any nonsense from this woman. 'I would advise you to have more time out of your bed. It weakens the limbs and encourages fluid on the lungs, sores on the skin. Let me see your buttocks.'

'How dare you order me about. When I bathe, then you can examine me further. I find you very forward in your remarks, and Scottish, to boot.'

'Correct, daughter of a shipbuilder, educated privately and four years under canvas. I'm a member of the Women's Suffrage society and I know ill-health when I see it.' Flora folded her arms in frustration.

'You are very sure of yourself, young lady.'

'Well, if I am to secure your recovery, I will devise a timetable of my own. It must be very boring to be confined to your room. How long have you been afflicted like this?'

'The Pickfords are not a strong family. Mama died when

I was ten, my brother left England for his health and Papa was sick for many years.'

'You looked after him?' Flora said.

'With help, yes, but he was very demanding. I was exhausted and now the same fate awaits me.'

'Only if you let it. I see no signs of an early demise. How old are you?'

'Thirty years of age – but why do you ask such questions?'

Flora suppressed a gasp – the woman in the bed looked so much older. 'Let me see your hair.'

'I wear it cropped to keep me cool,' Miss Pickford said.

'If you had no fire and opened the window, you would be cool enough. Fresh air fills the lungs with good breathing. Who is your doctor?'

'I got rid of him; nasty man wanted me to take walks and take a strict diet. I need the flesh around me to protect my bones.'

Flora tried not to smile. 'So, you think a thick layer of blubber is a cure-all?'

'I don't like your tone, Miss Garvie. I'm not accustomed to being questioned by an employed nurse in such a manner. Perhaps it's better you don't unpack and take yourself back to London.'

'Perhaps you are right, Miss Pickford. When people are dying in their thousands of this terrible sickness, I do not have time to waste on a perfectly healthy young woman who is convincing herself into an early grave. You are to be pitied for wasting the many years you have yet to live, when you could marry and bear children, do good to those around you. For those of us who have wealth, there are duties as well as privileges. To lie in bed and do nothing is death indeed. I do pity you though. I could help you but better I leave now than to waste both our times. I wish you well.' Flora turned towards the door to beat a retreat.

'How dare you foist your opinions on me and then turn your back. Do you not think I wish to be as other women are?' Miss Pickford sat up.

Flora turned round and, seeing the helpless look on the woman's face, she paused. 'I will stay until the morning and we'll discuss this further, if you feel it would be worthwhile. We have got off to a bad start.'

'Do you really mean what you say? I can get well again?'

'Of course, but it will take an effort on your part and mine... cooperation is the best tactic in facing a challenge.'

'But I'm afraid it's too late for me.' Her voice took on a pitiful edge.

'Ah, there's the rub! Fear is a great challenger. When we want to try something new, facing fear is the first step and you have just named it. Well done.'

'I don't understand...' Miss Pickford sank back into the pillow.

'You will, if we both tackle it together, but it is up to you, Miss Pickford. God helps those who help themselves and others. But I see I have tired you out.'

'Please stay,' Miss Pickford said.

'If you so wish.'

'I've never met a nurse like you before. You don't know your place.'

'Perhaps that's just as well, because my background is not dissimilar to your own. My name is Flora Garvie. You can call me Garvie if it suits. There is one thing I would like to suggest.'

'Name it.'

'Your four o'clock tea should be served, but with no cake,' Flora ordered.

'But I like my cake,' Miss Pickford whined.

'Better to have it once a week on Sunday as a special treat, understood? Bones are stronger if not weighed down with too much flesh.'

'If you say so, Miss Garvie.'

This was a start, Flora thought, realising there was quite a journey ahead to release Miss Pickford from this bedroom prison. The woman was sick but not in a way she was ready to acknowledge.

Chapter 11

In the late summer of 1919, Kit left Marseille with his new identity and took a train to Nîmes. He was sick of life in the busy port, with its quayside haunts and rough streets, and of working in the kitchen of a man who hated anyone with an English accent. He was a mean, foul-mouthed tyrant who cheated his staff, ran them ragged and pimped girls for sex-starved sailors. Here was a seedy side of life far beyond anything he had witnessed in Glasgow, with its brawls, beatings and drunken assaults.

One night, when Marcel was trying to persuade one of his waitresses upstairs, Kit lunged at him. 'The girl does not want it… leave her alone.'

Marcel turned his bulk on Kit, in an attempt to thump him senseless, but Kit was ready for the attack and threw his assailant on the floor. Marcel yelled out in pain. 'You bloody shirker, I know your sort, a deserter if ever I saw one. Wait till I stand… Get out of my bar before I set Pépé on you.'

Pépé was his flea-bitten mongrel, biting any customers

who got close to his master, but this threat meant nothing to Kit. Unknown to Marcel, the mutt had taken a shine to him. 'It will be a pleasure, *monsieur*. The *gendarmes* will be eager to inspect your premises for the rats that shelter here.' Kit pulled the waitress away to the other end of the bar. 'Go away home, lassie. This is no place for you.'

She shook her head. 'I must stay here. Marcel took me in when no one else would.'

'What hold does he have over you?' Kit felt pity for the half-starved waif.

'I went with a German soldier, a prisoner of war. My family disowned me so I had to leave the village. This is where I choose to stay. I don't mind the life, or the men; some are kind, like you.'

'Marcel is a bully… come away. We can find somewhere better for you.'

'No, Christophe, you are kind but you are not one of us. It's you who had better leave quickly. Marcel has friends.' As she was speaking, the girl rushed to the till and emptied it of notes. 'Take these… I will make up a story. You are owed wages, please go now!'

Kit went back to his room to collect his knapsack and headed towards the hills.

Nîmes was a beautiful city, full of Roman remains, but it was the hills of the Cévennes that took his eye. There was a majesty and mystery to these mountains. They were not the hills of home, but they called to him nevertheless. He bought a map, a ticket to Saint-Hippolyte-du-Fort, heading upwards, curious as to what he might find there.

It was hot and dusty and he was glad of his espadrilles. After taking water from the fountain, Kit bought bread, cheese and a hunk of *saucisson*. Following the nature trail through thick forest tracks, he climbed uphill beside sheep tracks worn by centuries of feet. From here, he could see plantations of vines, and chestnut groves. Trekking ever higher, sitting down to take in this beautiful landscape, he filled his lungs with the clear fresh air. These hills were empty of city noise and smoke, with only the chatter of birdsong in his ears. The track was dotted with bushes of gorse and juniper berries. Below him the course of the river valley snaked its way through the shrubs and rocks. The sun beat down ever harder and he sought shade for a siesta. Suddenly the thought of Christ alone in the desert came into his mind but he pushed such thoughts away. Sickening guilt and doubt always lay waiting to pounce.

Where was Flora now? He knew he looked like a tramp, his trousers tattered, splattered with dust, his ginger beard betraying his Celtic origins. Not many Frenchmen sported such flaming hair. Yet there was something in the wilderness of this landscape that spoke to him. Here he would be safe, but he must find work. It was the *vendange* season – the grape harvest. He realised he would stand out as a stranger, but somewhere there might be a place where he could take stock. In Marseille he had survived, keeping his head down doing menial jobs. No one gave him a second glance for the port was full of foreigners. In the countryside it might be different. There would be suspicion, so his story must be convincing: a British soldier wounded in the war, wanting to explore the country that had sheltered him before returning home.

The first shock on asking directions was that he could not understand the responses of the farmhands. It was not a dialect but some strange ancient language. With the help of gestures he just about understood enough to head north and west until he came to a hamlet with stone houses and slate roofs.

Below, in the fields, he saw men in broad straw hats working in the vineyards. The street was lined with purple-blossomed trees and mulberries. It felt so peaceful after the city, welcoming him in some strange way. Kit walked on until he came to a bigger village, with a well in the middle of the street, tall houses and, to his amazement, what looked like a familiar-shaped church with plain and simple architecture.

The door was open and the coolness of the building drew him indoors. There were benches, a pulpit unadorned. How strange, he thought. No images, no crucifixes or candles.

Sitting down, he felt suddenly overwhelmed with heat and tiredness. Walking for two days, sleeping under the stars, finishing off his meagre rations had exhausted him. His eyes drooped, his body relaxed, he lay down across the bench and fell into a deep sleep.

He awoke to find a man with a long beard standing over him. Kit jumped up. '*Je suis désolé,*' he mumbled, rubbing his eyes.

'You are the Englishman with fox-coloured hair that workers have noticed in the hills?' replied the old man with white hair and pale blue eyes, smiling.

'*Je suis écossais,*' Kit replied. 'I came in out of the heat. I do apologise.'

'*Mais de rien...* This temple is a sanctuary to all who seek peace and shelter.'

'Temple?' Kit said.

'Yes, this is a Protestant church and I am the pastor, Nicholas Vries from Holland,' the man replied in good English. 'In fact, I once went to a church convention in Edinburgh. Do you come from that magnificent city?'

'No, *monsieur*, I'm from Glasgow. But I must be on my way…' Kit rose to leave.

'Where are you heading? It is late in the day for a walk.'

'Not sure, it is such a magnificent countryside. When I saw the hills, I just had to climb them. I have a map,' he replied, not wishing to detain the pastor from his duties.

'"I will lift up mine eyes unto the hills".' The pastor smiled. '*Exactement*… You must dine with us.'

'*Mais non*, sir, I am not fit for company,' Kit said, looking down at his dusty clothes.

'We have water and soap, come, meet my family. It is not often we meet a Scotsman in our village, and one with such magnificent hair.' Pastor Vries took his arm.

Kit knew he could not refuse such kind hospitality. He was badly in need of a wash and a change of shirt, knowing he must stink to high heaven. '*Vous êtes très gentil…*'

He followed the old man up the cobbled street, aware of people looking at him with interest. They entered a tall house through a stone archway and emerged into a courtyard. Kit felt wary of what questions they might ask him but decided he would be as honest as he could.

'Marie, we have a guest. *Pardon*, I forgot to ask your name,' said Vries.

'Christophe… Chris Carstairs,' Kit answered, not looking his host in the face.

A tall woman in a long black skirt and apron came to greet him. 'Come, you look tired. When did you last eat?'

Kit smiled. 'This morning, but please, *madame*, I will sit outside. I am unwashed for many days.'

'Come then, Christophe, I will boil water. There is a washbasin in your room.'

'But *madame*, I have no clean clothes,' Kit protested, blushing.

'We have shirts, sadly no longer in use since our son, Simeon, fell at Verdun.'

'Marie could not part with them,' said Vries. 'Now we know why. They were waiting for you to come to us in need. Do not be shy.'

Kit was ushered upstairs to a bedroom, a maid brought hot water, shaving soap, a clean linen shirt, underwear and thick trousers. He dunked his head in the water, as if baptised afresh, then put on the dead man's clothes in trepidation. He had not asked for such hospitality and he felt humbled by the generosity and trust of his Christian hosts, unsure of what to say or how to explain himself to them.

He looked at his new self in the tall mirror. He was thinner to the point of being scrawny, there were even more streaks of grey at his temples, and his arms were mottled with brown freckles. He wanted to weep with gratitude at this unexpected kindness, knowing, as a passing guest, he must do his best to be honest.

'*Voilà*, a new man,' said the pastor, smiling. 'I think you will feel better, yes?'

Kit nodded. 'I thank you, it's a long time since I sat at such a beautiful table.' He looked around the room and saw a silver framed photograph of Simeon in his uniform, staring out proudly at him.

'You have a wound to your face from the war?' Marie said with concern.

'Yes, the war,' he said, pointing to his scar. 'A sad time for all of us.'

'You were in a Scottish regiment. You wore the kilt?'

'Of course,' said Kit smiling. 'In battle we wore aprons, but now there is peace at last.' He wanted to get off this subject. The door opened and in walked a young woman, who stared at Kit in shock, then made to leave.

'Liliane, come back, sit down… we will explain.' Marie rose to welcome her.

'Liliane was our son Simeon's betrothed. It has been hard for her. So many young men went from here, but few have returned,' Vries explained.

Marie ushered Liliane to the table. 'Come, sit with us and meet our Scottish guest.'

Liliane nodded, her eyes wide with surprise.

'He fell asleep in the church, his clothes were… well, they needed a wash. Simeon would want us to share his own with him.'

Liliane said nothing at first except, 'Pardon, I have little anglais,' she whispered.

'Liliane teaches at the village school and our children love her,' Marie continued.

They said grace and ate in silence, a wonderful rabbit stew laced with herbs. 'Our rabbits are fed with rosemary, thyme and juniper. Can you taste them?' Marie continued.

Kit had not had a feast like this for months, with delicious juices dripping from his lips onto his napkin. He nodded energetically, agreeing, then said, 'Pardon, madame, excuse me dribbling.' They laughed at his words.

'It is good to hear that accent again. I loved the hills of Scotland. The people were very kind, too,' Pastor Vries said.

Kit sat back enjoying this civilised company, aware that Liliane was eyeing him, her eyes darting away when he returned her gaze. She was a pretty, birdlike creature with sharp features, her hair tied into a plait across her head. She was wearing the black clothes of a widow.

'Do you know the history of our people?' the pastor asked.

'I'm afraid I don't. I know a little of the Huguenots and their persecution.'

'Here we have many Protestant temples. When our faith was threatened, our people fled to the hills to worship in the mountains. We live at peace now with our Catholic neighbours. We worship apart and live as plain folk do, some more than others. The mulberry trees provide leaves for the silk mills, but in the war there was little call for silk, which is a worry as we have many weavers. Our people farm and grow vines and chestnuts, but we are a scattered population. Are you Catholic? Not that it matters to us.'

Kit shook his head. 'I was brought up Presbyterian. My parents were missionaries.'

'Then will you stay awhile amongst us, explore our beautiful country and worship with us? You look as if a rest might help you on your journey.' It was if the pastor was looking into his heart, recognising his troubled soul.

'Sir, I have nothing with which to fund my stay here,' Kit replied, not sure if he wanted to remain under scrutiny.

'Who asked you for money? There are plenty of tasks for a young man to help those who have lost their sons and husbands,' Vries continued.

Kit was tempted. 'I'm not sure, sir...'

'Who but the Lord himself would send me a Presbyterian Scottish soldier down on his luck and plonk him on a bench in our temple, like a fallen angel with flame in his hair?'

Kit sat back and laughed. 'If you put it like that...'

'Good, that's settled then,' said Nicholas Vries, nodding to his wife and Liliane with satisfaction. 'We can find him plenty to do here, can't we?'

Chapter 12

In the glorious autumn colours of the Cotswolds, the rehabilitation of Drusilla Pickford began in earnest. Flora was not going to waste time pandering to the silly woman's excuses and there were many battles ahead. First, was persuading the invalid she would not collapse if she left her bed each morning, dressed as if ready to receive visitors, and read the morning paper.

On Flora's afternoons off, she left the house to explore the beautiful lanes and villages of the county while Minnie took it upon herself to stand guard and record any tantrums. It was the lushness of the area that half persuaded Flora to stay at this post. What struck her though, was the ruinous state of the estate cottages, so in need of repair, the sight of tired women tending their vegetable patches while ragged clothes fluttered along the washing lines. There was an air of neglect and sadness. No one looked up to greet her. Children rushed past her, shoeless. How did they fare in winter?

Going back to Bordley Court with its sunlit aspect and

sumptuous furnishings made the contrast all the more uncomfortable. It was hard to see Drusilla in all her fussy surroundings and not feel determined to change some things. When was the last time this pampered woman had seen the condition in which her tenants lived? She was not a 'Miss Havisham' yet, but where would her selfish isolation end? Flora was eager to shake her out of her lethargy.

'I went for a walk in Bordley this afternoon. It is a sad place.'

'The war took our men. Barnes has no under gardeners to train up and the borders are neglected. I don't like to look out of the window at such mess.'

Trust Drusilla to think only of herself. 'I was thinking more of the children without shoes, or warm winter coats. That is what I call real neglect,' Flora replied, hoping for a sympathetic response, but Drusilla said nothing, turning her attention to the fire. 'It's getting cold, Minnie must attend to it.' She rang the servant's bell to summon her. 'Where's my tea, it's late…'

'For someone so frail, you care a lot about your stomach,' said Flora.

'How dare you question my condition?'

Flora was not going to be distracted, putting a log on the fire herself. 'There are so many of your tenants in need of firewood and good food. As their landlady, perhaps it's time for you to take more interest in them.'

'There you go again,' Drusilla said. 'I do not employ you to question me on things the estate manager can see to.'

'But if only you could visit to see for yourself, I'm sure it would help speed things along.'

'How can I go out in my condition?'

'And what condition is that, exactly?' Flora shook her head in frustration.

'Don't be impertinent, I've had enough lectures from you.'

'Miss Pickford, I haven't even begun yet, but if you are not prepared to cooperate, there's no point in my staying. As I keep saying, you could be such a force for good, if only you got off your daybed, put on a pair of stout shoes and made an effort. Before we have tea, it's time for your daily walk in the fresh air. Come on, it will do you good to see your borders for yourself. I'll get your coat.'

'My fur coat... I expect it's chilly out there. The nights are drawing in, or hadn't you noticed, half dressed in that cape?'

'I'll have you know this cape was a lifesaver in France. When we were frozen in our tents, we slept fitfully, fully dressed, with blankets, capes, and newspapers underneath to keep warm. Sometimes we bundled in together,' Flora added.

'There you go again, war, war, war. I'm sick of such talk.'

Flora felt her fury rising. 'Meanwhile, some of you lay snug in your beds, well fed and pampered, while others starved. No more excuses, it's a beautiful afternoon. The trees are turning gold and russet. You are lucky to live in such a gorgeous setting.'

'If I must,' Drusilla sighed. 'You are a hard taskmaster.' Wrapped in her fur coat and hat, she descended the stairs like a Russian princess. At the door to the portico entrance, she hesitated, as if the very act of leaving the cocoon of her house took some enormous effort. Flora recognised this hesitancy.

'Deep breaths, Miss Pickford, smell the autumn air, the woodsmoke. This is the season of mists and mellow fruitfulness.'

'Don't go spouting poetry at me... I'm here, aren't I?'

They walked slowly round the garden path, Flora pausing to point out apples, berries and the late Michaelmas daisies and asters. Then she settled herself down on a seat. 'I have something to ask you.'

'What now?'

'I wondered if I might borrow the car. I've been driving for years. Perhaps we could take a tour of the area together, to Cirencester, go into the country to view some other villages and old churches.'

'Whatever for? When you've seen one street, you've seen them all. They're all the same round here.'

'I doubt it,' said Flora. 'I've been reading about the wool merchants' churches. There's one in Burford I would like to see. Have you visited it?'

'No, but I suppose I'll have to. Is this another part of my treatment?'

'Not exactly, but I'd like your company, just the same,' Flora replied with a smile.

Drusilla shook her head but there was a twinkle in her eye. 'You are exasperating at times, Flora Garvie...'

'Good, we can have lunch out and make a day of it.' Flora sensed she had overcome another obstacle of Miss Pickford's resistance to change.

From bed to daybed, down the stairs into the garden, touring in the car along the leafy lanes, to draughty golden stone churches, admiring stained-glass mediaeval windows, statues and beautiful landscapes, Drusilla began to take notice of the world around her. The attacks of panic at leaving the house lessened. Her attendance at church increased as she ran out of excuses, but the taking on of responsibility for her estate was still a far-off dream. In the end it was to be a simple request that brought Drusilla closer to her tenants.

The nearby village of Lee Stowe had formed a Rural Women's Institute where women of the village could meet together once a month for practical demonstrations, talks and social events. It was presided over by Lady Olveston, from Olveston Hall, and her daughter.

Mrs Repton, the vicar's wife, spread the idea that perhaps Bordley cum Magna might like to form its own society. Resistance was firm from farmers and some husbands, who felt a night away from the home and hearth was solely their prerogative.

Not to be deterred, Mrs Repton came to call on Drusilla with a request. 'If you were to encourage your tenants' wives, as their landlady, to form a monthly meeting, there would be fewer arguments. Would you consider standing as their chairman?'

'Oh, I couldn't... I don't go out in in the evening.'

'This will be an afternoon meeting to fit in with chores and school. Everyone would be back in time to make meals. We would value your presence to add weight to the proceedings.' Mrs Repton nodded in Flora's direction for encouragement.

'Indeed, I think it's most suitable that the lady of the manor should take the lead. Lady Olveston is doing her duty,' Flora added.

Drusilla waved her hand. 'Well, if you put it like that... but I'll not be expected to make an address, will I?'

'Perhaps later. We will need a pianist, so perhaps Miss Garvie will oblige us? She was a great success in the Sunday school. The meetings open with a hymn. A committee of members will deal with our programme of events and all you would have to do is introduce speaker or topic and the members will do the rest. Can I leave it in your capable hands? I'm sure Miss Flora will help you.' Drusilla nodded weakly and Flora smiled with relief. 'Good, I knew you would come on board.'

Flora sensed this new meeting might overcome Drusilla's shyness and help her to mix in the community. She was afraid her employer was in danger of becoming over-dependent on her as a companion, but soon, she thought, it would be time to return home. She had stayed much longer than expected. Her sister, Elvira, wrote screeds about new friends, parties, meetings and dances. There were lengthy details about all the pretty dresses, with short skirts, she was buying in Sauchiehall Street. This frivolity worried her but it was Pa's news that was more serious.

He was worried that now the demand for warships was over, he would have to lay off men in the shipyards. He also mentioned that Aunt Jemima was not well. He couldn't manage Kildowie without Mima.

Staying here in Bordley Court now felt like an indulgence but it had served two purposes: one, that Drusilla was coming back to life, and secondly, Flora had had time to mourn Kit's loss in privacy. The anger she felt at his leaving her was fading. All that was left was a deep sadness for what might have been.

Like so many wartime women, she was having to face a future that no longer included a lover. Lady Olveston's daughter, Petra, lost her fiancé at Gallipoli. Drusilla Pickford limped through life not knowing the joys of lying in the arms of a loving man. Flora felt perhaps she was better off not giving her heart and then feeling the agony when all hope was gone.

Mrs Repton told her there was a mother in the village who kept the door ever open in case her son, George, returned in the night. Even when she received the bronze memorial penny, given to all families who lost soldiers, she did not open it, shoving it in the back of a cupboard. George would not want to see it when he returned. False hope was eating her from within and the doctor did not think she would last out the winter.

In the next month or two, Flora decided, she would hand in her notice, giving Drusilla time for the women's meeting to be established. She hoped that when the time came to leave, they would remain friends, but Flora knew Drusilla Pickford resisted change and there might be battles ahead.

Chapter 13

Kit did not mean to stay so long with Pastor Vries but
there were many tasks for a fit man in the valley that
he could not ignore. He turned his hand to whatever was
asked of him. At the time of the *vendange*, he joined the
villagers stripping the grapes from the vines and putting
them into pails. It was late summer and a scene worthy of
sketching; the green-gold valley, the river racing through the
rocks, the hillside vineyards and the broad straw hats that
kept off the fierce sun. The tubs of grapes were loaded onto
horse carts bound for Monsieur Causse's yard, where they
would be crushed.

Then came the chopping of old chestnut branches into
logs, beating walnut trees to collect the nuts while the scent
of woodsmoke perfumed the air. On Sundays he joined the
family in the temple out of courtesy, aware that Liliane
Causse sat on a bench watching him. She was the *vigneron*'s
daughter, forced to live at home with her little brother, Jean,
who liked to play football with Kit and practise his English.

Liliane watched them from a distance, but spoke few

words to Kit, if they ever found themselves alone. She often walked the schoolchildren to the river to bathe their feet and collect flowers for the classroom. She helped the older girls with sewing lessons. Many worked in the silk mills, others took the bus as far as Saint-Jean-du-Gard.

No questions were asked of him, except those of a spiritual nature. He listened to the pastor preaching, agreeing with much of what he said. Vries was not a hell and damnation kind of pulpit firebrand, but spoke of love and redemption. 'To love is great, the great gift, which makes the world a garden of hope. This solace comes to all who trust in the Lord's words.' Kit felt the quiet passion of the man's conviction and mourned the loss of it in himself.

'Are you at one with our Lord?' Vries asked him afterwards, as if it was natural to expect a direct answer. Kit did not reply, turning away from his piercing gaze, embarrassed. How could he explain how angry he felt and how hopeless after all he had witnessed on the battlefield... Where was the God of love in all that chaos? At such times, he would drown his sorrows in spirits. Now all he could do was to refrain from drinking in the local inn, respecting his hosts teetotal beliefs. It was as if in this year he was gaining strength and health through this outdoor life but it could not last; this hiding away from the reality of his predicament. He was living a lie amongst them. They were assuming he was a true Christian when, in reality, he was no such person; far from it.

He had lived like a tramp, taken refuge in the mountains, and now, in the comfort of their home, he sensed he was being looked to as a suitable replacement for the Vries's lost son, Simeon.

They often asked Liliane to supper, expecting Kit to escort the girl home to her parents' house. They, in turn, invited him in to sample their produce.

'Judge the flavours. Each batch is unique, because it takes on the *terroir*, Christophe.' Liliane and her mother sat listening, with embroidery or mending on their laps, looking up at him with a smile, while little Jean jumped on his knee and prattled away.

Kit was sure he had given Liliane no encouragement but somehow his reticence had made her family all the more eager to embrace him.

He was beginning to feel trapped by all these expectations. And soon, a harsh winter would wrap itself around the village roads and tracks, with farms hidden by drifts for days. It would be time to leave and trek back down to the warmer coast to find work again.

As the first Armistice anniversary dawned, Kit found himself in the crowded temple while the names of the dead were read out. Suddenly all the grief of the past year flooded over him. All over the world, this day would be marked with solemnity, the sacrifices of so many, never to be forgotten. He thought of Fergus, Bertie and those of his regiment. Were they now in a better place, looking down on him? He could not bear the thought of Fergus condemning his betrayal of his sister and he wondered whether Flora was suffering somewhere in Scotland.

He walked down to the river in the late afternoon, but his black shadow of sadness and doubt followed him. He had not walked far when he glimpsed Liliane trailing behind him. 'I came to see if you were… This is a hard day for all of us... all those lost men. It is too much, is it not?' They were almost the longest words she had spoken to him.

He paused to let her join him as he sat watching the river Hérault and thought of the famous lines from 'Abide with Me': *Time, like an ever-rolling stream, bears all its sons away...* He recalled all the drumhead services and burials he had taken. Had it really brought any comfort?

'We who are lonely should share our grief,' Liliane said, touching his arm.

Kit tried not to wince. 'Please, Liliane, I have nothing to offer you.'

She smiled. 'I ask only for comfort, a warm touch. I would love to have a child from your body,' she said.

Kit was shocked at this unexpected boldness, especially from such a shy woman. 'I'm sorry, I'm not free to give such a thing. As I said, I have nothing to offer... if I have misled you in any way...'

'Many say I am a fine woman,' Liliane continued. 'I have thick hair and my body is strong. I ask for only one night or two...' She was ignoring his resistance.

'Please, Miss Causse, enough. I am not the right man for you. You're too kind and spiritual.' Kit shook off her hand. 'I love another who is not free... You have all been so kind, but I can't give you what you ask. I do not want to compromise you.'

She paused, turning to him. 'I could tell them we are lovers and you must marry me then,' she said.

'But you won't, you're not such a woman. You have your pride, as I have mine. There will be someone waiting to give you what you need one day, but it is not me. I am so sorry...

please go. I came here to be alone with my memories.' He was being cruel to be kind.

Kit sensed she was crying as she slipped away from his side. How ever did this happen? Now there was no decision to make. He must leave before things got worse.

This respite here had been a gift but the price of past betrayal was restless nights and regret. He could no longer live among honest people. His name, his history, were all fabrications. Liliane's approach was a signal that his time in this remote sanctuary was over. How they must wonder about the man who arrived from nowhere, who received and sent no post, who had a scar of war on his face and in his soul. There would be talk when he disappeared overnight, but he would soon be forgotten. Then he recalled a text from St Paul: *Here we have no abiding city*. The price of his freedom was always to be on the move.

Chapter 14

Flora sat on the window seat overlooking the garden to read Pa's letter.

My dear Flora,

We are beginning to fear you will never return to us. I do not understand your absence. Why have you not come home? All is not well here. Jemima is in hospital and not likely to recover from an operation to remove a blockage. Elvira is away in Glasgow, with a gang of young agitators of whom I don't approve. She has formed an attachment to one of my shipyard workers, Sandy Lennox, who she met in some Clydesider rally. She'll not listen to sense and spouts such political nonsense. I fear for her sanity. Perhaps you could reason with her before the whole thing gets out of hand.

The Armistice Memorial has come and gone with thousands attending in George Square for a moving service of remembrance. We will never forget our lost boys...

Flora folded the letter, knowing it was time to depart. Why had she put off her return for so long? What was it about returning to Glasgow that made her reluctant? How unkind and selfish it was to persist in hiding away here.

In her heart, she knew losing Kit was behind everything. Here there were no reminders of him, or what might have been between them. Now, she was dreading her return. It made no sense. There were no memories of him back home either, only his visits to Kildowie when she was a girl. It was memories of Fergus, not Kit, that would haunt the house and yet... She shook her head. If only we had known each other in friendship then, not ignored each other. The Kit of Glasgow was not the tortured soul she had loved in the Rose Villa. In the south of France, they had brought each other to life. His death was still raw, an open wound that wouldn't heal. What would be waiting for her back home but tension and loss? Elvira had not written to her lately and Hector's wife, Rose, made no mention of any troubles. Time, then, to face the journey north.

Drusilla sulked at her news. 'How can you abandon me when I'm still struggling?'

'Nonsense,' Flora chided her. 'You are back in perfect health and much-needed in the church and the village. You've entertained Lady Olveston here and she's proving to be a good friend to you. Now there is so much to look forward to in life.'

'Can't you stay on for Christmas?'

'No, because my family need me, and I'm afraid my aunt is dying. My father has many worries and my younger sister needs some guidance.'

'You are lucky to have a family.' Drusilla looked towards the piano top, glancing at photographs of her late parents.

'You could always invite your brother, Lionel, to visit for the festive season. You've not seen him for many years. Friends can become like family, too. It's up to you now to fill your days and this house with noise and laughter. It's a beautiful home to be shared, not shuttered away. The gardens are a delight, and a garden party for church funds would give everyone a chance to admire them. Perhaps you might even venture north and visit me at Kildowie and see all our beautiful countryside for yourself.'

'Really! Do you mean that? But it's a long way...' Drusilla perked up before subsiding again.

'Barnes could drive you to Cheltenham to take the train and you could be with us in a day,' Flora replied.

'I would have to wrap up warm, if it is as chilly up there as I've heard.'

'As you please, but just think about it. September is always a lovely month to visit Loch Lomond.' Flora felt Drusilla relaxing.

Three days later, Flora sat in first class, heading north through the Midlands and up the west coast to Carlisle. She tried to ignore the signal box at Quintinshill where the accident had robbed them of her brother. How could she not recall the terrible flames and fumes, the screams of dying men as she sat helpless on the upbound train to Glasgow? Theirs should have been a family reunion, but Fergus had no time to meet them. This event convinced her that nursing was the role for her. Now that career was closed off. Going home was all she had left.

Pa was waiting in the December chill. His hair was white

and he was sporting a thick beard. He was still a handsome man for his age, but looking drained and tired. They hugged each other warmly.

'Home at last... we thought you'd forgotten us. There's just time for a quick visit to the Western Infirmary to see Mima. She's been asking for you,' he said, ushering her to his limousine.

Her aunt lay in a side ward. Mima had shrunk into a little old woman before her time. Her eyes, though, lit up at the sight of her niece.

'Come closer, hen... Good to see you. I knew you wouldn't stay away. We've missed you, but now you're here.' Flora clasped her bony hand with care. 'When I'm away to my rest, make sure you have my jewels. I'm no' letting yon flibbertigibbet sister of yours have the whole of them. She would be selling them for the Bolsheviks in the Gorbals.'

Flora wasn't sure what this was all about, but she smiled and nodded. 'We'll see about that,' she said.

A nurse came in and ordered them out. 'She's awful weak, we want her to sleep.'

'Ach away with you, I'll be asleep soon enough,' came the voice from the bed. Aunt Jemima wanted the last word. 'Let them stay.'

'Just five minutes. They can come tomorrow.'

'Perhaps... let me look at you, child. You're like a drink of water and pinched in the face. Who's been hurting you?'

Flora smiled and avoided answering. 'It's lovely to be back for good; no more gallivanting for me.'

'You always did have itchy feet... One day you'll be back

in France, back to where your sorrows began and where they'll end, lassie.'

Flora looked at her father. 'What does she mean?'

'Let her talk. She tells me I'll find a wife before long and Elvira will be a mother… Where she gets these notions from, I've no idea,' Allan Garvie whispered, with tears in his eyes.

'Whisht, young man, I'm no' finished yet. Don't you give up on the shipyard… A time will come when you'll be needed again.' Mima smiled, shaking her head. 'My mother told me just the other day, sure as death, war is coming. She was sitting by my bed and held my hand. '"It'll no' be long now, my bonnie bairn," she said, "and we'll be together again. Fergus will be waiting tae greet thee."' The talking exhausted her. She closed her eyes. 'Away home now and see to things. I'm fine. It won't be long.'

They tiptoed out. Flora took one last lingering look at her aunt. She was right, death was waiting patiently to take her in the wee small hours. She had felt the cold feet, weak pulse and the beginning of the rattle in her chest. There was no point in staying, as the dying often liked to depart alone.

'Good night, dear Jemima.' Flora turned back and kissed her forehead. 'All will be well.'

Chapter 15

1922

Antibes in winter was bustling with tourists wanting warmth and bright skies. Kit had found garden work at the Hotel du Cap, an ochre-coloured mansion built on a promontory jutting out into the Mediterranean. Monsieur Sella, the manager, liked having Britishers on his staff to help the wealthy American and English guests, who spoke little French, to enjoy their stay. By now Kit knew many of the best places to visit, the mediaeval villages and forts, castles and churches, but most guests just wanted to recline in the sun and dine at the finest restaurants.

He had a room over a stable block, his wage was modest but he lived mostly on generous tips. This gave him cash on his days off to buy art materials, to pursue the urge to capture the brilliance of the light and scenery around the bay. He took lessons from an old man who had once trained alongside Monet in Paris but his approach was old-fashioned, preferring statues or buildings: 'Look, look and really see...' he would say, which Kit found hard to understand.

He was more into technical draughtsmanship, a good disciplinarian but boring and Monsieur Heget lost interest when Kit did not bring his set pieces but produced brightly coloured seascapes. There was no point in wasting his hard-earned cash this way. Perhaps he was not cut out for the artistic life after all, impatient as he was with his progress.

The sketchbooks from the war, buried in his knapsack, had much more expression and fluidity than these lifeless and rigid exercises. He had kept them as souvenirs, including a brief sketch of Flora that always made him feel sad and guilty.

Then Monsieur Sella decided to open his hotel for the summer and not close down during this quieter season as was usual. He was further encouraged when an American couple rented the whole hotel for the summer, inviting as their guests artists and writers, much to Kit's amazement and relief. He need not lose his living but could stay on to greet all the new visitors. By midsummer, the hotel was bustling. A troupe of dancers arrived from London and Paris, gorgeous girls with lithe bodies in flimsy tunics. They cavorted around the hotel swimming pool, sat among rocks topless, not caring who viewed them. Kit was elevated to working in the bar, wearing a smart uniform. He did not know where to look when serving cocktails, but he soon found himself relaxing on the beach on his afternoon off, curious as to how these young women came to be such bold and imaginative dancers.

'Madame Morris has a studio in Chelsea. She's a marvellous ballet dancer who's created a new movement,' replied one pretty dancer, called Sylvie, who promptly jumped up to demonstrate. 'It's based on Greek movements,' she said, posing like an image from a Minoan vase. 'Come and meet her and her lover, he is a famous Scottish painter.'

Kit recoiled at the thought of meeting a fellow Scotsman but curiosity got the better of him when he served drinks to the couple lounging on the sand, smoking.

'Sir, Sylvie told me about you. I'm ashamed to say I've not seen any of your work.'

Mr Fergusson looked up, cigarette in mouth. 'Not many have yet, but we live in hope, don't we, Meg?' They both laughed.

'He's being modest. He's exhibited in Paris and been very well received,' his wife replied.

'But what's brought a braw Scotsman into this den of iniquity?' Fergusson eyed him with interest. 'And a Glaswegian – or have I mistaken your accent?'

Kit nodded. 'I'm just travelling. I'm learning to paint a little in my spare time.'

'That's no use, laddie, you have to give yourself up to it, not dabble. An artist must live to paint, not paint as a hobby. Don't get me wrong, there's nothing wrong with amateur art, but I guess that is not what you're after? Come and show me what you've done some time.' Kit backed off, embarrassed by this generous offer. Who would want to see his scribbles?

Sylvie saw his hesitation. 'Believe me, he'll give it to you straight, because who learns without criticism? They're a kind couple, and encouraging. Look at me, I thought I had two left feet. My own ballet teacher despaired of me, but Meg Morris showed me a different style and method. I never thought I'd be in her troupe but she drills us until I could dance in my sleep.'

From her plummy voice, Kit guessed she was a girl from some affluent southern family who let her roam with the company, free of all home commitments. She was fair-haired, with the type of skin that tanned into a golden hue. Her blue eyes were pale, almost Scandinavian.

'Would you like me to pose for you?' she said. 'I can stand still, or lie, as you wish. You should see Fergusson's nudes – they're stunning and erotic.' She winked at him.

Kit didn't know what to reply, but something in her bold stare challenged him to agree. 'I can't pay much,' he replied.

'Dearie me, what a buttoned-up creature you are… I'm doing it for fun, to see if you can make a go of my body. All artists do life drawing. How else can you really connect with the human form?'

'Do you paint? Everybody here seems to be artistic,' Kit said, aware that he must seem an ignoramus.

'There's more guests to come. It's going to be one long summer party. Some of the Frenchies are, well, very bohemian in their tastes.' Sylvie paused. 'Don't be shocked. I'll meet you on the beach after your shift. I'll be waiting.' She smirked, making Kit blush.

Kit found her lying naked by a rock, with a silk paisley shawl draped discreetly across her groin. 'Thought you'd never come,' she said impatiently, pointing to her rug.

'Sorry I'm late. We're busy with new arrivals from America.' He sat in the hot sand, feeling awkward at her obvious pleasure.

'Come on, just look and see the shapes and lines. Don't spoil the light and shade… You're at the wrong angle.'

Kit felt himself tensing up, his fingers tightening, unsure how to start. He could see an outline and carefully pencilled this in, finding himself stirred by her languid pose. Resisting an embarrassing surge in his groin, he tried to concentrate on the task in hand. 'This is no good,' he sighed. He got up to leave, shaking his head.

'Oh, do sit down and loosen up. Have you never seen a naked woman before? Honestly, you're strung as tight as piano wire. What you need is a stiff drink. Let me see what you drew.'

Kit recoiled, pulling his sketchpad into his chest. 'No, I'm showing this to nobody. Thank you for your time, but I don't think this sort of drawing is for me.' He had found the whole episode uncomfortable. It was as if his hands were laced with rope, unable to express any movement in his fingers. Now he avoided the dancing troupe, keeping busy behind the bar as it filled with families and artists. He was ignorant of who they all were, until the waiters pointed out Pablo Picasso and his cronies. Then another Scots couple arrived, older, gentler, the Rennie Mackintoshes... The very man who had designed the Willow tea rooms and other famous buildings in Glasgow. Kit felt tongue-tied, knowing here were some of the giant artists of his age. He desperately wanted to meet and talk to them but he was a barman, not a guest.

Kit watched the golden couples lounging, drinking cocktails, off for drives in expensive limousines. This was a world away from his provincial city home, a world underpinned by old and new money and privilege. What would Pastor Vries make of this gilded cage? There was a part of him that stood back, observing the pampering these visitors expected from staff. Some screamed and shouted all night, demanding drinks, others passed out drunk, while no one seemed to sleep in their own rooms. It was siren country and he was an outsider, not sure if he ever wanted to be in such a clique. Was this what the war was fought for? The boys who died, who he'd buried in pits, many unknown, boys who would never know what their sacrifice was worth… surely not for this, Kit thought, not for this decadence? Some evenings, the girls gave concerts on the shore, silhouetted against the setting sun. He had never seen bodies so liberated and sensuous. One night he went back to his room and sketched out the scene from memory, the shapes, the angles and the colours that had fired his imagination. In the morning he rose and saw what he had done, and for the first time he felt satisfied. It had life, colour and movement. Perhaps that was something he might show to Mr Fergusson if the opportunity arose later. There was a knock on the door and, without hesitation, Sylvie bounced into his room, wearing silk pyjamas and carrying a bottle.

'Come on, Chris, it's time you had a lesson or two that's strictly not on any curriculum. Have you been avoiding me?' Sylvie took his hand. 'Time to show you horizontal poses.'

Chapter 16

'What did your last slave die of?' Flora snapped at her sister. Elvira had dumped all her clothes in a heap on the bedroom floor. 'You can jolly well pick them up. We can't expect Mrs Quinn to traipse after you... Come on, chop, chop!'

'You're as bad as Aunt Mima, ordering me about,' her sister sulked, but she pulled her clothes off the floor and dumped them on a chair. 'Satisfied?'

'Will you be in for dinner tonight?' Flora asked.

'What's it to you?'

'I'm only asking you, so I know. If there's just Pa and me, we'll eat in the kitchen, not the dining room.'

'I've got a meeting and I'll be staying with Isa Lennox.'

'I see. When will you be back then?'

Elvira shrugged her shoulders. 'How do I know? I'll be in the campaign office all morning, and meeting some friends for lunch. And by the way, everyone calls me Vera now, I don't like Elvira.'

'But it's your given name, Mummy chose it for you. What's wrong with it?'

'It smacks of money and private education and all that stuff.'

Flora shook her head. 'So, *Vera*, we'll see you when we see you. I was hoping we could go shopping and take in a matinee, a film. We never seem to have time together, nowadays.'

'I've no time for pictures... they're all sentimental rubbish and a waste of good money, a sop to the downtrodden...'

Flora made a hasty retreat. She could not face another of Vera's political lectures.

It was strange how Flora seemed to take up the mantle left by Mima after she passed away. Back at Kildowie, life went on almost as she'd left it in 1915, but there were subtle changes. Often there was just Pa and herself for supper, and lately there were no more cooks or maids, just a daily from the village. Vera was always out at political meetings with Sandy Lennox and his crowd of agitators. She used her home like a hotel and often stayed over in the city with friends. Flora suspected it was Sandy who took her back to his tenement flat at night.

Since the war, Vera had changed from a schoolgirl to an argumentative idealist full of theories on how the working classes must rise up and take their rightful place in government. There seemed a gulf between them. The war years and Flora's experiences meant very little to her sister. For her generation, it was the past and best forgotten. The future was working for social equality, peace and liberty for the downtrodden. Deeds not words.

Vera had her own allowance. She drove a modest saloon car, but still liked to appear in smart outfits and wear her cropped hair in a Marcel wave. Appearance mattered, even if Sandy dressed like a tramp most of the time. What the attraction was puzzled Flora. She found him sullen and contemptuous of their background. Pa would not let him in the house, after his first visit.

Her one comfort was Rose Murray, her practising doctor friend, still happy in Bearsden with Hector and their children. They had a nanny for Hamish and Iris. Now she ran a surgery in the rough end of the city with a welfare clinic to help nursing mothers and babies. Hers was the true concern for the downtrodden and burdened women of the slums, Flora thought, restless to be useful outside the home. Their house was too empty now, but Pa clung on to the hope that one day it would ring with childish noise.

'What can I do?' she complained to Rose over supper one night. 'I've done nothing useful but keep house and moan to you, since I came home.' She sighed, as Rose was collecting up the family clutter in their drawing room; toys, papers and empty cups.

'What you need is a job and some fun.'

'Easy to say, hard to find, with things as they are,' Flora replied.

'I've been thinking about that and I have a solution,' said Rose. 'There's a move afoot to provide advice to women from nurses and midwives. Birth control is what I mean, but it is a delicate subject, especially among certain churches. I see women worn down with too many mouths to feed, men, unemployed, with the fear of yet another pregnancy held over them. Many are coming for help too late. You've no idea to what lengths some will go to prevent another child. We have simple devices to help, but the very suggestion causes great disgust. Many are too poor to buy them. This is a battle worth fighting, Flora.'

'I take your point, but I have no experience. I'm unmarried. What can I do?'

'Read up on it: *Married Love*, for a start. I have a copy somewhere. We need to set up premises, form a committee, advertise discreetly… all the usual stuff. I know it will be opposed, but we both know deeds not words win the day. What do you think?'

'I'm not sure I am qualified for this sort of work.' Flora hadn't heard of any of these ideas before.

'Perhaps you could come and help in my clinic sometime and get a feel for what we are dealing with. I really could use your help.' Rose had a gentle way of coercing that Flora couldn't ignore. 'As for the second of my plans for you, we have a concert party starting up, raising funds for limbless soldiers. I think you'd enjoy being part of it. There are lots of sketches and singing – do say you will join us?'

The thought of prancing on a stage did not appeal, but then she had entertained wounded soldiers in the war. This was a worthy cause, so how could she refuse? Hector's work was connected to the hospital for the limbless soldiers and sailors at Erskine House across the Clyde. It was a mansion dedicated to helping war veterans. There were articles in the *Herald* about how they desperately needed funds, comforts and extra equipment. How could she ignore this, after all she'd experienced behind the trenches?

In the months that followed this conversation, Flora came to Rose's clinic in a church hall close to the surgery to watch babies being examined. She made endless cups of tea, observed the poverty that brought mothers in shawls, lugging ragged toddlers while heavy with child. The kiddies often had skin rashes, headlice and rotten teeth. There were children with bandy legs, runny noses and squinty eyes needing light treatment. It made her think of her own privileged childhood and she felt ashamed that the accident of birth and family income gave some people great advantages over others. Life was indeed not fair.

Their newly formed committee began to make plans for a clinic in town but opposition was immediate. Landlords would not rent premises for such an immoral purpose. The local parish priest got news of their plans and began the protest, forbidding the women in his congregation to attend. Donations were slow to arrive. It was all taking time.

Only married women were to be advised but if someone wore a brass curtain ring, who would know, Rose said. As for unmarried women, such information might encourage sinful living, said one woman, who Flora recognised immediately as none other than Muriel Clegg, née Armour-Brown, Kit's intended.

It was strange to think of Kit Carlyle once being her beau. Muriel was now a plump mother of twins and involved in charitable work across the city; a doctor's wife, still connected to her father's church. Her principles did not waver.

'We must not risk inviting the wrong type of women into our office, to take advantage of devices. There's enough immorality in this city as it is.'

Little did Muriel realise how close Flora had come to being such a woman. It was only luck that she was not carrying Kit's child after that night together. They had taken no precautions. Flora had briefly hoped that she had conceived his baby. It would have been something of Kit to live on. Her life would be more fulfilled than it was now. Doors would close to her, though, as an unmarried mother.

Flora also turned up to the church hall rehearsals for the Starlight Troupe, at first out of duty, then she began to enjoy being back in a choir. The concert party consisted of about twenty volunteers. Billy Sanderson was the director, a dapper little man with a wispy moustache and wearing an obvious toupee. He lisped out his directions with flamboyant gestures that reminded Flora of one of her orderlies. He was called Cedric and had flounced around the ward like a pantomime dame. Yet he was one of the bravest men, carrying on under bombardments, when others were running for cover. Effeminate or not, Cedric won her respect for his courage and his care for patients.

Billy drilled his troupe like a sergeant major and at teabreak she was sitting down, when Rose brought over a young man.

'I'd like you to meet Ivo Lamont. He assists Hector and has a wonderful tenor voice. This is Flora Garvie, my friend.'

Before her stood a tall, dark, handsome man with a patch covering his right eye. He smiled and held out his hand. 'Pleased to make your acquaintance. I gather you were in the last show in France?'

Flora nodded. 'Seems a long time ago now.'

'Not to those of us who were there,' he replied.

'I'm sorry, I didn't mean to be insulting.' She had clearly touched a nerve.

'You'd rather forget things, perhaps?'

'Exactly,' Flora said.

'I suppose it is time to move on, but it feels like yesterday. Some say those who keep remembering can never move forward.'

Flora saw the twitch in his cheek that so reminded her of Kit. This was not the sort of sad exchange she expected at a rehearsal. She turned away from him.

'Have I said something wrong? I'm always putting my foot in it, Miss Garvie,' said Ivo, smiling.

Flora stood up to take her cup back.

'I'll take that for you.' He bent down, but then dropped it with a crash. 'Sorry... mistook the distance.'

'No, let me. I can see Billy champing at the bit to get on with the sketch.'

Rose helped her to clear up the mess. 'Ivo's a bit ham-fisted, badly wounded, but an excellent soldier. He works as a volunteer at the hospital.'

'He's not fit for work then? He seems fit to me.' Flora gave him a nurse's appraisal.

'He's not quite recovered yet. His family own an estate out by Loch Lomond. Money is the least of his problems; a nicer chap you couldn't meet and I think he likes you.'

'Rose Murray, are you matchmaking?'

'Would I?' Rose laughed, getting the evil eye from Billy.

Flora thought no more of this encounter with Ivo Lamont, but it appeared he had other ideas and made a point of seeking her out each rehearsal night. One night, after they had finished, he followed her out.

'Look, I know it's a bit of a cheek, but I have tickets for a symphony concert in the St Andrew's Halls. I wondered if you'd like to come?'

Flora hesitated at first, but there was no harm in this invitation. When was the last time a man showed interest in her? 'I'd be delighted,' she replied.

To her surprise, for the first time in years, she meant it.

Chapter 11

Kit lay back on his lumpy bed after Sylvie had left, feeling exhausted, exhilarated, surprised that she was able to arouse him into such a frenzy of lovemaking. She didn't laugh at his inexperience.

'Slow down,' she whispered, pausing while he recovered before gently massaging him into yet another blissful arousal. Then she lit a cigarette for him while he stared up at the ceiling, stunned by how he had responded to her caresses.

Sylvie was no amateur in the art of seduction. As she wrapped her limbs round him, her deep kisses took his breath away. What had he been missing all these years? Kit felt lighter, freer, introduced to another world far away from his past.

Yet at the very climax, he thought of Flora in his arms, receiving him so willingly. They had fumbled their way into the act of love. Sylvie showed no such tenderness as she pounced on him.

She came to the bar two days later and whispered over

the counter. 'Come to my room, number thirty-one. I'll be waiting and I've got a little surprise.'

Kit couldn't wait for the end of his shift but some of the French artists were roaring drunk and singing.

She was waiting when at last he got away but to his disappointment, she was not alone. 'Denise and I, we're going to put on a little show for you. Sit down and drink this, and I promise you'll have fun.'

The two girls danced around and then jumped up on the bed, shedding their clothes, garment by garment, laughing until they were both almost naked. They lay down and proceeded to remove their silk undies and caress each other, until Sylvie opened her legs to Denise's fingers.

She moaned with ecstasy. 'Come and join us, darling. Don't be shy.' She beckoned to Kit.

Kit was feeling a strange drowsiness as they undressed him and began to work on him, first one, then the other, until they were a tangle of writhing bodies. He entered first the one and then the other in blissful ignorance of which of the girls was which. It seemed that they played together for hours but then suddenly Sylvie jumped up.

'You'd better leave, darling. Don't want you to be found, or you'll lose your job. Monsieur Sella is a stickler. I hope you enjoyed our little soirée. Plenty more where that came from. Perhaps we'll bring a boy for you?'

Kit stumbled out, creeping away in a drunken stupor down the corridor. He couldn't remember much, but what he could recall felt oddly uncomfortable. He woke in the morning with a thumping headache and was late for his morning shift. He had strange bruise marks all over his body and needed a swim in the sea to freshen up but there was no time. Had he really slept with two women or was it some fantastic dream? He couldn't quite recall how it had all happened. All he could remember was a gilded headboard and the scent of warm perfumed bodies. Now he found it hard to concentrate, as if his mind was strangely disconnected from his body. There was a dry taste at the back of his mouth. What had Sylvie put in his drink?

The life of the rich was different from anything he had ever known. They lived in a dream world of sunbathing, dining and dancing. They had a coterie of hangers-on, artists and writers, even the dancers who rehearsed each morning for Miss Morris.

Kit watched Sylvie leaping recklessly off the rocks into the sea. A photographer was capturing her dancing shapes. What had this got to do with Glasgow tenements, battlefields or beggars on the narrow streets? He hoped that at least the wealthy paid for wages that found their way back into the pockets of the poor. He never passed a street urchin without giving something. In those first days, when he fled from Cannes, he had come near to begging himself.

When he met up with Sylvie again on the beach, he insisted they be alone. 'It's you I want to be with.'

But she sighed. 'Darling, don't be clingy. We'll be leaving soon.'

'Will you write to me?' Kit asked, stunned by her coolness.

'Of course not, I'm a dancer, not a secretary. Besides I'll be too busy…'

'I could come along with you and find work.' Why was she saying such things?

'Now you're being tiresome. We've had fun, haven't we?

You'll know now how to please a woman. You're quite sweet, but not really my type... you think too much.'

'I've been your summer distraction?' Kit snapped, realising Sylvie was dumping him.

'Precisely, darling, time for both of us to move on.' Sylvie fingered the waves in her hair. 'Look, I'll be late for my hair salon. I'll come up for a nightcap before I leave, if you like.'

'Don't bother, I can drink alone,' Kit said, turning away from her.

'Dangerous pastime, sweetie, you'll turn into an old soak.' With this she darted away. Kit was shocked. How could he have dreamt Sylvie would want him sticking around? It amused her to seduce him, tantalising him with her beauty and experience. He felt ice water rushing through his veins. To be just a summer fling left him feeling cheap and redundant. Time to move on indeed.

Rejection was not the only legacy of his summer affair. Kit soon began to feel pain whenever he peed. A humiliating trip to the hotel doctor confirmed his worst fear. Sylvie had given him more than a good time. The mercury treatment was painful and expensive, taking up all his savings.

Worse still was that feeling of being corrupted by a superficial and dazzling world. He was not a millionaire, nor ever would be. Sylvie would find new lovers who would suffer the same fate as himself. He thought of Liliane's invitation to love her and of how he had deserted Flora Garvie. He felt ashamed. There was a saying back home: 'If it's so pleasurable, it's sinful', especially when it came to sex. Perhaps there was truth in that after all.

Chapter 18

On the morning of her wedding to Ivo Lamont, Flora awoke early and surveyed her old bedroom. Her cream silk wedding dress was hanging up and everything else was laid out ready for the ceremony in the Lamont estate chapel. Next door slept Maudie, who had come home from Switzerland especially to be her bridesmaid, since Vera had refused to oblige, saying marriage was bourgeois and unnecessary. This hurt Flora more than she could say. Across the landing, in the spare room, was another unexpected guest, none other than Drusilla Pickford who, much to Flora's surprise, accepted her invitation, arriving by chauffeur-driven car – some things would never change – all the way from Bordley.

It was going to be a quiet service, with the reception in Ivo's family house, on the edge of Loch Lomond. His parents had given them a small cottage for weekends while they lived in Ivo's fine Glasgow apartment close to the university in Park Circus. This way they could continue their voluntary work, with less travelling and more time for themselves.

Flora smiled, thinking of Ivo's gentle courtship of her, of the beautiful diamond ring he had produced one evening, taking her by surprise. There was something about Ivo that was safe, comfortable and reliable. She felt cherished.

The June day had dawned perfect and Flora's father, Allan, presented her with a two-strand string of exquisite natural pearls that had belonged to her mother. He had kept them just for this day.

'Your mother would have been so proud of you.'

Pearls were the perfect jewels to set off her dress and the bouquet of cream and pink roses. Rose had given her a blue garter for luck. Maudie produced a beautiful veil of Swiss lace to fix in her hair. Ivo invited guests both from the hospital and from his former regiment. They included Virginia Forsyth, widow of his colonel, who had died in the last month of the war. She had been left with two young boys, Callum and Duncan, resplendent in their kilts. Drusilla wore a loose *eau de nil* coat and dress, pretty cloche hat and stylish shoes. Maudie promised to look after her.

'She sings your praises at every turn. I remember your letters... How she must have changed. What did you do?'

'Nothing,' said Flora, struggling with her satin elbow gloves. 'A little chat and a few home truths. I told her with privilege comes duty and she took that on board. The rest is all her own hard work. I think she was lonely and now her brother has taken over the estate, a little side-lined. At least he's insisted on repairs to their rundown cottages. Recently she has become a manager at the local school, as well as president of the Women's Institute. I am so pleased for her.'

Ivo's family had made Flora very welcome, but his mother

took her aside on the day their engagement was announced in the *Scotsman*.

'My son's health is not strong. The war changed us all, when his brother was killed. I think he feels it should have been him. I know your family suffered a similar loss. He does have down days sometimes. Be patient with him, he always rallies if left alone. Forgive me being so frank but as a former nurse, you will understand these things, I'm sure. We're so relieved you've brought a smile back to his face.'

Flora was not quite sure how to take this. Ivo did go quiet, but seemed to pull himself back. If she was honest, theirs was not a passionate romance, nor as stormy as things might have been with Kit. They were good companions, the same age and from the same backgrounds. It augured well for future happiness. The only cloud was that Ivo wanted to go back to France for their honeymoon. Flora did not. Instead, they settled on a long tour of Devon and Cornwall, staying in fine hotels, visiting historic houses and museums. Then they would stop off with Drusilla and Lionel for a few days, exploring the Cotswolds together.

'This is where I found some purpose after the war,' Flora said. 'It was a strange time, wasn't it? I had to adjust to not being a nurse.'

Ivo looked across the rolling hills. 'I try not to think about that time. I went a little crazy.'

'We all did,' said Flora, knowing it was time to tell him about Kit Carlyle, their brief love affair and his death. They sat in the garden at dusk while she explained.

Ivo held her hand and kissed it. 'Don't be hard on the poor chap. Given enough stress, we can all crack up. I know I did, for a while. But I am surprised by a chaplain taking his own life and leaving you in the lurch. He didn't deserve your loving. I'm sorry, I shouldn't say this, but his loss gave me the biggest gift of my life.'

How could she not love this man? It was she who didn't deserve him.

They had the perfect wedding day. The only cloud in the sky was Vera's absence. Flora tried not to let it spoil a memorable day. On the way home from their honeymoon, Ivo suggested she go to visit her sister in person and express her hurt and disappointment.

'You must build up the bridge between you before it falls down.'

It was not that far to Sandy's tenement building in Anderson Cross. It was a down-at-heel district. Men were being laid off and hung about the streets, aimless and downtrodden. There were many dismal areas, now the city was in the grips of a deep depression. Allan Garvie tried to hang on to his best workers, but times were tough and there were barely enough orders to keep the yard open. No wonder Vera disliked the luxury of the Lamont nuptial.

Flora tried to look inconspicuous by leaving her car in the drive and taking a bus. She walked along, clutching her purse, just in case… The tenement close was depressing, with peeling plaster walls. Women at the stairhead ignored her enquiries for the Lennox's room.

'Are yous frae the factor?' She assured them she was not the rent collector.

'I want to visit my sister.'

'Ach aye, yon snobby one… not so stuck up now,' said one wifie with a sneer, pointing up the stairs to the right.

Flora climbed them, aware of the smell of stale urine, and

knocked on the door, secretly hoping Vera would not be at home to witness her nervousness. The door opened. Her beautiful sister stood unwashed, bleary-eyed, staring at her.

'What do you want? Come to gloat, Mrs Lamont?'

'Oh, Vera, I just wanted to know you were safe and well. We missed you. Why didn't you come?'

'Well, what do you expect?' Vera pointed to her swollen belly. 'Who would want the bride to be shamed by an unmarried sister looking like a bloated sack of potatoes and with not a wedding ring in sight?'

'Darling, why didn't you tell me? I thought you hated us. I'm your sister. I only care about you,' said Flora.

At these kind words Vera's face crumpled and she fell into Flora's arms.

'I'm sorry. It's just a mess, a bloody mess. You'd better come in. Those nosy bitches below will be earwigging. Now you'll see for yourself how the other half lives but don't tell anyone, especially Pa. He was so angry at me for not coming to your wedding. He sent me a letter full of fury. He didn't know, nor shall he. He'll find out enough when the bairn arrives. I'm not afraid of him, you know.'

Her words did not convince Flora for one second. Her sister was in trouble, isolated and afraid. Vera needed help.

'Ivo, what shall I do to help? Vera's near her time and is living in such a squalid single end – one room stuffed with books and pamphlets. There's a box bed in the recess, a cold tap and a fire they can't afford to light. How can she bring a baby into that?'

'Sadly, love, that's true of so many families in this

depression. What about the father, Lennox? A bit of a rabble-rouser, I gather,' Ivo said.

'He's out of work, dismissed for trying to set up a trade union, Vera says.'

'Are they going to marry?'

'That's another complication. Sandy was married young, to Betty McPhail, a Catholic girl, so no chance of divorce; not that it bothers them, but I fear for Vera's health in that damp place.'

'Then we'll find them somewhere better. I'm sure we can get them somewhere in Partick or Maryhill. You can leave it with me, but will they accept charity? People have their pride, Flora.'

'I want that man to get off his soapbox and put his lover first, after all she sacrificed to follow him.'

'Steady on, we don't know how hard he's tried to find new work.'

Ivo went to visit the couple the very next week, taking with him the offer of a job with a craftsman boatbuilder, who was repairing pleasure boats on the Clyde. He was a veteran soldier from Ivo's regiment and willing to give Sandy a chance to learn a new skill. To their amazement Sandy agreed, knowing that this would please Vera. Finding a flat was more difficult, but eventually Ivo came up with a two room and kitchen apartment, not far from the Clyde. It looked as if all their worries were over, until one night, Sandy phoned from a callbox.

'Vera's asking for you… to let you know she is in labour. They've taken her to the women's hospital in Rotten Row. Something is not quite right. Can you come?'

Ivo and Flora drove at speed through the dark streets

to the hospital. They were ushered into a ward with a side room. Flora was glad she had given Vera their mother's wedding ring as a safeguard.

'Mrs Lennox is resting now. She lost a lot of blood but she will mend,' said the sister.

'And the bairn?' Sandy asked. The nurse shook her head.

'There was a bleed in the womb, preventing… when he was born, there was no life, I'm afraid.'

'I had a wee son,' Sandy cried and for the first time Flora saw the boy behind the mask of the fanatic. 'Can I see him?'

The nurse shook her head. 'He was taken away. It's for the best.'

'Elvira is going to live?' Flora looked the nurse in the eye.

'Oh, yes, she'll recover but will need some care.'

'Was it placenta previa?' Flora asked.

'You are a nurse?'

'A VAD in the war in France,' Flora answered with pride. 'I served with the Scottish Women's Hospital Unit in Belgium.' A look of instant rapport passed between them. 'I'm sorry for your loss, Mr Lennox. There really was nothing we could do.'

They were allowed five minutes with Vera, who looked exhausted and unsure. 'What happened? They knocked me out when the baby arrived.'

The sad news was left to Sandy, who held her hand. 'I'm sorry, hen, our wee boy didn't make it. There were complications.'

Flora found herself weeping at his tenderness. 'She must have rest to recover her strength. Another time, perhaps.'

'Oh, no, I'm no' putting her through all that again, I could have lost her.'

Flora looked at Ivo. Vera was loved and that was all that mattered now. 'Shall I get Pa to visit?'

'No, no, I don't want anyone knowing our business. What he doesn't know won't hurt him or shame him. Just tell him I've not been well and needed a rest, that's all.'

'When you come out, you must stay with me in the cottage for fresh air and a good rest. Is that all right with you, Sandy?' Flora didn't want to tread on his pride.

'For as long as she likes. I can manage. I want to distemper the apartment.'

'What about the campaign?' Flora knew how committed he was to his socialist party.

'One less won't make any difference. Your health comes first, Vera.'

Flora didn't like the idea of Pa being kept in the dark but at least he was no longer alone these days. At the wedding, he had escorted Virginia Forsyth to the reception with her boys and later invited them all to play tennis and go fishing. Flora hoped their friendship would develop into something more.

It had been a turbulent two years of depression, riots in the street, strikes and unrest, but their Hogmanay supper was shared with all the family, including Sandy and Vera. Over the past months, Vera had begun to unbend a little and accept their paths might take them all in different directions. Underneath, Flora mused, what mattered was love and compassion. She hoped the coming year would be better for them all.

Chapter 19

The flight from Antibes seemed a lifetime away for Kit, who was now carving out a path, literally, making gardens for villas around the coast. Nothing was too strenuous for him to tackle, digging out rocks, mending walls, setting steps up steep inclines. It was strange how, along the way, one job led to another, and other opportunities grew from the simple act of sketching the beautiful houses. He took his siesta during the fierce afternoon heat, studying each house and drawing sketches. When once a client saw his artistic talent, he was asked to paint their house and garden. He added his own colours and texture to the paper. With the glorious Mediterranean light, he gave each painting shadows and depth.

Word got around and he received commissions to paint more villas and their surroundings. For the first time in years, he was able to rent a decent room, enjoy the cafés and bars from Avignon to Arles, slowly moving west towards Montpellier and Béziers. He signed his pictures simply: Carstairs. Some of his work even hung in cafés. They had such bright colours and the beginnings of a style that was all his own.

Yet the more successful he was, the lonelier he became. He had achieved a goal in earning a living as an artist and yet there was little satisfaction in his new-found career. Depression dogged him and there were days when only the need to work got him out of bed and onto his bicycle for the next assignment.

One morning, on a whim, he travelled back and visited Pastor Vries in the Cévennes. They welcomed him warmly but he still felt he didn't deserve their kindness. He was tempted to share his secret with the old man but could not bear to see the look of shock and disappointment when he discovered Kit was a pastor with no faith, living a lie under a false name.

Sitting once more among the hills, watching the clouds building, threatening a storm, he began to sketch the sloping roofs of the village houses down below. They made lines and shapes that intrigued him. Across the valley was the very farmhouse where Liliane now lived and worked as a farmer's wife. From his perch he was able to sketch out the old farmhouse building, sheltering under the slope of the hill. When he had finished the painting to his satisfaction, he gave it to the Vries family, as a gift for Liliane and her new husband.

He was now unrecognisable as the Scottish padre, his skin burned to chestnut with flecks of mottled brown on his arms and across his face. Only his Titian hair, bleached by the sun, drew attention. He wore a beret to hide his thick locks. Winter was fast approaching and soon most of his work would dry up. The heat had burnt shrubs and flowers, leaves wilted and dropped to the ground. He would have to go back to bar work, not to the fancy hotels on the coast, but inland where he could spend his evenings painting.

Ever the wanderer, Kit drifted along the coast, never settling, with one eye over his shoulder as if he was being stalked. There was no one to recognise him. He was burdened by guilt that seemed to weigh him down. It was as if a dark cloud circled above his head. When would he ever find peace again?

Chapter 20

In 1930, the headaches started. Ivo would sit in a darkened room until they passed. It was just migraine, his physician advised, but Flora worried quietly. Sometimes, during the night, she found him groping in the darkened bedroom to find aspirin and then he would creep back to the warmth of Flora's body.

'Another bad one?' she asked. 'I think we should explore this further.'

Ivo fobbed her off, preferring to keep busy. It was when he said, 'I can see two of you,' that Flora became really alarmed, thinking of those poor boys on the ward with shrapnel wounds to the head who often joked about having two nurses at their bedside.

She spoke to Hector secretly. He knew better than anyone how stalwart and uncomplaining his friend could be. He also knew a good eye specialist in the city and together they set up an appointment. Ivo went along with reluctance.

'You two are fussing over nothing,' he said. 'It's just a bad migraine.'

They arrived at the surgeon's consulting room in the row of fine terraced houses by the Botanical Gardens. Ivo went in alone, while Hector and Flora sat reading magazines. Then they were both called in to the room and Flora's heart began to thump. Something was wrong. She could feel the tension building. The surgeon sat her down.

'Now, Mrs Lamont, nothing to alarm you both, but there's something at the back of his eye that I'm a bit concerned about.'

'Alec, she was a nurse in the war, there's no need to waffle,' Hector interrupted the doctor.

'And I'm here, too,' snapped Ivo. 'Give me it straight, man!'

'I suspect there's a growth behind the eye. Unfortunately, it's your good eye, but we'll need X-rays to identify things more clearly.'

'I'm going blind, then,' Ivo said. Flora held his hand.

'First things first, let's explore further… a small operation, perhaps, some radiation treatment, if needed.'

They left the room, silent. Hector tried to chivvy their spirits. 'It may not come to anything. Better safe than sorry. Alec is the best, a belt and braces sort of chap, and he will be thorough. You're in very good hands.'

They drove to Bearsden in silence. Rose took one look at Flora's face. 'You need a stiff whisky. Try not to worry.'

'He can't lose his sight, it's so unfair,' Flora cried in the kitchen, out of earshot. 'He talked about a growth. We both know what that can mean. They'll cut out the eye. It happened to one of the nurses I met in France.'

Rose hugged her. 'Let's just wait and see what they find.'

'Diana and Ross Lamont will be devastated. If the worst

happens, Ivo will lose his independence and I can't bear that for him,' Flora said, feeling sick.

'You'll bear it. You've been brave before. Why don't you both go out to the cottage, drop everything and enjoy the autumn together, all those golden colours and the peace?'

Flora packed a few walking clothes and they drove off to the loch, avoiding the Lamont house. They walked by the water's edge, where Ivo pointed to a spot.

'This is where I want to be buried. It's so peaceful.'

'Oh, don't be morbid,' Flora replied, tugging him away. 'Let's just walk in the woods and see autumn in all its glory.'

'I suppose it may be the last time I'll see it, if I go blind,' Ivo sighed. 'What a blasted turn-up... not sure how I feel. I'm going to be such a drag on you, my sweet. And if the worst happens...'

'Never,' said Flora. 'I love you and we'll fight this together. Our marriage has been the best thing ever. I'm not letting you go.' She hugged him tight. The thought of losing him was too much to bear.

'There's no bonnie bairns for you, I'm sorry,' he added.

'We tried... we took advice. Perhaps it was just not meant to be, but we've got Hamish and Iris and now Duncan and Callum – lots of children in our lives,' she said, to comfort him.

'But it's not the same and I fear it's my fault.'

Flora wanted none of this depressing talk and tried to distract him. 'Enough of this – look at that glorious copper beech tree and the berries on the rowans. Tonight, we'll go to the Buchanan Arms in Drymen and have a feast. We deserve a fine dinner and if you have to have an operation, then we must build up your strength.'

'Yes, nurse.' Ivo smiled and Flora's heart flooded with love for this man. After only six wonderful years together, surely nothing could blight their future?

In the months that followed, Ivo's condition worsened, despite Alec Henderson's best efforts. He was referred to a surgeon for removal of the eye, only to find that the malignancy had spread and hope of recovery was slim. Flora never left his side. Rose and Hector took turns to help. Maudie wrote every week, enquiring after his health. Even Vera came, grateful for his earlier kindness.

Flora could not believe how rapidly Ivo's strength ebbed. Soon he could no longer walk. He slept most of the time, but enjoyed listening to the wireless. He was not happy that Germany was rearming and building wide roads. 'The autobahns are just like the Romans built, straight and fast. Now why would they be doing that?'

'To give the unemployed work just as we have done, with the Boulevard out of the city from Anniesland. Now rest,' Flora ordered.

'I'll rest soon enough,' he replied.

'None of that talk. We will find a way through.' Flora refused to think of an alternative.

'But we must talk, my love. You will be well provided for, so have no worries… This apartment is yours to do with as you please.'

'Please, Ivo, I don't want to discuss it. How could I live here without you? It's just not fair.'

'We both know that life isn't fair. After all we went through in France, you surely know that by now. I don't want to be a burden.'

Flora clung to him. 'Never, never, don't leave me,' she cried.

'We've had some wonderful times, more than many... Fergus, Bertie, Kit. Think of all the people we lost – Alexander, my brother. I look forward to seeing them in another life...' Ivo whispered, with a faraway look.

· 'You have to go on fighting for me. What shall I do?' She could hear the panic in her voice.

'You'll find a way, with the help of friends and family. Just keep me in your heart for a while. Perhaps one day you won't be alone.'

Flora stood up. 'How can you say such a thing? How could I love anybody, after you?'

'Never say never, Flo. You loved Kit once. Your heart is so full of life and loving, there'll be room for another.'

'Please, no more of this. Shall I put on some music?' They had purchased a fine gramophone in a cabinet and a collection of classical music.

'You choose something cheery. Harry Lauder, or that little boy who sings "O for the wings of a dove".'

They sat in silence listening to the boy soprano. Flora was weeping with tiredness and grief. She was losing him day by day and soon there would come a time when he would sleep more than he woke. It was nature's way. She had seen it in the wards and now her beloved husband was fading away from her. It just wasn't fair.

Chapter 21

1932 was not a good year for Kit. He hurt his back wrenching rocks in a garden where the owner complained the renovations were not happening fast enough. First, he wanted a rock garden, then decided it must be shifted to a different spot. When Kit failed to keep an appointment, due to excruciating pain in his sacrum, the owner dismissed him and began to badmouth him as a lazy slacker. It was time to move on, but with little money in reserve, his comfortable lifestyle was over and it was back to hand-to-mouth menial work when he could find it. As the months turned into years, he fell back onto sketching houses to pay for his living.

The pain was so bad he began to drink spirits to ease the spasms and he found himself drifting westwards again, homeless and almost destitute. He dossed down wherever he could find shelter, with a bottle for sustenance. He ate little and no longer had the desire to paint or sketch to support himself. Then, to make matters worse, he got an infection in his chest that made him so breathless, he could hardly walk.

When he passed out on the outskirts of Béziers, people took him for a drunk and left him prostrate on a bench. It was only the kindness of an old widow woman that saved him. She took pity on him, gave him water, felt his head and sent for the local doctor.

They laid him out on the grass in the shade. By then he was delirious, tossing and turning, singing 'By yon bonnie banks and by yon bonnie braes' over and over again.

'What language is this?' said a passer-by suspiciously to the old woman. '*Allemand?*'

'*Mais non,*' said the doctor. 'I'd know that anywhere, *madame*. He's in a bad way. Let's see if there are papers in his knapsack.' The doctor rummaged in it. 'What a state he's in!' They found his identity. 'He's *anglais*, English... Christophe Carstairs. What on earth brings him down here? I have no English but I know a *médicin* who can help us. Don't let him move. I'll be back.'

A crowd was gathering, curious. 'Another tramp on the road to hell, by the look of him,' said a sour-faced man in black, crossing himself.

'He's English,' the old woman replied.

'*Les anglais...* what did they do for us in the war?'

The man made to pull him up. 'We don't want the likes of him spreading disease. Look at him, what use is he to us? Redheads have the devil in them.'

Madame stayed firm. 'The doctor's coming, leave him alone. He is at the door of death.' She put a blanket over him.

★

It was hours before the doctor returned with a tall man. Kit was barely conscious, but he heard a voice that rang in his ears like a gong.

'What the blazes...? Is that you, Carlyle? Jesus, Mary and Joseph...' The doctor sounded his chest, felt his pulse. 'He's barely alive or sober and stinks to high heaven. Kit... Padre... it is you.'

It was then that Kit opened his eyes to see a man with bushy eyebrows and dark Celtic looks bending over him. Through the fog of fever, he recognised the face of his old comrade Sam O'Keeffe, and thought he was dreaming. But the voice continued to bawl in his ear. 'What the hell are you doing here? You are supposed to be dead!'

Chapter 22

Flora stood at Ivo's grave, surrounded by many mourners. His mother, Diana, was ashen-faced, bravely bearing up while his father stood gazing ahead, stoic in his grief. Flora felt nothing but fury. This was not how it was supposed to be. It was like Fergus all over again and she felt the same rage she had felt for him, and all the other lost ones. Rose stood close by, with her son Hamish who loved his uncle Ivo. Everything was a blur of greetings, condolences, and trying to be brave, as he would have wished. He was a military man and she must not let him down. It was the gathering of the clans and colleagues. So many had come to pay their respects.

A lone piper played the lament 'Flowers of the Forest' as they processed slowly towards a beautiful spot at the edge of the estate under a fine oak tree. It was here Ivo had wished to be buried. The loch water rippled gently and lapped over the stones; the sky glowed. It was a fine resting place for a hero. Flora felt numb.

'I'm so sorry,' said Vera, shaking her head. 'He was so

good to us.' The sisters had drawn closer to each other during Ivo's illness. Vera and Sandy knew what loss was like, and Vera's eyes were full of tears.

'Aye, a rare soul was yer man,' said Sandy, dressed, for once, in a suit. Flora was glad they had come, even though they stood apart from her father and his companion, Virginia.

Vera had still not made it up with her father. After all the family had been through, surely now was the time to draw together, whatever their political differences. They were all that was left of the Garvie family. But Flora had neither the will nor energy to intervene, lost in her own sadness and frustration. It was as if there was a glass wall between her and the other mourners. She wished they would all go away and leave her be. It was selfish. Ross and Diana Lamont needed her. She stood looking out at Loch Lomond in all its glory. How could it be so beautiful, when she was in such a place of pain? The world would keep on turning but it would never be the same again for her.

Flora turned to walk back to the house, knowing she was expected to be on hand to greet everyone at the reception. All she could think of was fleeing back to the safety of their cottage where Ivo's presence felt very real. Then, looking up, but still lost in her thoughts, she saw a lanky figure come into view, and she recognised the gawky stride of one of her oldest friends.

'Maudie? Is it really you?' She fell into her arms. 'You came all this way.'

'Do you think I wouldn't be there for you, Flo? Bit of a rush and I got leave... I am so very sorry.' Flora tried not to cry, but the tears just poured out. Maudie took her hand.

'There's nothing I can say that will make any of it better, but I just had to be here.'

'Has Olive come too?'

There was a silence. 'Olive has left me to go travelling with her new chum. We grew apart, but that's a long story for later.' Arm in arm, they strolled back to the house.

'Wait till Rose sees you,' said Flora.

'It was Rose who telegraphed me. I'll be staying a little while, so there will be plenty of time to talk later. *Courage, ma brave.*'

'How do I live without him?' Flora sobbed.

'One day at a time.'

Chapter 23

Kit had no idea how he had arrived at the farmhouse. He woke in a room with a beamed roof. He lay in a large bed opposite a carved armoire. The air smelt of lavender and polish. Who had brought him here, bathed his filthy body, put a clean cotton nightshirt on him? He could smell roasting coffee beans and it made him hungry. Then he recalled Sam O'Keeffe's face staring down in disbelief at him. What could he say to his old friend? His first thought was to climb out of the window and escape, but he was too weak to move.

A dark-haired woman, with beautiful olive skin, came in with a tray of coffee, warm bread and peach jam. She smiled at him. '*Bonjour, monsieur*, I'm Sam's wife, Consuela. Welcome to Magret and excuse, please, the noise of *les enfants*...'

Kit smiled back. Trust Sam to keep his promise to find a fine-looking wife for himself and father a brood of children. He didn't know what to say except '*Je vous remercie, madame.*'

'Now you must eat and then you will be stronger,' she

said. 'Sam is taking the children to find mushrooms for supper in the woods.'

'How many children do you have?'

'Eleven, so far,' she replied.

'Eleven!' Kit gasped. That was going some for an ex Catholic.

'Ah, Christophe, you don't understand.' She laughed, seeing the look on his face. 'They are not our children, but ones who needed a home, orphans, refugee children from Spain. There's bad trouble there. They come to us and we find them homes. Some are sick and weak, so we build them up.'

Kit had no words with which to respond. While he had been bumming around the Côte d'Azur, Sam was caring for lost children. It made him feel ashamed to have been discovered. How could he face his old friend?

'*Madame*, I must leave. You have enough to feed, without me imposing on your hospitality.' He tried to sit up, but a fit of coughing made him lean back on the pillow with exhaustion.

'You go nowhere but the grave, if you try to walk. Your chest is bad and you are so thin. How can you recover without help?' Consuela said.

I don't deserve to recover, he thought. This is the last place on earth I want to be, but I'm trapped.

'The good *seigneur* brought you back from the dead,' she added. 'One more night in the open and you would not have survived. Sam will look after you. He is a good doctor.'

'Yes, I know that, but I'm no longer a good man. There's much to explain. I fear he will ask me to leave, once he knows the truth of the matter.'

Consuela nodded, making no reply, but straightened his bedclothes and pillow. 'Now rest, it is an order,' she said when she had finished. But she left Kit deeply troubled. Of all the doctors in France he had to find Sam again. This was surely beyond coincidence. For all his faults, betrayals and deceptions, was there a higher hand at work here, forcing him to face who and what he had become?

Later that morning, Sam came through the door and closed it firmly. 'I hear you want to leave us. Sorry, chum, here you stay, until I say you're fit. What a mess you've made of your body. Do you know it was only your hair I recognised at first? The rest of you... I couldn't believe the wretched wreck I saw before me. Whatever made you do such a thing... fake your death? Someone sent me your obituary. Who is this Christopher Carstairs? Why?'

Kit shook his head. 'It's a long story,' he replied, turning away from his friend's gaze.

'I'm going nowhere and neither are you.' Sam pulled a chair closer. 'I'm listening.'

Out it poured, slowly at first: his wounds, his failure to rescue the boy in the mud, the officers' hostel, about meeting Flora Garvie and causing her disgrace, his loss of faith. Kit held nothing back, his cowardly escape to Marseille and the time in the Cévennes, even his seduction by Sylvie and his dose of the clap.

'I thought I was destined to be an artist but when I saw the real artists at work, I realised I am nothing but a house painter, an odd-job man, a failure in everything I've done. I hate myself for letting everyone down.'

'So, you are feeling sorry for yourself, then?' Sam probed.

Kit continued to confess. 'It's worse than that. I'm weak and cowardly.'

'Never, my friend. You were badly wounded. I gather from your obituary that you won a DSO. Could have had a VC. You saved men's lives and their minds. I don't call that cowardly, just exhaustion. I think you've had what us quacks call a breakdown of the mind. I'm not excusing everything, but you've punished your body almost beyond the point of repair. The congestion in your lungs, your liver, your back discs are compressed... What on earth are we going to do with you?'

'Patch me up and let me go. I'll manage, I have so far,' Kit replied. 'There is nothing to live for now.'

'That's self-pity talking. You're still breathing and you are not an old soldier yet. There's a lifetime to find purpose. I can help you heal. We have fresh air, good food and rest for you here. We can help you heal but you also have to help yourself. Think of all the boys you buried, who would love to be alive and kicking. We were the lucky ones, never forget that. Sermon over...' Sam smiled. 'What do you think?'

'I hear your words, but they're all scrambled up in my head. How can I forgive myself?'

'Look, we are all weak at times, full of faults, treacherous even, but accepting those bits of ourselves means we can choose to live in another way,' Sam replied.

'But I have hurt so many – Aunt Jessie, Muriel, Flora... I can't go back.'

'Perhaps it's better if you don't. Just make this Christopher Carstairs someone worthy of respect and ask for guidance.

Where from… is up to you. Don't wallow in the past, move on towards another life. We do have choices.'

'I can't live off your kindness, with all those mouths to feed,' Kit said.

'When you're stronger we can discuss that. I do need a handyman. There's plenty of work you can do here to help us.'

'How did you find this place?' Kit wanted to change the subject.

'I met Consuela after her father was murdered in Spain. I'd read what's going on there. She was a nurse and escorting some orphans to a nearby convent. You've seen her – who can forget a face like that? Talk about sparks flying. I touched her hand once and almost got an electric shock. I knew I had found the woman of my dreams. We did hope for our own children, but it appears when I had mumps as a schoolboy, it blighted any chance…' Sam paused. 'Now we have our hands full of frightened, sick children who need a lot of attention. I do have a practice down in the village and we get a small grant from a charity to feed and clothe the children so we just about manage.'

'I don't want to be a burden. I have nothing to offer.'

'Oh, but you have. I have plans to extend into the barn. Students will come during vacations to help, but they need supervision and I do have my medical work. There is work for you here, once you're well again. Just rest up, search within yourself and paint for pleasure. The land is beautiful. We all can't be Leonardos or Monets. Don't be so self-critical, paint what gives you joy.' Sam added, 'Just don't ask me to pick up a paintbrush. Though maybe you could teach the children a little, when you are stronger. And there's plenty of manual work here at Magret.'

Kit smiled. 'I've done plenty of that over the years. You can count on me.'

'Splendid, but take your time. I've tired you out now.' Sam left the room, while Kit lay back, exhausted but relieved. Was it possible to forgive yourself for past mistakes? Could he ever hold his head up high again?

Chapter 24

Maudie insisted Flora came to visit her in Lucerne. She was working in a special lakeside clinic for nervous disorders, with its own private beach. Maudie's generous heart wanted Flora to have a change of scene, away from the Lamonts.

It had been a year of visits to the Highlands, with Allan and Virginia and the boys. They were planning a quiet wedding. Flora had also been down to the Cotswolds to spend a holiday with Drusilla and Lionel in Bordley Court. The old house had been transformed by Lionel into a luxurious residence. He had brought in a designer to redecorate the rooms, improve the kitchen and freshen up all the bedrooms.

'I can never thank you enough for bringing my sister back to life again,' Lionel said, when they were alone after dinner one night. 'She's even learned how to drive!'

They spent meals discussing the rise of Herr Hitler in Germany. Lionel was convinced war was on the horizon. Drusilla shuddered. 'Then we must make provision for food and plant out the kitchen garden immediately,' she said.

The brother and sister proved such kind hosts, driving Flora to villages hidden in the beautiful countryside. They begged her to stay on, but she was homesick and made excuses to leave.

Once home, Rose insisted she carried on with the new clinic in the city. Flora was shocked more by what poverty, unemployment and ill-health did to families in the city. She could see that the worst of the depression was receding. Pa's shipyard had new orders for frigates. There were more saloon cars on the streets and skilled men back at work. But the threat of war was hovering over them like a dark cloud. It was a threat no one wanted to think about yet.

Keep busy, everybody kept advising, but sometimes Flora felt exhausted just filling her days. Maudie's invitation for a lengthy stay was timely. Her friend was grieving the loss of Olive's friendship. As they sat sipping a chilled Riesling, looking over the lake, Flora felt it was time to probe Maudie's unhappiness.

'What went wrong between the two of you?'

'I wish I knew. One day we were bosom pals, the next there was a coolness on her part. She said she wanted to move on and visit Italy, so I suggested a holiday but she turned up her nose, saying I was a stick in the mud for staying here so long.

'"I'm sick of nursing nutcases," Olive said. "Inge says some of them should be put to sleep. They are no use to society." I was shocked but said nothing. This was the first time she mentioned Inge Muller, one of the sisters in charge. Ollie began to go out on her own in the evening, to meetings, she said. I suspected it was to meet Inge. That's when they decided to leave for Italy. Inge was impressed with some leader called Mussolini and Olive wanted to see Italy for herself, so that's about it.' Maudie sighed, looking Flora straight in the eye. 'We were more than friends. We shared a bed. Are you shocked?'

Flora touched her hand. 'Why should I be shocked? She made you happy. But I'm finding happiness doesn't last, does it? I heard someone say you must measure success in life by your laughter. I'm not sure we've had a lot to laugh about so far.' She paused to sip the wine, savouring its flavour. 'I think you measure life in friendships and at least in that, I have been blessed. You all held me up. I'd like to think you will find another companion, but I doubt I'll ever find another Ivo to love.'

Maudie stood up. 'Come on, let's not get maudlin. I know a wonderful taverna across the water. They do the most delicious cheese fondue. It comes sizzling straight to table in a pan and you'll love it; Gruyère, Emmental, wine, crusty bread. That'll cheer us both up. When in doubt, eat, I say!'

Chapter 25

The rehabilitation of Kit Carlyle began in earnest at the farm in Magret. It was a house of hope. In the fresh air of the hillside, he began to breathe in the scents of rosemary and thyme. Consuela made him drink funny-tasting tisanes. Booze was forbidden, not even wine. His body protested with night flushes, sweating and restless sleep. He was given chamomile infusions, vervain and other potions to help him relax. Sam insisted he pottered about in the garden with a sketchpad.

Sitting in the shade to draw whatever he fancied, he found himself sketching an outline of the Rose Villa with its steps down to the beach and the wrought-iron balcony. It was painful at first, recalling those happier times, remembering the pink blancmange stucco plasterwork, the icing sugar cornices, the terracotta roof, the chatter of the nurses knitting in the sunshine, drinking in the Riviera view. He recalled Flora racing down the beach, thinking he was walking into the sea. Was she married with little ones by now, safe in the knowledge that her former lover was long gone from this earth? He hoped she was at peace.

Coming back from the dead would serve no purpose at all, bringing only hurt and recriminations from those he had betrayed. As for the war, the grief of such losses would live with him for ever. There was nothing he could do to alter that either.

Sam was right. He owed it to everyone to pull himself together and make amends for all he had done in the past, make a fresh start, a new life. He might not be Monet, but he could be Carstairs. He may not be Rennie Mackintosh, but he could learn from his style. Kit felt the first stirrings of hope and strength returning within him.

His first job was to repay his hosts in any way he could. He had not been around little children since Sunday school days, but he might learn to entertain, help out, enjoy their joie de vivre and comfort those who were still suffering. He used to do party tricks with the infant classes. Would they like Punch and Judy, games of football? He could give them time, time that allowed Sam and his wife to have some leisure to themselves. While he was recovering from all his infections, he would make a role for himself and then move on. There were artist colonies on the west coast, close to Spain. Perhaps there, he might find another way to live.

Chapter 26

The first Flora knew about the Spanish *coup d'état* was when Vera came rushing to the apartment in Park Circus.

'Sandy wants to volunteer and go to Spain. I'm so worried,' she cried. 'He says he must go, that this Fascist movement of General Franco's is a great danger. They are bombing innocent people. His group are gathering up anyone ready to fight.' Vera plonked herself down on the sofa to light a cigarette. 'I want to go with him, but they're not taking women. What shall I do?'

Flora's heart sank. 'Does he know what he's letting himself in for? War is no picnic, I promise you. It's bound to be chaotic at first. Aren't we supposed to stay neutral?'

'How can you say that, when innocent people need our support?' Vera leapt up and paced the room. 'They're setting up a Spanish Aid committee so at least I can drum up funds from this end. Can you help us?'

'Let me think about it,' Flora replied, realising what Sandy needed was a decent coat, sturdy boots and some first-aid kit. She could help with that. 'It's funny there's not been much in the newspapers.'

'The Establishment is against intervention, typical bourgeoisie head in the sand,' Vera said. 'They think Herr Hitler is a great leader, but Sandy says wait and see what he will do...'

Two weeks later Flora went with Vera to wave off the men from George Square, joining a group of weeping women in shawls, clutching children crying for their daddies. The volunteers were taking a bus to Dover via London. Then they would travel through France to the Spanish borders. Sandy had waved his visitor's pass for Paris at them, valid only for a day trip, but after that, Vera explained, they were on their own, making their way to Perpignan and hoping no one would ask why only one of them had a passport.

Flora was uneasy, but Vera was busy raising funds for their men. It gave her something to focus on, while she waited for his letters to arrive. Flora admired her sister for her earnest belief in their cause but when had anything good come out of civil war, she wondered?

On cold winter nights, Vera came to stay over. It was good to have her company and Flora persuaded her to take in a film at the Picture House. She refused to go back to Kildowie House now that Virginia was there.

'It's nothing personal but it's not my home and it has too many memories. I don't belong to that life anymore.'

She was adamant about her priorities. Flora was not so full of certainty, no longer sure of anything now Ivo had gone. For her part Vera was living with the worry of separation. Those fireside evenings, when silence reigned and only the ticking clock disturbed their thoughts, were precious. Flora thought of her own rebellious self all those years ago, defying the census, marching for the women's vote. Perhaps they were both cut from the same cloth, after all. Flora wondered what ancestor had given them such defiant spirits.

In some ways she envied Vera, knowing her own life was now quiet, uneventful and a little boring. Was she settling into a matronly middle age? How she hoped not.

Chapter 27

Kit stayed on to help Sam finish the farmhouse extension. Earlier in the year, a contingent of young students on an international exchange helped them to paint the walls, make shelves and clear another vegetable patch. Kit enjoyed their youthful enthusiasm. Many were Quakers, intent on promoting peace instead of war. This long break on Sam's farm helped him regain strength, stay sober and teach the children painting, drawing and a little English.

Sam's wife was worried about her family in Barcelona and the news that the Republicans were retreating north alongside an ever-growing influx of refugees into France. There were rumours that desperate families were searching for work and places to rest, but they were not always welcome. Many were turned back at the border but then took to crossing the Pyrenees at night and on foot.

The Magret farm housed mothers and children, who rested in the renovated barn. But Sam was facing a dilemma. 'We can't take them all in. Just look at their sores and the state of their feet. We can only do so much here,' he confided to Kit. 'Consuela would have us pack them in like sardines so I only hope there are other agencies closer to the border. I'm afraid this trickle will become a flood, if things go on as they are.'

It was then that Kit knew his time was up here. He owed it to Sam and his wife to move westwards, to find out what was going on. 'I can always go down to the border and see if any preparations are being made for refugees. I have a notion to visit the coast. They say the light is wonderful for artists. I owe you both so much, but it is time I made my own way.'

'Are you sure?'

'Look at me, I am as fit as a butcher's dog, thanks to you. Time I did something useful. Having seen the state of some of your guests, perhaps it's time I saw things for myself. You have saved my sanity.'

'Dear old Kit,' Sam replied. 'This house will always be here for you but stay safe, old boy. Your chest will always be weak and mind you keep off the booze. It won't help anything.'

'No booze, no women, no exertion – that's quite a prescription,' Kit laughed.

A week later Sam and Consuela saw him off on the train with a packed lunch, a case full of artwork, shirts, knitted jumpers and a little book full of the children's drawings, along with a photo of Sam smiling into the camera in front of the farmhouse.

He travelled along the coast road towards Perpignan, stopping off at the resort of Collioure. He wanted to explore around the area – Port Vendres, Banyuls, Saint-Cyprien – so his first purchase was a bicycle. He was back to painting villas, selling pictures of houses to owners wherever he stopped for a few days. There was even enough money to rent a small room.

Collioure was a quaint, colourful village that dipped down to a harbour where a large castle loomed over the bay. There was a labyrinth of narrow streets and passageways, fishermen tending nets, women sitting in the streets knitting. It was crowded with many nationalities, because this was the holiday season. Further out of the town he saw a different reality: families in rags, sitting in the shade, barefoot children with staring hungry eyes. In his heart he wanted to feed them all, but his pocket was empty and he felt ashamed. When he asked the concierge of the rented room what was happening, her reply dismayed him.

'Poof! They are like stray dogs, mangy, covered in fleas, and they should stay in their own country, not burden us with their filthy diseases.'

Surely there had to be some centres where they could be resettled? Kit was determined to find out more. His first call was to the local church, knowing they must be aware of the plight of those poor folk on their doorstep.

It was strange, entering the portals of the Catholic church. It was cool and peaceful. His footsteps echoed around the building. This bore no resemblance to his former church in Glasgow which was plain, austere, with very little ornament.

The priest was sorting papers and looked up. 'Can I help?'

'Father, I am new to the area but I am seeing things that disturb me: the beggars, the ragged children, families living on the street. What can be done?'

The reply was chilling. 'We are trying to move them on,

because it's not good for the district to be filled with Spanish rebels. It frightens the tourists to see beggars,' he said. 'You are English?'

'*Ecossais*. Are there places of refuge somewhere? They are innocent women and children: "suffer the little children to come unto me..."' Kit quoted.

'Ah, you are Protestant. The British have left us to pick up the pieces of a righteous war. General Franco defends the country and the church...'

'I have little knowledge of the rights and wrongs of this war, but we can't let children starve in the streets.' Kit was shocked by his indifference.

'Then you feed them, sir. We have our own poor to attend to.' The priest did not flinch from the look of dismay on Kit's face.

'Thank you, Father, for you have given me an idea...' he replied.

There must be someone, some agency, some charity that was taking action. He would need a place, a feeding station, such as they had had in the trenches. Suddenly ideas flooded into his head and Kit rushed back to his digs to pen a long letter to Sam. He had not felt so energised for years. Here, at last, was something useful he could do.

Chapter 28

In April came the terrible news of the bombing of Guernica. 'They were not Spanish planes,' Hector said, pushing his paper aside. 'Just a practice for foreign allies. This is a rehearsal for war.'

Rose and Flora were busy distributing leaflets to churches and committees, appealing for aid and clothing to be shipped across from Britain. Flora took up the cause, alongside Rose and Vera. It felt like old times, but Vera was looking very strained. She had not heard from Sandy for over a month and was beginning to fear the worst. It didn't help matters that the government had made it illegal for British nationals to fight in Spain. That did not stop Glasgow men from enlisting, nor had it stopped Maudie Wallace from joining the fray with the Swiss Aid. She sent a letter from Lucerne to her friends.

By the time you get this letter I shall be somewhere in Spain with the Swiss White Cross. I could not stand by and watch. Don't worry, it's a spiffing unit and we will not be partisan to either side, no matter how or where our sympathies lie. With the war experience I've had, I can be useful, especially to the young nurses, who I feel will be shocked by battle conditions.

I know you will all want to be useful, so raising funds will help us deliver clothes and food where it is most needed. The innocent bystanders suffer the most, I fear. I will write when I can, but don't be surprised if the letters are delayed…

Dear Maudie was heading into danger once more and Flora felt a stab of envy. They were comfortable and settled in a rut here.

Flora was still working at the clinic, hearing stories of injured fighters returning home, restless and lost from a world their wives couldn't share. Vera was tireless, speaking at the Women's Rural Institutes, explaining the need to make homes for Spanish orphans, little colonies where they could recover in fresh air. Much fell on deaf ears, but there were some willing to offer their empty country houses.

Then came disturbing rumours of many Scotsmen held in prisoner-of-war camps, where treatment was harsh, with regular executions. This sent Vera into a frenzy of despair.

'I have to go and see for myself,' she said. 'I can't wait here, not knowing if Sandy is alive or dead. You have to help me, Flora. I have no means of going by myself. My bank account is almost empty.'

'Steady on, you won't be able to cross into Spain. All the border posts are closed.'

'Then I'll walk over the mountains.'

'To do what? Get yourself arrested as an alien? You have

no passport. Think about it… you'll have to go through proper channels, consuls, whatever. Be patient, there's nothing you can do but wait.'

Vera stormed off, yelling, 'You don't understand. I can't bear to think of him suffering in a prisoner-of-war camp.'

Oh, but I do, Flora sighed to herself, thinking about Kit's struggle with depression and despair during the war. She could never believe he walked into the sea to end it all and yet it must be true. She would never get over all the losses in their life, but worst of all, she had failed to save him from himself.

Vera deserved her help. How could she risk her sister rushing into this wild scheme? What if she disappeared one night and tried to enter Spain? That must not happen. Who better to accompany her? Come to think of it, what was keeping her in Glasgow?

What if they went down into France together? What if they filled her old car with relief clothes and tins?

They could pass this off as a holiday, collect a proper passport for Vera, book into a hotel somewhere and see what news they could glean. It was a crazy notion, but the idea gripped Flora. She would make sure Vera would not cross into Spain illegally. As far as Pa was concerned, she was taking Vera on a much-needed break. No one would object to this holiday, not Rose nor Hector.

Flora was sure Ivo would think it a sensible solution. He was such a generous soul. She missed him dearly, but it was five years since he had passed, another world away. When she dreamed of him, his face would always fade, to be replaced by Kit's, smiling at her. She awoke with an empty feeling in her stomach, knowing she would never love again in her life.

Why not ask Drusilla and Lionel for support, too? Then there was 'Cyril' to consider. Her saloon was getting on in years and perhaps not up to the long journey. Time to retire him to the country cottage, time to purchase one of those station wagons with plenty of room for boxes in the boot. They could share the driving, buy maps and compasses. It would be an adventure, with purpose at the end of it. Now Flora couldn't sleep, as the scheme buzzed in her head like a demented bee.

Chapter 29

The letter from Sam was encouraging: *Consuela knows a doctor in Collioure who will help you, a refugee friend of her late father, called Pedro Ortega, look him up.*

It didn't take long to search out Dr Ortega, who was busy taking a makeshift clinic in a backstreet room, where queues of patients were sitting around the doorstep, dejected, smoking, nursing small children sleeping on their laps.

Kit walked around until the queue shortened and then made his own entrance to find a white-haired old man, bent almost double, smoking a cheroot.

'Yes?' he said, peering over half-moon spectacles.

Kit spoke French at first, but the man looked puzzled. 'Who are you?'

'A friend of Sam O'Keeffe and his wife, Consuela.' He broke into English. 'They told me you could help me.'

'Are you sick?' Ortega replied, in broken English. 'Republican soldier?' He was suspicious.

'Not at all, sir. Sam and I were in the Great War. I stayed with them, as I was sick there...'

The old man was still suspicious. 'Why are you here, then?'

'There are people starving outside, and all around the country. They need food and medicine. If there was a van that could go out to distribute food… But I see you are very busy.'

'Yes, you have seen the queues outside my door. How can I leave my patients here? I'm sorry.'

'Do you know anyone who might be willing to help in this way?'

Ortega shrugged his shoulders. 'Go to the authorities, ask them to see the crisis for themselves, or get the priests to leave their altars.'

'I got no help from that quarter.' Kit described his visit to the church.

'Not all priests are heartless, I know one who might listen with sympathy to you. Tell him I gave you his address, but be careful who you talk to. There are Nationalist spies looking for rebels to force back to certain death in Spain. Come, have a drink with me. How is my beautiful Consuela, any babies yet?'

'Eleven and counting.' Kit smiled, seeing the shock on Ortega's face. 'They host orphaned children in their farmhouse. We've just built an extension.'

They sat down and over a glass of fine Banyuls he described the house at Magret. Pedro wrote down an address.

'Be discreet, go to confession. Don't draw attention to yourself. Father Antoine will listen. As a refugee, I am not registered to practise here, but they turn a blind eye and I get some supplies.' He paused, coughing loudly. 'I am reduced, at times, to hedgerow medicines, tisanes, poultices. So many are malnourished and covered in sores and many have no money to pay me. Others give me what they can spare – watches, rings. It is hard to accept... Border guards search them for valuables, but some are lucky, hiding precious things in very strange places.'

'Thank you, Dr Ortega.'

'What's a man like you doing here, so far from home? In fact, where was that?'

'Just travelling, since the war.' Kit did not want to reveal anything more. 'I'm from Glasgow, but I've no ties to the city now. I prefer to travel and paint.'

'An artist then?'

'Sort of...'

'Either you are or you're not. What do you paint?'

'Houses mostly, villas. I sell some to the owners and it gives me enough to move on. Now I will sell what I can to raise funds.'

'You should ask your friends back home to support you.'

'I can't.'

'Why is that?' Ortega moved forward.

'They think I am dead.' Kit waited for the shocked response but Ortega shook his head.

'You committed a crime?'

'No,' Kit replied, 'it... it was just...' The third glass of Banyuls had made him relax and he found himself telling his history for only the second time.

'So now you want to redeem yourself by helping refugees. What happened to this Flora?'

'I don't know and I will never know. How can I go back, after what I did to her?'

'You could be honest and write to her,' the doctor suggested.

'And blow a hole in her life? No, never. I loved her too much to disrupt her life.'

'I think confession will be good for you, so get yourself down to Father Antoine. That will be a good start. Your heart is full of charity. You will find a way forward and I will do what I can to aid you.'

'I might as well tell you I was a Protestant priest, a chaplain in the army, but I lost my faith after the war. I was so sure of it before.'

'Now you're beginning to rethink everything and perhaps find another rock to lean on?'

'I don't know about that.'

'I wish you good luck. I think you have found something important to do and love for others is never wasted.'

Kit walked back to his digs, slightly tipsy. His life had turned around after Sam rescued him. Now he had another ally in the old doctor. Was there a pattern to this? Was something guiding him ever forward?

Chapter 30

Collioure

Flora parked up close to the harbour. Vera was hungry, eager to stretch her legs. She'd been very silent for the last stretch of the journey, taking in glimpses of the high peaks of the Pyrenees. Their route had taken them from the Normandy coast, down into the hills of the Auvergne, filling up at little petrol stations along the way. Flora was glad to see France at peace. She kept stopping at war cemeteries to pay her respects to the *poilus* who had made such sacrifices.

Her heart leapt at the sight of the Mediterranean, glistening in the sunshine. She stared with delight across Collioure harbour, full of fishing boats, bobbing in the turquoise sea.

It was somewhere close to here that the famous Scottish architect and his artist wife had settled for a while. Pa had acquired one of Rennie Mackintosh's paintings of a spot close to where Matisse and those French artists formed a colony. The Scottish artist had made such a mark in their city, with his School of Art design.

Finding shade in the tall buildings of the backstreets, with winding steps and narrow alleyways, Flora wandered along to the great *bastide*, perched on the rocks. Then she turned back to admire the quaint shops and doorways, while Vera went racing ahead, eager to find news of the war in Spain.

Flora dawdled, admiring the little art galleries. There was one with its door open onto the street and she found herself drawn to peer into the window, full of colourful landscapes and sea pictures. Her attention was grabbed by a bold oil painting of a large pink villa, perched on the edge of a rock. Seeing her transfixed by the image, the gallery owner beckoned her inside. 'You like this, *madame*?'

'Who did it?' she asked, when she had composed herself.

'A local artist, English. I have some of his other works. He specialises in houses. I think it has taken your eye?'

Flora paused to collect her thoughts. 'It reminds me of somewhere I once knew, a long time ago, but I'm sorry...' She backed out of the gallery, almost falling down the steps. '*Merci*,' she muttered, her heart beating fast.

How strange after all these years to see this reminder of times past. Could it be the very same villa she had known so well? Common sense told her there were many such rose stucco villas dotted along the Riviera. It could be any one of them, and yet there was something familiar about the steps winding down to the beach.

Feeling faint, she went in search of shade and a pastis to calm her nerves. How could this simple image, by some unknown artist, bring back such powerful memories?

'Oh, there you are, I thought I'd lost you,' said her sister, standing over her clutching a French newspaper. 'I want you to translate this for me. This place is heaving with Spaniards and I want to know what's going on. Flora, are you listening to me? I'm starving. We can have lunch right over there.' She pointed to a restaurant. 'The seafood looks wonderful…' Vera paused to catch her breath. 'It's hot here. What's the matter with you? You look like you've seen a ghost.'

'I'm tired, that's all. Let's find a hotel. I can translate better in the cool and after that, I'd like to visit Port Vendres to see Rennie Mackintosh's place. Pa would be interested in the view that inspired his own painting.'

'This isn't a holiday, Flora. We are here to distribute our boxes and explore a way for me to find Sandy, don't forget.'

'I've not forgotten. I've driven most of the way here, so surely I'm entitled to a day or two to rest and get my bearings?' Vera was younger and fresher but burdened by fear and doubt, just as Flora had been in the war. Yet there was a sense of entitlement about her sister that demanded people listen to her opinions and do her bidding.

She was as sure of her own cause as Flora had been of the suffrage campaign. Sometimes she felt Vera's head was in the clouds about practical things, such as collecting clothes, preparing the Morris 10 for a long journey, or collecting passport signatures. Vera had mostly left this venture to her big sister. It was hard at times for Flora not to resent her young sister's thoughtlessness. When would she ever grow up? The whole world did not revolve around her and Sandy Lennox. There was no rush. Their boxes were full of clothes, not perishables.

The image of that villa was still pressing on her mind. Should she buy it as a keepsake, or not? Was she being sentimental? Why did she want any reminder of that time? It was a good likeness, well executed, and it captured the brightness of the place but it held so many painful memories. Ah well. Flora sighed, knowing she must sleep on it before making a decision.

Chapter 31

Kit found volunteers to take a rusty old Citroën van out into the hills that bordered on Spain. There they would distribute what supplies they drummed up from Father Antoine's congregation and friends. It was tiring work, with wheels that kept puncturing on rocky tracks, and a tank that kept running out of fuel. The heat of the day was so fierce that they began to make night runs, to reach groups who had crossed over the peaks in secret. They were almost always exhausted, hungry and in need of shelter. The volunteers soon ran out of baguettes, dried milk, fruit and drums of water.

It was here Kit joined up with other groups of charity workers, more organised than his own, and they talked about how holding camps close to Saint-Cyprien and Argèles were being set up to shelter the escapees from bombing and persecutions.

After days out in the hills, he was glad to return to the coast and the bustle of Collioure to rest. He had transported wounded Republican soldiers and their women to Dr

Ortega. From these men, he heard tales that shocked him; how prisoners of war were shackled to each other with barbed wire, and children were forced to watch their own parents being shot. Had the world learned nothing from the Great War? He called in at the art gallery to see if any of his pictures had been sold. Funds were running low.

'Sorry,' said the owner. 'Though I had a woman in, who took a great interest in your pink villa. She thought she recognised it. An English woman, I think. It seemed to upset her and she backed out, but perhaps she may return. I could see it meant something to her.'

'Did you get her name?' Kit was curious.

'No, we never got round to that. She did ask about the artist. All I could recall was she thought Carstairs was a good Scottish name.'

Kit suddenly felt alarm at this enquiry, but curious nonetheless. 'Do you think she will come back? What did she look like?'

'Tall, dark-haired, wealthy, judging by her dress and pearls. A typical tourist of a certain class,' he replied.

'How long ago was this?'

'Just a few days ago, so she may return. You could give her your address.'

'No, Claude, do you mind if I take back the villa? It's no longer for sale. I should never have put it in the gallery.' Kit couldn't wait to have it back.

'I did sell a small painting of a farmhouse, but nothing else. Why remove one of your best pictures? I don't understand. She may want to buy it,' Claude said, lifting the painting from the window with reluctance.

'No thanks, I'll take it back with me now.'

'Please yourself, but it is a pity...'

How could Kit explain how nervous he was, knowing that someone out there recognised the Rose Villa? Someone might recognise him from the old days, a nurse who knew all about Flora and the scandalous romance with the chaplain. No, it was too risky. He carried the painting under his arm through the streets, like a criminal hiding his loot, making for his own room above the Café Maritime. He found himself shaking, and pulled his straw hat over his face to hide his ginger hair.

Why was he running away? Because somewhere out there was a woman who might recognise him, even after nearly twenty years? Don't be ridiculous, he chided himself, but he was taking no chances. *The Rose Villa* was no longer for sale.

Chapter 32

The two women drove into the beautiful city of Perpignan to visit the consulate. Vera was anxious to glean any news of the Scots contingent in the International Brigade. The staff were sympathetic but not very helpful.

'All international soldiers will be told to leave shortly. The war is not going well for them. Many injured have been deported already, so I don't see how we can find Mr Lennox... a bit of a needle in a haystack, I'm afraid. Anyway, it's now illegal for British citizens to enter the war. Go home, ladies, you'd do better to wait for news from the Scottish Red Cross... It's a waste of time crossing into Spain at the moment. Go to the border, if you must, or to the station and ask there. Trains go straight to Paris with some of the troops.'

Vera slumped in her chair in tears. 'I haven't heard from him for months. What can I think?'

'Perhaps there's news waiting for you back home. This city is full of spies, fraudsters promising safe passage, making false promises for a fee, then vanishing into the hills. Go home, ladies.'

Flora felt patronised, but the consul spoke the truth in many ways. This was a wild goose chase, if ever there was one, and they were out of their depth. Helping Vera come to terms with this disappointment was not going to be easy, though. At least they had registered details of Sandy so if anything was discovered, they would be informed, but it felt like a forlorn hope.

Her first task was to cheer her sister up. 'Come on, let's find a restaurant and explore the city while we're here. We can make our way back slowly. The consul is right. There may be news waiting at home.'

Vera was rummaging in her bag. 'I did get something from the Republicans in Glasgow. They said there is a friendly restaurant somewhere in the city. I've got the address in my bag.' She fumbled around until she found a slip of paper: *The Continental Bar, Place Araga.* Comrades meet there and we might hear some news.'

It was a smoky, crowded bar and their entrance was noticed. No one spoke, until Vera marched up to the bar with a snapshot of Sandy.

'*Ecossais, mon mari...*' The men shook their heads, suspicious of them both. There was no point in staying any longer. A black-eyed waitress followed them out.

'Many men pass through. Give me that photograph to pin on the board. I can ask... I like the Scotsmen. They can drink the bar dry but it is not going well for them, many are leaving.'

They found another, quieter, restaurant in which to lick their wounds of disappointment. 'If only there was someone else to ask.' Vera brushed her hair off her face, shaking her head, defeated.

'There's always Maudie Wallace,' Flora suggested. 'She is out in Spain somewhere. We can write to her. It's a long shot, but Maudie is our best bet.'

Vera shrugged her shoulders. 'Even I know Spain is a huge country. Maudie could be anywhere.'

'She's with the Swiss White Cross and they'll be close to all the action.'

'What a waste of time this has been. I'm sorry, we should never have come.'

'At least we've got close to the border, had a restful stopover by the sea and had time together. It's a beautiful area. I wish we could explore more.'

'If you say so,' Vera replied.

Flora decided to change the subject. 'Let me tell you something very strange. When we were in Collioure, I saw a picture of a rose-pink villa. I'm sure it was the very place I stayed at on the Riviera in 1919. You know, where I met Kit Carlyle, before he died... all history now.' Flora didn't want to go into any more details.

'The painting was done by a chap called Carstairs and I'm sure it was the very place. It upset me at first, so I didn't buy it. Thinking about it later, I decided to go back and bargain for it. After all, why shouldn't I have a memento of those days? So, I went back, but it wasn't in the window. I presumed it had been sold, but the owner said the artist had removed it himself. He decided it was not for sale as soon as he heard someone recognised it, so he just took it away. What do you make of that? I asked for his address, but the owner didn't know it. All he said was that he's a funny chap, and a bit of a recluse, and that it would be best to leave him alone. That he went out on some secret missions with the local priest.

'The owner offered me some of his other work but I only wanted the Rose Villa. It's puzzled me ever since. Why would an artist put it up for sale one minute and then change his mind the next? What was so off-putting about my interest in it?'

'Who knows, Flo? The artists I've met are a law unto themselves,' Vera replied. 'One less thing for us to take home.'

'Do you want to leave now?' Flora said in surprise at this turnabout.

'Yes, no point in staying.'

'We could explore a bit longer, as we've only just reached the coast.' Flora was finding the landscape dramatic and interesting.

'It's too hot and dusty and it'll take days to drive back north. We've delivered the boxes. There's nothing for me here.'

Flora was disappointed and reluctant to leave now. That painting had unsettled her, reminding her of the light and warmth of the Riviera and the love that might have been. She thought of Maudie Wallace somewhere in danger, and of the poor, foot-weary peasants trundling along the highways in rags. Who was the strange artist, Carstairs, who didn't want to share his rose-pink villa with anyone?

Kit wrote to Sam O'Keeffe, as promised.

It's so crowded here with tourists, refugees and security men that I've not done much work except transport food and blankets to those who are on foot. There are so many small children being dragged over the mountains. Many have no parents and are collected up by strangers. I fear for their safety and health. Would it be possible for you to take in some more? Winter is coming and this is no place for shoeless orphans. Father Antoine has sent some to the nuns, but there's not enough room for all of them.

Our provisions are running low and I am tempted to write to a newspaper with a description of conditions here. I fear it will get worse once the floodgates open. There must be generous people in Britain prepared to help. It's at times like this that I realise what a huge mistake I made all those years ago in hiding my identity. I can never forgive myself, but it is too late now, so I will write under this name. Although it has served me well, subterfuge no longer sits easy upon me.

Only the other week a woman came into the gallery and recognised the Rose Villa convalescent house. She seemed very interested but I couldn't bear to part with it and took it off the wall. I keep it in my room, to remind myself of my perfidy. My stock of work is dwindling rapidly, but I sell enough to keep a shirt on my back. Father Antoine is the first priest I have warmed to since the old padre in our battalion. I told him I had no faith, but, like Dr Ortega, he just smiled, saying that I must think things through for myself from now on. He is devout, but in a way that feels honest. Love is not what we say, but what we do. I thought of Flora and the Suffragettes, 'Deeds not words.'

I feel I have a purpose here, something I've not felt for years. There are rumours that the Civil War will soon be over but heaven help those on the wrong side. I fear a bloodbath. Let me know what you think about my idea? Consuela would be such a mother to these weary little ones...

Kit was glad to have kept in touch with his old friend and he had kept his word not to drink, tempting though it was when he was tired, alone and wondering how they would fund their next vanload of supplies. True, also, to his word, he wrote a detailed letter to the London *Times*, the Glasgow *Herald* and the *Manchester Guardian*, describing the fate of innocent victims of war. After the bombing raids on Guernica, readers would be in no doubt about the suffering of millions in Spain, on both sides. Whether it would be fruitful or not he didn't know, but it was an effort worth making. He signed himself Christopher Carstairs, with a *poste restante* address, and also added Father Antoine's details for good measure. All he could do was wait and see if there was any response. For the first time in years, he prayed that aid would come, and soon.

Chapter 33

The journey back to Scotland was tedious, knowing as they did that it had been a wasted visit for Vera. Flora blamed herself for suggesting it. This civil war was complicated and now that victory for the Nationalists was assured, the future for Republicans was dire.

Rose welcomed them back and Pa was relieved to see them safely home. The ice between him and Vera was melting. He could see how concerned she was for Sandy, fearing the worst. No news is not always good news. To keep busy herself she started attending meetings once more.

There were so many factions, all with different views about what should be done that even Vera was losing heart. Labour stalwarts, trade unionists, Communists, all squabbling.

'I'm sick of it,' she announced. 'The real heroes are out there, shedding blood for freedom. When will it end?'

When any wounded brigadiers returned, she pounced on them for information. The only fresh news was the ban on internationals crossing the border to fight. Now and again, there was an exchange of prisoners.

The Duchess of Atholl's appeal for Spanish relief came as a welcome distraction. Here was something of which everyone could approve. Tins of dried milk, beans, cocoa, herring, salmon and cash flowed in, and the first of many aid lorries were sent off. Flora was impressed by this energetic aristocrat who could fill a concert hall with her stirring speeches.

There was talk of bringing shiploads of orphans across to Scotland, making hostels for them and sending them to school. Together Vera and Flora forged a common bond on Flag days, garden parties and church collections. Even Pa and Virginia opened Kildowie grounds for a fund-raising event. It raised enough to fill a lorry with tinned goods and fresh clothing.

In the streets around the city, working women knitted comforts for the Scottish Brigade to wear during the winter. There were baby layettes for newborns and warm jumpers for children. Rose held a cake sale for the cause.

In January 1938 after Hogmanay, Flora and Vera were sorting clothes in a church hall in Shettleston, when a man walked through the door who Vera recognised.

'Patrick! You're back!'

The man was muffled, with a thick bandage around his throat. He could hardly speak. 'There you are... Ma told me where to find you. It's from Sandy...'

Flora thought her sister was going to faint. 'Is he home? Is he...' She couldn't finish her words.

Patrick shook his head. 'Nae, missus, he's been wounded and is in hospital. He gave me this letter. Some of us were bussed out, part of some exchange. Sandy was too sick to be moved.'

'He's alive, Flora!' Vera burst into tears, crumpled into a ball with relief.

'Come away, so you can read your letter in peace.' The other helpers put their arms around the sobbing girl. Flora drove her back to Park Circus, where her cleaning lady made strong coffee. Vera sat hugging the letter, almost too scared to open it.

Dear lass. I hope this reaches you. We were unlucky, got caught in crossfire, made a bit of a pig's ear of it. Got a bullet in ma leg and it went awful septic but thanks to the doctor I got seen before it went green but its gey stiff.

Don't you worry, hen, I'll be shipped off. I'm nae use with a gammy leg. Getting letters out is not easy or I would have written sooner. Bit of a hellhole here, on all fronts. I will write more through the Red Cross. Take care and keep up the good fight...

Vera read the page over and over. She sniffed the creased paper. 'It smells of Lysol.'

'That's good, then, it must be a clean hospital,' Flora said. 'Does he say where?'

'No, if it was seized, it might be dangerous but I'll see Patrick again and get the full story. I know which street he's on.'

'It's a rough district. Shall I come with you?'

'I'd rather you didn't. I know these people and they'll not open up with a stranger in the room.'

Flora felt left out. 'I understand, but I'll worry.'

'Look, I can take care of myself. I'm one of them,' Vera replied, jumping up ready to leave.

No, you are not, Elvira, Flora thought to herself. You're a Garvie, you have the use of my car. You do charity work and have an allowance from your father. You don't have to watch the pennies. Dear Aunt Jemima left you provided for and I see you never go without. You can go where you please, with choices those women can only dream of. Vera did have an entrance into that community through Sandy, but she was an outsider, however much she supported them.

Two days later, there was a letter in the tray in the hall, with a familiar scrawl that made Flora dash to tear it open. Maudie Wallace had been in Barcelona, when they were almost in Spain. Their letters had crossed. Her news made Flora shudder. So many innocents killed and wounded and so little help on offer. No wonder they wanted to flee into France.

Flora put the pages down and looked over her city, the park, the fine buildings, folk going about their business, with no fear of fire raining down on them. That was the moment when she knew she had to do something more than raise cash. Vera would carry on the good work and Sandy would return. Sadly, there was no one waiting for her.

When Allan Garvie heard Flora's plans, he paced the floor in the drawing room.

'You're not home five minutes and you want to go back into France. Whatever for?'

'It's been months and Maudie's letter has been on my mind. They need support, not just food and funds but practical help. I was a nurse and there's nothing holding me here. There's plenty of folk who can do the meetings, collections, dances and tea parties. I can do more. Listen to what Maudie says: *If only you'd come and help. There are feeding stations, collecting stations for orphaned children to drive them to safety. It's pitiful to see the state of them. I'm due leave. We could meet in Perpignan.'*

Allan was not convinced. 'Virginia and I are worried. The continent is in turmoil. Can we believe this Herr Hitler is to be trusted? Better to stay here and continue the good work. It's not safe out there.'

'It wasn't safe in the war, Pa. I just have a feeling I can be of use down there.' How could she explain that, ever since her return to Kildowie, nothing felt right? She wanted to see more of the coastline, the hills beyond and the rugged landscape. Were those hills calling her back for a reason? Their visit had been all about finding Sandy. He would return to Vera, of that she was certain but Pa still needed assuring.

'It would be so good to meet up with Maudie again.'

'But you're no spring chicken. In your forties, or have you forgotten?' Pa argued.

'I play tennis, golf, hike in the hills. I am strong. I'm not your little girl. I'll promise to go back by train this time, if it makes you feel better,' she said, knowing he was right. One look in the mirror showed lips tightening, little crows' feet by her eyes. It was not as if she was husband hunting. She was returning to be of service.

'I don't know, Flo, you're getting as bad as your sister, on your soapbox…'

'I'm a widow with means. I'm a war veteran. I have seen death and destruction in so many ways, things you can only imagine. I've never talked about that stuff. It's in the past.

I will write and stay safe. I don't want to spend my life playing bridge, entertaining Ivo's old comrades, much as I like some of them. I am not in the marriage market, nor am I Aunt Mima.'

'You always were a gey stubborny piece of work, lass, once a notion gets in your head. I haven't forgotten how you defied yon census count, tearing a strip off anyone who thought women not worthy of the vote. I can't stop you. I know that and I am proud of you, always have been.' He turned to Virginia, who had stayed silent but now nodded in approval.

'No heroics, Flora, please, and come back to us when it's all over.'

Flora smiled with relief. She had talked Pa around and knew she had his reluctant blessing. 'Thank you.' She hugged him tightly. 'Now I must go and pack cases and make my peace with Vera. When Sandy returns, they'll battle on together. You will see them right.'

Chapter 34

Kit drew the truck up the long drive to the O'Keeffes' farmhouse. In the back he had ten children, squashed together, but they did not speak much, staring out, wide eyed, numbed by the strangeness of their surroundings. His Spanish was improving but it wasn't good enough to explain just where he was taking them.

At the sound of his rackety entrance, Consuela came to the door. 'At last, *les pauvres enfants*,' she said, greeting Kit with kisses on his cheeks. 'Who have we got here?' She spoke in Spanish as he brought them out, one by one, to meet her. 'I am Consuela... what are your names?' Her gentle voice seemed to relax them.

'This is Juan and Maria, Ignazio, Marcos...' Kit announced the first ones. To be truthful he had forgotten the other names. 'It's been another long journey. I hope you can find room for them.'

Consuela sighed, 'There are others here, but we will manage. First to the kitchen, to wash hands.' She whispered, 'Have they any clean clothes?'

Kit shook his head. 'Nothing but the rags they stand up in and none too clean, many with sores. We think these children have no parents. Sorry to dump them on you at such short notice. After nights in makeshift shelters, and a trek through the mountains, they're done in. Sam will need to check them over.'

'He's out somewhere visiting a patient, but won't be long. I have made a bean stew and we've bread and apples. We'll try to fatten them up.' She looked across at the children huddled together. 'Look at their eyes, they have seen the unspeakable.'

'I can't thank you enough. We were at our wits' end not knowing how to find them safety. My friend, Father Antoine, will do his best to find them homes, but it's not easy. There are just too many climbing over the border under cover of darkness; women, babies, wounded men.'

'Is it that bad? We can keep them here for a while, but there are plans to ship children abroad, Sam heard.' Consuela ushered the children into the big kitchen, giving them each an apple to chew while she boiled kettles on the stove. Then she proceeded to dunk their hands into the cooled water, examining each one carefully, shaking her head at the state of their arms. 'Scabies, ringworm and dirt. You have a look round and see what progress we've made, while I see to these. They must be so hungry.'

Kit wandered around the field, where there was a large vegetable plot and two young boys busy weeding through the crops. '*Hola!*' he shouted. The boys looked up briefly and carried on as he passed by.

There was a swing tied with sturdy rope to an oak tree and a worn path down to a stream, perfect for bathing and swimming. There were two donkeys in a paddock, goats for milk and a hen coop. Here were supplies for fruit, vegetables and eggs. He felt humbled by their response to his plea for help. Playing here might give these children time to heal from their ordeals. Their futures were uncertain, but hope lived in this children's house. It was a refuge from war and suffering.

The sickest children had been too ill to journey here. They were farmed out to hospitals in Perpignan. Kit stood silent for a moment, thinking how his life had changed since those first days in Collioure. Driving trucks along the coast, delivering children to safe houses, bringing in supplies from aid societies: the Red Cross, Society of Friends, Swiss Aid and the ever growing band of volunteers arriving daily. It was not a moment too soon. Thousands more would flee into France and preparations were inadequate, if rumours were to be believed.

Later he stood in the kitchen, watching the older children hanging back to let the new arrivals wolf down their soupy stew.

'Eat slowly,' Consuela said, 'or you will be sick.' She cut chunks of bread and the young ones dunked them into the stew, looking around at the strangers as if their hosts might steal their food. Some were shaking. When they had finished, they stood up to let the others sit down and fill their bowls.

'Now it's rest time.' Consuela led them out to the bunk beds, but not before examining them for infections and lice, stripping those infected and bandaging any sores and finding replacement underwear from a large blanket box.

'We've had a collection in the village, so generous... but

our supplies are dwindling. Tonight, we can try to bathe them.'

An hour later Sam arrived, looking weary and stooped. 'Good to see you, old chum. Great work you're doing.'

Kit shook his hand warmly. 'Not as much as you're doing here.'

'How's that chest of yours? I'll check it over later.'

'I'm fine, never felt better, but too many gaspers at times,' he confessed. 'How can I thank you for taking this lot in? It's getting worse. I don't know how it will end.'

'This war might end soon, but there's another on the horizon,' Sam replied. 'Herr Hitler has plans to take us all over. Still, we're safe enough down here. I've got an Irish passport and Consuela a Spanish one. How about you?'

'Registered as an alien, as the law demands, but I'm not thinking about another war.' Kit wanted to change the subject. 'I can always marry a French girl, but who would want an old soak like me?' He laughed.

'Why not? You're not getting any younger. A wife and a baby is what you need.' Sam smiled.

'Far too busy to tie myself down. With a false name and no proof of identity, that's the last thing on my mind.'

Since Antibes and the episode with Sylvie, Kit had steered clear of any romantic entanglement. He wanted time to paint and wander around on his bicycle to the ports and harbours to paint seascapes. His money was running out, so a pile of saleable canvases was useful. *The Rose Villa* stayed covered in his room. Occasionally he took it out, recalling those never-to-be-forgotten days, making sure it was dry and safe, then put it away.

Tonight he would kip down in the farm, in front of the

log fire with a nip of brandy and a cigarette. He was tired, the old lorry was on its last legs and the roads leading to Sam's place were little more than dirt tracks.

This friendship renewed was one of the anchors in his nomadic life. There was time to sit and share, reminisce about times long past. How could there be another war, when the last one was supposed to end all conflict? It was like a dark cloud building up to a storm.

As he drifted off to sleep, Kit relaxed. Perhaps it was all just a rumour and would come to nothing. The Germans would not dare to trample over French fields, not after their last humiliating defeat.

Chapter 35

Flora was relieved to see Maudie Wallace waiting at Perpignan station, waving wildly, rushing to help carry the heavy suitcases along the platform.

'Good to see you. Let me look at you! It's been ages.' Maudie hugged her. 'What on earth have you got in there, a body?'

'You said bring clothes, so I did. I made my friends clear out their wardrobes.'

'Golly, you're a brick, carting that monstrosity from Glasgow. Let's get a taxi to your hotel. I can't believe it's really you, like old times… but not quite.'

Flora noticed how gaunt her friend looked, with hair that was turning grey and scraped into a bun. She was the one who looked worn out: her eyes were sunken, with shadows under them. 'Are you well?' Flora asked, with concern.

'Ach, just a bout of the usual gut rot and the trots… They sent me across the border for a rest. I'm fine. You, I must say, look beautiful, not a day older.'

'Pull the other one, I can't believe we're over forty... fair, fat and forty,' she joked.

'Rubbish, you always look so elegant. Enjoy it while it lasts. Once you see what's happening down here...' Maudie paused. 'But that's for later.'

They arrived at the Hotel Continental and Flora made for the bathroom. The train from Paris had been packed with families who had too much luggage to be tourists. Many spoke German and languages she didn't recognise. They seemed nervy and didn't sleep. She was puzzled, until a woman whispered across the table, '*Juifs*... on the run.'

Maudie waited downstairs, ready to hit the town. Flora felt exhausted, but they found a little bistro and tucked into a bowl of *moules* and *boeuf en daube*. 'How are things back home? What is Elvira up to now?'

Flora rolled her eyes. 'You must call her Vera now. She's still living with Sandy who returned from Spain, half the man he once was. They are still waging war against the Nationalists here, but Sandy, thank God, is out of it. He's holding down his job, much to Pa's surprise. Pa married Virginia Forsyth. Her two boys are racing around the gardens, much to his delight. I think he has plans for them in his business. His order books are bulging. They were asking after you and send their regards. You know the Scots are doing so much with their Spanish Aid Fund. There's talk of making hostels for refugee children across the country.'

'Why have you come back?' Maudie took off her glasses to peer at her friend.

'Something I can't explain. I suppose a need to be needed. Your letters brought home to me just how awful things are and how there's a shortage of nurses and doctors. I know I'm rusty, but as a nurse you never forget the basics. All I want is to find a place where I can be useful.'

'This is where I can help… There's a hostel I want you to see. They could do with extra hands. It may be humdrum at first, manual labour, but it needs nursery nurses. I met this girl on the trek north, called Esme, who was working in Barcelona. She told me the terrible tale of planes dropping little packages of chocolate and toys. When the children ran to pick them up, they exploded in their faces and hands, killing or maiming them. Can you imagine a mind that makes these devices, knowing full well a starving child would be tempted? May they rot in hell! What a sick world we are living in. Esme was so disturbed by what she witnessed that they are sending her back to the States. But I digress. There's plenty of work waiting for you.'

'Will you go back into Spain?'

Maudie shook her head wearily. 'No, I have work here on a ward, but to know you're not far away… It will be like old times.'

'We never did work together in the war, did we? I promised to write to Rose with all your news. There's another baby on the way, a bit of a surprise, but Rose will take it in her stride with plenty of help. Ironic really, as she's still working at the clinic helping women prevent unwanted births.'

'Come on, let's get some fresh air and explore the city. Tomorrow we'll take a bus to the chateau at Brouilla and you can see the hostel for yourself.'

The night was clear and crisp as they strolled past the castle and the cathedral. 'Why don't you come and stay at my hotel?' Flora offered, but Maudie smiled.

'I've got a place and I think you'll need to rest and sleep in. I can talk the hind legs off a donkey, as well you know. I'd only wear you out. We'll meet tomorrow. Thanks for asking though.' They stopped back at the hotel entrance and Flora waved goodbye to her friend, as she disappeared into the busy street.

How unreal this all was, she mused later, lying in a strange bed, listening to the night noises of a city. She was beginning a new adventure but what was she letting herself in for? What if she couldn't cope with the language, or the conditions? What if her face didn't fit?

You're here now, so make the most of it. Change is always strange at first, stop chunnering and get some sleep. Maudie will set you up. Be thankful for the dearest of old friends.

Chapter 36

At first it was a trickle coming into the makeshift border camp, on a cold December night. Kit was shocked by the sight of barefoot children, some wrapped in newspapers, half dead from the mountain trek over the Pyrenees. All he had to offer was stale loaves of bread and water, as some collapsed crying out, 'My mother is left on the mountainside, she could go no further. Help us find her.'

Then he saw a mother in labour, clutching her swollen stomach, crying as the man with her yelled for help. '*Por favor, señor.*'

He opened the van full of empty boxes, to let her climb up as she cried out in pain. Kit was panicked and shouted across for a nurse, but none was in sight. Then a woman in khaki slacks ran over, jumped into the open van and began to soothe the frightened girl in Spanish. Laying her down, she lifted up her ragged skirt to see how far she was in labour and Kit looked away. This was women's work.

'She needs help.'

Kit was so relieved to hear an American voice.

'Shall we get her out of here?' he said.

'Are you serious? Where else can she go in this crowd... Do you want her to give birth on a filthy beach? Looks as if the baby's on its way, poor kid.'

Kit nudged curious onlookers away while the American tried to make the back of the van into a kind of bed from flattened cardboard. Kit pushed his way out of the crowd, to find hot water that was boiling over a fire, where children huddled for warmth. Towels were needed to wrap a baby, but there was nothing to hand. The cries of the woman grew louder, her man was shouting for something, taking the very shirt off his back to use as a cushion for her head. Kit felt helpless.

At least the American had turned up or it would have been him in the back of the van acting as a midwife. There was a strange silence before each scream pierced the air and then a cry, a gurgle of protest as the baby was brought into the world.

People cheered with relief and clapped. Kit remembered it must be nearly Christmas Eve. A cloth suddenly appeared and a blanket given by someone in the crowd; most had little more than bundles with them.

'It's a boy!' yelled the American woman in Spanish and she lifted him up quickly to show to the onlookers.

'His name is Jesús,' the father proudly announced. 'And he is free, French born, so he will be safe.' They cheered congratulations. Kit felt himself praying gratefully.

'Phew!' said the girl. 'That was close. I'm Frankie Menkel. I've never delivered a baby before, just foals. Thank God it was her fourth baby. Two died in the bombing and another is with his grandmother somewhere, who knows?'

'Your Spanish is good,' Kit said, in awe. She was little more than twenty, dressed in corduroy breeches and her dark hair wrapped round with a scarf.

'So it should be. My mother was born in Madrid, emigrated to the States. And you?'

'Chris.' He smiled. 'You saved my bacon there. I wouldn't have known one end from the other.' They both laughed with relief.

'No sweat,' Frankie replied. 'She did most of it herself. Come on, let's get them hot drinks. Where are all this lot coming from?'

'Heaven only knows. I think we need to move them on and fast. The holding camp is full.'

As he spoke, a group of dark-skinned soldiers with hard faces marched up. '*Marchez*,' their officer ordered, pulling up the sitting refugees and shoving them into lines. '*Marchez vite!*'

'Where're you taking them? They're exhausted. It's dark and cold,' Kit interrupted him.

'To the beaches. Plenty of room there for beggars, thieves and all this riff-raff.'

Frankie pushed in. 'This gal is goin' nowhere with a newborn. There's a place further along, a maternity hostel. We're taking baby Jesús there, and quick, before he freezes to death. Can I borrow this van?'

'I'll drive,' Kit offered.

'No thanks. You're needed here. I don't trust these troops; they're Moroccans. You go along with them and see where these poor sods are deposited. The van's safe with me. I'll catch up with you later, promise.' Her dark eyes flashed. Kit sensed he could trust her. 'Be seeing you...' she yelled.

Kit escorted the stragglers as best he could, gathering two other volunteers en route. It was going to be another exhausting trek for them and he didn't trust the scar-faced officer one iota. There would be no Christmas cheer where this lot were heading. How could a damp beach keep any of them safe?

Chapter 31

M audie escorted Flora to the makeshift maternity hostel in the little town of Brouilla where a young Swiss nurse was organising patients into the crowded rooms.

'This is Miss Elisabeth Eidenbenz who is in charge, with Karl Ketterer.'

A pretty young woman hardly looking out of school with her coronet of plaited hair and her smile that beamed a welcome. 'We are understaffed and overcrowded. Wallace tells me you were a nurse in *la guerre*. There will be plenty to do here. You have had injections?'

Flora nodded, glad that Rose had insisted she was inoculated before she left. She glanced over to the beds where sad-eyed Spanish women were holding newborns and eyeing her with interest.

'We have midwives, a local doctor, but we need a driver to collect women in need of confinement. You drive?'

Flora smiled. 'I once drove from Scotland to here,' she said in her best French, hoping to impress, and a little awestruck by the young woman's dignity and confidence.

'Why did you return here?'

'Because in Scotland there are many women raising funds for the Spanish refugees. I wanted to do more than shake a tin on a street corner.'

'You know the battle for the Ebro is lost, and the war is almost over, but punishments are harsh. We expect many more women such as these. You have seen the conditions on the beach.'

'Yes, there are hundreds there, sleeping in trenches in the sand. Why are there no proper camps?'

'Sadly, the French were not prepared. You can see how full we are. The worst cases go to hospitals in Perpignan, but we do what we can with the aid we are given. I'm afraid it will seem menial work.'

Maudie butted in. 'Flora is no shirker. She worked on the ambulance trains up and down France. She once cleaned a warehouse on her hands and knees, to make a sterile ward...'

Flora blushed. 'Not just me, of course, but VADs had to make the best of things.'

'Excellent,' Elisabeth said. 'Welcome aboard our crowded ship.'

Over the days that followed, Flora sensed Elisabeth was a powerhouse of calm efficiency, sending out search parties for desperate women and children, giving expectant mothers a chance to give birth safely, in clean conditions, away from the stench and filth of the coastal camps.

Flora drove volunteers and nurses to check those near their time, distributing tins of clean water, dried milk powder and fresh bread. She had never seen such desperation. It was a living hell on earth. There were families using the sea water to relieve themselves, to wash, and some elderly, devoid of hope, just lay ignored, dying on the sand. The soldiers roughly dragged the bodies out of sight, without bothering about decent burial rites.

It wasn't long before Flora itched with lice. Her skirt was stained with dirt and she begged for slacks and a long-sleeved shirt to protect herself from biting insects. This was exhausting work and she felt every one of her years. In every letter home, she pleaded with Pa and Vera to do their utmost to send aid down to the coast.

How could she describe the chaos? There were many aid workers from all nations: American Quakers, Swiss and British individuals like herself. Coordination between charities was often fragmented. Christmas and New Year passed, with a few ceremonies and little extra rations to lighten the darkness and ease the cold of winter shelters. It was Dante's Inferno without the heat. Her only relief was in knowing Maudie was not far away and if she took a bus or train into Perpignan, she could collapse for a night in a clean hotel.

By February of 1939 the floodgates opened as expected and thousands upon thousands of refugees surged across the border into France. Every available beach was choked with newcomers, corralled behind barbed wire. Children were shipped out across Europe, separated from desperate families who only wanted their young ones to be fed, sheltered and safe. It was a time of tears and sorrowful partings.

The incessant search for pregnant women went on. They escorted them to the bathhouse, boiled up the clothes that would stand washing and hung them out to dry in the weak sunshine, where the wailing of hungry babies filled the air.

Mothers took turns to help where they could, in the kitchen and wash house.

So strict was their regime of cleanliness and effective midwifery that there were few deaths among mothers, but some babies were too premature or weak to survive.

The nurseries were full of laundry baskets used as cribs. Once rested, the women worked in the garden, digging or planting vegetables, and fathers came to help with repairs and carpentry, building fences and freshening up paint.

Each family was registered and places were found for the lucky ones to work or be shipped far away from the beaches. Flora had never worked so hard, her joints ached at the end of every shift, but it was satisfying work and there was no time to be homesick, or plan her return to Scotland. Here she was determined to stay.

Chapter 38

Kit spent a whole week at the O'Keeffes' farm, helping out with older children who were in need of discipline and occupation. They were troubled souls, old before their time, still shocked by what they had witnessed on their trek across the mountains.

Sam tried to get them to open up about their experiences but it was Consuela who had the knack of giving them sweet cordials and biscuits, sitting them round the table and coaxing them gently to tell each other how they made the journey into France.

Ricardo shook his head at first. 'I don't know, it was dark. My father carried my little sister. We had to be quiet, but Paula wailed. The shepherd told them to shut her up. "There are guards!" Papa tried to quieten her but she struggled. If you don't shut that baby up, I will shut her up for ever, they said, and made me put a scarf around her mouth.' Ricardo stopped and began to weep.

'She kept on crying and Papa wound it round her face... She was silent after that. It was too tight and when we were allowed to rest, Mama pulled the scarf away but Paula did not move or breathe... no life. Did I kill her?' Ricardo's head fell on his arms. 'They took Papa away to another place.'

'The cold killed her.' Consuela put her arms round him. 'It isn't you... you were being kind, giving her your scarf.'

Kit could barely listen to this sad story. So many of them here were separated from their families, lost in a confusing, silent world, with no ruins, bombs, or familiar voices, just strangers.

The O'Keeffes were doing their best to find work, by fishing and giving French lessons. The village school was too full to accept any more refugees and there were fights with local boys, who called them names. Some were offered a chance to be taken to Sète, where ocean liners would take them to another Spanish-speaking country, in South America. Some were heading north to Britain. Sam was reluctant to let his charges go, until he heard that Scotland was settling children in the countryside. 'Do you know where Perthshire is?' he asked Kit.

'Perth will make a fine place with its rivers and lochs, lots of fruit picking and open spaces for them to play. Our schools are first class.'

'Will you escort them then?' Consuela asked, but Kit shook his head.

'Sorry, my place is right here. I have no desire to return...'

Sam smiled. 'Of course not, how could you explain your new lease of life? Lazarus returned from the dead. One day you'll have to make your peace with all your lies, you know.'

Kit ignored this jibe. *La Retirada*, as they called the invasion of Spanish families, was in full flow. Exhausting though it was, there was always this haven to return to, for some peace but not quiet. This children's house was anything but. He arranged for a football match with local boys, ordering mixed teams to battle it out on the field next to the school. The locals were in for a shock, for some of Sam's boys could duck and dive and shoot fast. Better to mix them up and then it would be a fairer match.

Kit had never lost his love for the game. Watching Glasgow Rangers versus Celtic was one of his fondest memories, even if the resulting skirmishes outside the grounds had bloody outcomes. He recalled the wartime soldiers' banter, as they went careering over rough ground before a stand-to. There were some professional footballers among them, but mostly they were just Saturday team lads. How many of them had survived to play again? Not many, he feared. It was hard to shake loose those images from his mind. No point in going back into the past. There were too many ghosts waiting to pounce on him there.

Chapter 39

In the summer of 1939, when Flora and other volunteers
were searching the camp at Saint-Cyprien, she came
across two women in the first stages of labour. Slowly they
extricated them from the beach, demanding their release
from the guards in order to get them back to the chateau at
Brouilla. The sun was blazing, and flies buzzed over them,
attracted to their sweat. The stench from the makeshift
latrines was overwhelming. The sooner Flora and her
helper could get them away from there, the better. She
parked their truck as close as she could, but the crowded
tracks were dusty, throwing sand into her face, blinding her
eyes with grit.

Another truck with children sitting in the back went
past them slowly, the children's hands hanging over the
sides, their dark little faces scowling into the sun. At least
they were being driven away from the crush of the beach.
The driver paused, caught up in the queue. As he wiped
sweat from his face, his beret slipped down the back of
his head, revealing a mop of sandy curls. He leaned out of

the window to see what the hold-up was and for a second caught Flora's eye, as she stood waiting to cross over to the other side. Flora froze. How could a dead man be driving a truck full of refugee children? How could a dead man be here in this hellish hole? Who was the ginger-haired man with the russet beard? It couldn't possibly be…

Flora had to know if she was seeing a ghost, or just another aid worker with reddish hair. She left the women with her colleague and raced alongside the truck.

'Kit? Kit Carlyle?' she shouted. As the lorry picked up pace, so did she. She had to know. Was this a never forgotten face from her past, a face lined with age, and leathered by sunlight but still recognisable? She was running.

'Kit, it's you!' The driver stared ahead, trying to ignore her.

'Stop the truck!' she ordered, but he edged away, shaking his head at the man in the seat beside him. The co-driver leant over. 'Out of the way, lady. Chris, she's a crazy woman. Drive on.'

How dare they run away? Flora flung herself in front of the truck and it screeched to a halt. 'Get out and face me, Kit Carlyle, or I'll climb on the bonnet.' She could hardly breathe, her voice cracking with shock and emotion. 'It *is* you.'

The stopped truck was attracting a crowd. Kit climbed down, his eyes avoiding hers. The face was thinner, but the tell-tale scar on his cheek was visible through his beard. They stood in silence for what seemed like an age. Flora found her throat was dry. 'How could you?' was all she could croak.

Kit bowed his head, raising both hands. 'Flora, I'm sorry.'

'Sorry? Is that all you can say, after all these years? I thought you were dead. What the hell are you doing here?'

'Flora, I can explain, but not here. I have to get the children away to the port. I can explain.'

'No, you bloody well won't. I never want to see your face again, you... hypocrite, you coward. You should be ashamed of yourself...' The crowd closed in, realising the altercation was getting interesting. 'You just carry on with all your lies. Drive on and don't look back!' she yelled, beside herself with fury as she turned back through the crush, her limbs fuelled by anger of a ferocity she had never encountered before.

She heard his voice yelling, 'Flora... wait...' She ran.

All these years of secret mourning for a lost lover and now here he was, alive and well. Was this some dream? Her heart was thumping, limbs wobbling and her head spinning with heat and panic. She felt she would faint and needed to sit down to catch her breath.

'Are you all right?' Anita, the aid worker, came running. 'What was all that about, standing in front of a truck? You could've been run down! Someone you know?'

Flora brushed down her slacks, mopped her brow and gathered what dignity she had left. 'I don't want to talk about it, not now, not ever... where are our mothers? We must see to them.'

'They're fine, waiting in the truck.'

Flora stumbled through the crowds, feeling sick, desperate to be alone to gather the shattered bits of herself, to blot out the scene, the look on Kit's face, a look of bewilderment, shock and shame. *You have a job to do, so get on with it.* There were two frightened women who were depending on her. She drove back slowly, distracted, crashing the gearstick, but once in the safety of her cabin, she pulled out her battered suitcase.

Her first instinct was to pack up and leave on the next train to Paris, to flee from the filth, the noise of the camps. The thought of sharing the same district with a man such as Carlyle was unbearable. She wanted no further explanation, excuses, apologies. Her hands trembled, her legs cramping with lack of water and shock. Collapsing on her camp bed, tears welled up, tears of pity for herself and frustration at such an unexpected encounter in the full view of an audience. She had made an utter fool of herself. Perhaps it wasn't him after all?

Who was she fooling? How many tears had she shed in dark places after news of his death reached her? The letter from his commanding officer, the pain of recalling those tender moments and caresses on the beach by the Rose Villa, the passion of that first lovemaking, the innocence of their bodies, were real enough. This betrayal was beyond words, humiliating, unbelievable. To fake his own death, to abandon her to face Matron's wrath. It still rankled. What cruel fate had brought them face to face in this borderland of chaos? There was nothing for it now but to leave, to find a hiding place to lick her wounded heart.

'Look out, Chris, steady on! You nearly crashed into those vans. What's gotten into you? Better let me drive. You're all over the show,' yelled Chuck Hauser, Kit's American co-driver, grabbing the wheel. 'Who was that crazy dame, calling you Kit, flinging herself onto the bonnet? You in some trouble with her? Just pull over, let's give the kids in the back a break. Tell Uncle Chuck all about it. I won't say a word.'

I bet you won't, thought Kit. Chuck was a good worker but young. He tried to make everything into a joke, to hide his shock at the job they were doing.

'Shut up, just give me another cig and keep your nose out. None of your damn business who she is and don't call Flora a crazy woman.' Kit jumped out of the truck, furious with himself for putting the kids in danger by reckless driving.

'Flora, so that's her name. Have you been having fun?' Chuck joked, but seeing the fury on Kit's face, he walked away. 'Okay, okay!'

Kit wanted to punch him but they let down the back of the truck in silence, so the children could let off steam. The Spanish nurse followed her charges into a field, leaving Kit to storm off alone to gather his thoughts. It had felt like a killer punch to his chest when he saw her staring at him from the crowd. The only girl he had ever loved was standing before him, recognising him after twenty years. He wanted to crawl into a hole and howl. The day of reckoning had come and now he must face the worst of himself. Just when he thought he was being useful here, he had been found out. Dragging on the cigarette brought no relief. The cheap tobacco made him cough, the smoke choked his throat. What excuse could he make that didn't sound trite and unconvincing? All he felt was for Flora. It pierced his heart like a spear to know how he had hurt her. He could hardly breathe, spluttering on his fag, spitting it out in disgust.

After her challenge, she had just walked away with dignity,

vowing never to speak to him again. Kit knew she deserved an explanation, even if she would never comprehend why he had been so weak. Anyway, why was she here, in the chaos of this filthy transit camp? Once a nurse always a nurse, he supposed. How brave of her to be battling with all that poverty and disease. An image of her in her VAD cap and cloak flashed into his mind, blushing as they touched hands in secret, all those years ago.

How could he not recognise her? She was older, of course, but the years had been kind. She was still a striking woman, with hardly a grey hair. Those dark eyes pierced him with an accusation all too accurate. He could not bear it.

He thought he had escaped but here was the *dies irae*, the day of wrath was upon him now. He could disappear again, whispered a tempting voice at the back of his head. Oh no, you don't, not this time. That was the old me, he argued. He was needed here. People were relying on him to help rescue families and children. Sam's children's house was a colony for these orphans, a respite before long journeys into the unknown. He would not be deserting them as he had deserted those loved ones in the past.

'On our way...' he called to Chuck.

'I'll drive then.' Chuck made for the driving seat.

'No, I'm fine.' Kit wanted to concentrate on the task in hand and push that shattering encounter to the back of his mind for now. He needed time to think, to prepare, to face Flora, but not yet. What to do next needed planning. There was a good man who might help him own up to twenty years of deception, one man he trusted to hear his confession with compassion. He would do nothing until he had spoken with him.

Chapter 40

Flora was due leave and had packed her bag. Her rescued mothers were settled in and ready to deliver.

'I've had some bad news but I have a nursing friend in the city. It would help to spend a few days with her, if it is permitted,' she said to Elisabeth.

'I'm sorry to hear that. Of course you can take a short break. We're waiting for a contingent of nurses from Switzerland, but we can spare you for a few days.'

Flora caught the train into Perpignan, drawing funds from her account and depositing her luggage at the hotel by the cathedral. She wired Maudie with news of her leave, hoping they could meet up soon. It was such a relief to get a reply saying Maudie was free, and could be there within hours. Flora flung herself into her arms, trying not to cry with relief.

'You won't believe what I have to tell you!'

'Calm down, Flo, what's happened?'

'Let's go somewhere. I need a gin, and a large one at that.' Flora grabbed her handbag and almost shoved Maudie out of the door. Once they were settled in a smart café, Flora took out her hankie. 'You won't believe who I have just seen. I'm so furious, after all these years. I can't breathe. I'm still in shock...'

'Whoa... whoa, slow down. Who're you talking about?'

'Kristian Carlyle. I saw him in the camp. He's been alive all these years, here in France!'

Maudie took off her spectacles to wipe them. 'Are you sure? There must be a mistake, a resemblance, perhaps?'

'No mistake; he was driving a lorry full of refugee children out of the camp. I was escorting two pregnant mothers in the hostel truck to Brouilla. There he was in a queue, laughing, smoking and then he turned his head and saw me. The shock on his face. He tried to drive on, but I stood in front of the vehicle. How dare he try to evade me... All he said was "sorry". I wanted to kill him. Pretending to be dead indeed! For heaven's sake, his name is etched in gold on the war memorial.' Flora began to weep. 'How could he do this to me?'

Maudie leaned over to hug her. 'I'm so sorry. It's hard to take in. What's he been up to all this time?'

'Who knows. I never want to see his face again and I want to go home.' Flora was trembling. 'I've mourned his loss down the years, wondering if he intended to lose his life. Here I was, feeling guilty that my love wasn't enough for him, and all this time the coward was living the life of Riley in the Riviera sunshine.'

The waiter brought their drinks and Flora gulped hers down. 'I'll have another,' she said.

Maudie stayed her hand. 'Calm down, Flo. Kit was never a coward in the battlefield, you and I know that. Something must have happened to make him do such a despicable thing to you, to Muriel, his minister and his church. Thank the Lord there's none of his family alive. You told me Aunt Jessie had died. Now he's helping out, like you. Kit was always kind and thoughtful, with a strong sense of duty.'

'How can you say such a thing?' Flora snapped.

'Because now he's seen you, he'll want to make his peace, if I know him. He owes you that,' Maudie replied.

'How do you know? After twenty years, how can I speak to him again? He's a stranger and I can't bear to think what an ass I made of myself in front of him.'

'He can't have changed that much, if you recognised him.' Maudie wanted details and shoved another glass of something sweet and strong into her hand.

'Oh, he's changed all right. He looked rougher, with a gingery stubble that didn't hide the scar on his cheek. His hair is still auburn but greyer, his eyes that peculiar blue, eyes never change, do they?'

'And feelings don't change easily. I still think of Olive and wonder where she is in the world. You must hear him out.'

'Never, I would only spit in his face...' Flora flung her arm out and spilled her glass. 'Now look what he's made me do...'

Maudie mopped away the spillage. 'Flora Lamont, listen to me. I'll say it again. He owes you an explanation. He may be ashamed to face you again, but he's an honourable man of the cloth.'

'Not anymore,' Flora interrupted. 'I saw no dog collar round his neck. Why are you taking his side?' She didn't want to hear Maudie's defence of the man who had wounded her heart.

'Because…' Maudie paused. 'Let me tell you that, if it were my brother Bertie who came back from the dead, I'd forgive him, whatever he had done. To see him in the flesh, full of life, would be such a joy, a chance to take him back home. You don't know how lucky you are. A man you thought lost for ever is still living and close at hand; a man you once loved has come back into your life…'

'But he's not come back to me, or sought me out. He went his own merry way without a thought for any of us left behind.'

'You don't know that. Perhaps you are meant to find each other again. You told me you came back here because something called you. He has found his way here, too. Don't you think that's a strange quirk of fate? Perhaps it is a gift. I'd seize it with both hands. I don't know if forgiveness is possible, but give love a chance…'

'Love! How dare you use that word! There was no love in what he did. I could never trust him again,' Flora argued.

'Then forgive him, go back home and forget him. You have a choice.'

'I can't leave yet. There's too much to do here and I have commitments to the maternity hostel.'

'And I guess so has he, commitment to whatever charity he is working for… The camps are huge, full of desperate people. You might never come across him again. Does he even know where you're based?'

'No!'

'There you go. He might remove himself, like you, far away, then you'll both be left with regrets and unfinished business.'

Flora jumped up to leave. 'I didn't come here to listen to this. I thought you would sympathise and support me.'

'Sit down,' Maudie ordered. 'Bitterness is not your style. You're my oldest living friend. I know enough about you to know you are strong. Kit has done you a great wrong. Give him a chance to ask for your mercy.'

Flora gazed down at her empty glass. 'I was hoping you'd see things from my point of view. You obviously don't...'

'Please let's not fall out about this. I'm your friend and I'm telling the truth as I see it, with love and affection for you both. I know these are hard words to swallow, but if I say only what you want to hear, I wouldn't be true to our friendship.'

Flora looked away. How could she doubt Maudie's sincerity? She was the bridesmaid who had stepped in when Vera wouldn't show up, the friend who held her hand when Ivo died. Her words made sense, but it was hard to swallow them. Running away was no solution. It left so many unanswered questions. She was here to help in terrible times and that must come first, Kit or no Kit. Had the will of divine providence brought them face to face for a reason?

If he turned up again, she was not sure how she would respond. The hurt was raw, unsettling, shocking, but it would be borne. As for forgiveness, that was another matter.

Flora drank the last dregs from her glass and looked Maudie in the face. 'So, what shall I do now?'

'I don't know...' came the reply. 'Only your heart can tell you that.'

Chapter 41

Once the new children were safely delivered to Sam and Consuela, Kit made his excuses and drove off. He claimed he had other places to go but their precious fuel was running out. He left the vehicle with Chuck and caught a train back to the harbour at Collioure.

The stations were crowded with strangers of every nationality, coming from both the north of France towards Spain, and refugees fleeing across the Spanish border. How would the camps cope with another influx of refugees? All he could think about was Flora, about the look of disdain on her face. Of course, she had every right to be furious. What had he been thinking of twenty years ago? Everything about that episode disgusted him now.

At that time, he was not thinking straight. Faking his demise seemed the right thing to do. Sam kept explaining that he had a breakdown of nerves. He was not the only ex-veteran suffering in this way. Kit had sought no help. An officer, a minister could not show weakness before his men. The sights he had witnessed still haunted his dreams, waking him up, leaving him shaking, disorientated, but was this just an excuse?

He prayed Father Antoine would be in the town somewhere. He must speak with him. Kit made his way down to L'église Notre Dame des Anges, to the chapel by the harbour, desperate for the coolness of the stone building with the vaulted roof, the grandeur of the golden altar. Someone was practising on the organ; a piece of Bach that made him want to weep with shame and despair. Looking around, he saw no sign of his friend. He trudged back towards the little centre for food and clothing, pushing his way through crowds of beggars, some drunk, slumped on the cobbles, and into the backstreet where the queue had formed. He stood in turn. 'I'd like to see the Father,' he said to the doorkeeper.

'He's busy, you'll have to wait,' she replied, looking at him with suspicion.

'Please tell him Chris is here. If he needs help...'

She inspected him for any weapons. 'Go around the back, then, he's got paperwork. Don't stay long.'

How many times had his old boss's wife been just such a guardian at the gate of the manse, when her husband was weary and in need of peace? He recognised the woman's devotion, but his need was urgent. As he opened the door, Antoine looked up over his spectacles and smiled.

'Christophe, how good to see you. It's been far too long, but I hear you are busy at the border. What an awful situation. Come, sit, take a glass of Banyuls with me.' Antoine rose from his chair and made for a cupboard.

'No drink,' Kit said. 'I need to talk... I'm in trouble and I have no one else to share this with. After you've heard my confession, you will not want to drink with me.'

'Then this is not the place. The accounts can wait but I see you can't.'

They left by the back door and went through the crowded streets, along a coastal path, now packed with families making camps and shelters. They walked in silence to a quieter spot overlooking the sea.

'What is so bad that you seek me out?' Antoine lit two cigarettes and passed one to Kit.

'I have lied to you, as I have to others. I'm not the artist Chris Carstairs, but a renegade Presbyterian minister, a Protestant, Kristian Carlyle, who deserted his post, faked his own demise and fled from the woman he loved…' He buried his head in his hands. 'I've lived a lie for twenty years and then three days ago in the camp, the very woman recognised me, called me by my real name. I fled from her. I don't know what to do, Antoine. Now you know the worst of me. I'm a fraud. What makes it worse is there was another girl, back home in Glasgow, waiting for me to return and marry her. It happened after the Armistice when I was wounded. We were sent to convalesce near Cannes.

'I'd known Flora for years in Glasgow. Her brother, Fergus, was one of my best friends. I met her again by chance on the Côte d'Azur, where she was posted. She, too, had been ill. We fell in love and I let her down badly. She was sent home in disgrace, but I did not follow her. I'm so ashamed. I was unwell, but I can't forgive myself for what I did.'

Antoine looked ahead, staring out to sea. 'Where is this Flora now?'

'Not sure, working in a hostel, I think. It's such chaos down there. I did promise to explain, but she ran away. I thought of following her, but the crowds pressed forward and I lost sight of her. I pretended not to know her at first… How do I ever make that right?'

Antoine puffed on his cigarette, looking out to sea. 'I'm hearing all this past confession and regret. Now you must confront the present and find her. Only then can you ask forgiveness. How did she come to be here?'

'I have no idea, but Flora was a nurse in the war and a good, compassionate one.'

'How strange that you're both engaged in war work again. Is it possible that this encounter was no accident?'

'What do you mean?' Kit sat up, curious.

'Maybe the hand of Providence is in all this, a chance for you to redeem yourself, to face the woman you hurt and see what's left between you?'

'But she said she never wanted to see me again. Those were her very words.'

'Spoken in fear, shock, anger, no doubt. Find her and talk together, or write. That's all I can suggest. Only then will you know if anything still exists that is worth saving.'

'But I've let so many people down.'

'You are human, frail, and let your own standards down. None of us are heroes, just fallible people trying to do our best and making a mess of some things.'

'But not you, Antoine…'

'You don't know me, Chris. I have a past too; things I can only share with my Maker. I know how caring and hardworking you are. Those actions speak for themselves. Just continue your mission and try to forgive yourself. There's still time to make amends. Leave the rest to higher powers than ours. Come on, confession is thirsty work.

Let's find ourselves a quiet bistro and drink to your future successes, whatever they might be...'

'If only...' Kit sighed.

'No more of that, my friend. Dig out some courage and find her.'

Chapter 42

In July came a welcome letter from Pa, waiting for Flora when she returned to the hostel after seeing Maudie, but it was not the usual cheery missive.

Flora dear,

Isn't it about time you returned to us? It has been months and I'm not sure now is the right time to be lingering in France. The news grows grimmer every week. Soon we shall be at war and there will be turmoil in Europe. I'd be happier if you returned to Scotland. We know you set off with such good intentions but we're not as young as we were and we worry for you. I fear Virginia's boys will be caught up in this conflict just as you were in the last. I could not bear to lose you.

I'm glad to hear Maud Wallace is working close by. She's a sensible girl, but Perpignan is such a long way from us. You have done your duty. The civil war veterans are returning home. Elvira is no longer so harum-scarum.

Her baby is due any time now. They kept things to themselves after the last one died. Yes, I do know about the wee bairn they lost.

Surely, you'll want to be home for the happy event? Sandy has proved to be a hardworking skilled boatbuilder and a decent provider. Please think of your status and the risks it may pose if you flout regulations and stay on abroad.

As for local news, we are so busy in the yards. Good to hear the hammer blows ringing and chimneys smoking down Clydeside. It's as if suddenly the country has woken up to the threat from abroad. Ships are an essential part of our defence...

Flora read on. What her father didn't realise was that she was miles away from danger, but that another war was on her doorstep; sickness, hunger and poverty. This was much more pressing. They had at long last erected wooden barracks and taken over an old military camp. These conditions were far from satisfactory. So far not a word or sighting of Kit had disturbed her mission. Then one of the American aid workers, Frankie Menkel, sought her out.

'There's some guy I know who's anxious to find you. He's been fishing in the HQ for your details. Can I tell him where you are lodged?'

'If it's the red-haired truck driver you mean, I'm not sure I want to meet him again.'

'I gather you met in another life in the war. How could you not want to catch up? I'd go after him myself, given half a chance, but he's no interest in me.'

Flora didn't want to pursue this conversation, but Frankie was not for being silenced.

'Chris is a guy with secrets. I know a few of them. When he's in his cups, he talks freely, and you are all he thinks about these days. He thinks you're hiding from him.'

'Look, I'm busy at Elne, helping prepare the new chateau hospital. Soon I'll no longer be in Brouilla.' Frankie was a coordinator of transport and they had met a few times before. She meant well and was a bit of a glamour puss who made Flora feel old and dowdy in her dungarees and headscarf.

'Did you know I met him during the *Retirada*? We delivered this baby in the back of the van. I thought the poor guy would faint, but he stuck it out. What have you got against him?' Frankie was curious.

'Oh look, baby Rafael has just soiled on the mat, must clean him up and check with Sister Elisabeth...' The little refugee was her priority, not sharing intimate details with an American girl who seemed to have a crush on Kit.

Since her tearful talk with Maudie, Flora had buried her feelings in work. She tried not to think of Kit nearby. Pa was right about war looming. The camps were filling with Jewish families trying to cross over into Spain. They had delivered three of their babies and watched as the rabbi celebrated their births. There was talk of shepherds acting as *passeurs* – smugglers – lining up to escort them in convoys across the mountains. To climb the Pyrenees was no easy feat, even in summer, and she feared for them walking at night. Plans for the new maternity hospital were coming on apace. Chateau Bartou was a strange edifice: tall, angular, with windows jutting out and in much need of repair. Elisabeth was excited, because there was much more room. Already the grounds were being transformed into allotments by Spanish men and women.

As the afternoon wore on, Flora relented and sought out Frankie's truck. 'If you see Kit, tell him to write to me here. I'm not promising a reply, though.'

'Why do you keep calling him Kit? He's Christophe, Chris, to us.'

'I knew him as Kit. You can ask him why he changed his name. Perhaps he might explain...'

A letter was the safest way of opening the communication between them. A meeting was too personal, too close for comfort. She was in no mood for another face-to-face confrontation. She wanted him to sweat and grovel, to beg for her forgiveness. She wanted to be the one in control from now on. Yes, she would read his letter, but nothing more, for the moment.

Kit sat in what was left of Sam's garden, now a soccer pitch, where the boys pounded the makeshift goal posts. '*Señor*, come play!' they shouted, but Kit waved them away. He had other things on his mind and needed some quiet space in which to write to Flora, as she had requested. Frankie had brought the message and he hoped it was a start of something more. He was nervous about getting the tone wrong – too light or too heavy.

This colony was teeming with children, some boisterous and full of mischief, others more withdrawn and silent like Marisa. Consuela was worried that the little girl had not spoken a word since her arrival. She trailed around after them like a lost lamb and for some reason especially followed Kit at a distance, hugging a bit of torn rag. He could see her now, peering from behind the fence, watching him. He waved, but she ran off. There was an old sweet chestnut tree, and he dragged a battered cane chair under its branches for shade. The August sun was fierce, but he was cool enough here to take up his writing pad and pen the most important of letters.

Dear Flora

Thank you for giving me the opportunity to write to you. I want to explain my behaviour twenty years ago and why I took the actions that will haunt me for the rest of my life.

I realised after hostilities ceased, I was no longer fit for purpose as a chaplain. All my certainties of faith were lost in the mud of Flanders. Please believe me when I say, hand on heart, the sight of you at that fateful soirée brought such joy. You were kind and reminded me of home. I looked to your bright self as my saviour and our loving was such a relief, an act of healing. I know that my selfish need for you to prop me up was unfair and greedy. In those precious weeks together, I could forget my troubled soul and lose myself in the romance I hoped would blossom into something more.

When I brought disgrace on you and you left, it felt as if a crutch had been whipped away from me. Thinking only of my own needs, I realised I had obligations in Glasgow that might complicate my return and our loving. I resented not being able to follow you at first. In my confusion I began to think that if I abandoned all my responsibilities to you, my church, soldiers and Muriel, my faith would somehow return. In my disordered mind, I saw my act as one of generosity on my part, releasing you from the burden that was myself at that time. All I can say in my defence is that I was living under a cloud of despair, loss of hope for the future and self-pity. I thought I would be free but the chains of guilt have shackled me at every turn since then.

I left you to suffer alone. I deserted everyone I held dear, but I hope I am no longer that pitiful broken man. I am no saint, anything but. Yet here in Dr Sam O'Keeffe's children's colony and in the camps, I can work for the good of others in need and be useful again.

I offer my humblest apology for all the hurt I have caused. When I saw your face in that crowd, I wanted to flee from you. You have found me out and have every right to hate my guts. I understand why you could never forgive my duplicity. I have destroyed the memory you held of me, the love we once shared. Fergus would be saddened by my betrayal.

I can't return home, as you will be free to do when the time comes. I fear a time is approaching when war threatens us once more. Your nationality may bring danger, so do take care to be safe. I have no ties now to Britain, having false papers and no desire to leave here.

I am not expecting any reply. I am better out of your life as I don't deserve your forgiveness. I intend to carry on here, come what may. I can't stand by and watch the sufferings of these poor people. Strange how we can say so much on paper, better than face to face. For what is in my heart, I have no words. Have pity on your erstwhile friend. Forget I ever existed. My weakness destroyed everything precious between us and I must live with that for ever.

Yours for aye

Kit

PS I am sending with this letter a token of happier times.

Flora read Kit's letter and wept. Her hands were shaking as she absorbed all the sadness and regret that he had poured onto the pages. She had made a good life for herself without him while he had wandered alone, drifting until now. The sincerity of the apology was real, with glimpses of the man he used to be. Here was the Kit of old, who she witnessed fighting in vain to secure Maudie's brother a place on the ambulance train, all those years ago. Watching from another ambulance train, unknown to him, she had witnessed Kit's strength and goodness. It was the moment she began to love him.

The letter was attached to a parcel that Frankie had left in the foyer of the hostel. They were stuck together with Elastoplast. She had gone to a quiet place so she could read Kit's letter and open up the package. It revealed the back of a canvas. Turning it round, she gasped with surprise. It was the very picture she had coveted in Collioure: the painting of the rose-coloured villa, the convalescent nurses' home in Cannes. It was the picture removed from the gallery when she showed interest in the artist called Carstairs. He had kept it all this time and was now giving it to her in remembrance of happier days on the Riviera.

Flora hugged it to her chest, tears rolling down her cheeks, tears for all the lost years, for what might have been between them, the children never born, the home they might have shared. When war came, she must leave, as directed by the consulate. Surely, before that, it would do no harm to meet him once more, face to face? This letter was softening the pain in her heart. Flora found her writing case and sat down to write a reply, knowing exactly the time and place for this important assignation.

Chapter 43

Flora sat staring up at the vaulted roof of the Cathedral of St John the Baptist in Perpignan. There was a stern, dark feeling of doom and judgement about this Catalan church and a coolness that made her shiver. The altar, by contrast, was a glorious gold extravaganza, strange to her Presbyterian tastes. Somehow it felt the right place to meet Kit again.

She had dressed with care. Slacks were too informal, but her summer dresses were bleached and faded by the sun, and felt too frivolous for such an important meeting. A thin blouse and her only skirt would have to do. She had washed her hair, coiling it into a topknot. Her skin was sunburnt, so she covered her arms with a shawl and put a lace scarf over her head. On her feet she wore espadrilles with laces tied around her ankles. In the camp she wore boots and shirts and a bandanna to protect her hair. She doubted Kit would notice anything about her appearance, but it mattered to her.

She suggested noon, so they could talk and then perhaps find somewhere quiet to lunch.

Looking down at her wristwatch, she noticed the hands were moving slowly past the hour, but she waited on, in case he was delayed. Perhaps this neutral place was not a sensible idea. There were tourists wandering up and down the aisles talking, but no sign of Kit. She sat facing the door, but he didn't appear.

She made excuses for him. Perhaps he had not received her letter, or perhaps Frankie had mislaid it. He was caught up in the crowded roads, crawling into the city. She waited for a full half hour more, just in case, but still he did not come. How quickly then her anxiety turned to anger. Damn the man! Flora shot out of her seat and made for the door, stubbing her toe on a corner stone. Damn, damn, damn. Why ever had she believed he would come?

Outside there was a commotion, loudspeakers blasting out over the streets and square. Crowds were heading to the source of the noise. It was an announcement in Catalan and French, hard to catch the gist.

Flora tried to push forward. What was all this agitation? Women were crossing themselves. One word she did catch was *la guerre… guerra…* war.

At last, the waiting was over. Tensions had been building over the past few weeks in the camp. Volunteers suddenly disappeared to enlist, leaving gaps and staff shortages. There was no cause for alarm, for France's borders were secured by the great Maginot line of defences. France and Britain together were a force to be reckoned with. It all felt so far away on this beautiful September morning.

Had Kit decided to enlist again? Surely not. He was

too old. But why wasn't he here to share this momentous moment with her? Why the hell was she bothering to make excuses for the inexcusable?

Her feet led her instinctively towards the hospital in search of Maudie Wallace. She suddenly felt very much alone and in need of a friend with whom to share this dreadful news. Why was she crying? Kit had let her down once more. Why was she surprised?

Kit had slept fitfully, anxious to be up in time to make his way to Perpignan. He was desperate to see Flora again, but his rest had been disturbed by fits of coughing. His forehead burned and his chest was so tight that his breathing became laboured. He tried to clear his throat, but his head was pounding, and there was a strange buzzing in his ears. He tried to ignore it. Nothing was going to stop his rendezvous but as he stood up to dress in a clean shirt and shorts, the room swirled around him and he had to hold onto the wall for support.

Chuck burst in through the door. 'Wakey wakey, today is the big day when Chris gets to meet his girl...' He paused. 'My God you look rough, are you okay? Better take a shower, a cold one. Did the nerves get you? How much did you have to drink last night with Frankie and her gang?'

Kit was not listening, finding it hard to focus because his hacking cough had started up again and his legs went from under him. 'Shut up and help me... I have to get dressed. I don't want to be late.'

Chuck stood back. 'Hell, Chris, you're as pale as a ghost. What have you—'

'It's just my old war wound come back to haunt me today, of all days. I have to see her.'

'You ain't goin' nowhere, chum. You're burning up. I'm fetchin' in the doc to look you over. Come on, it's back to bed for you...'

'But I can't...' Those were the last words Kit could manage. The room went black and he collapsed in a heap on the wooden floor.

Chapter 44

Flora pushed her way through the crowds to the hospital, which was bustling with anxious patients and families. This was not a time to be interrupting Maudie's shift. She left a note and hung around the city streets, restless and angry. How dare Kit let her down again? How dare the world go to war, after all it had suffered in the last lot? She resented the blue sky, the sunshine, the swaying palm trees and the cooling fountains. There were smiling faces. Did they not know what a war might mean for them and their sons? She ought to be heading back to camp, but Flora needed her friend's company.

Maudie came, hours later, to their favourite café. 'Sorry, but it's bedlam in there. No one can talk about anything else but the war. It reminds me of 1914 all over again. There's been announcements all day and talk of curfews on the streets. As if anyone is going to bomb us down here.'

'They did in Barcelona, not a million miles away from here,' Flora reminded her.

'How did the meeting with Kit go?' Maudie paused,

eyeing Flora with concern. 'Not very well, by the look of you.'

'He didn't turn up.' Flora pulled a cigarette out of her silver case and handed it to Maudie. 'You'd think he'd have the decency, but that's it. I'm finished with him. He's not worth the bother. I tried.'

'There must be a reason. Today has been worrying for all the volunteers.'

'Why?'

'Think about it. Most of us are aliens with foreign passports. Germans, Swiss, American, Irish as well as Brits. There's bound to be panic and controls on our movements, in case some of us are spies. We've no idea who can stay and who must leave. I'm going to leave. I've had plenty of time to think about it. Someone will be able to use me back home.' Maudie puffed on her cigarette. 'Besides, I'm homesick for Bonnie Scotland, for Rosie and the "dear green place" we call Glasgow. How about you?'

'I'll be joining you, but I must help get this new maternity home open in time for winter. They've reached a critical stage. I can't just desert my post yet and there are going to be so many more refugees trying to cross into Spain. How can it have come to this again? Did our brothers die in vain? I just don't understand what's gone wrong.'

'Ours is not to reason why, Flo. I just want to see the Clyde, the great cranes in the shipyards, the trams rattling up Sauchiehall Street and hear the skirl of the bagpipes, sentimental fool that I am.'

'You're making me homesick, talking about home. I'll write home to the family with my plans, when the time is right. I know you must go, but I'll miss you like hell.

Without you, I'd have gone mad with this Kit business. But that's all over. Let's not talk any more about him.'

'Then let's eat.' Maudie shoved a menu in her hand. 'My treat. You look as if you need a good meal inside you, you're far too thin.'

'It's the heat and the trots, usual gippy tummy and the curse, it's getting heavier each month.'

'It's our age, our bodies are changing.'

'Oh, surely not yet,' Flora sighed. She hated to think of being middle-aged. She still felt eighteen in her head, full of plans and energy, even if she had felt more than usually tired of late.

'Let's not depress ourselves even more.' Maudie ordered a large bowl of *potage*, followed by fresh grilled sardines, with ice cream as dessert, plus a carafe of good Roussillon wine.

Arm in arm they strolled through the streets to the square, as the sun was setting.

Flora paused at the sight of it slipping down behind the buildings. 'I always feel sad when I see the sun going down. Silly, I know, but it reminds me of darkness ahead and the end of another day of life.'

'Plenty more days ahead for us yet, old girl. We're still in our prime.' Maudie ushered her away. 'I'll walk with you to the train and let you know when I'm leaving, just in case we can go together. Don't stay if things get rough. I don't want you trapped here, if borders are closed. You can always walk over the Pyrenees and out through Spain.' She nudged her friend. 'Now that would be some expedition.'

The platform was full of families holding carpet bags and valises, and troops in uniform, heading north. 'You see what

I mean, about getting out now. We all need family at a time like this. If we're lucky, it will only take three or four days until we cross the Channel. Don't leave it too late.'

'I promise, but let's meet again before you leave. I can't bear to think of you not being down the road, as it were. I owe you so much.' Flora felt tears welling up.

'Steady the Buffs, Flo, you'll have me greetin', too. Cheery bye for now.' They hugged each other tightly. Maudie strode back through the crowd and Flora felt a stab of fear that she might never see her friend again.

Chapter 45

The Chateau Bartou in Elne was a hive of activity. Walls needed new plaster, pleas for hospital beds to arrive on time went unheeded, extra linen and equipment had to be found from somewhere and the whole place was still covered in dust. No one was spared in the rush to open the doors of the maternity hospital. Elisabeth Eidenbenz had set aside a bright and sunny room as a special labour suite. There was a bathroom and laundry store. Mothers were still arriving daily from the camps and they would need delousing and fresh clothes.

There was no time for Flora to think of Kit, except at night when she tried to reason with herself and mull over what might have been. On the day of Maudie's departure, they said a tearful goodbye on the platform, and Flora gave her chum letters for her father and Vera, wondering all the time if it was sensible to stay on. Maudie made things worse by humming an old song through the carriage window:

I'm no awa' to bide awa'...
I'm no awa' tae leave you.
I'm no awa' to bide awa',
I'll aye came back tae see you...

At last, the day came for the big move into the shiny new premises. It was exciting to see it filled with babies and mothers. Perhaps when the New Year came around, Flora herself would depart, leaving the bitterness she still felt behind her.

Sometimes, when they took aid to camps further out in the countryside, it was hard not to look around for Kit. She hated herself for such weakness but a bit of her heart was desperate for an explanation from him. She could collar Frankie Menkel when she saw her, but pride stopped her. In any case, Frankie wasn't around, busy at the transport department where they were beginning to be short-staffed.

New midwives from Switzerland arrived, leaving volunteers to go out further afield to pick up expectant mothers and bring them back for care. As they feared, most of them were coming from the north, not the south, from Holland and Belgium and elsewhere in Europe, with terrible tales to tell of new laws, requisitions of property and valuables and assaults in the streets. Most wanted to get into Spain and Portugal and onto ships to America. Once again, Pa wrote to Flora begging her to leave, in case the borders closed, and she promised to make suitable arrangements.

One morning in February, when she was collecting yet another group of women from the makeshift medical post, she bumped into Frankie who was hurrying past her, but

Flora grabbed her arm. 'You must come and see the new maternity hospital.'

'Sorry, been busy.' Frankie was not meeting her eye.

'Have I done something wrong?' Flora was puzzled. Frankie was usually chatty and friendly, but not today. 'It's been ages since we met. I thought you might have left.'

'Americans are neutral and safe here for the moment. It's you who should be packing up.'

'All in hand,' Flora replied, sensing the name Kit hung between them, unspoken. Taking a deep breath she said, 'Have you seen Kit lately... I mean Chris?'

Frankie looked away. 'Not recently, he's been convalescing in the hills and back with the O' Keeffes now.'

'Convalescing?' Flora picked on this word. 'From what?'

'Oh, didn't you know? A bad lung infection. He was in hospital for weeks and up in the hills for fresh air.'

'When was this?' Flora felt her heart pounding at this news.

'About the time war broke out in September.'

'That's months ago. Why did no one tell me?'

'He was too ill for visitors and not up to recriminations. He needs peace and quiet.'

'I'm a nurse, Frankie, I know what a patient needs; someone could at least have sent me a note,' she snapped.

'It's up to Chris who he contacts and not my business to intervene.'

Flora sensed Frankie was holding something back.

'A friend would let everyone know about his condition, surely?' Was this girl anxious to keep her away from Kit? 'Where is this O'Keeffe place? I must visit him to see things for myself.'

'In the hills, not easy to find, but I must dash… Better to leave things as they are. I hear you're leaving soon.'

So that's your game, Flora thought. 'So you can have him all to yourself? You could have told me, but you chose not to, am I right?'

'Think what you like, Mrs Lamont. He's not been the same since you arrived on the scene. You're not good for his health…'

'That's for me to judge for myself, don't you think?'

Frankie did not reply, but scurried off leaving Flora shaking. All this time she had imagined he was indifferent to their meeting again, but he'd been seriously ill, thinking it was she who didn't care. How could she find time to visit him? *You always make time for what is important to you*, she heard Aunt Mima whisper in her ear.

There was one young man who might just help her but how to find him? He could be anywhere in the area. She could not settle until he was found. Kit had to know she had not ignored his sickness. What if he had died and they'd had no time to make their peace? Nothing and no one was going to stop her from seeing him, face to face, once more.

Chapter 46

Kit was feeling a fraud, now his breathing was much easier, his limbs stronger and he was able to take daily walks with little Marisa, who tagged alongside him, picking wild flowers. She seemed to have taken a shine to him but still never spoke. Sam thought she might be dumb, but every now and then she moaned in her sleep and cried out if she lost her rag cloth.

The kids playing around him were a welcome distraction, but he was not up to a game of football yet. They listened to the news of troop movements, the Allies gathering, as they had in 1914, awaiting a battle. It all seemed quiet on the western front.

Kit was trapped with a false name and papers and too feeble to be of use to any army. Father Antoine visited him. He was hoping to enlist as a chaplain, leaving Kit sad that he wouldn't see his friend for months.

The garden was his useful place, making sure they had plenty of vegetables. There were shortages already in the village shops. Some were hoarding tins and oil. There were no cigarettes, except on the black market, and Sam forbade him ever to touch them again. It was a miracle that Consuela and her Spanish helpers kept everyone fed and watered. He thought about the parable of the loaves and fishes, feeling guilty he had nothing to offer but time with the colony of children.

Chuck and Frankie were constant visitors, but one visitor stayed away, no doubt having returned home as the Brits had been advised. He had hoped his letter would have explained why he didn't make their appointment but Flora did not reply. Frankie said she had no news of her. That was it then, but it left him hurt and confused. It was not in Flora's nature to be uncaring and yet twenty years was a long time. Perhaps her heart was hardened.

One day, though, he heard a familiar truck rattling up the stony track towards the farmhouse. He was at the far end of the garden, sitting under the chestnut tree, reading a story in French to a group of small children. Marisa, as always, had wanted to sit on his knee, but he could have no favourites when he was teaching. It was cooler than normal, with a chilly wind, and he thought of the poor folk trapped in unheated wooden barracks, at the mercy of the rain and icy draughts.

It was Chuck, on his rounds. 'Someone to see you, Chris...'

Kit wasn't expecting anyone, but then he saw Flora, wrapped in a shawl, her hair covered in a scarf. Flora, here at last! He rose, wanting her to see he was well again, but he stumbled and Marisa cried out in alarm. The children helped him up.

'Thank you, go and play. We'll finish the story later.' He

felt such a fool to be weak at the knees but the sight of her had taken his breath away first with delight and then with fear. 'Flora, you came,' was all he could manage. Consuela was watching from the doorway. 'Welcome... It's too cold, come inside, by the stove, and get warm.'

Kit couldn't take his eyes off his unexpected guest. 'I thought you'd gone home.'

'Not yet. Soon, but I wanted to see you before I left. Are you recovered?'

'Better for seeing you. I'm sorry I couldn't make our meeting. I tried but my body had other ideas. You got my letter?'

'What letter? No, I thought you'd thought better of meeting.'

'But I gave Frankie a note. She didn't give it to you?'

'Until the other day, I'd not seen her for months. I expect she was busy. We did meet last week, though, and she told me then. I'm sorry... I would have come sooner had I known. You must think me unfeeling.'

Consuela shoved them into the living room and shut the door, giving them privacy to talk.

They sat in silence, each staring at the other.

'There's so much I want to say,' Kit offered.

'I think it was all said in the first letter. Are you really better?'

'Almost. Being an invalid is so boring but I'm on the mend and it gives me time to help the children with their work. The village school is too full to have them, so I am doing my best to give them lessons.'

Flora leaned forward. 'What happened?'

'I caught some bug in the camps that played havoc

with my breathing. Travelling around from camp to camp doesn't help, what with infections and the poor diet. I have a weakness in the lungs, but months up in the hills have worked wonders. It is so beautiful up beyond Prades. Smoking didn't help, of course, but Sam has given me my orders. I'm not to take another drag...'

'I'm glad to hear it. You must take care of yourself from now on.'

'Yes, nurse.' They stared at each other again. So much to say and yet where to start? It was Kit who broke the silence. 'Have you been happy in your life?'

'Yes, for the most part. I had a good marriage to Ivo Lamont, a friend of Hector and Rose Murray, but it didn't last. He died from the effects of an old war wound in 1932.'

'And children?'

'No. I wouldn't be out here, if there were any. My sister, Vera, is expecting a baby, though. And you?'

'I've lived alone since... There were a few brief liaisons. I was lucky to find my old comrade and his wife, Consuela. I owe both of them my sanity and my life.'

'Why did you run away from me?' Flora said.

There was no escaping it. 'As I said in my letter, I tried to follow you, but I lost you and now you're leaving. You and I, we never seem to be in the right place at the right time, do we?'

'There is no you and I, Kit.'

'But there could be, now that we've found each other again. I don't want to lose touch... as friends,' he offered.

'It's all too late, Kit. Too much time has passed. I ought to go back home, Pa is worried. Maudie has already left.'

'Maudie Wallace?'

'Yes, she was in Spain and in Perpignan, but she left two weeks ago.'

'If only I'd known.'

'Known what?'

'Oh, nothing, I feel so ashamed. I didn't expect you...' His words faltered.

'You can thank Maudie for that. She was the one who talked me into meeting you. She said if I didn't, I'd never know.'

'Never know...?'

'If I could forgive you for what you did.'

'And can you?' He grabbed her hand.

'A little, Kit, but I'll never forget what you put us all through.'

'I can't believe I was so spineless.'

'You were never spineless,' Flora said, as he bent his head to avoid her gaze. 'You won medals for your bravery under fire. You tried to save Bertie.'

'But I couldn't save that young laddie, stuck in the mud. I had to watch him sink under, still holding my hand. All I could do was pray and tell him his mother was waiting for him. What use was that to him? It haunts me still.'

'That must have been awfully hard to bear, but at least you stayed with him.'

'Most of the time I was just as afraid as my men, but I couldn't show it. I had to give them hope that they would survive to go home.'

Flora's hand reached out to cover his. 'They tell us courage is about being afraid, but doing what is needed anyway. After too much of it, the strain will take its toll on minds and bodies. You stayed with him and gave him comfort to the last. He didn't die alone.'

'And now some poor sods will have to go through it all again.' He shook his head, suddenly weary. 'We fought the war to end all wars…'

'Am I tiring you out? Perhaps I'd better leave. I can see it upsets you to remember.' Flora stood up. 'I must meet Consuela and thank her for being so tactful.'

'No, please stay… I enjoy the peace and calm you bring. We could have been a team and I let it all go.'

'I'm here now, so let's make the most of being together. No morbid thoughts, Kit. By the way, thank you for the painting. Do you realise I was the woman who wanted to buy it in Collioure? I came back for it but it had gone. We must have passed each other in the street. Strange, isn't it, how we nearly met then.'

'I couldn't bear to part with it to a stranger. I'm glad you like it.'

'I shall treasure *The Rose Villa* always.'

'I couldn't have parted with it to anyone else but you.'

He could see her relaxing, her expression softening at his words. Pity that he was a man no longer young and eager, full of certainties, but a man broken by war and guilt. He sensed she could see how he had changed, become stronger and with more self-knowledge. She might learn to admire him but could she still love him? 'Do you have to leave so soon?'

'I haven't booked my ticket yet, but my passport has almost expired, so I'll have to go. How about you?'

'Granny Nora, on my mother's side, came from Ireland. Sam says I could apply for an Irish passport but I'd have to come clean about my true identity. I'm not sure I can do that. Besides, I like what Sam is doing here. I would love to hear little Marisa talk again. She follows me round, my little shadow—' They were interrupted by a tap on the door.

'Luncheon is served, only soup, but I have a decent bottle of wine and freshly baked bread.' Consuela burst in. 'Flora, I am so glad to meet you at last. I've heard so much about you from Christophe.'

It was hard to believe that Flora was sitting by his side, smiling, chatting, charming everyone with tales of her maternity hospital. 'We put new babies in little laundry baskets out in the shade, when the sun is up and their mothers are busy knitting. It's a happy ship, thanks to Elisabeth. She's young, but so capable and determined. I shall be sad to leave.'

Kit watched her. How could he let this woman go? How could he have ever deserted her? The realisation that this was, perhaps, the last time they would meet stung him to the core. Soon she would be out of reach, back over the Channel, in the land to which he had forfeited his right to live. Later they walked to the end of the far field. 'I wish we had met sooner but something always gets in the way.'

Flora ignored this. 'Don't lose your talent for painting. You are good and I'm glad you found something precious for yourself while staying here. Once back home, I'll do my bit, too. I would like to have met Sam. I gather he's out on his rounds.'

'Stay for supper and meet him,' Kit said.

'No, it's time for me to leave, and Chuck will want to be off, too.'

'I can drive you back,' he offered.

'In your pyjamas?' They both laughed and he held her hand. 'There was only ever you…'

'Aye, I ken,' she replied in Scottish dialect. 'We could have done some good work together, but our stars weren't aligned. I shall think of you here, in a lady's dressing gown and pyjamas.' She smiled, but her eyes were sad. 'Write to me, sometimes. I'd like to know you're happy. I shall keep our meeting to myself. No one need know. Maudie will say nothing.'

'You must give me the date you're leaving.'

'I will, but not through Frankie. She can't wait to see the back of me,' Flora murmured. Outside, Chuck was already waiting by the truck. She waved to them all and then was gone.

What might have been, that phrase said it all. Kit felt the ground sinking beneath him. He grabbed the fence to steady himself. This was all his doing. How could he expect anything more?

Flora drove back in silence, wanting to savour everything about that afternoon – the view from the farmhouse, the curious children milling around, little Marisa clinging onto Kit's hand and the look on Kit's face at the sight of her.

'You okay?' Chuck asked.

'Fine,' she replied.

'What is it with you two? What went wrong?'

'It's a long story, but we've made our peace. I can go home knowing Kit is settled here, and if he gets an Irish passport he can stay as long as it's safe. You've all been such good friends to him.'

'Sure, he's safe, for now, but for how long? You've seen the shape he's in. He'll burn himself out, with no one to steady him.'

'I'm sure Frankie will step up to the mark, once I'm gone.'

'For a while, but she's young and romantic. She's no idea what he's been through, none of us has, except Doc Sam. He's one hell of a good guy, but complicated, I guess. Generous to a fault and great with kids, especially the little orphan Annie who won't speak. If anyone can get her to open her mouth, Chris will. I'd hate to see him make a false move with Miss Menkel. She don't deserve him.'

'That's for him to decide,' Flora said, opening the door to jump down. 'Thanks for the lift. Be seeing you.'

Chuck's comments were unsettling. It was all too late. They were not meant to be together and the sooner she left, the better. Tomorrow she would begin to prepare for her departure and share her plan with Miss Eidenbenz. Most of the Brits had already gone home. That night she tossed and turned, unable to sleep. *Am I doing the right thing?* Seeing Kit again dredged up all the old feelings from the past. She had planned that visit to Magret to be formal and a little cool. Behind Kit's cheerful bonhomie lay a wounded man, deeply saddened by his past mistakes. He had been open and honest and those blue, blue eyes still had the power to unnerve her. How easy it would be to fall in love with him again, but to do so was unthinkable. Or was it?

Chapter 47

Kit waited for Flora to write with news of her departure date, but nothing came and he wondered if she had decided to slip away without any farewells. He hoped to goodness that was not the case. Sam was pleased with his progress. The three of them sat listening to the wireless but nothing seemed to be happening after six months; except skirmishes at sea and strict blackout notices. Everything went on as normal there, except for shortages of imported foodstuffs in the shops. The markets sold out early and there were fewer men on the streets.

Consuela was determined to give the Spanish children a traditional Easter celebration. It was going to take some planning. Spring was burgeoning around them, with flowers blossoming in the hedgerows and woods, for the girls to make garlands with. The hens were laying and Consuela stored the eggs away carefully for boiling. How she found the other ingredients for a colourful cake and pies was beyond Kit and Sam. This was to be a secret surprise treat. Holy week was a time of fasting and there was a vat of *potaje de vigilia*, a hearty soup filled with garden vegetables, spinach, garlic, dried peppers and chick peas.

Kit boiled the eggs with onion skins to turn them a deep golden colour. Later, he showed the children how to decorate them with paint brushes. Chuck found bars of chocolate, but no one dared ask him where from. They were hidden away to share out on Easter Sunday. Kit wrote, inviting Flora to visit again, but she sent a postcard from a place in the foothills of the Pyrenees, where she was helping out. At least she was still in France.

His only other visitor was Frankie. 'Chuck tells me Mrs Lamont came, after all,' she said.

'No thanks to you. What did you do with my note to her?'

'Sorry, I lost it somewhere. I didn't know it was important. I told her about you being sick. Has she gone yet? We've heard things are hotting up in the north. I suggested she'd be better off in Spain.'

'I bet you did,' Kit snapped. 'Why don't you like her?'

'These Limeys, here today, gone tomorrow. Some of them were useless in the office. One gal arrived, took one look at the mud and filth and turned right back. No staying power.'

'Is that what you think of Flora? I bet she didn't tell you she scrubbed her hands raw, nursed wounded men on trains, skivvied as a volunteer in the worst conditions imaginable. Her kind saved hundreds of lives, gave us men hope in the darkest hours and watched their own colleagues blown to bits in shellfire. No staying power? Sure, she comes from a wealthy family, but she didn't hesitate to come back here to serve once more.'

'Okay, so I didn't know that. I'm sorry.'

'It's Flora you should apologise to, young lady. You've

no idea what you nearly did.' Kit was having no truck with her arrogance and watched her face crumple. 'Don't meddle where you're not wanted.'

The children went to mass on Good Friday and Easter Sunday, joining the crowds of worshippers in the village church. Sam, his wife and helpers stayed behind to prepare for the feast. It was a warm spring day and they brought the big table out onto the grass, decorating it with vases of wild flowers. Consuela made her version of the famous Catalan pie: pastry filled with eggs, lardons of pork and chorizo that had hung in the cellar.

The children returned, awestruck by the scene before them. Everyone sat down, excited by the feast. Then came the masterpiece, *mona de Pascua*, the Easter cake. Consuela found remnants of cooking dye to layer up the sponge and topped the cake with the colourful boiled eggs. Each child received a piece of chocolate, to wolf down before it melted in the sun.

One of the older refugees brought out his guitar and began to play, castanets were found and soon the children joined Consuela in dancing, clapping their hands and swirling. Right in the middle was Marisa, lost in her own world, stamping her feet, twisting in a flamenco dance learned from her lost family.

'Do you see that?' Sam whispered. 'There must be gypsy in her blood.'

Kit was speechless, watching the little girl smiling and laughing. Then she turned to him and beckoned. 'Come, Papa, come and dance with me!' He jumped up to join her with tears in his eyes. They were the first words he had ever heard her utter.

Chapter 48

The internment camp was hidden, miles away from Elne, in the foothills of the Pyrenees in the Ariège district close to Pamiers. It was a dark, forbidding setting, with rows of barbed wire and armed guards at the gates. Their truck was brightly labelled AYUDA SUIZA. No one could be in any doubt about their permit to visit. Documents were handed over, read and scrutinised. They were counted in and it felt like entering a prison, not a refugee centre. Flora shivered as they went into the miserable rows of shanty town barracks. They were directed to a hospital post, which was little more than a large shed, with camp beds and hardly any blankets. It was none too clean. And the medicine cabinet was empty of supplies.

The nurses immediately set to work examining the patients, filling the cupboard with bandages, antiseptics and medicines, while Flora, Anita and two others unloaded tins of dried milk, eggs, and whatever produce they had been able to acquire, into a wheelbarrow. They found what passed for a kitchen, where the women eagerly awaited them. Most were thin, with pinched cheeks. One woman was in tears, holding her hands in gratitude. 'Thank you, thank you,' she cried.

Today they would make a soupy broth, first for the children. Word got around that there would be a hot meal. Families began to queue, helping old parents, babies and young children to the front. Flora was glad she had delayed her departure to help out after two nurses fell sick. There was something sinister about this place, so carefully hidden from view. At least by the sea there was light, but here it was dark and must be grim in the winter snows. They set to chopping vegetables, slicing bread. Children were ushered to a large bench, where they could sup their broth. Some, without spoons, just licked the bowls like dogs. They were barefoot and covered in sores. Flora was used to the stench of unwashed bodies, but this was something else. One pregnant mother showed signs of a fever. They began to separate the sick children and babies, dishing out medicines with heavy hearts. Their supplies would not last long.

'We can't leave them here,' Flora said and Anita nodded. It wasn't the first time they had been faced with this dilemma. There was only one solution. 'We can't leave them here, or they'll die while infecting the whole camp. The mothers must come with their babies.'

'But how?' said the lead nurse. 'We have to abide by the rules. We are here under sufferance.'

'I know what Elisabeth would say... "Suffer the little children..."' Anita looked to Flora for support.

'We back the lorry up and reload,' Flora whispered. 'With a few additions...'

'We can't smuggle them out. What if we're caught? The trucks won't be allowed back again. We have to think of the rest of them here.'

'It's a risk, but it's been done before,' Flora said, knowing other teams were smuggling children in the boots of their cars. The nurses huddled together to discuss what to do. Rebellious feelings were running high.

'On your own head be it, Flora, but we'll risk it.'

'Then here's the plan…'

They brought two of the sick mothers and babies to the hospital post for treatment. The babies were dosed with a sleeping draught, to quieten them, and the mothers inspected, washed and given aspirin. The nurses didn't ask for names. That would come later. They waited until dusk, then hustled them deep inside the truck, covered with empty boxes and blankets.

Then slowly, ever so slowly, they crawled towards the entrance gate, hearts in mouths. 'Look natural,' Flora whispered. 'Don't look shifty. Look ahead, look at the map, anything but anxious.'

The guard peered into the cabin, checked the back of the truck, but the nurses were sitting forward, blocking his view. He counted them out and sent them on their way. They drove for miles, with pinprick headlights, and then stopped to let the mothers out to relieve themselves. Flora was driving. It was a long journey back, with many wrong turns, and her eyes began to close with weariness. It was not until the small hours of the morning that they finally arrived. The two girls and babies were taken to an isolation room, while staff looked on without comment. They all knew that the less they were told, the better.

Flora climbed up the stairs to her bedroom, barely able to move for exhaustion. If she was sent home tomorrow, at least two mothers and their babies now had a chance of survival.

Chapter 49

It was late April and Flora knew she was dithering about booking her ticket home. There was a new influx of Jewish refugees filling the hospital, tired pregnant mothers preparing to hike over the mountains to freedom if their transit papers were refused at the border. Part of her wanted to stay on to help, the other part knew she must head north. The day came when she could delay no longer and sent a card direct to Kit with the date of her ticket; there was no time to visit the O'Keeffes' farm, much as she would have liked to do. Kit had been very much in her thoughts and it was hard to push him to the back of her mind.

It was a tearful departure from Elne in May. How she would miss that powdery scent of babies in the nursery at changing time, the playful bath times, the smile on their mothers' faces and the delight of the nurses when a new baby was born. It was such a special place. She would never forget Miss Eidenbenz, with her girlish and yet deeply spiritual face. Her warmth created a wonderful family atmosphere among staff and mothers. How Flora was going to miss all the fun they had managed to create in the hardest of times.

On the doorstep of the chateau, she was presented with a posy of flowers made with sprigs of mimosa. Anita was driving her down to the city, so she could collect what remained of her funds from the bank. She clutched her ticket and passport tightly, hoping the train would be on time and she would not have to sit on her suitcase. She would telegram Pa later from Paris and give him a surprise.

Kit awoke with a start. Had he overslept? Flora was leaving today and he had made sure he kipped down with Chuck Hauser, closer to Perpignan, so as not to be late. He had talked half the night with him. There were so many things he wanted to say to her and he rehearsed them with his young friend.

'If you don't ask, you'll never know.'

'What if she's already left?'

'We can ring the maternity hospital to find out. Leave it with me. Don't get in a sweat or you'll set yourself back. Get dressed and we'll borrow some petrol coupons. There's a guy at the gasoline pump who will oblige.'

'It's a slow crawl into Perpignan. I don't want to miss her.'

'If it's today, we've plenty of time, just get dressed.'

Kit pulled on his baggy shorts, a moth-eaten jumper and cotton shirt. There was no time to trim his beard and he ruffled his hair into some sort of order. He had to be on time for once, to wave her off. *Please God, give me a chance to make things right. Merciful Father take pity on us*, he found himself praying.

As they were leaving, one of Chuck's mates waved his hands to stop them. 'Have you heard? The Germans have broken through into Holland and Belgium and are crossing into France. All hell has broken loose! Now the war has really begun.'

Kit looked at Chuck and shook his head. 'She'll walk right into a storm if she heads north. We have to stop her!'

They drove through the camp and the rutted dirt tracks. It was windy and wet and Chuck had difficulty seeing through the glass. Kit felt panic rising as they neared the city. Chuck jumped out, to make the call from a café.

'*Do hurry up.*' Kit felt his anxiety rising once more.

Chuck gave him the thumbs up. 'It's okay, she's only just left.'

'Thank you, thank you,' he whispered to himself. He must stop Flora. She was walking into danger and almost certain internment.

The queue for the Paris train was long and the engine was puffing steam, smoke and dusty smuts as they stood in line. Flora gripped her ticket, in case it blew away. She was early coming, prepared for a wait. The wind blew along the platform, ruffling her thin skirt. How long before they were allowed into the already crowded carriages? Faces peered out at the travellers on the platform. She wanted a carriage full of chattering women to distract her from this painful departure. She could see Anita walking back, after driving her into town. Dear Anita, she would miss her. She glanced back again in case by any chance Kit had remembered the date, but then again, why should he drive all this way to see her off?

At last, she was allowed into a carriage full of ladies in black, knitting furiously and talking amongst themselves in the Catalan dialect. It was going to be a long and lonely journey with just some apples and a chunk of bread and cheese to eat. There were also some precious chocolates, given to her as she left, and a flask of strong coffee. She hoped there was a dining car to break the monotony.

Why hadn't she returned with Maudie? Duty had held her back, or was it that unfinished business with Kit? Now she had seen him and they had spoken some hard truths to each other, there was no reason not to leave and yet... She felt a sadness envelop her like mist. The two of them had come to the end of the road, with nothing left to say to each other. Flora sat back with a great sigh, wishing the engine would fire up and depart.

'The train's in... I can see it,' Kit said as he leapt out of the truck. 'It's on time!' He dashed past the porter, while Chuck bought the platform tickets. He was desperate, peering into each crowded carriage, searching in vain for Flora. She mustn't go north, not now. Was he too late? Had he got the wrong train? He could feel his lungs tightening with each stride. Don't give up on me now, he thought. Breathe slowly, calm your pace. He had to find her and warn her. Oh please, Lord, let me warn her... He strode down the whole length of the train and back again. Chuck was doing the same. Then he saw Flora's face peering out in surprise, just as it had when he'd first seen her on the ambulance train, all those years ago: nurse and chaplain fated never to meet.

'Pull down the window, Flora, please,' he yelled and gestured.

Curious, she did just that, to his relief. 'You came to see me off, thank you,' she said, leaning out further. 'And there's Chuck waving.'

'You have to get out, there's war in the north. France may fall and you'll be trapped... Don't go!'

'I'll be fine. My passport is in order now. Don't worry about me.'

'But I do, you don't understand... They're fighting for the Channel. You could be killed.' Kit was pounding on the window. Chuck stood further down the platform, shaking his head and yelling. 'Ask the damn woman!'

'Ask me what?' Flora shouted, as the engine revved up, steam puffing out.

'Marry me!' Kit shouted back. 'Marry me, Flora. I love you... Please don't let us part all over again...'

Flora couldn't quite make out what he was shouting. 'What?' she yelled, as the train slowly edged its way out of the station.

'He asked you to marry him,' said one of the sprightly widows, in perfect French. 'What are you waiting for, *madame*?'

'Kit, Kit, I can't hear you.'

'Don't let him slip away without an answer,' the lady added, smiling. Flora felt panic as the train began to pull away. *Not again*, pounded her heart, *not again. This is your last chance.* It was now or never to follow her heart, as it screamed: *Go, just go.*

The door opened and the widow woman threw her suitcase out. 'Jump, *madame*, jump!' The smoke swirled around as she leapt, hands first into a sprawling heap. When she recovered from the shock of her landing, she stood up, breathless, but Kit was gone.

★

The two men walked away as the train chugged out of the station, gathering speed. *Too late, too late*, it rattled on the lines. Kit walked slowly, breathless, despondent. Was it happening all over again?

'No luck, chum. Sorry, but you tried.' Chuck took his arm and they made for the exit.

Kit turned back, for one last lingering look at what might have been, and, as the steam cleared, he saw a woman running with a suitcase.

'Kit, Kit Carlyle... yes, yes, yes.' He ran towards her and she collapsed into his waiting arms.

Chapter 50

Flora woke early, the June sunlight streaming through a chink in the blackout curtains of the hotel in the square in Prades. The town nestled in the foothills of the Pyrenees, in view of the majestic mountain, Canigou. Last night they'd heard the Spanish refugee cellist Pablo Casals playing a Bach partita. The sonorous music was still ringing in her ears.

By her side Kit slept on, not stirring as she gently opened the curtain to welcome the day. This was the first morning of their new life together, a couple at long last. She smiled, wondering how to explain their relationship to her faraway family. How all her plans had changed now Kit was back in her life. She must write a letter, so they were not alarmed by her absence.

Officialdom required birth certificates, passports, all the rigmarole of waiting weeks for permission to marry. There was now no time for any of this, but it was Consuela's idea to ask Father Antoine for a simple blessing, however unorthodox. He was happy to oblige. It was the perfect solution to seal their union.

A strange dream had disturbed her sleep last night. They were walking up a rocky track into the rough garrigue, the blue mountain peaks ahead. Then a fingerpost appeared out of nowhere. 'Time for you to go on,' Kit urged but she refused to budge, clinging to him. 'Where you go, I go from now on.'

'It's not safe for you to stay.'

'I don't care.' Suddenly he turned to retrace his steps, ignoring her, but she ran back. 'Wait, wait... we are one now...'

Flora had woken up with a start, relieved that the dream wasn't true. There was no going back. They were making plans, war or no war. She looked at Ivo's ring, still on her finger, touching it, sensing Ivo, Fergus and Maudie would approve. When you find something precious, surely the future must hold some hope. Outside her window, they were setting up the market in the square. She could hear the bustle of farmers and women laying out their stalls. Life was going on, no matter what.

Flora turned to see Kit watching her. 'Come back to bed.'

'Aren't we lucky?' she whispered, nestling back into his arms. 'What shall we do today?'

'Wait and see. I've something I want to show you.'

'What do you think?' Kit asked Flora, as they stood in front of an old farmhouse high in the hills above Prades. The tiled roof was slipping, the shutters were hanging off their hinges. The barn door was on the floor. This old place had been empty and neglected for years, almost beyond repair.

'Do you really want to know?' She shook her head. 'Only you could find such a wreck.'

'But it's cheap to rent. It can be fixed, made watertight and the barn is sound. It will make a perfect children's hostel. The air is fresh and there's plenty of wood.'

Flora took his hand. Kit shared this dream of creating another refuge place for the many displaced children who were racing around the camps. Children in need of schooling, discipline and a place of safety from predatory men who used them to steal, beg and worse.

If the aid charities would allow it, they could create their own colony.

'We're high in the Pyrenees, hidden from view, and not far from the village school below. There's a stream for fresh water,' he continued. 'Sam came across it by chance, on a walk when I was recovering here. He brought me to inspect it, thinking it had possibilities, but we'd need funds and help. It's too much for you and me to tackle alone.'

Flora knew funds would not be a problem, if she could somehow transfer moneys from the rental of the Glasgow apartment in Park Circus. Now, however, was a different matter.

'It will need paperwork and permissions. Who are the owners and what will they think of our scheme? We'll have to be registered here as aliens. France has fallen. We could be expelled… We can't just start work. It will take months to renovate.'

It was good to see Kit so animated. Since their reunion on the platform, they had barely spent a minute apart. However uncertain the future, nothing was going to separate them again. With her nursing experience and voluntary work, with Kit's ability to organise renovations and his command of the language, they would make a formidable team.

As far as the village of Montze was concerned, she would be Madame Carstairs. There was a wedding ring on her finger, even if it was Ivo's. He would be proud that she had found her vocation and a loving companion who she had known most of her adult life.

She smiled, thinking of the precious ceremony shared with Father Antoine. He came to visit Magret, taking them aside in Sam's garden to give them his blessing. 'I wish you well on your journey together. It has taken you both a lifetime to find the love you both deserve, my dear friends. May God go with you.'

The party afterwards was as good as any wedding breakfast. Chuck and Frankie came together, unaware of the significance of the celebrations. Someone brought an accordion and they danced until the stars came out. The one thing Flora knew she must do now was to write to her family, explaining everything as best she could, without revealing the strange truth of her secret relationship with the man they knew as Kit Carlyle.

Dear Pa

This is a difficult letter to write and with war in the north I shall have to send this via Spain. You won't like what I'm going to say, but hear me out. I can't come home now as I promised. I'm sorry to worry you, but rest assured we're quite safe down here in the south-west.

A few months ago, I came across an old comrade-in-arms, a Scotsman. He was badly wounded in body and soul by his war experience, but now is restored to health. We have decided to pool our resources to open a refuge hostel for orphaned and homeless children. The camps are full to bursting with families fleeing from persecution and in need of shelter, the children most of all.

We can offer them a home and safety. Chris has a soldier friend and his wife who are doing the same thing and they have been an inspiration to us. We have both worked down here since 1938 and we met up by chance.

I know you will be disappointed, but after such a long time here, I just couldn't leave. Maudie will explain my dilemma, but not all of it. Trust me, I have found my vocation and much joy in this shared venture.

Give my love to Virginia, Vera and Sandy and keep me informed about their new baby. I will write to Rose, Hector and Maudie with updates which I hope they will share with you both. Do not worry if postal communications are slow. I'll find a way to keep in touch.

Please understand that I must stay. Be happy for me.

Cheery bye

Flora

She cried over each sentence, not knowing if they would ever see each other again. Protecting Kit was important now. There was so much to do, if this dream of his was to become reality. It would take much longer than he thought and much more cash than they could afford.

Flora had to admit this was a glorious spot, surrounded by thick oak forests that led up to the higher slopes where there was a view down the valley. There were still roses struggling in the dry soil, but their pink buds made her smile. 'You'll need vision to turn this wreck into a children's house,' Sam said, smiling, when he came with Consuela to encourage them. 'If anyone can do it, Kit can.'

'We can put a swing on that tree for Marisa and her friends,' Kit said, pointing to a huge chestnut tree. The little girl now spoke freely and looked on Kit as her papa. She would be the first to join them when the home was fit to live in.

'I think it will take more than a swing to mend their broken lives, but fresh food and space to play is a start,' Sam said.

Converting the barn into a dormitory was first on their list. 'This is going to cost,' Flora sighed, knowing if the war in the north drew any closer, her own supply of funds might dry up. 'We'll need help from somewhere,' she added.

'Father Antoine knows someone who will help,' Sam said. 'His only proviso is that you welcome children of all races and creeds. You know what he means? We have to trust him in this.'

Was Sam referring to the Jewish migrants and other German dissidents who had fled from their own country?

'I may no longer be a preacher, but one thing is true. Love must be at the heart of our venture. Love can break down barriers, bring healing and peace. Love is stronger than hatred and good must prevail over evil regimes. There must be hope. Our refuge must be a house of hope.'

'That's quite a sermon,' Flora replied, kissing him. 'Hope would make a good name for this farmhouse: a place of hope. Come on, let's look around for a chicken coop, a suitable sunny plot for vegetables. Sick children will bring us problems, diseases, sleepless nights.'

'I will lift up mine eyes unto the hills,' Kit quoted, pointing to a stream cascading down the hillside, 'From whence cometh everlasting streams of abundance,' he laughed. 'I haven't forgotten all my texts. Water will not be a problem but we'll have to utilise the energy of our children, teach them to grow things. We must also hope the local priest will be on our side. He will find us volunteers.'

'You are very trusting. We're strangers here, Protestants, British. What if they think us spies? It's a lot to ask them to shield us, if anything goes wrong.'

Kit was not going to be defeated. 'We're Scots, don't forget, and there is the tradition of the "auld alliance". We'll take just one day at a time, darling Flora. We found each other, after all those years. That's miracle enough in my eyes. To be sharing my venture with you is more than I could ever hope for.'

'Perhaps this is what we're meant to do, to build a place of hope and healing, just as Rose Villa was all those years ago. It will be our little fortress on the hill, a place of safety for all who need it,' Flora whispered, as they inspected the boundaries, making plans in their heads. The future was uncertain and this was no easy billet. Even now the thunder of war was rattling over France, but today was for living. They must cling to hope, like those little roses blooming in neglected borders, trusting in the goodwill of friends and strangers to help make their children's refuge a reality. That was enough for now.

Chapter 51

Flora had many weeks to rue Kit's dream to rebuild the old farmhouse. The winter of 1940 came early and they were unprepared for the harshness of the wind whistling down from the peaks, lifting tiles, finding the gaps in the doors and windows, piling snowdrifts against the barn. First, in October, came terrible floods, roaring down, turning their stream into a raging torrent, dragging branches and rocks in its race to the valley below. News came of drownings along the river Tech and great loss of life. Flora prayed that the chateau refuge in Elne was spared devastation but what of the camps on the coastline?

They struggled to keep a fire from smoking and the iron stove from belching fumes. Their water supply froze. They were reduced to living and sleeping in one room, with thick curtains to hold back the draughts. They piled on every layer of clothing they could. How Flora longed for her sturdy Scottish tweeds and brogues. Galoshes were impossible to buy. They were reduced to wearing wooden clogs that clattered on the stone-flagged floor.

With the last of the precious wool she had gleaned from a farmer's wife, she knitted scarves and bonnets on makeshift wooden needles. The wool was rough and scratchy. Kit grew a grizzly red beard, impatient that the storms were hindering his progress. Everything was in short supply: tools, nails, timber. What kindling they foraged from the forest floor was dried to feed their hungry stove.

Flora scavenged in the scrub for berries, nuts and chestnuts to dry off and grind. The chickens were snug in the storage cave under the house, out of harm's way, and laid well, until the light faded. The nanny goat still had milk, enough to store as soft cheese. There were sliced apples drying in the rafters, salted beans and puréed tomatoes. There was no sugar for jams but they could barter eggs for honey, if there was spare. Kit filled their stewpot with rabbit, but meat was scarce and he eyed the older hens with longing.

Down in Montze, they were known as Monsieur Christophe and Madame Fleur, the strange couple who lived high on the mountain path and sometimes rode down on a bike. If folk were suspicious, they were always polite and formal. When word got round that Madame had been a nurse in the maternity hospital in Elne, a few intrepid mothers climbed the path with reluctant children. A trip to the nearest doctor meant a bus ride. Some were close to their delivery time and asked Flora to check all was well. Their dialect was incomprehensible at times, half French, half Spanish, but somehow she was able to offer herbal tisanes and poultices, and give reassurance where needed. Some were thin to the point of emaciation. The working men and their precious children were always served first. Too many lived on scraps, Flora feared.

Any visitor to the house could see how spartan their conditions now were. One day, a grateful grandfather brought them a thick rug, with a precious jar of hedgerow jam and a pound of fresh butter. For all that it was a region full of rich vegetation, vineyards and good soil, the best produce went to market to pay for extras and clothes. Oil was in short supply, the bus ran on a gasoline contraption, only officials and delivery vans had their own transport. Kit's bike was their lifeline. Flora hated the long trek back when the tyres were punctured by sharp rocks and she had to drag it uphill for yet more repair. They strapped a wicker basket to the back, but on most visits, it was half full. There was little to glean from the *boulangerie* or the *boucherie*, with their meagre ration cards.

Not everyone was friendly to them. Conversations stopped when Flora entered the village store. Madame Arnot nodded, speaking slowly and loudly, as if she was deaf, while Flora struggled to make herself understood. Mostly they were left to themselves, no doubt the object of gossip and suspicion as to why two *anglais* were hiding in the hills. The scuttling of the French fleet by the British navy had turned many against their allies.

There was one friendly face in the *mairie*, the girl who renewed their official papers and identity cards. Her fiancé was now a PoW, somewhere in Germany. She spoke a little English and assured them she hated the Boche. She did not query their status and, in fact, she carefully changed their names from Carstairs to Carrier, but one day curiosity got the better of her. 'You stay here, why?' she asked.

Kit explained about their hopes of making a rest home to give sick children fresh air and respite.

'Ah, like the one in Mosset... they have refugees there, but Monsieur Pik and his family are not safe. When they come, *les pauvres petites*, you will need permits for extra rations. When do they come?'

Flora shrugged. 'We have to make the old house fit to live in and it's a slow job.'

'Then you will need my young brother, Sebastien. He has too much time on his hands, too old for school but too young to join up. He will help you when the spring comes.'

Within weeks the snows melted and a gangling youth with a thin moustache and cheeks covered in acne arrived. Seb was a hard worker, whose first love was the vegetable garden, where he cleared rocks and spread chicken manure to enrich the soil. He seemed to have hollow legs and an appetite for Flora's soups. Sometimes he brought little gifts from his family: a loaf of bread, honey and precious seedlings.

Flora was embarrassed not to have anything with which to thank his sister, Sandrine, until she remembered a pretty blouse. It was worn out, but the handmade lace collar could be removed to dress up any plain outfit. In these small kindnesses was this friendship cemented.

Suddenly spring erupted with a flush of new leaves, the scent of garrigue shrubs, carpets of wild flowers and the hum of bees. Windows could be opened onto the snow-capped peaks that encircled them. Flora felt her spirits lifting.

At the end of the day, though, she watched Kit sitting by the fire with pale sunken cheeks. Had they taken on too much? Was it realistic for two middle-aged people to create a refuge here? Sam wrote encouraging letters and sent welcome funds for repairs. The refuge would have to be basic: an attic full of bunks, a big table in the kitchen. There were only poor mattresses for bedding, the best she could procure from the market stalls. This was Kit's dream. She knew she must never discourage him.

One afternoon, much to Kit's surprise, Sam O'Keeffe arrived on foot, carrying a box.

'How are things going? Trust it to be the worst winter for years.' He surveyed the vegetable garden and the swing already waiting, roped to a sturdy chestnut tree, for Marisa and other children to play on.

'To what do we owe this unexpected honour?' It was good to see his old friend. 'Flora is down in the village.'

Kit felt relieved that thanks to Seb's strong arms, most of the obvious repairs had been completed. Sam must have made the long and torturous journey by train and bus for a reason. What was so important that it could not be sent in a letter?

'Let's take a wander up the track. The mountains look splendid from here.' Sam pointed to the old stony path away from the farmhouse, into the hills.

Kit paused to get his breath as he followed behind, resting to admire the view. Above them a raptor soared on the slipstream. His eyes strained to watch its flight.

'You've done well, old chap. It couldn't have been easy, but there's been a slight change of plan,' Sam said. 'I thought I'd better tell you in person.'

'What do you mean?' Kit felt the first stab of alarm. 'I know the house isn't ready yet.' He felt protective of all they had achieved so far and against the odds.

'No, no, don't get me wrong. It'll be fine for our purposes… it's just that…' Sam hesitated.

'Spit it out.' Kit was impatient.

'I don't suppose you hear much news about the occupied quarter?'

Kit shrugged his shoulders. 'Nothing we can believe or trust, just rumours in the market. I know it's all over for France, but we are safe enough here in the mountains.'

'I've brought you a wireless, old but reliable. I left it on the table. We are still in the unoccupied zone, still under Pétain and Vichy, but laws are changing all the time, and not for the better. My Irish credentials still hold but you should not be here. I am relieved that you're only a five-hour walk into Spain, should the worst happen.'

Kit sat down on a rock and looked up at Sam. 'What are you trying to tell me?'

'I've been studying the map. The path to Spain is tough from here, but doable. It's just that there are people we're anxious to get across the border… people who might be more useful back home, if you catch my drift…'

'You mean escapees,' Kit replied. Trust Sam to be involved in rescuing army stragglers.

Sam nodded. 'Airmen, soldiers, politicians. People like that need our support. We want to make a route, with safe houses, where shepherd guides can collect their parcels. The border is hardly guarded at the moment. Now is the time to take our chance.'

Where was all this leading? This was not what Kit was expecting. How had Sam got involved in such dangerous work? Kit was no fool. He had heard rumours of smugglers and shepherds guiding strangers in the dead of night, on treks across the mountains. Some returned with pockets of cash to spend. He recalled one day, when the ice had melted, finding a suitcase nestling in a gully, its lock broken and half-rotten books scattered around. No one in their right mind would ever lug heavy cases up the steep rocky wilderness. 'I thought we were taking in sick children.'

'And you will. You must when the time comes but we also need you to take in a few kids who are in danger because of their race. These are children whose parents have been shipped off in cattle trucks from the camps at Gurs and Rivesaltes. These are children who France no longer wants to protect. You've seen conditions there and now they are even worse. Many aid workers have been expelled, leaving just a few doing the work of ten. I'm asking you to stay on up here and guide whoever comes to your door, shelter them, ask no names, no pack drill, just send them with whoever calls for them. Could I ask this of you?' Sam paused, taking in a deep breath. 'Flora must be sent into Spain at the first sign of danger. Let me assure you, we don't trust everyone who offers to help. There have been betrayals and false go-betweens they call *passeurs*. It's only for a short while until one of the other compromised routes is repaired.'

Kit sat silent, winded by Sam's explanation.

'There are funds supporting us. It is vital work. Can I count on you?'

'Stop right there... Flora must know. She must know the score. If the worst happened...' He felt sick. How could he ask his wife to risk her life?

'Of course, but this is a remote spot, off the beaten track. You have decent cover and will be safe. Your children must become a familiar part of the village even though some will have false names and papers. We can go into all this later.'

Kit turned back down the track, thinking aloud. 'How long has this been a plan? Did you bring me up here all those months ago, with this in mind?'

It was Sam's turn to fall silent. 'Only when France had truly fallen and stranded soldiers were being passed around. You were so keen to create another Magret. I sensed there were possibilities here.'

'Now I feel we're here under false pretences. I did hope you'd bring little Marisa to join us. This is a whole new enterprise. I'm not sure I can involve Flora.'

'Then keep her in the dark, say nothing. The less she knows the better. If things get risky, she won't be compromised.'

'And Consuela?'

'Oh, she is deeply involved. Someone has to prepare the children for the journey, get permits to travel, tickets and escort them to a pick-up point.'

'I see,' Kit replied, with a curtness he couldn't help. This was too much to take in now. Sam had been devious for all the good reasons. He was protecting the lives of innocent children, just as he had once protected Kit when close to death. Sam had brought him back to life, and thus he had found Flora once again. He owed his friend so much. How could he deny him this request?

To keep Flora in the dark was another matter. If silence kept her safe, then so be it, but it would not be easy. Suddenly Kit felt as if their dream idyll was over. They were in the grip of forces over which they were no longer in control.

Chapter 52

Flora sped down into the village with a smile. The sight of those sloping tiled roofs and honey-coloured stone houses lining the cobbled streets lifted her spirits. War or no war there were still red geraniums in clay pots on steps, laundry fluttering in the breeze and people in the streets. She parked by the *boulangerie*, just as a woman came out of the shop to glare at her and her bicycle.

'All right for some… with fancy cycles. Why does your sort find fresh tyres, when my poor son can't find work for love nor money? Go back to your own country!' Flora stepped back just as Sandrine's mother, Lise Quintana, came out to hear this tirade.

'Take no notice of Madame Bernat. If the mayor himself sent round a taxi for her son, he still would find an excuse not to work…' The woman scurried off, muttering to herself. 'Sorry about that, Madame Fleur, but since her husband ran off with a waitress from Prades, she is bitter. Have you got your new arrivals yet?'

Flora shook her head. 'There's been a delay, but any day now.'

'I'm glad I've caught you. Sandrine told me to tell you there's been some new missive from Vichy about clearing out any foreigners in a fifteen-kilometre radius close to the Spanish border. There have been sightings of escapees and controls are to be tightened. You are not so close that it's a threat and the *gendarmes* know who you are. It is rumoured your husband is sick and needs the air for his health. No one will bother you.'

Flora was taken aback by this news. 'But what about the children coming from the camps?'

'They know all about that, too. Nothing passes their notice here, but you are doing a service to poor infants. No one will denounce you if they wish to meet St Peter at heaven's gates one day.' Lise crossed herself. 'All the same, I don't trust this government. Sandrine says they are making so many rules and regulations. Where will it end?'

Flora clutched her bicycle to steady herself. It was hard to take all this in. Time to head back to warn Kit, but first she would send a telegraph to Sam, to check all was well with their plans. It was a slow, hot climb back to the farmhouse, with only a meagre loaf and some roots to show for her journey.

Kit took her news calmly. 'By the time all the red tape is unwound, permits are stamped and re-stamped, they will have forgotten we exist. It's good to know that keeping the border to Spain open is seen as a threat to the new order. If there is any danger, I'll know you will be able to cross into safety.'

'Not without you, I won't,' Flora replied, her heart thumping at this idea. 'We're in this together, no matter what.' Her cheeks flushed at the very thought of separation.

'We can't stay here for ever if things get rough,' Kit said.

'But we've not even started yet. After all the work we've put into getting this place fit for a hostel – don't tell me it's been for nothing?' She looked around at all the improvements they had made, remembering the back-aching work to clear the soil and manage their stock. Neither of them was getting any younger.

Kit held her close. 'None of that, lassie. We're here for a purpose, even if it's not quite what we bargained for.'

'What do you mean?'

'Nothing… it'll be fine. Here we are and here we'll stay, until our mission is over. It's God's work we'll be doing.' Kit smiled. 'But I could murder a fag right now.'

'Over my dead body!' Flora pushed him away, but he held her tight. 'I have a feeling our life here is about to change.'

Why did Flora not share his confidence, or his faith in the future? Madame Bernat's words had stung. Did the village really want them? Would they protect them if the worst happened, or would the likes of Bernat point a finger in their direction? Who could they really trust down there? After all, she sighed to herself, we're just a pair of aliens, middle-aged Scots. How can we affect the outcome of this terrible war? What could we possibly do to defy the enemy?

A few days later Flora's fears were forgotten when a small group of children arrived on foot, from a van left at the foot of the hill. One look at the state of them and Flora's heart melted with pity. An Irish woman called Mary had collected them from Rivesaltes camp and hidden a couple of extras in the base under the floorboards. She handed over their papers and permits.

'I had to smuggle out these two. They can speak French, but are still recovering from tummy troubles. They have papers.' She gave Kit a strange look and whispered, 'You'll find their true identities in the lining of their jackets. They answer to Joseph and Carlotta, refugees from Belgium, brother and sister. They were on their way to join relatives in America, we think, but the parents...' Mary shook her head. 'We must get them across into Spain, when the time comes, but first, they need to gain some strength for a mountain climb.'

Flora looked down at the two refugees with their dark soulful eyes, sunken cheeks and stick-thin limbs. No doubt they were Jewish children, caught up in the exodus after the fall of the northern countries. Taking them in was part of the bargain they had made with the charity that funded them.

As for getting them over the mountains, they would not last a night up there where the air was so thin and the wind chill like ice. First, they must put on weight, so she and Kit must let them rest and play and find them warm clothes. She looked at the other four orphaned children, just as thin and starved – Maria and Pia, Paulo and Jorge – who clung to each other, not sure who these two strangers were. And, of course, little Alphonse.

'How long can they stay?' Flora asked.

'Until we can find them shelter in a convent school, or a home. The longer the better away from that dreadful place where they are allowed to roam into danger. We will send you three more, when it is safe.'

Mary looked around. 'This is a perfect hideaway, and

near enough for guides to pass by.' She stayed to eat, to introduce each child and their medical history, but then was anxious to be off, away down the track.

Once Mary had left, Flora felt panic rising. How were they going to manage these orphans of war, with their haunted faces and wild eyes? She, who had been an aid worker not that long ago, felt her confidence sinking. But then she pulled herself together. This was a safe place to let these children learn to be children again. This was what all their hard work had been about. She must not shirk her duty now.

'Come along.' She smiled, pointing them towards the stream. 'Let's see if we can find some little fish.' She wanted to show them there were no fences or dogs here. They followed her silently with heads bowed and shoulders hunched like old men and women.

Kit stood watching, shaking his head. He glanced at Flora and whispered, 'At last, our work begins.'

Chapter 53

'What am I going to do, Lise? I asked for warm coats and they've sent blankets...' Flora showed Lise Quintana a pile of army blankets sent by the charity. 'Not that I'm not grateful, of course.' It was good to express her frustrations to the one friend she had made in the village. 'With winter coming, they all need something warm to wear. I could just about manage capes. Sewing was never my strength at school.'

'*Tante Lise*' was always a welcome visitor, trudging up the track whenever she was free, bringing treats for the little ones who fished in her pockets to find them. There were eight of them now, living in the eaves. At last, little Marisa, Kit's first conquest from Magret, had joined them and bossed the infants about.

Lise smiled, looking around at the gaggle of children stretched out on the rug. 'Don't worry, I can help you make them up. I marvel how you manage to keep them fed on these meagre rations.'

Joseph and Carlotta were fighting over pieces of the

Noah's Ark that Kit had built out of scraps of wood. Flora no longer minded the tears and squabbles. In some ways it was their proudest achievement, to have turned silent sullen arrivals into children who felt safe enough to open up, talk, play and fight. They fought about whose turn it was to feed the chickens and collect eggs, who could stroke Gigi, the goat, and her kid, or milk her without spilling the bucket.

Flora was fearing the arrival of the snow, hoping their fuel would last and she could preserve enough from their stores to make something for Christmas. The children were kept isolated from the village, registered at the *mairie* for their ration books. The priest called to invite them to Sunday mass, but so far none of them had gone. The school had no room for them anyway. Flora made the excuse that they were still recovering from deprivation in the camps. Berthe Bernat and her cronies made it known that they were dirty and full of diseases.

In a strange way, the woman was doing them a favour. It kept this little colony isolated and safe from prying eyes, all the more important now they had four Jewish children with false names and identities hidden amongst them.

Kit was making himself responsible for their education. He sat them round the kitchen table each day after chores, the littlest practising letters and learning to read from their few books. He emptied his precious paints, so they were free to express themselves on paper, but it was scarce. He took them out into the garrigue, among the shrubs and rocks, to search for wildlife, leaves and berries, making them aware of anything poisonous. The boys loved football and tagging games. Fresh air was filling their lungs and strengthening their muscles. Keeping them fed was a daunting task, even if

Sandrine Quintana from the town hall and Lise made sure they received children's full rations. Supplies in the village were getting scarce and Flora noticed they would always be last in the queue for anything extra.

By the time they flopped into bed, Flora felt every one of her forty-four years. Most nights were still broken by the cries of screaming children, by the bed soiler or Alphonse, who crept down in the night to steal food from the cupboard to hide under his pillow. Kit was patient, sitting with the little thief, trying to explain that there would always be food on the table and sharing it out fairly would mean no one would go short, but old habits were hard to break.

Both Kit and Flora had seen the chaos in the camps, how people secretly grabbed whatever they could to eat. It was taking time for each new arrival to learn trust. Sleepless nights took their toll and Flora worried about Kit. Strong willed as he was, he was still physically weak. He needed help. She had never loved him more than she did now. It was time to find someone to take on all the more demanding repairs.

Once again Lise came to the rescue. 'Let Sebastien return. My son is in need of direction. He spends too much time with that Bernat boy, who's always in trouble with the *gendarme*, Jean-Baptiste. Berthe Bernat spoils him.'

The following week, Seb set to work helping Kit muck out the cave under the farmhouse, so they could shelter the stock there along with the chickens. They collected ferns for bedding.

Lise had made a simple pattern for the coat making, to pin onto the blanket cloth, and they cut out the shapes into different sizes, using every inch of fabric. 'I'll take them back and run them up on my machine. You can finish off the hems and fastenings later.'

'How can I thank you?' Flora was tearful, knowing she had nothing with which to repay her friend.

'We are on this earth to help each other,' came the reply.

One day Flora vowed she would find some way to repay this kindness. One by one the coats were completed, lined with flannel from old bedsheets. Marisa and Carlotta were taught how to knit simple scarves and hoods. Flora cut up the last of her thicker skirts, to make leggings for the youngest ones. She lived in a pair of Kit's trousers, patched at the knee. They looked like raggle-taggle gypsies but at least no one was here to see them. When she went into the village, she made an effort, wearing a threadbare coat and a silk scarf.

Now it was time to turn her mind to Christmas, to brighten the darkness of the long winter ahead. It would take a miracle or two to achieve this, she sighed. The cupboards were bare of anything not essential, money was tight and to give eight children a present each was nigh impossible. It would be the bleakest of celebrations. In desperation she wrote to the Children's Aid in the hope of some supplies.

As she sat by the fire sipping what passed for coffee, she recalled all those nights on duty in the hospital tents on the western front; she remembered the efforts nurses made to cheer the wounded soldiers, the pleasure that came from simple things, such as decorating the ward with greenery, the Christmas trees, the little treats they made for the men, lavender bags to take the smell of sepsis away, tangerines and nuts. They made the best of times, in the worst of times. She smiled, thinking of how during Christmas on the

Riviera she had met Kit again: two wounded Scots who had found love among the bougainvillea. It was not beyond them to make the children's Christmas Day special. They would find pleasure in games and singing. All the rest she would have to leave to the Almighty. Did it not say in the Good Book, 'Ask and ye shall receive?'

Chapter 54

Kit was busy putting the finishing touches to a nativity scene carved from scraps of wood. There was a manger, little animals and the holy family. The wireless was broken, so they heard snippets of news from village gossip. Kit's most reliable source was Jean-Baptiste Latour, the policeman. There was no further post from Sam O'Keeffe and he wondered if the scheme for passing escapees over the border was proving too difficult and dangerous. In many ways he hoped so.

Flora still knew nothing about this idea and the more he thought about drawing attention to their refuge, the more he disliked it. As he paused to look out over the bleak mountain track, with the frosty stillness in the air and silence, he felt relief in knowing no one would be mad enough to risk this path in the ice and darkness. He found Flora huddled over her herbal nightcap. When she looked up, he could see she had been crying. Now the children were safely upstairs for the night, this was the special time they could share together.

'What's happened?'

'Everything. I so wanted to make our Christmas Day special, but I've got nothing and no parcel from the Children's Aid, no party food or presents...'

'Whoa!' he replied. 'We never celebrated Christmas all that much in Scotland. Why this sudden panic? We'll find a few branches to decorate...'

'What with?' Flora snapped.

'Don't be defeatist – pine cones, cut-outs. You can tie on those sweeties you bought.'

'They've vanished. Alphonse has been ferreting in my cupboard again. I thought you'd sorted him out.'

Seeing her distress, Kit took her hand. 'Don't begrudge the poor lad. Heaven knows, he has nothing else in his life now but danger. We can still have a special day and make it different.'

Later, Kit lay by her side, wide awake. Sam had warned them that taking in frightened camp children would not be easy. They had made progress with Joseph's sullen silences and Pia's pants-soiling and Alphonse's stealing, as well as Marisa's demand to be always by his side. Were they too old for this caper? Flora looked gaunt at times and he was feeling every one of his years, but now was not the time to falter. Who else had their orphans got to protect them?

Next morning broke clear and bright and on his way to open the chicken run, he saw Jean-Baptiste climbing up the track whistling, carrying a parcel. The Children's Aid had sent Flora something after all.

'From the post office? Thank you.' Kit stepped forward.

'No, *monsieur*, these are a few things from your friends in Montze. Lise Quintana wanted to thank you for keeping

Sebastien busy. I have enough with the other troublemakers. Now I have one less to cuff round the ears.' He laughed.

'Thank you. Flora will be delighted and so surprised. And you bring it all this way for us...'

'*De rien*, I was coming this way on purpose. Have you seen any strangers on your track?'

Kit shook his head. 'Surely, no tourists in this weather?'

'Not exactly. Word has it that *passeurs* are preparing to climb routes into Spain with groups of aliens. All illegal, of course, and the border is lightly guarded at this time of year. Vichy wants to stamp out any such pathways. I must report any sightings of suspicious activity. Don't worry, it is helpful you keep your head down here. Your status is irregular but you are not the only foreigners doing good things in the hills. It's just I'd...' Jean hesitated. 'I thought I'd better warn you, in case you are approached. But, as you say, Monsieur Christophe, this is not a safe time to go climbing.'

They shook hands formally. Kit was touched. He was relieved he didn't need to lie for there had been no one knocking at their door. Carrying the parcel in to where Flora was sitting with the children, he announced, 'Père Noel has sent us a box.'

'Open, open!' yelled the children, flocking round in excitement.

'No, not now, it must wait for Christmas Eve, or Père Noel might return in the night and take it away to give to other good little children.' He waited until the children were settled for their lessons and recounted everything about Jean's visit.

'And you never invited the poor man in for something to drink?' Flora replied.

'He was on official duty and still had other farms to visit.' He didn't mention Jean's warning about secret travellers. There seemed no point.

This time they took no chances and hid the packet under their bed, away from prying eyes. 'How kind of Lise and Sandrine to think of us. They have so little these days for themselves,' Flora whispered.

'It's put the smile back on your face, though,' Kit teased.

'I've been thinking up games to play. Do you remember our own children's parties? There's pin a tail on the donkey, the memory tray, the farmer wants a wife and pass the parcel. Now they have a surprise to open on the day, too.'

On Christmas Eve, they brought in some greenery and decorated the branches. They made a tableau for the nativity scene and then opened the parcel sent by the Quintanas. It did not disappoint. How had they found tiny oranges and walnuts, a packet of dates and a box of biscuits, plus a few well-loved toys? Flora led them in singing carols and they dined on a small chicken supplemented with many vegetables.

They were in the middle of a game when Kit heard a faint rapping on the shutter. The others were too engrossed, but Marisa rushed to the door with him. Outside in the falling snow, he saw the outline of a man covered with an old blanket.

'It's Père Noel come to visit us,' Marisa yelled, and everything stopped as the children rushed to greet him. The man almost fell through the door. Kit stiffened in alarm, seeing the desperate look in his eye. 'No, back to your game. I will deal with this.' He pushed the man back outside. 'What do you want?'

'I am lost, said the voice in appalling French. '*Aidez-moi, monsieur…*'

'But who are you?' Kit could see he was exhausted and frozen.

The stranger loosened his scarf and pulled out a dog tag. '*Anglais.*'

Kit relaxed. 'Come inside,' he said in English. 'Say nothing. I will do the talking.' He let the man into the kitchen and the children stared. 'This poor man is lost in the snow. He is very tired, so we must let him dry off by our fire and find him a drink to warm his bones.'

Flora looked at him in alarm. 'What's going on here?' she mouthed.

Kit shook his head and whispered, 'Not now.'

Kit let the frozen young soldier sip his drink in peace. What on earth was the fool doing out on the track, at dusk? Was he a genuine escapee on the run, or a spy? Had he been sent to check them out? Was Jean-Baptiste aware he was in the area? Was this some test?

Once Flora had taken the children up to bed, Kit gave the soldier a grilling. 'What the hell is going on? No one climbs up this rocky track in the dark. Are you mad? Who are you?'

'Captain Gower Wyn Jones. Can't tell you nothing else. I was passed on from Marseille. There is a mission there and a reverend who hides stragglers. Got split up at the station somewhere. I was told to make for the hills… another priest told me that there were English speakers who might help me.'

'Who sent you?' Kit waited for a satisfactory answer, but the captain fell silent. 'Haven't a clue, all hush-hush, no names, not real ones, an absolute nightmare, the whole bloody way. Now I'm stuck waiting for the guide.' He gave Kit a look of utter weariness and despair.

'Don't look at me, I can barely climb half a mile with my lung trouble. Who told you where we lived?' He had to check this out. 'There are sick orphan children living here. This is their refuge, supported by a Swiss charity. I can't do anything to risk their safety.'

'No one said anything about refugees.'

'I bet they didn't, whoever they are, but we can't take a risk. You can sleep in the cave tonight. After that you're on your own. Have you a rendezvous to meet with this guide?'

The captain pulled out a rough map on soggy paper. Kit looked at it. 'You are miles away from there, on the wrong track, and if you go through the village, you'll get picked up. Before it gets light, trek down and skirt round the road, take the track on the far side of the village. There's a farm high up. Perhaps that is the one you need. I'm sorry I can do no more.'

Kit led the soldier down under the house to the warmth of the goat pen and a pile of dried ferns. He grabbed a moth-eaten blanket. 'This is the best I can do. No one must know you have been here. I'll pack you some bread and cheese. I don't want to see you in the morning.'

When he returned to the kitchen, Flora pounced on him. 'What's going on? Who is that man?'

'It's better you know nothing. He made a mistake and lost his way. He'll be gone in the morning. We can give him food.'

Flora stood with her hands on her hips. 'This is not like

you to turn a stranger away in the night, and on this night especially.'

'Why?'

'It's Christmas, after all. No room at the inn... or have you forgotten how many strangers took you in, when you were desperate? Is there something I should know?'

It was no use, Flora would have to learn the truth of it all. 'You know we have to be careful. Our own status is fragile. We are being watched. Not everyone likes our presence in the village, as well you know. I can't jeopardise your safety, or that of the children we have hidden here.'

'I must speak to him,' Flora said, with that determined look in her eye he knew so well.

'Better not, he's safe for the night. That's the best we can do.'

'Is it?' Flora answered.

Kit could see she was not going to be fobbed off. Part of him was relieved. They were a team, after all. Still, he had to be sure that the soldier's arrival was not some test of loyalty. The trouble was, loyalty to whom?

Chapter 55

O ne look outside next morning and they knew no one would be going anywhere. It had snowed heavily, with drifts high against the walls. The children rushed to play outside, but not before Flora wrapped them up against the cold. Kit was about to dig his way downstairs towards the cave.

'We can't send the man away in this... He will freeze or fall into a ravine. Bring him into the warmth,' Flora ordered.

'The kids will see he's not Père Noel,' Kit argued.

'I can fix that,' Flora replied.

Here was one of their British men, a stranger in a hostile land. The poor guy had made it this far and she was not going to fail him at the last hurdle. First, she sent him into the back store to freshen up, while she searched out some of Kit's clothes. Luckily, they were about the same height, though Gower was much thinner. He came back looking brighter and ready to wolf down a plate of what passed for porridge. It was made from ground chestnuts and stale bread, soaked in water and sweetened with the thick grape juice that Lise had brought up, after the wine harvest.

'Don't speak English in front of the children, only when we are in private. Just smile when I'm talking to them, as if you understand, and nod. They must still believe you are Father Christmas, come in secret.'

Carlotta rushed in, with soaking mittens. 'Who's that man?'

Marisa was quick to reply. 'Don't you know? It's Père Noel come to bring us toys but they got buried in the snow. Now he has nothing to give us and is very sad.'

Kit looked at his wife, shaking his head. Only a child could make up such an explanation.

'Listen,' Flora said, gathering the children together. 'Poor Père Noel is too tired to go on his journey, so we must take very good care of him for a few more days. He has far to go so when the path is clearer, we will show him the way. Now he must rest, so try to be quiet.'

'Will he tell us a story?' Alphonse asked.

'He lives far away in the north, so his French is not good, but he will listen to all your stories.'

'Can he tell my momma where I am?' Joseph tugged at Gower's sleeve. 'She lives in Berlin.'

'I'm sure he will do his best, but he is our secret visitor. No one else must know or they will be jealous that he hasn't visited them.'

How can I be telling such lies? she thought. Gower's presence spelt danger to them all. At least the storm had covered his tracks and no one would come visiting, but come New Year Seb and his family and maybe Jean-Baptiste might return. Their visitor must be gone by then.

In the evening, the three of them sat by the stove and the

captain told them his extraordinary story of escape from the debacle at Dunkirk.

'We were lined up as prisoners, to be shipped to Germany. I was in a queue, when suddenly a hand pulled me behind a wall. An old woman standing in the crowd yanked me to safety and shoved an old coat over my uniform and a tattered beret on my head. I was hurried away to a house, where they hid me and then, at night, I was passed along. The kindness they showed can never be repaid, but one day I will return to thank them all. I found there was a group of us. We were given dungarees and papers and we worked in the fields all summer. After months of working, we were sent south and that's where that Scottish padre, Reverend Tuskie, hid us near the Seamen's Mission. There's a fine group of patriots down there, feeding us and bringing things, while we waited for instructions to proceed down the coast to Perpignan. That's where it went wrong for me.'

'How?' Flora was thrilled by this news of escape committees organising routes to freedom.

'I was separated from the others and got on the wrong train. It took me into the hills here. The guard guessed I was British, but didn't give me away. He sent me to a priest, an old man who knew there were English hiding in the mountains. He gave me directions to find some hotel for people wanting to cross over. I walked and walked by night and slept in barns by day. No one turned me away when I asked for bread or milk.'

'So, you have been seen in the area. Word always gets around,' Kit said, worried by his story. 'You may have to double back again. The peaks are too dangerous now for a man without a guide. You can stay here but keep away from the children. I daren't risk their safety, not all of them are French.' He gave Gower a meaningful look.

'I see,' Gower replied. 'I must say you have saved my life. Let me make myself useful in any way I can.'

'Don't worry, there's plenty to do indoors and out, but first, are you any good with a wireless?'

'Take me to it,' Gower laughed. He settled down and took the old set to pieces while Joseph and Alphonse watched every move.

Kit took the girls down to feed the last of their hens with scraps while Flora attacked the mending basket. How rough the children were on their threadbare clothing. They wore warm coats and mittens in the house, to save fuel. How she longed to throw open the shutters to feel the summer heat on her skin and smell the aromas of the garrigue. Now there was an extra person to feed. It would take a miracle to eke out their meagre rations. The children must have any extras. The adults would go without, for a while. Harbouring an enemy soldier was a dire offence. Locals must be protected. As for Kit and Flora, they were only looking after one of their own.

The following morning Kit composed a cryptic letter to Sam O'Keeffe. It was brief but subtle in case it should fall into the wrong hands.

Thanks for the parcel. It was most unexpected, delivered on Christmas Eve. I'm afraid the size was incorrect so I will be returning the item by train to Béziers when the weather improves. Be sure to be at the station to collect. I would hate it to go astray in these uncertain times.

Christophe

With any luck, Sam would grasp the message and make sure Gower was handed into safe keeping. It was the best he could do. Involving his old friend would suggest to Sam that Kit and Flora were willing to take risks. Where would that end?

Putting the soldier on a train required a travel permit and papers, so he prayed Gower's were valid enough. How to get him there unseen was another matter. This problem kept Kit wide awake all night. Once again it was Flora who came up with a workable idea.

'When the weather lifts, we can take Gower down to the village and make it known he brought a parcel from the Children's Aid charity, but then got snowed in. Now he needs to get back to his base in Béziers. The organisation is Swiss but his French is poor. What do you think?' she said, leaning over to kiss Kit.

'Brilliant, and if Seb or Lise ask why the children mention a Père Noel, we can say it's his nickname. Jean knows we were expecting a parcel.'

That night they listened to the newly mended wireless and realised they were about to miss New Year. 'Come on, it's Hogmanay,' Flora shouted. 'Gower must go outside and find a log, wait until our clock strikes midnight and then bring it in.'

'I'll freeze,' he protested.

'No, you won't. You will be our first-footer, first to cross over the door and bring in the New Year and good luck. Heaven knows, we need it!'

Kit shoved him out of the door, laughing as they waited for the chimes of the clock on the wall. As soon as Gower came back inside, the men toasted in 1942 by shaking hands and kissing Flora on the cheek. There was only grape juice to drink. Flora and Kit burst out laughing at the look on Gower's face.

'Come on, let's go the whole hog,' Kit said, linking arms with them to sing 'Auld Lang Syne'. 'Where will we all be this time next year?'

Chapter 56

It was late January when winter lost its iron grip. Kit made snowshoes to strap on his leaky boots and ventured down to the village to claim their rations. He stopped off at the local bar, where the men gathered over what passed for coffee, to let it be known they had sheltered a visitor who needed transport back to civilisation. There was a chance a delivery driver might stop off on his route, but no one offered.

As luck would have it, he bumped into Father Xavier, the local priest, scurrying down the street. Kit took the opportunity to sound him out.

'Leave it with me,' the priest offered. 'I may need a lift myself, because there is an old priest, near Prades, who needs a sick visit. I'll send word with Sebastien. I must say you've sorted out that young man, and set such an example to a fatherless boy. He even attends mass with his mother. Lise sings your praises.'

It was time to post his letter, hoping that Sam would

be able to organise Gower's safe passage. He was sure his friend knew all the local escape routes.

Three days later, the priest sent word. Their visitor was to call at the presbytery. Flora went with Gower to make sure he didn't get waylaid, or arouse suspicion. Gower wasn't eager to be sent back in the opposite direction.

'All this way and for nothing,' he moaned.

'We're taking no chances. Better to be late than end up a prisoner again,' she snapped.

'I'm sorry, Flora. I owe you both so much... just nervous. The priest will suss me out, once I open my mouth.'

'If he guesses, I don't think he'll betray us. Say nothing, except you lost your way in the snow and you don't want to put anyone in danger.'

There was a strange three-wheeled contraption waiting by the church. Gower was squeezed in through an opening in the back. Flora waved him off. She had instructions to telegraph Consuela, to say the parcel was on its way to them. There was time to visit Lise, who was busy unravelling an old jumper. Flora held out her arms to be the wool winder.

'You had a visitor, Seb tells me.' She raised her eyebrow knowingly. 'Stupid man, trying to make a crossing in such weather.'

'You know, then?' Flora confessed. 'Does everyone in the village know?'

'Father Xavier and perhaps Jean-Baptiste. Seb, of course, but you know the old saying: tell three people and it's no longer a secret...'

'What could we do? It was Christmas Eve, so we let him

sleep in the stable. The children were convinced he was Father Christmas.' It was a relief to share all this with a friend.

'Be careful, Fleur, it is thin ice you are treading... We know it's going on. There are folk with generous hearts, but you have children in your house. Not everyone is as sympathetic as my Sandrine in the *mairie*. Some have their eye on promotion in the future and support Vichy.'

'It won't be happening again. We are off the beaten track. There will be no more travellers,' Flora replied.

'Don't you believe it. Our shepherds know every gully and path over these mountains. Who can resist the offer of riches in return for acting as guides? There are rumours that men pay hundreds to cross into safety. It will be hard to refuse such a chance. It is a dangerous time.'

Flora tried to change the subject; Lise had unnerved her. 'Do come and visit us soon. The children love to see you, especially Marisa. She now thinks Sandrine is a heroine from her story book, so pretty and kind.'

'When are you going to find them homes? Surely they are well enough now, after months in the fresh air? I have a cousin who might take two little girls.' Lise always had good suggestions.

'We think it best they stick together, until the warmer weather. I must admit, it's hard to keep them clothed and fed. We are waiting for more books and pencils. Kit is diligent and has them reading. We give singing lessons and there are plenty of chores and playtime but really they ought to be in school, learning to mix. There may be more children coming from the camps on the coast, but we can't house them until this lot find homes.'

'You will need help, then. I can ask in the village for a young girl to cook or clean.'

'No, Lise, thank you, not yet. The children who come to us aren't all French or Spanish orphans.'

Lise dropped her wool. 'You mean to tell me you shelter children of... Jews? They have false names and cards?'

Flora nodded. 'They have a right to life and freedom. What have they done wrong but be born into a different faith? Our Saviour was a Jew, wasn't he?' Flora's cheeks flushed, knowing she was taking a risk in divulging this secret to her friend. 'When they are stronger, they'll be guided to safety, too. That's why they are brought to us.'

There was a pause while Lise gathered her wool. She bent her head. 'Does my daughter know what you are doing?'

'That's not for me to say, she is being very helpful...' Flora sensed she was indeed on thin ice now.

'I don't want Sandrine in danger because of your scheme. Is it not enough that her papa died of wounds in the Great War and that her fiancé is a prisoner? How could you ask her to get involved?' Suddenly the atmosphere in the room had turned chilly.

'Lise, I'm sorry. I thought you knew. Without Sandrine's help, we would get no extra rations, or papers for any of them.' Flora could see she was outstaying her welcome and rose to leave. 'You are upset by all of this.'

'Upset... I am furious. All this going on behind my back, my family put in danger by a bunch of foreigners. I have no words to say to you.'

'You've made yourself clear. I'll trouble you no further. I apologise for the position I have put you in and understand how this must make our friendship difficult. How can I ever thank you for all your kindness to us over the years and your companionship? I realise that when trust is gone, friendship soon follows, but I shall miss you.' Flora fled through the door, blinded by tears of frustration and sadness. Had she lost a dear friend by assuming Lise approved of their little colony? Now there would be trouble between mother and daughter, because she had opened her big mouth. Flora knew what it was like to have tensions in a family. She recalled arguments with Vera back in Scotland, the agony of keeping her secret, being blamed for not returning home when the war started. Climbing back to the farmhouse, she felt drained of all feeling. Something she held precious had been lost that morning and it was her own fault.

Kit sensed a change the minute she came through the door. Flora pulled off her scarf and flung it on the table. 'That's that, then,' she announced.

'Did Gower not get off? Oh, don't tell me he's got arrested, or did he refuse to go?'

'What, Gower? No, he's gone. It's not that.' Flora flopped down in the chair and out it all came. 'It's Lise, she hadn't twigged how much Sandrine is helping us and now she's distraught for her daughter's safety. She blames us... Oh, Kit, when will this ever end?' Flora bent her head and wept.

What could he say? They had chosen to stay, against advice. Everything on the surface seemed safe enough, but Gower's arrival had brought home how easily it could go wrong. Now there was a risk of exposure down in the village. There was nothing he could do to make things right between Flora and Lise. What mother doesn't want to protect her child? Sandrine had chosen to keep silent, to protect her family. This bloody war was dividing not only countries, but also families and friendships. He just prayed Lise Quintana wouldn't make a formal complaint to the authorities. That would put their hidden children in danger. Only time would tell.

Chapter 51

One morning in high summer, Seb Quintana arrived, with a face like thunder. 'I'm not going, Monsieur Chris!' He threw his beret onto the table.

'Going where?' Kit could see the lad was upset by something.

'Sandrine told me... there's new orders coming from Vichy. We have to report for labour duty, for compulsory war service in Germany, and only essential workers and invalids will be exempt. What can I do?'

'Sit down and let's think this through. Are you sure? You know what rumours are like.'

'Sandrine wouldn't spread lies. It is for boys born between 1920 and 1922.' He put his head in his hands. 'It will kill my mother. I'm not going, I'll hide. If I have to, I'll disappear deep into the forest. I'll ask Dr Fournier for a certificate of exemption. The war killed my father. He died of his wounds, after I was born. Who will protect my sister and mother?'

Kit poured him a drink. 'Calm down, young man. You

say essential workers will be exempt? You work for old
Maurice Tessier, you work for me, and agricultural work is
important. It will be all right, you'll see. How is Lise?' They
had not seen his mother for months.

'They do nothing but snap at each other and don't tell me
what it's about. I'm not a baby.'

Kit guessed just what this was all about, but it was not
his place to inform the boy. He was just grateful Seb still
came to help with the heavy work. Over the months, Kit
had stored up his ration of cigarettes to share out. It was his
secret currency. He liked to visit old Maurice Tessier who
lived alone on a farm higher up with his flock of sheep. He
exchanged ciggies for honey, the liquid gold that provided
the children with some sweetness.

Two weeks ago, they had said goodbye to Marisa, Maria
and Pia who were being schooled in a convent. Father
Xavier had found homes on a farm for Paulo and Jorge.
Marisa was not happy to return to Magret, but Kit insisted
she was ready for better education among her peers. It was
a tearful parting. Now there were just the four refugees,
Joseph, Alphonse, Carlotta and Ruth, a new girl who was
proving hard to settle in with the others. Then there were the
occasional night visitors wanting soup and warmth, before
heading into the peaks, to freedom. With the summer heat,
Kit felt he could relax. Life had its own routine here. The
children ran around half naked and barefoot, growing fast.
They were dependent on the additional clothing and extras
from the Children's Aid. Flora had barely visited the village
since the fallout with Lise. Kit hoped that the children,
being out of sight, were almost forgotten.

He took his bicycle down for supplies and made sure to

call on Father Xavier. Gower did catch the train to Béziers. One day a postcard arrived from Magret, thanking them for the safe return of the parcel.

Restrictions were hard to ignore. The atmosphere was changing, with the order that forbade anyone to listen to foreign broadcasts, especially Radio Londres. They got little accurate news of the war but enough to realise it was not going well. There was a census being planned but Jean-Baptiste whispered their own details might get conveniently lost somewhere in the *mairie*.

He called one evening, bringing a basket of tomatoes and a bottle of wine. 'Maybe it's time you took your charges over the mountains. I can't guarantee your safety. Orders have come to round up aliens in the cities. It is only a matter of time before they come into this district for you.'

Had they outstayed their welcome? Kit thought. It was time to make preparations, to find a reliable guide, or join a party of fellow escapees.

Two days later, Flora received a letter from the Swiss Maternity hospital in Elne, asking her to shelter a mother and baby who needed to be hidden. This refugee had given birth to a girl but she was in a weak state and needed fresh air and the chance to build up her strength for the long journey ahead.

I hope you can receive her and give her the hope she so desperately needs, to make a future for herself and her child. We have given them fresh papers under the name of Juliette and Francine Morrel. Please make sure all her other documents are kept safe, until such time as she can reclaim her true identity.

Kit read the letter with a sigh. 'A mother and baby are not going to be easy to hide. I don't feel I can ask any more of Jean-Baptiste, or Sandrine. I think we're on our own with this. When is she coming?'

'Who knows?' Flora replied, realising to take the children across the Pyrenees was one thing but a mother and baby quite another. 'She'll need time to build up strength. How can they bring her here, without being spotted?'

'That's not our problem. We'll have to feed and prepare her when she arrives. It means we may have to stay much longer now.'

'So be it,' Flora said. 'We knew this day would come, so we need to find a trustworthy guide. I can see to the mother but you must see to the rest.'

Suddenly the false security built up over the year evaporated. That night they clung to each other as never before. At least together they could face everything, but the thought of leaving all they had built here filled Kit with sadness. They had so many happy memories of the house; taking a ruin and making it into a home; a haven in the darkest days. Even the dusky pink roses had been brought back to life, then there were the goats, chickens and all the harvests of vegetables. To leave it all behind and climb those fierce mountains carrying children, the very idea filled him with alarm. To put their lives into the hands of strangers, to risk accidents in the harsh terrain, was a hard decision. Then he smiled, recalling one of Aunt Jessie's sayings: 'The good Lord made yer back for the burden.'

Chapter 58

In early autumn the mother from Elne arrived at dusk, carrying a battered suitcase with a baby slung in a shawl on her back. Whoever escorted her disappeared into the shadows, leaving the exhausted young woman wearing a threadbare jacket and skirt, trembling and close to tears.

'Come in, come in, *madame*.' Flora ushered her into the living room. 'We've been expecting you for some time. Who brought you here?'

The woman shook her head. 'I don't know. He never said his name,' she replied in halting French.

'Perhaps as well. Come, sit, your baby is fast asleep. I must call you Juliette, and the baby, Francine,' Flora explained, feeling awkward. 'It's better to start this way,' she added, as Juliette unravelled her sling. Flora could see how small the baby was, with her mop of dark hair and skin already bronzed by the sun. She recalled how the newborns were carried out into the fresh air each day, to strengthen their bones. The time at Elne had been filled with the joy of watching puny babies filling out, and their mother's faces relaxing with decent food and rest. The strain on Juliette's face was all too obvious. Flora pressed a cup of mint tea into her hand.

'This is all we have at the moment,' she said.

Juliette looked up and smiled. She had the most startling green eyes, fringed with dark lashes. 'You are English, I am told, so why do you stay?'

'This is our home now and we are needed here,' was all Flora could think of to say. In fact no one knew how long they would be permitted to live here. There was no need to alarm the new arrival, though. 'We'll have to register your false papers in the town hall and hide the real ones.'

Juliette dived deep into the lining of her jacket and placed them on the table. Her real name was Esther Heilbron, *Juive* was stamped over the card. Baby's name was Malka. 'And your husband?' Flora didn't want to interrogate, but she needed to know the facts.

'I don't know,' she began to weep. 'He went ahead, to get us visas for America, but never came back to us and then the *rafles* began, the sudden roundups of people in the streets and the camps. Miss Eidenbenz hid me among the Spanish mothers. It was a fisherman who came for us. You can smell fish on my clothes. He delivers his catch to the hospital and then took me... How can I ever thank him?'

'You are safe here. We'll tell them you have a serious chest infection and must be isolated in fresh air. Can I hold the baby, to give you a rest?' Flora stretched out her arms to receive the sleeping child, with a sigh. How she had longed for her own little one to nurse, but her womb had stayed empty. Now in her forties, all hope of being a mother was over, but at least she had the consolation of caring for these children, children nursed over the years in the camps and in the hospital and here in the hills. She stroked the baby's soft downy hair. 'What a beauty she will be.'

Juliette smiled. 'Malka's dark like her father.' This thought made her weep again. 'If only I knew where fate has taken him.'

'Come, you are exhausted. I will show you to your room. It's small, little more than a cupboard, but you will be private. In the morning, there will be four more little people wanting to hug Francine. She won't be Malka until you are free again, Juliette.' Just at that moment, Kit appeared, looking grim.

'Have you heard?' Then he saw the stranger. 'Ah, *madame.*' He smiled, stretching out his hand.

'Juliette, this is my husband, Kit. What's happening?'

He held up his hand. 'I'll tell you later,' he whispered and turned to the mother. 'You must have had a long journey,' he said, sitting down, ready to listen to her story.

Flora interjected, 'I think Madame Juliette is exhausted and needs to eat. There's a little bread and chestnut preserve for you. Tomorrow will be time enough to hear all about the journey.'

Kit took the hint and went in search of a candle to guide their guests up the wooden stairs. Flora carried her case that did, indeed, stink of fish. 'You rest and I'll bring up the food and goat's milk. We'll not disturb you further.'

When they were alone and settled, Flora joined Kit at the table. 'What's the matter?'

'It's terrible, they are clearing out all the camps of Jews, packing them in rail trucks to send north. Our guest got out just in time, if they searched Elne. Everything's changing,

Jean-Baptiste says. They have to fulfil some quota and are searching for refugees and even local Jews. We must be careful with her.'

'But no one knows Juliette is here and it must stay that way,' Flora said. 'No point in registering her now. Even Sebastien mustn't know she's here. Lise has never forgiven me for risking her family. Just look at the girl. We need to build her up and find a guide to move her on. Have you spoken with Maurice Tessier?'

'Not yet, there's nothing for it but to send Seb to his farm, to help with his harvest. I'll make some excuse to keep the boy away from this house. He's still smarting about the conscription. He is hoping Maurice can make full use of him, then his exemption papers will be legal. Sandrine will see to that, I'm sure.'

They sat in silence over their cups of tea. Juliette's arrival was fraught with danger. Everyone must get across to Spain as soon as she was fit. Flora's heart sank at the thought of those two, out there in the cold, at the mercy of more strangers. What about her own little charges? They must be moved, too.

She passed the identity cards across to Kit. They loosened the floorboard, hidden under a sheepskin rug. Kit knelt down to pull out the large tin which contained all their documents: Flora's passport, the children's real identities and now two more. He paused and turned to Flora.

'If anything should happen, get this out and bury it.' Flora could see the pulse on his temple throbbing, as it did whenever he was worried.

It was strange having another woman in the house, but she loved the presence of the baby. The children were fascinated, too. The girls wanted to play with her, watching as Juliette opened her shirt to feed the hungry mite. Joseph and Alphonse soon lost interest and scampered out into the fields, searching for mushrooms with Kit. Over the weeks that followed, Juliette recounted the story of their journey from Belgium and across the Occupied Zone to Perpignan. That was where their luck had run out. Juliette was sent to Rivesaltes, where she lay in the beach prison, until a team from the maternity hospital brought her to Elne to deliver in safety.

Flora could picture it all so well. Juliette came from a family who had owned a lace factory. Her life was changed now beyond all recognition, but she rolled up her sleeves to help. Sometimes she fell silent and stared out anxiously across at the mountain range. How on earth were they going to get her over those peaks?

Restrictions grew even tighter, but Kit persuaded old Maurice to take on Sebastien, while he himself explored a possible safe route. When the time came to leave, they must have a reliable guide. Food was now so precious that even one extra mouth was a problem. As a nursing mother, Juliette needed extra, so Flora cut down on her own meals. They went foraging in the forests, as a way of strengthening the children for the long journey ahead. None of them had decent shoes, or boots, just espadrilles, and now the weather was changing again. The heat of summer was followed by torrential rain, turning the path into a mudslide. Those were the hardest days, when Juliette's gloom and fear enveloped them like a fog. They cheered themselves by listening to the wireless, but the news was bitty; something about war being waged in North Africa.

'If there's a victory in Africa, our coast will be occupied, as a defence against invasion,' Kit said. 'If Jerry comes here...' He stopped. There was no point in worrying them further.

The enormity of their situation filled Flora with panic. They were not yet prepared for flight. Looking around the house with pride, she wondered how she could let it go. Years of love and effort had gone into making this a safe haven. Now the winds of war were rattling its very foundations. What they needed was more time, time to gather essentials like clothes. The lives of six others were in their hands. It felt like a heavy weight on her shoulders.

Chapter 59

'You might know someone who can help us?' Kit leaned forward towards Maurice. They were sipping a heady wine in his farmhouse kitchen. 'How much will they want?'

'Do not insult him, Christophe. Albert is a man of honour. He will do it for France and to help win the war. There are others who will demand hundreds of francs but Albert is not one of them.' The old man sucked on his pipe, shaking his head.

'Pardon, *monsieur*, but it's such a dangerous occupation. If the authorities catch wind of this, surely there will be punishment?'

'Not round here,' said the old man. 'Our policemen are honest… what the eye doesn't see. How many parcels need delivering?'

'Three big ones and four small… no, five now,' Kit replied, almost forgetting the baby.

'You may have to join another group. It will be a night journey.' Maurice paused, looking up at his guest. 'We will be sorry to see you go. You and your wife have brought life back to the old place.' He dragged on his pipe. 'And I will miss my supplies of these.' They both laughed as he gestured towards his tobacco hoard. 'When will you leave?'

'When we are instructed by the guide.'

'You will need stronger shoes than those straw things, if the snow comes early.'

'There's nothing I can do about that,' said Kit, looking down at his battered espadrilles. 'Don't tell Sebastien, until we are gone. He was upset that I let him go.'

'You don't know, then, that Sebastien left me? He's joined the other boys, to work in the forest. They're all eager for adventure, away from the threat of forced labour. His mother will be distraught.'

'So who will help you now?' Kit knew that Maurice was no longer agile.

'Don't worry, I have a cousin who has a son. He will be kept occupied on the farm. Don't worry about me, it's you who must be ready to leave at the midnight knock on the door. We are living on borrowed time, I fear. There are whispers that our occupiers are making their way south. The Spanish border will be guarded on both sides, so any lookout posts must be avoided at all costs.'

Kit knocked back his drink. 'Thanks for that stomach warmer. I must go and make sure our little band of travellers have supplies at hand, should the time come sooner than we think. First, though, find me an axe and I will chop up those branches. It's the least I can do.'

'I'm not an invalid yet.' But Maurice did not protest too strongly. 'When you finish, take a look in that old chest by the door.'

Kit set to his task with gusto. They had a plan, a safe route to the border with a trusted *passeur*. The weather was fine enough. After that, they must trust their escape to Albert's skill and knowledge. He felt his spirits lift; *All shall be well, all manner of things shall be well*, he prayed, almost forgetting to open the wooden chest. Perhaps Maurice had a store of honey or apples. But inside was something more precious than gold. Here were three pairs of leather shoes, too small for his own feet. He lifted them out. The old man smiled, pointing to a faded picture in a frame. 'My wife, Louise, and the little one, Céline. I could never part with them after they went to live with the angels.' His voice croaked with emotion.

Kit stared at the little girl with ringlets, smiling, in her confirmation bridal dress and veil. 'I can't take these.'

'You must. What good will they do mouldering there, when they can carry some poor child over the mountain? Perhaps they've been waiting for just such a purpose. I don't need shoes to remind me of them. They live in my heart. Now off you go.'

'How can I thank you?'

'Just get across to Spain to freedom, before winter comes. Perhaps one day we will meet again.'

'We can only take what we can carry on our backs,' Flora tried to explain, as she sat with Juliette who had her leather case crammed with her baby's things.

'If I am going to America, I cannot go without my lace,' the girl protested, fingering some fine pieces. How she had managed to preserve the Brussels lace from the salt, sand

and thieves in the camp was a mystery. 'This is all I have left of home. Tomas would not want us to go empty-handed to my relatives.'

Sometimes Flora wondered if Juliette lived in another universe, oblivious to the reality of her predicament. She must be brought down to earth. With a baby on her back, she would struggle to carry much more than a little sack. They were making the last of the blankets into capes and shoe wrappings, for the children to wear over their espadrilles

The pair of child's shoes only fitted Carlotta, but Juliette had squeezed herself into Maurice's wife's leather lace-ups. This left one pair no one could fit yet, but they would come in useful for bartering, Flora thought.

As September drifted into October, they waited each night for the rap on the door, but it never came. Perhaps there had been a change of plan. Kit climbed up to see Maurice but there was no further news on offer.

'We have to go before the snows come. This waiting is getting on my nerves,' Flora moaned.

They had told the children nothing and tried to act as if the autumn harvesting would go on as normal; foraging for kindling, finding nuts. Maurice promised to see to their animals when they left, but Flora feared they would all go into the pot. Kit cut long poles to act as walking staves. Everything was ready, as ready as they could make it, and the warmth of the season still held.

One Monday, Kit decided to make another of his weekly trips down into the village to collect supplies and to speak to Father Xavier. It was a decent morning, and he sped down on his bike looking like a workman, in his faded dungarees and beret, carrying a battered knapsack in which to bring home supplies.

Juliette was in one of her tearful moods and went about her chores, sighing and staring up at the mountain. 'We'll never climb over those hills. Oh, why did I come? It was better to stay down in the camp. I'll never see Tomas again. What will become of my baby?'

Flora bit her lip and went outside to calm herself. If Juliette was like this now, what would she be like, struggling up there? Kit would have to cajole her out of this mood. He had a way of teasing people in a patient, pastoral manner. In some ways, he'd never lost his calling. What a good padre he must have been, far more patient than she ever was.

By the time she'd prepared the meagre supper, Flora realised Kit had been gone for hours. Surely, he had found some rations, but perhaps he'd got waylaid by Jean-Baptiste in the café. It was not like him to be late. Flora felt a flutter of fear gripping her. It was getting dark and her hands started to shake as they cleared away the cracked plates. Juliette saw her anxiety. 'You know what men are like,' she offered. 'One drink leads to another... He'll have to push his bike uphill.'

Keep busy, Flora urged herself. It was time for bed and prayers and stories, but her mind was racing ahead. Something was wrong, very wrong. She felt sick, biting on a dry crust of bread to steady her nerves, throwing another log into the stove, before sitting huddled over its meagre warmth, wrapped in a blanket. She dozed a while, waking up chilled, with the knowledge that Kit had not yet returned.

Chapter 60

Kit woke, reaching out for the warmth of Flora by his side. It was daylight but he could see the room was not their own, so he tried to sit up, but his head was spinning and he felt sick. There was a crucifix facing him on the wall and on the bedside table an enamel bowl. He leant over to grab it and retched, but nothing came and still the room was spinning. It was then he felt two stiff boards strapped to his left leg. He was trapped, unable to move and feeling faint.

A familiar face peered round the door. 'At last, the warrior awakes – good morning, Christophe.' It was Xavier's smiling face.

'What am I doing here? Flora will wonder where I am. How long have I been lying here?' He struggled to rise, but Xavier held him back.

'You, my son, are going nowhere, I'm afraid.'

'What happened? Why am I strapped? I can't seem to remember anything. How long have I been lying here?'

'Long enough. You had an accident and came off your bicycle, knocked down by a motorbike and out cold.

Luckily Jean-Baptiste got to you, before you yelled out in English, and brought you here for safety. Dr Fournier thinks your ankle may be broken.'

'No, it can't be, I can't feel anything.'

'Not yet you won't... the doctor used all his precious painkillers to knock you out.'

'I must get up. I can manage on crutches.'

'It's not that simple. It wasn't any old bike, but a brand-new German machine that hit you. The officer knows it was his fault. The Boche are coming up the valley.'

'Whose fault? Who had a fancy bike?' Kit did not understand.

'They are coming. An officer was on a recce and took the corner too fast. He wanted to see you to apologise, but I told him you are unconscious and not to be disturbed.'

None of this was making any sense, but Kit heard enough to know he was trapped. 'How bad is it, then?'

'Dr Fournier is taking no chances, because he fears it is a fracture. We will know more when he calls in. This has got to be handled sensitively. At least your papers, such as they are, are in order. What we feared is happening. Vichy is now under German control and we are to be occupied. The soldier told me that much.'

'Who?' Kit struggled to catch what he was saying.

'The German officer, nice enough chap, Catholic, but we must make sure he doesn't meet you.'

'Someone must warn Flora,' Kit said, beginning to understand how critical his condition was. 'We were all set to leave. If there are troops arriving, we have to get out now.'

'I'm sorry, with that leg you will go nowhere, not for weeks.' Xavier shook his head.

This can't be happening, Kit thought, not now. If only he hadn't cycled into Montze. If only their guide had turned up sooner. He wanted to lash out with frustration at this cruel turn of fate.

'Did many people witness my accident?' It would be all over the village that the foreigner was struck, or worse. What if news had already reached Flora? What a bloody mess! He looked towards the crucifix, as if to apologise, and ask what do we do now?

'Wait and see how bad your injury is, first. We'll make sure your identity is hidden. No one down here will betray you. Word will reach your wife. It's no longer safe for you to remain, especially as you don't live alone. Those poor children will have to be removed from danger, and soon, but now you must rest. You'll not be disturbed.' Xavier was trying to be reassuring. 'My housekeeper knows what's happened. No one will be allowed through the door. I have let it be known you must have complete silence.' With that the priest withdrew.

Kit lay back, his head throbbing with frustration. His misfortune had now put them all in danger. How would Flora ever forgive him?

Flora was woken by Ruth tugging her arm. 'Tante Fleur, why are you sleeping in the chair? I'm hungry.'

She looked up to see if Kit's beret was on the hook. Had he let her sleep in, after his drunken arrival? She could hear the baby crying upstairs. Her limbs were stiff, her arm tingling. Her stomach was churning, sick with fear. She realised Kit had not come home. Something was wrong and she must find out what. Juliette could see to the children's breakfast gruel, but she would not settle until she knew why he was delayed. Ruth began to cry. 'My tummy hurts.' There was nothing for it but to see if the hens had laid enough eggs to share out. Now daylight was scarcer, they would stop laying.

'Come on then, we'll go and see if Mitzi has some eggs for us.'

The panic she was feeling was not going to keep Ruth calm. Even after all these months, the little girl would freeze and howl for no reason. The chickens clucked at their arrival, hoping for seed or scraps. It was safe to let them run free, while Ruth opened the box. There were only two to collect, not really enough for a meal, but better than nothing.

She looked up to see a figure in the distance coming up the path, a woman in a scarf, hurrying in their direction. It was Lise Quintana, and Flora felt anxious at the sight of her former friend, fearing the worst. Her legs gave beneath her and she clung to the fencepost. All she could think of was not to break those precious eggs.

'They've arrested him...' she shouted.

Lise ran to help her. 'No, no, nothing like that. He's had an accident on his bike. The priest is looking after him. He's safe. I was sent to warn you. German troops are in the vicinity. We don't know much more.'

'Then I must go to him at once,' Flora said.

'No, Fleur, that would not be wise. Better to stay here.' Lise looked down at Ruth, who was hiding behind Flora's skirt. 'I see you have another of those children,' she said.

'Of course, but don't worry, we'll not be staying when Kit comes up. We have plans.'

'Wait,' Lise replied. 'Christophe has broken his ankle. He

can't be moved for weeks. But don't worry. Even if we get some unwanted guests, no one in Montze will betray him. I'll let it be known that my cousin has come, to recover from infection. Kit will stay with us, until he can walk safely.'

'Why are you doing this, after all that passed between us?' Flora recalled their bitter argument.

'Because things have changed. Father Xavier told us of the terrible conditions in the camps, the cruelty to foreigners and their children. It made me understand why you are doing what you do and I felt shame. I don't know what else to say.' The two women looked at each other.

'You'd better come inside then,' said Flora breaking the silence.

'I've not come empty-handed.' Out of her bag Lise brought a fresh loaf, precious butter and some bonbons for the children. They clambered up into the house, where Juliette was stirring the gruel. Her eyes darted with fear at the sight of the stranger.

'It's all right, this is my friend Lise... Juliette's helping me in the house. She was sent from the Maternity Suisse, at Elne, with her baby. I don't know what I would do without her.'

The children's eyes never left the loaf, which was being sliced thinly enough to go round.

'Monsieur Christophe has hurt his leg but the doctor will mend it soon,' was all Flora could manage. 'Tante Lise came to tell us the news.' She cracked the eggs into the last of the goat's milk and melted butter in a pan, to scramble the eggs, into which she'd snipped herbs and tomatoes. Everyone got a spoonful to enjoy, while her own mind was racing. What did Lise mean by unwanted guests?

Lise didn't answer this question right away but when the children had left the table, she explained it was an enemy soldier who had knocked Kit off his bike. Juliette gasped in panic. 'We must leave at once.'

Lise shook her head. 'They won't come up here. There's nothing but sheep and scrubland, nothing to interest them.'

'I'm not leaving without Kit,' Flora said.

'He would not want you in danger. It's a pity you delayed.'

All these autumn weeks waiting for a guide and now this. Flora felt sick.

'Christophe will be safe with us. Sebastien is in the forest working with the charcoal burners. He can stay in his room. Sandrine will keep an eye on any developments. Better you get your guests across the border and then return here. Kit will meet you when he's better. You said you had plans.'

Flora knew no one else must know any details, not even a friend. 'Nothing is settled,' she replied. 'Thanks for bringing me up to date. I was thinking the worst. Give him my love.'

'Good, I'll let him know. You pass your guests over, and then you can make plans together.' How simple that all sounded in theory. When the *passeur* came, she would hand over Juliette and the children and return to await Kit's recovery. Then they would escape together. As long as Juliette and the children escaped to safety, her duty was done. Or was it? Those little ones had been part of her life for months. How would they cope on a mountainside in darkness? How could she entrust them to strangers? The journey must be done in daylight. Which was the best route to follow? How could she even think of letting them go alone?

Chapter 61

Kit was relieved by the news that Flora was safe and ready to hand over her parcels. Dr Fournier assured him the fracture would heal, but he must rest and be shielded by the Quintana family until such time as it was safe to return to Flora.

'Don't worry,' Lise assured him. 'She will see to her guests and stay until you're fit again.'

He didn't like the idea of Flora alone, with all that responsibility on her shoulders. The sooner their guide made himself known, the better.

Now there was a constant clatter of enemy vehicles up the cobbled streets. Kit peered out of the window, sickened to see those dreaded steel helmets and grey field uniforms. The sky threatened another storm.

Jean-Baptiste visited in secret one evening. 'We must be more careful now. Too many village boys fled into the hills to avoid the conscripted labour and there's sullen resistance to the foreign troops. They demand to be first in the queue for provisions, stripping apple lofts of fruit and *caves* of wine.

No one knows how to react to them. Some are just boys, others are like hungry wolves. The mountain-trained men will soon scour the countryside for resistors and refugees.'

'Then I must go now,' Kit replied, trying to stand.

'Don't be a fool. For all your years in France, your accent is foreign, good but not local, and you can't crawl uphill. Be patient. You are safe here. No one will denounce you, but they are searching for strangers, so don't draw attention to yourself. Stay indoors, out of sight.'

'But the longer I stay, the more this house is in danger,' Kit argued.

'Besides, you and your wife are doing good work by protecting those poor children. We must all help each other, until the day of liberation comes.' Jean paused. 'And it will come.'

Kit could hardly believe that day would come, a time when he and Flora could live out the rest of their lives together, without the dread of a knock on the door. Jean-Baptiste's words were meant to give him hope but all they did was fill him with gloom. He was a useless drain on this family, a magnet for treachery. How long would his wretched leg take to heal? How long would he be imprisoned here?

It was Juliette who noticed the paper slid under the door. Silently, someone had passed on the message they had been waiting for, and then disappeared. It just read *Maurice says, tomorrow*.

'What does that mean?' Juliette watched Flora's face for a response.

'It means it's time to meet Albert, the guide, who must

be ready for us. We have to get everyone organised.' Flora's stomach churned at the summons. At last, the party would be on its way to freedom.

She hadn't told Juliette that she was staying on, or that Juliette must guide the children, alone, to freedom. Every time she opened her mouth to speak, someone or something seemed to interrupt the conversation. Better to wait until they were at the farm. Better that they meet Albert first. Yet why did it feel as if she was abandoning them to an unknown fate? It was making her feel sick. Leaving Kit behind was unthinkable. They had spent so much time apart, most of their youth, and this past year had been so happy, so fulfilled. They were a team, two horses hitched to the same wagon. Flora could not bear to think of them being separated again. *Then just keep busy.* She began to gather the little sacks for each child to carry. It was time to dig out the tin box that held all their identity papers. Nothing must be left to show evidence of their presence here.

The women lined up the children for the visit to Maurice's farm.

'We're going to take a long walk in the hills to find the farmer's lost sheep, a really big adventure,' she lied.

'Is it a game?' Ruth asked.

'Perhaps,' Flora replied.

'Then I don't want to go walking.' Ruth stamped her feet and sat down, ready for another of her famous tantrums, but Juliette stepped in.

'My baby will cry if you don't come with us. Francine likes you to tickle her.' Ruth smiled at this.

'Thanks,' whispered Flora, seeing Juliette was a natural mother and had a calming way with the group. Surely, she would manage them all on the journey? It shouldn't take two of them to deal with four children and a baby.

Flora sat down to write a letter to Kit, for Maurice to deliver. It was just a note to say she was staying on until he could join her. She made no special farewell to the children's house, as they had named it. Once the party was safely on their way, she would return. Just in case proof of identity was required by the guide, she took her own papers along, concealed under the shoulder pad of her coat.

Maurice was waiting, with a swarthy bearded man. So, this was Albert, the guide. He eyed them all up slowly. 'You didn't say anything about a baby,' he commented. 'It will be extra.'

Maurice shrugged, as he introduced the women. '*Mesdames*... I'm sorry but there is a change of plan. Albert is sick, but here is Monsieur Paul, who's volunteered in his place. He knows the route Albert takes, but you must wait until first light, in case there are any border guards on patrol. Things are busier than they were, now the Boche are in control.'

Flora didn't like the sound of this. 'Do they go alone, or join another party?' she asked.

'If we make good time, there's a meeting point by a shepherd's hut and shelter for the night, but I can't stop for stragglers,' Paul replied. 'You have brought food? The children must be quiet and not attract attention. There are bears and wolves roving about, but I have a gun.' He smiled, revealing a line of broken teeth.

'Bears... wolves? What does he mean?' Juliette clutched Francine closer to her chest.

'Don't worry, these guides are experienced. He'll know

where they hide up,' the farmer replied. 'I have a rabbit stew, come, eat while you can.' He ushered them to the table, where they sat together in silence, filling themselves for the journey. 'Now the children must nap, rest for the hike ahead. Five or six hours should do it, if we are lucky,' he added, drawing Flora to his side. 'I'm glad you are going with them. I would not like to think of that lady alone. There is something about this Paul. I'm sure he is honest enough, but with a woman alone, I'm not so sure... I have heard tales... With two of you, I feel he wouldn't dare take liberties.'

This was the moment to confess her own selfish plan, to admit to her desire to stay put, but Flora looked down at the sleeping children, her darling little ones: Alphonse, Joseph, Carlotta and poor, troubled Ruth. What on earth had she been thinking? How could she abandon them all now? It was just a flight of fancy to think that Juliette could manage to do everything all by herself, and with the baby, too. Even if they found another group to join, there was a glint in Paul's eye that she didn't like, a cold calculating look. Every instinct in her body screamed that he was not a man to be trusted. She could not give up her precious charges into his keeping, unless she was there by their side.

Flora nodded in agreement. 'Don't worry, *monsieur*, we will keep him in his place, but what did he mean that baby was extra?'

'*Mais non*, there's no money involved, I'm sure. If Albert recommended him, he may want a tip but nothing more. You must rest now.'

Flora felt the note in her pocket, but didn't pull it out. 'Please let Kit know once we are safely over the border. I will return and wait for him.'

'Of course. May the Good Lord rain many blessings on you both for what you are doing.' Flora found a corner to rest, checking the list, checking in her mind what they might have to carry. She was tired, but relieved that her little family would be safer with two pairs of hands to protect them. How could she abdicate her responsibility to get them to safety, no matter what the cost? Only after that would she be free to return, but first she must sleep. Tomorrow would be a long day.

Chapter 62

At first light they set off from Maurice's farm in high spirits, each with a little sack on their back, following the stream until they reached stony boulders. Paul pointed upward to a sloping terrace and a rocky path. It was a slow climb and Flora stopped to admire the view, but Paul chivvied them onwards, towards a forest of old pines and the stream that became a waterfall.

It was Joseph who noticed an iron cross fixed into a rock. 'Come, look! Why is that there?'

Paul laughed. 'Two imbeciles tried to cross the torrent and were swept away in an avalanche in 1870.'

'How terrible,' Juliette said, clutching her baby tighter. '*Monsieur*, can we rest now? Baby needs to feed.'

'Later,' Paul snapped. 'There are rocks to climb and you can rest then. It's going to rain, but we'll find a grotto to shelter in. Just keep moving.'

Flora recognised that Ruth and Carlotta were flagging. 'My shoes hurt,' Carlotta cried. Paul ignored her.

The skies were darkening and the slope was getting even

steeper. Thank goodness they were not attempting the escape in wintertime. The wind was whipping up into a storm and the rain came pelting down. They made to shelter under a few trees, but their guide was having none of it.

'Do you want to cross the border, or not?' he snapped again. 'There's a shepherd's hut further up… keep going and you can dry out.'

Ruth was dragging behind where the path was narrow. One careless slip and a child could fall over the edge, onto the rocks that bordered the river Rotja. Flora coaxed her back, holding out her hand. The last thing she wanted was one of Ruth's tantrums.

It felt as if they'd been walking for hours. The boys were game, but Juliette was so very tired with her little case strapped on her back and Francine began to cry.

'Shut that thing up!' Paul shouted. 'Do you want the field *gendarmerie* to hear us? Their trucks are patrolling up to Mantet, just looking for any Jews and escapees.'

'But she is hungry,' Flora pleaded. 'Shouting doesn't help. We are doing our best.'

'I should never have taken you on. At this rate it will be nightfall before you cross over and that was not my plan.' Paul was in no mood for excuses, striding ahead, muttering to himself.

At long last they came to a ruined hut, hardly big enough to give shelter. Juliette began to feed the baby and Paul's eyes never left her breasts. Flora brought out their meal, sharing it out equally. It did not go far because the children were ravenous. 'We must rest before the next bit. How long will that be?' she asked.

'It's up to you. This is where I leave,' Paul replied. 'I'm

not sticking around waiting for you lot to get a move on. Stay here and try again in the morning. Just follow the path towards Mantet. The trail is well used, but keep out of the town. It's guarded.'

'What do you mean, you're leaving us here?' Flora stood up, to argue with him.

'Just what I said, but I won't go without my dues. I charge for each parcel, you understand, and you have one extra.'

The two women looked at each other in horror at this news. But we were told you *passeurs* did this for the love of France, not for money.'

'Whoever told you that was a fool. I have mouths to feed and food to buy. France can go to the devil, for all I care. This is my work and people must pay for it, or else...' There was no mistaking the threat in his voice. Suddenly the atmosphere was charged with menace.

'We don't have much money.' Flora's throat tightened, knowing this was true.

He was staring at Juliette. 'Jews always have gold in their hems,' he replied. 'Come on, sister, deliver.'

'Search me then. I have nothing of value. Everything was stolen in the camp.' Paul snatched her hand. 'You have a ring, and you, too. Give me what you have got or I'll throw your identities down into the river and the baby too... just shut up.'

Flora pulled off Ivo's wedding ring. 'Here, take it, and my watch. You're a disgrace to your country. May you go to hell for this.'

Juliette was tugging at her finger. 'Take mine, too. We can find our way to freedom without his help.' Flora threw the few francs she had on the floor.

Paul grabbed the notes with a sickening grin. 'Safe journey, ladies.' Picking up his knapsack, he raised his hat in a mock gesture of respect and disappeared. Afterwards Flora looked at Juliette, both close to tears. The children were fast asleep, unaware of the danger they were now in.

'What can we do now?' Flora croaked, knowing that if she had not come with Juliette, she might have left the girl to a worse fate. 'We have nothing to barter with.'

To her amazement Juliette smiled. 'Oh yes we have, the thief is right. Our race has learnt to survive searches. Few men will look into a dirty nappy, will they?' She pulled out the soggy towel wrapped around Francine and brought out a leather pouch. 'With this, we buy freedom.' Flora saw gold coins wrapped inside. 'How did you...?'

'Never you mind. I can buy a new ring, but freedom is beyond price.' Juliette winked at her friend.

'That doesn't solve how we get through to Mantet,' Flora sighed. 'I suppose we'd better rest here until morning comes and just follow the path. I just hope to God he's told us the truth. Wait until I see old Maurice again... We've come so far together, there's no going back for us now.'

Maurice sent news that the 'parcels' had departed with a new guide. By now they would either be over the border, or arrested and on their way back in France. This gave Kit little comfort. He cursed his bad luck and his ankle which was now encased in plaster. He was trapped indoors and out of sight, with only Lise and Sandrine for company.

They were worrying about young Sebastien being caught, but so far there had been no alarms or arrests in the district.

Kit received briefings from Jean-Baptiste to the effect that there were few troop movements in the area. There were, however, mountain-fit soldiers from the Austrian region who could scale the Pyrenees with ease when the time came. Only last week Maurice had a visit from the field soldiers. They had searched his barn thoroughly and he feared they knew the likely mountain passes that hapless refugees might attempt to cross.

'Don't worry,' he assured them. 'We sent Flora's group on a little-known trail – difficult, but not impossible. Paul came back the next day to say all was well.'

Kit was feeling helpless, trying to make himself both useful and invisible. There was a space in the cave with a trapdoor, through which he must escape. How was this possible, when he could only hobble?

A few times, Xavier came to play cards until curfew. Over a bottle of Banyuls Kit confided his whole life story, their decision to stay on in France, when common sense told them to leave. The priest took it all in his stride.

'I've never sat down with a Protestant minister before.' Xavier reminded Kit of his old friend, Father Antoine, in Collioure.

One evening he borrowed a pencil and began to sketch the priest's features, having not picked up a pen for months. It helped to pass the time. Lise and Sandrine giggled as he tried to capture their sharp features and dark eyes.

'When can I leave?' he begged, but Dr Fournier shook his head.

'Patience. You want it to heal? Don't force your weight on it. When the plaster is off, we'll test with a little exercise... then and only then.'

Montze was changing, with the arrival of foreign soldiers, the clatter of boots on cobbles and the constant drone of lorries and motorbikes uphill. Kit hoped his secret presence was long forgotten by villagers, but one night Xavier arrived, his cheeks flushed with anxiety.

'Jean-Baptiste has warned me. You have been denounced to the authorities. A letter, anonymous of course, saying there was an *anglais* hiding in the hills, whose children were not his own, but refugees. A search party has been sent to your farmhouse. Whoever it is, still thinks you are there.'

'I bet I know who that will be,' Lise said. 'The blessed Berthe Bernat, but at least she doesn't know you're here. When they search, they are thorough. It's no good, Christophe.'

He could see the anxiety on Lise's face. 'I can't put you in any more danger. I must leave now,' he replied, trying to stand.

'Don't be a fool. You're not fit to go anywhere. No one will search here,' Sandrine said. 'I have an idea – leave this with me.'

'No, you can't get involved again,' Lise shouted. 'Father, tell her not to be so silly.'

Sandrine was having none of her mother's caution. 'He can't stay here, *Maman*. I know people who can help us.'

'Who?'

'Never you mind.'

'Tell her, Father. She puts herself in mortal danger. Do I have to lose everyone I love?' Lise pleaded. How Kit hated to be the cause of such arguments.

'It's madness to break cover now, or draw attention to your house. Let Sandrine make her enquiries. There has to be a plan, a safe one. If Kit can be spirited away quietly, then no one will be any the wiser,' said Xavier.

'But I can't walk,' Kit added, his heart sinking at this news.

'Who said anything about walking?' the priest replied. 'There will be a way. I shall pray for guidance: "I will lift up mine eyes unto the hills…" The answer must surely be up there, Sandrine?'

Later, Kit lay on his bed unable to close his eyes, listening for any car drawing up in the street. Only the enemy could afford petrol. How could he be spirited into the hills? To break curfew was asking for trouble. To be seen in broad daylight, unthinkable. He was trapped and to be sent miles away from Flora was the worst of outcomes. Where was she now? Waiting in Spain for him? Or putting herself in danger trying to get back home? Fear was nestling, not in his mind but deep in his gut. It was all going so very wrong. His stomach was churning with the knowledge that it was all his fault.

Chapter 63

At first light, Flora stretched out her frozen limbs with relief. They had survived the night, huddled together for warmth and comfort. Even Ruth had settled but Flora's stomach was rumbling and she felt sick with hunger. Not a crumb of provisions was left, so they must make the most of the light and head along the path. Nobody wanted to leave the shelter of the stone shack.

It was time to keep the little ones in a line, walking between Flora and Juliette for their safety. Francine slept, oblivious, but once awake, her howling might attract unwelcome attention. Maurice had warned them of mountain troops with dogs, but so far their luck had held. In the distance was a snow-topped mountain that heralded the Spanish border, but the trail was rough and unclear. Flora trusted it would lead them to safety.

'How far is it now?' Juliette asked. 'My legs ache from the long hike yesterday.'

'I reckon it can't be too far now,' Flora replied, more in hope than conviction. If ever she needed faith and trust in her instincts, it was now. To get them all lost in these cruel mountains, with no guide, was terrifying. She must show confidence and pretend, when in fact she felt only fear and foreboding.

'I'm hungry,' Joseph cried. 'Is there nothing left?'

'I'm sorry,' Flora answered. 'We can drink at the next stream.'

It had been raining in the night and the shrubs smelt fresh, as on they walked towards the summit. It rose in the sky to the south. There was a sullen silence from the children, but then the baby began to whimper again.

'We have to stop,' Juliette cried. 'I can't go any further.'

Ruth was always quick to pick up on an atmosphere and sat down, refusing to budge.

'Just a little further. I'm sure we're close to Spain,' Flora lied.

'How do you know?' Juliette snapped. 'With no proper map, no guide, no food. It's all been for nothing…' She was at breaking point.

Flora sensed rebellion on her hands, lost for words, until she heard movement by the rocks. 'Take cover!' She gathered the girls to her side. Her heart was thumping. To be so near and yet so far, she thought. They hid as best they could but Francine began to howl. Their cover was blown, but instead of soldiers in field grey, it was an old man and woman, picking something from the ground, who now looked at them. Flora froze, not knowing what to say. To her surprise they beckoned and smiled.

Flora hesitated, recalling a few phrases she had learned at Elne. '*La Francia o España?* France or Spain?' she whispered.

The old woman nodded, beckoning them forward with a smile.

Were they really in Spain? Had they crossed the border so easily? What if this was a trap? She looked at Juliette, knowing they had all had enough. There was no other choice but to follow. After about half an hour, they came to a little house with a stone barn hewn out of the rock. 'Come, come, come.' The old woman beckoned, pointing to the barn. She did not seem surprised to be welcoming visitors. The children saw chickens running about and goats tethered. This was something they recognised. They sat down, loosening their makeshift capes and hats.

'Are we safe?' Juliette looked towards Flora.

'I hope so,' was all Flora could say. It was not long before the woman brought out a large pan of polenta, soaked in goats' milk. The children pounced on it with relish, each taking their turn with the spoon, until the pan was scraped dry.

'Thank you,' Flora said to the woman, who smiled back with a toothless grin. She brought out rough blankets. They lay down to rest their weary limbs. Had they made it to safety? If not, a night's rest would give them strength to carry on. If only Kit was there, too, her joy would be complete, but it was enough that the first part of her duty was done. Flora's eyelids drooped with tiredness and she snuggled down to sleep.

A dog barked, waking her. Suddenly alert to the fading light, she could hear voices outside the barn. Oh, surely not – were they betrayed? The barn door opened and a man in a strange uniform and funny hat was staring at them. Flora shot up, expecting the worst and promptly bent over to be sick. Juliette took the children to the far end of the barn.

'Papers,' he demanded. This was the moment she had dreaded. Had they fallen into a trap, by following and trusting the couple?

Juliette started to weep. She pulled out her papers and Flora took her old passport out from its hiding place, alongside the children's real identities. It was all over, then. Time to be sent back over the border, or worse. Her hands trembled as she held them out. '*Por favor.*'

The guard examined them carefully, looking them up and down. 'You come with me,' he replied, in halting French.

Flora clung on to Juliette, as the children clung to them. She wanted to curse the cunning of the couple who had tricked them. At least they had a good meal inside them. To be sent back over that cruel rocky trail once more was unbearable. How would they survive? And how could she have been so naive?

In the middle of the night, Kit was bundled into a cart and covered up with straw.

'Don't move,' Jean-Baptiste ordered, as he supervised this hurried departure. There was hardly time to make his farewells. Every second mattered, if they were to creep out of Montze without attracting the guards billeted down the street. The decision to remove the plaster cast was not ideal but with his ankle strapped tightly and a stave for support, he was now at the mercy of a stranger with a mule, whose hooves were wrapped in cloth, to silence any sound. Kit crouched low, wanting to sneeze as straw tickled his nostrils.

He hugged a bundle of clothes in a sack which also contained bread, cheese and his papers. It was an ignominious leave-taking, at the mercy of whoever was spiriting him away to safety, somewhere up in the hills, no doubt.

It was a slow, painful drive in the darkness, but then he saw streaks of lemony light as the dawn broke. The jagged mountain peaks emerged and they climbed towards a forest of holm oaks and pine trees. What a relief to hear the driver calling him, and pulling away the straw, to reveal the beauty of this new terrain. 'Where are we now?' he shouted, but the driver ignored him. Every muscle in Kit's body ached with stiffness, his ankle throbbed.

So far there were no checkpoints or barricades. They must be far into the hills, miles away from Montze and far from any connections to Flora and the children. He could see wisps of smoke rising out of a clearing ahead. Was this his destination? The mule was slowing down and the old man turned to him. 'You stay here… someone will come.'

'How can I thank you?' Kit replied, trying to ease himself out of the cart with difficulty.

'They say you are an English soldier. You clear the Boche from my land, that will be your payment.' The guard guided him down and gave him his sack. He left Kit waving, as he hunched over his reins and disappeared. The smoke, Kit noticed, was just wisps. There were the fading embers of a fire surrounded by stones. The ground was pressed down by bootmarks and cigarette butts but there were no signs of the men who had camped here. He could hear buzzards circling high above him, the rustle of wind in the new leaves. He felt a strange, eerie emptiness to be alone in the middle of nowhere and hardly able to move without wincing.

If someone was expecting a fit soldier, ready to take up arms against a mutual enemy, they were in for a big disappointment. Here was only a middle-aged cripple, who had never carried a gun in his life. Kit stoked the fire with what was left of the dry brushwood, laid down his jacket and stretched out his legs to eat his breakfast. Was he being watched? Had somebody noticed his arrival? He put his arms above his head, knowing he was going nowhere, sensing that when they were sure of him, someone would emerge to check him over. Until then, he would siesta, stretch out and rest his weary body. It gave him time to pray that Flora and her little troupe were safely across the border. When she was ready, she would return and wait for him. He felt the dappled shade and sun on his face and knew no more.

Chapter 64

'Where are you taking us?' Flora watched the stern face of the *guardia civil* as he drove the car down the winding path from Mantet. Ruth was sitting on her knee; the others were squashed in the back of his official car. To her surprise, they had not been taken to a police station or another guard post, but bundled into this car and whisked away in the opposite direction. Juliette had pleaded with him to go slowly, because it was making her feel sick, but he ignored her and drove at a terrifying pace down the winding pass. Flora shut her eyes. The boys pressed their noses to the window with sheer pleasure at the speed.

'You stay in here,' he ordered, when they stopped at the petrol pump in the middle of nowhere.

'I want pee-pee,' Ruth cried.

'We all want to pee-pee,' Flora replied. They could wait until he went, or might they be able to make a run for it from here? But where were they? She had seen no border posts, just signs prohibiting entry. Were they still even in Spain? Perhaps they were not being sent back over the

335

mountains but taken to a border station and escorted back by train. Flora cursed those traitors who had tricked them into trusting them. The guard came back, carrying a bag of oranges and bottles of water. 'This is all I can find,' he said.

'Thank you, sir,' Flora replied. This man had a heart after all. They peeled the oranges into segments and the children wolfed them with relish. Juliette squeezed juice into water, for Francine.

'Where are you taking us?' Flora asked again.

'You go to the women's camp in Gerona to check your papers,' he replied in French.

'Do we go back to France?'

He shook his head, looking at Juliette and the children. 'It is not a safe place for them now.' Flora could have wept with gratitude. 'Or for you also, I think... There are rules. You stay there, *madame*, you're lucky it was me on duty. There are many who want you back in France. To cross the Pyrenees with children, two women alone, takes great courage. My French is poor, but I know what is happening, now the Germans have come.'

'Can we get out, please? I feel sick. The children need relief,' Flora begged.

'What has he been saying?' Juliette grabbed Flora's arm in alarm as they stretched their legs outside and took in the fresh air.

Flora retched, but nothing came. She felt faint and wobbly. 'Don't be afraid... of all the border guards, we have found a good man. He will take us to the coast. It's not far from Barcelona and I hope we'll get help there.' She was sick again.

'Take little sips, Flora... don't gulp. I am worried. You have had the sickness a lot.' Juliette was staring at her.

'Only when I get up quickly, with not enough food.'

'Perhaps.' Juliette smiled. 'Perhaps, but I hope there is a doctor to check you over, when we reach the camp.'

They all squeezed back into the car. It was hot and steamy and the children dozed but Flora stared out of the window. There was no going back to Montze now. What instinct had made her grab her own long-out-of-date British passport? Without it, she would be a stateless person. Would she be sent back, even so? For the moment, she must return to being Mrs Flora Lamont, née Garvie, or even Madame Christophe Carrier. She must claim all the rights of protection of a British citizen, but Juliette Morrel – Mrs Esther Heilbron – would she and the children get the same rights? One thing was certain, Flora would not leave their sides until she was sure of everyone's safety. They were her family and only when they left would she be alone once more. Yet somewhere out there was Kit, her other half. Would they ever be together again?

'This can't be right.' Flora looked up at the grey walls of the fortress. 'Why are you taking us here?'

'You must stay here, until your papers are checked,' he replied, staring ahead.

Juliette burst into a wail. 'It's a prison... Oh Lord, no, not again.' The children sensed her panic.

'You put children in there?' Flora cried.

'No, no... they will go to the nuns.'

'Not my baby, you can't take my baby!' Juliette clung to Francine, who was beginning to grizzle. 'Flora help us.'

'Surely a nursing mother can't be separated from her baby?'

'That is not my business. Illegal immigrants must be checked. This is where women go. Children go to the orphanage… that is all I know. You are better here than in the hands of German soldiers. It will not be so bad, you will see,' but he still couldn't look them in the eye as they drove through a large gate, and suddenly it became dark and shady.

Flora felt sick again and turned to the children. 'Don't worry, you've not done anything wrong. They will take you to a safe place by the sea to play, until we come to collect you.' She saw the fear in their eyes. Now she must be strong and calm for all of them. Her heart was thudding with fear of the danger they were in, but now was not the time to panic. As they were escorted out of the car, a woman in uniform came to collect them.

Flora felt her stomach clench. Not now, she prayed, forcing down the phlegm, standing upright, clutching her passport like a shield. They were taken into a bleak hall where a warden was waiting.

'I am a British citizen. This is a neutral country. I demand to see the consul,' Flora said, first in English and then in French, looking him straight in the eye, as if waiting for a reply. He took her passport. The photo was old.

'This is out of date. Why did you not leave?'

'Because of these orphans and many others before them, sick and needing shelter. Now they can't stay in France. They are all Jewish refugees, their parents left them in our care. How could I desert them?' He made no reply, turning to Juliette and her papers. 'Another Jewess?' He turned back to Flora, who stood firm.

'I am Scottish and Presbyterian. I have nursed in France since the Great War,' she lied.

'I see.' He paused. 'You will stay here… the baby with the mother until such times… The children must leave.'

'Where to?'

'That is our decision. You are not the first to burden us with your presence.' The wardress made to take the children, but they clung to Flora and began to cry. Flora knelt down. 'It won't be long, I promise. We will find you. The holy sisters will keep you safe.' But they were all crying now. Flora tried to hold back her own tears. 'You are my special children, I'll not desert you, as God is my witness. You are in His care, so be good for me.' She turned to Ruth who was sucking her thumb. Her dark eyes were wide with fear. 'We will find you, I promise.' She watched them walk back through the door, turning their heads as they went, and then she collapsed with exhaustion and fear. Juliette held her.

'You've been like a mother to them.'

Flora vomited onto the tiles and fainted.

She woke to find herself lying on a bed in a ward. A nun was watching her with interest as she tried to rise up but then fell back, sick. The nurse gave her a sip of water.

'Slowly,' she said. Flora felt panic in her chest. Where was Juliette?

'You stay here, don't move. A doctor will come, Señora Lamont.'

It seemed hours before a woman in a white coat came to examine her, relieved when she spoke to her in broken English. 'How long have you been sick?'

'Weeks… months. I can't remember. Did I eat something bad?'

'No, *señora*, it is not that. You are thin, but your breasts are full and your stomach round. There is a baby growing there.'

Flora shook her head. 'That's not possible. I am forty-five. I've never conceived. You are mistaken.' She was not making any sense.

'Are you telling me my job? Who knows when the good Lord in his wisdom grants us the gift of new life? You are not old.'

'But the others, they are my adopted children. What will become of them?'

'Don't worry, there are people out there who will make arrangements for them to join their own kind, to reunite them with family. You must stay here until the consul in Barcelona is informed. Arrangements will have to be made. You're not the first Englishwoman—'

'I'm Scottish. I have a family in Glasgow. They must be informed.'

'You stay here. You must rest and get ready for your baby, when the time comes.'

'Not in a prison,' Flora said.

'Be patient, woman.'

How could she rest with this unexpected news? She was carrying Kit's child, a child brought through the rocks and mountains and still secure inside her. She fingered her belly. It was full and firm. How could you not have known? She sighed. Perhaps if she had, she might not have risked this trek to freedom. How could she return to France? What would become of them now?

Chapter 65

K it found himself once more on the move, with the motley band of young men who had picked him up. They lived in the forest in a makeshift camp that could be struck and raised whenever danger loomed. Most of the boys were *réfractaires*, escaping forced labour with little experience of fending for themselves. It was no holiday camp, living in rough shacks and tents, with few regular food supplies and poor hygiene. Discipline did not exist at first. They would forage, then steal chickens and livestock, raiding remote farmhouses and demanding supplies. Robin Hood and his merry men they were not. There were divisions and cliques within the group.

At first, Kit observed and said little, aware he was an extra mouth to feed and crippled by his injury. He had nothing to offer in physical terms, but his years as a padre with unruly squaddies taught him that what was lacking here was respect and purpose. One night, as they sat around the firepit, he decided to ask them, straight out. 'Are you going to sit out the war here? Must your families go without in order to support you? What is there to show for this shadowy life? Are you real resisters, or not?' No one spoke, sipping their stolen wine, staring at him with suspicion. One boy looked towards the others before speaking.

'What is it to you? Old man, we took you in and fed you, what have you done for us?'

'I take your point and I thank you for sheltering me but if we are to be effective as opposition to the occupation here, it's time to take up arms, to make life difficult for the enemy, to attract new recruits and to train ourselves until we are a force to be reckoned with. Then we can all hold up our heads and demand supplies from locals.'

The boy laughed, shaking his head. 'Easy for you to talk… you can hardly walk, and where do we get weapons to fight the Boche? We are farm boys, not soldiers. We fell lumber and make charcoal. Better to stay hidden, I say.'

Kit could see they were unnerved and unsure of how to be useful. 'There are other ways to fight than with guns,' he offered. 'Railway lines and signal boxes can be destroyed, anything to disrupt supplies, help refugees escape across into Spain, make life uncomfortable for the enemy. When the war is won, you want your families to be proud of your actions. Stealing chickens and lounging about in the woods is hardly action.' Kit could see embarrassment on their faces, so he continued. 'There has to be order and discipline, as in any army. You will have skills and the tools of your trade. To be a good unit, we must work together, not bully and fight each other. We need a cook and a provision master, a fitness instructor, a uniform of sorts, even if it is only a beret and armband. If we don't respect ourselves, who will then respect us and be prepared to risk everything to join us?' Kit prayed they were taking notice.

'You make it sound easy. We're surrounded by field troops and our own police searching for us.'

'But you know the terrain better than they do. Let that be our defence. In Scotland we called it fieldcraft. There are families who will help shield us, just as you once protected me. I can lodge with them and pass messages. I have my exemption card. Who will notice a limping old veteran, a recluse who lives in the hills? That's what I can offer, till my leg is mended. We must take the precaution of never using our real names. I will be known only as Bruce. Security is key, because there may be men, eager to join us, who are not who they seem to be; spies ready to betray us.'

'How come you know all this stuff?' Interest was now rising.

'Did my bit in the last war,' Kit said. 'Do you see my point? It would mean a different way of doing things, from now on.'

Kit knew he was asking these inexperienced boys to come out of hiding and risk their lives. Did he, a stranger, have the right to ask this of them? As the embers cooled and the flies began to bite, Kit lay on his groundsheet, staring up at the leaves. His ankle was stronger now. He might be able to attempt a crossing, should the chance arise, but now that he had outlined this plan to the boys, he could not walk away. It was up to him to lick them into shape, but how he would do it without carrying a gun, he had no idea. There had to be a way.

★

343

Flora quickly recovered from her bout of nausea and was sent back to the cells to join the other illegal women. Juliette hugged her, relieved that they were together again. 'I've news. We won't have to stay here long. Someone told me to contact the Joint. I thought she was crazy but there's an organisation called the American Jewish Joint Distribution Committee in Barcelona. They're on the lookout for children and separated families like us and they visit prisons to pick up detainees.'

Flora smiled with relief for her friend. 'And I've got good news, too,' she replied, patting her stomach. 'Would you believe I'm having a baby and at my age? All these years I've yearned for such a gift...'

Juliette smiled. 'I did wonder, when you were so sick and dizzy. I'm so glad for you.'

'I've asked to be sent to the British Consul in Barcelona. I can't stay here now. Our baby can't be born in this place. I never thought we'd end up arrested, but perhaps it was meant to be.' She looked round. 'Where are the children?'

'Out playing in the yard. That's another thing – they were brought back here,' said Juliette. 'This committee will take them to a home for unaccompanied children, where safe passage from Spain to America can be arranged. Do you realise, if we hadn't come here, Flora, I'd never have known about all this? Perhaps I will hear good news about Tomas. I have to know where he is, too.'

The following days were bearable, if only because they didn't have to worry about food and lodging. They waited and waited, until one morning Flora was ushered to the warder's office. A dapper young man was standing by the desk, holding her old passport. 'Mrs Lamont, I've come to escort you to the consulate in Barcelona for an interview. Please gather your things. My car is waiting.'

'But I must say goodbye to my friend. We made the journey together, and the children, too.' She looked to the wardress for her permission.

She nodded. 'Ten minutes.'

It was a tearful farewell. Ruth clung to her skirt. 'Don't worry, I'll find out where you are living, I promise.' Flora was shaking as she clung to her precious charges, one by one.

'Are they sending you back into France?' Juliette asked.

'I hope not,' was all Flora could say. She must think first of her baby's safety. It changed everything. If only Kit could hear this exciting news. Surely it could only be a matter of time before he, too, crossed into Spain. She couldn't think of leaving here until they were together again.

As she sat in the consul's car, staring out over the sandy tracks leading to the coastline in the distance, Flora wondered what the diplomat would make of her perilous journey and the truth of her relationship with a man who was presumed dead.

Chapter 66

1942

'This is what happens if you're caught!' Kit pointed to a body on the rocks. No one wanted to look at the tortured, mutilated remains of the young fighter; even his eyes had been gouged out. Raoul, still a young boy, was sick at the sight, and Kit put his hand on his shoulder to steady him.

'War is a terrible thing,' he whispered, thinking of the bodies he had collected and buried all those years ago, sick to his soul. Over the past weeks, they had wandered ever westward and then northwards to join up with a fighting outfit of the Maquis, a battle-hardened group who hunted down lone guards, ambushed motorcyclists with tripwires, destroyed railway tracks. If captured, this was what they could expect in return.

Now winter was coming but no sign of the usual snows creeping down the mountains. Their tracks were easy to follow, food was scarce and shelter depended on farmers willing to harbour them, at the risk to their own lives. Some of his group had drifted away, back to work on farms, others stayed hidden with villagers. As Kit looked up at the peaks, he knew his own chances of crossing over into Spain were on hold. The boys, toughened as they were, still needed him. They had suffered losses from gunshot wounds going septic, and from fever and desertion. Morale was low and they were now heading into dangerous territory.

Life in the children's house seemed a far-off idyll. If he was caught, there would be no mercy. He would be shot as a British spy. His hair had turned almost white, but his beard was still foxy red. Although he could not pass as a local, he played his part as a tramp, drawing little attention in the streets as he knocked on doors, begging for food and passing messages to sympathisers. He was usually safe with priests, but no longer with the police. They heard rumours of a new force being recruited. There were spies infiltrating the Maquis camps in order to do untold damage, and it was hard to trust anyone new.

How were they to survive the winter without coming down into the valleys and risking exposure? Kit thought. They must find refuge, but where? There was only one place he could think of, but it was miles away and in the wrong direction. If they could hole up for the winter, though, out of sight and silent, they might live to fight another day.

By night, they crossed the tracks with icy patches, one false slip could send them hurtling down the rocky slopes to certain death. Walking silently in single file, listening for troop movements, was unnerving.

'Where are we going?' Raoul asked.

'Somewhere to hole up until the worst of the storms are over,' Kit replied, knowing the boy would pass this information along the line.

They were heading south and east on high ridges, avoiding any farmhouses and guard posts, at the mercy of the sharp watching eyes – wolves, bears, foxes – but nothing attacked them as they passed by. Kit could sense the boys were restless, having been separated from the larger Maquis group after the last skirmish. Survival was the name of the game and he prayed his farmhouse was still standing. At worst it would have been searched and ransacked, but that was bearable, so long as Flora was safely in Spain.

As they approached those familiar thick walls, he looked for a spiral of smoke, listened for the bark of a dog, but all was silent. The studded oak door yielded to his hand, while something scuttled across the floor, in protest at their arrival.

'Where's this?' The men paused. 'It's someone's house.'

'Not sure, but it looks as if it was deserted months ago.' His band mustn't know it belonged to him. To them he was just Bruce on the run, an old British veteran from the Great War. 'Come in… it won't bite you.' He laughed at their hesitancy, lighting his torch.

As he feared, the place had been searched, chairs thrown down, pictures broken on the floor. The wall clock and wireless gone. He dreaded to think what they would find upstairs. In the bedrooms, floorboards had been prised open by soldiers in search of cash, looking for loot; it might have been just local ruffians, or another resistance group, but it didn't matter. The roof was standing. The stove was intact, crockery was smashed, but they had lived rough for so many months that this was luxurious. Damp though it was, it would soon dry out.

'What a mess they've made.'

Kit shrugged. 'Let's hope no one will come back again. It will give us time to regroup and rest. No one must ever be visible, and that means no smoke, no lights. I have allies down in the village of Montze, but only I must make contact with them. One false step and we'll be arrested. You know the rest. Time for some shut-eye; we can straighten the place up in the morning. I saw a stream at the back, so you can wash and bring water, but only when it's dusk or first light. Remember, no one must know we are here.'

Flora stared in wonder at the precious bundle lying in her arms. How could she have given birth to such a miracle? The nuns glided around the room in their starched uniforms, smiling. It was as if she was back on duty in the Swiss maternity hospital in Elne, and yet not. Now Flora lay back, with her son cradled in her arms, while the nun helped the baby to the breast. The past few months had been unreal. The consul had listened to her story and sent her to a small hotel close by, offering light work in their office until her confinement. Nothing was too much trouble and the consul's wife made sure she was prepared for the big day.

'It's not often we get a Scottish lady on the run,' the consul laughed. 'You escaped internment by the skin of your teeth. Now we need to get you to Gibraltar and a safe passage home.'

Flora had other ideas. 'My baby must be British, of course, but I have to wait here for my husband to join me. He's British, too. I won't go without him. I must find work here, until he comes to fetch me. Then we can return together.'

'But your papers say you are a widow?' the consul quizzed.

'Yes, for many years, until I met Christopher in the aid camps. We knew each other as schoolchildren, back home. He was my brother's best friend. The brother who died in that dreadful railway crash at Quintinshill. Now Chris travels on false papers, so our marriage is irregular.' She found herself blushing. 'We were sheltering Jewish refugees, but it was time to bring them out of France. Chris had an accident and we had to leave without him, but it can only be a matter of time before he arrives.' She sighed, more in hope than expectation. Kit could be anywhere in France.

The consul looked out of the window, shaking his head. 'The borders with France are much tighter now that the Allies are heading through Italy. Germany fears a southern invasion. I fear you may have to wait many months.'

'Then I will wait.' Flora was adamant. The long journey to Madrid and on to Gibraltar with a new baby was unthinkable. 'I do have means to support myself, but I'll need to contact my family in Scotland in order to release property and assets and I must tell them I'm still alive.'

'The Red Cross can help with that, I'm sure. Your parents will expect a letter of explanation about your present situation. The letter may be able to go through the diplomatic bag, when the time comes. You're free to visit around the city, but it's full of spies and enemy agents, so be wary who you speak to,' he added.

'Don't worry, I'll be careful, but first, I'd like to find my little charges. They are housed by the Joint, I'm told.'

'Ah, in Caldes de Malavella, the orphanage… you may find them there. Señor Seguerra and his committee are very thorough in getting sponsors from America to find them safe passage to the States, but Atlantic crossings are still dangerous.'

And now, as she nursed her baby, still exhausted from a long birth and tearful about being alone in a foreign country where she had little of the language, it was time to write home. The letter she had put off for so long. They must have presumed her imprisoned, or worse. She felt guilty keeping her father and sister in the dark about meeting Kit Carlyle and all the lies she had fed them, giving excuses not to return when the war began. How would they react to her deception? It was time to tell the truth, the whole truth. She fondled the baby's downy head. Already his hair showed signs of redness like his father's. 'Christian Fergus, you will be known as Christy,' she whispered into his ear, kissing him, sniffing that familiar warm toasty odour she had first encountered at Elne. 'Christy, you and I are going nowhere, until your daddy comes for us.'

Chapter 67

Kit had no qualms about holing up his boys in the children's house. Most of them were little more than kids themselves. Their recent skirmishes over in the Ariège area had given them a taste of hand-to-hand battle and the inevitable sequel of wounds and septic limbs, fever and death. He dressed them as best he could, but to see the eyes of a dying boy glaze over, sickened him. They were like lambs to the slaughter, innocent and no match for trained soldiers, armed only with courage. Retreating to the safety of this farmhouse was a relief all round, but he was leading them into danger, nonetheless.

Only Maurice Tessier knew of his return to the area. Rumours hinted that change might be coming at long last. Life was still harsh, with searches, arrests, executions and curfews, but there was no sign of anyone returning to the farmhouse.

Living on scant rations, poaching, snaring, boiling up whatever they could find, made them edgy and quarrelsome, with fights breaking out over little snide comments. Fuel was low and they chopped down anything they could, including precious furniture hidden in the barn, to feed the fire. Clothes were patched and threadbare from scrabbling and sliding down rocks, which tore them to shreds. Clogs and boots were stuffed with straw or paper, anything to keep out the rain. Raoul spoke for all of them when he snapped, 'We're hungry and bored here. We ought to be down in the valley, showing our faces. We live like cowards up here. Better we beg help down in the village than die of starvation, Bruce. This is not what we joined up for.'

Kit nodded. 'I know, but you left home because you didn't want to serve the enemy as slave labourers. I just want to keep you safe, so you can return to your families. We have to have faith that the day will come when you will be free to do that openly. Going down into the street now is risky. I rarely come back empty-handed. I can make out I'm just travelling through. No one will betray me.'

'Are you sure... What if...' Raoul hesitated and Kit patted him on the arm. 'If I disappear, you are the pack leader. You do what you must. Spring is coming. We can move on then.'

'When the war is won, will you go back to Scotland?'

'Only if my wife is with me. There's nothing waiting for me there.'

'But you always sing the old song when we march... "You'll take the high road and I'll take the low road but I'll be in Scotland afore you",' the boy mimicked.

Kit smiled, surprised, not being aware of doing any such thing. 'Enough of this sentimental talk,' he said, pulling out the tattered map of the area. 'You need to study this and avoid any cart tracks and mountain trails. Always stick to the higher trees. The holm oaks will give you cover. Circle round the house to look for new signs of disturbance. There's always a chance someone has spotted smoke. Hide in the scrub and always put someone on watch in the tree hide.'

They still did not realise this was his home. Personal details were unsafe and so he bit his lip when they were careless with crockery, or damaged what was left of his life with Flora. The laddies were thoughtless, needing to let off steam, but when they broke the bedstead, his temper flared.

'Get off there! Someone may come back and find it wrecked enough… How would you feel if your *maman* had nowhere to sleep?' That had sobered them up for a while. Now it was time to visit his few safe contacts in Montze for news. Was there anyone left, willing to open their door to him? Only one way to find out.

'Now what are these?' One by one, Flora held up pictures of a bus, a car, a bicycle, horse and buggy. Today, she was taking her pupils through modes of transport. Her class consisted of many nationalities; all of them children eager to learn English, with the prospect of being shipped across to America one day. Once the exercise and recitals were over, they were allowed to draw and colour in their favourite vehicle.

She could not believe her good fortune in finding this modest position with the Joint Committee, preparing their orphans and adults for the big journey ahead.

'Anything that helps them assimilate when they arrive will be to their benefit,' said Mr Seguerra at the interview. Christy was placed in their makeshift nursery while she was at work. Being reunited with Juliette and toddler Francine was a wonderful bonus. Juliette and the other mothers took turns to help in the nursery. With their help and that of the consulate wives, she had been able to kit out and clothe her baby.

'He's growing fast,' Juliette said, sharing luncheon with her friend, admiring the baby's tufts of red hair with a smile. 'Just like his father… any news of him?'

Flora shook her head. 'And Tomas?'

'I pray he's crossed over to his cousins in New York, as we planned, but there's nothing official yet and I'm trying not to lose hope.' Juliette sighed, grabbing Flora's arm. 'Surely this cursed war will end? It can't be long and then you can return home.'

'I've sent letters to Lise and Sandrine in Montze, just in case they have news of Kit, but how do I know letters aren't read or censored? As soon as it's safe, I'm returning by rail with my new passport, but I hear things are chaotic, so we'll have to stay on longer than I'd wish. Everyone has been so kind and helpful and weren't we lucky, when we made our crossing? I hear tales from other refugees at the consulate, of nightmare journeys, arrests and possessions confiscated to search for valuables.'

'But that horrible Paul, may he rot in hell!' Juliette swore. 'He took our wedding rings.'

'But not your stash. How can I ever thank you? Dear God, you deserve to find Tomas waiting for you over there!'

In this refuge Flora was finding friendship and distraction, helping to pass the time. Every day she waited for the post but nothing came. Flora didn't like to think how long Juliette had been separated from her husband. She told herself no news was good news, for both of them. The liberation of all of France was surely not far off. The consul still wanted her to be repatriated through Gibraltar, but she had stood firm.

That night, with a large glass of wine by her side, Flora began to write the long overdue letter to her family in Scotland. For almost a year now, she had come home to her little apartment, tired, ready for the nightly routine, baby's feed and bath, supper to cook, too tired even to find pen and paper. This was always her excuse, especially if Christy niggled and wouldn't settle in his borrowed crib. Tonight, there was no excuse. Her son was asleep and the evening stretched ahead. It was time now to reveal her true story.

Dear Pa and all,

Forgive me for my silence and causing you such anxiety over these past years. There's so much to tell you as to why I have remained illegally in France and am now a temporary resident in Spain.

One of the reasons is that this story is not mine alone to tell and goes back long before this present war, but to the one we hoped would end all conflicts, to a time when I was invalided out from nursing, to be sent to the Côte d'Azur... What a strange time that was, living in such luxurious convalescence by the sea.

There is no logic to what happened then, other than, war throws us together in strange circumstances. What we least expect can spin our lives out of control. Living all these years with love's lies has not been easy. The future is uncertain, so I owe you an account of my current situation. There's no way I can return home without you knowing how things stand with myself, my husband

and the child born from our love. Everything you read here is as honest as I can recall, after all this time. It's an account of both separations and loss, bitterness and now hope. If none of this preamble is making sense, do please read on...

Out it all poured. From her first meeting with Kit, to the reason why she was so eager to return to France, their reunion and blessing, the children's house, the mountain crossing into Spain and the birth of their son. Nothing was held back. How Pa would respond, she had no idea but the thought that he had another grandson might soften the shock of her confession. It was midnight before cramp in her wrist forced her to complete the letter. A weight was lifted from her shoulders. Letters to her old chum, Maudie, and Sam O'Keeffe would follow. With luck, they would be sent through the diplomatic bag, to save time. This was highly unlawful, but just one more act of kindness shown to her by the consul's office. How could she ever repay them?

Chapter 68

Carcassonne

Kit sat on the cold stone shelf that passed for a bed. The walls were splattered with expletives, the cross of Lorraine, symbol of resistance, last messages and addresses, some written in blood. He was incarcerated in the prison at Carcassonne, awaiting a trial, as a spy. It would have only one outcome.

How long was it now since he was captured? He was amazed that he was still alive. In the darkness, hearing only the screams and curses of other men in the cells, it was hard to sleep. There was too much time to mull over the careless slip that had brought him to this terrible fate.

Rumours of Allied victories in the north had put the garrison at Montze on edge. Preparations for a possible landing on the south coast meant beaches were cleared, concrete defences built. They were searching ever harder for the Maquis and their supporters. Kit's group was tasked with disrupting the railway line that snaked through the valley to Foix. Months were spent spying on suitable weaknesses on the track. They were scattered across the terrain, reporting any troop movements and escaping traps set out for Resistance fighters.

A box of explosives was hidden for collection, waiting for the darkest of June nights, when, kitted out in balaclavas, masks and dark clothing, they must make their way down to a secret point and begin preparations to wire up the track for detonation.

Raoul and the boys, strengthened by a winter hiding in the mountain house, were in good spirits, confident and ready for action. A sympathiser from the nearby station arrived with a timetable. Orders were to wait for a train full of fresh troops, who would flood the Ariège area and protect this main line from just such an action as theirs.

Kit could imagine the inevitable mutilation and destruction and the fate of the nearest villages, when reprisals for their action were blamed on men and women and children. The enemy would take no prisoners. His instinct was to warn them to flee into the hills and hide, but there was no time for him to act on this. In the chaos of the attack, perhaps he could slip away and warn as many as he could to escape from the coming vengeance.

Everything went as planned. In slow motion, he watched the engine hurled on its side down the bank. Flames shot out, men were screaming, with their clothing on fire. Dense smoke billowing out acted as a screen to give them time to escape, but the rear carriages stood upright and troops spilled out, ready to attack, shooting at anything that moved. Kit fled down to their rendezvous point, knowing the village was aroused by the explosion and smoke.

'Get out! Get out!' he yelled to anyone he could see. 'They'll be coming soon... get out!' It was the best he could do to salve his conscience. Finding the priest's house, he knocked on the presbytery door.

'Father, you'd better leave now,' he warned.

'Oh dear, are you one of them?' The priest looked over his spectacles. 'Come in, son, you look as if you need a stiff drink.'

'No, Father, there's no time. Hide with your parishioners. I can show you a secret trail. You'll be safe, if you hurry.'

'Then I must ring my curate, to warn him, too.' The priest disappeared to make his call. He didn't seem in a rush at all.

Kit made for the door but found it was locked. He rattled it hard and made for the window, but the shutters were boarded up from outside. 'Father, what's this?' he yelled, but there was no reply. He was trapped, imprisoned. What the hell was going on? He did not have long to wait.

When the door was unfastened at last, the priest was not alone. A German officer and two men stood by his side. 'Well done, Father Pierre… another in the mousetrap, good work.'

Of all the priests in the district, Kit had knocked on the door of the only traitor among them.

'This one is not French.' The priest smiled. 'A spy, British, I suspect…'

'May the Lord forgive your treachery,' was all Kit could mutter, his mouth dry with the knowledge that he would not survive this betrayal. He was manhandled out of the presbytery to join men rounded up from the village. He had tried to warn them, but to no avail. Already he could see troops were shooting and burning folk out of their homes. There would be no mercy. Was a trainload of burning soldiers worth such terrible sacrifice here?

Now Kit lay on the stone bench in his cell, feeling sick, recalling how they were packed into a stinking cattle truck, on the long journey to the ancient city of Carcassonne. Unloaded, they were sectioned off, but Kit was pulled aside and pushed up stone stairs to a room where he was lined up with others he didn't recognise, perhaps other *maquisards*, or resistance men. They would be in for interrogation, before a certain death.

How sad to know he would never see Flora again in this life. How many of his own group had escaped? Who would lead them to safety? This was the risk they ran, every time they went out on a mission. His luck had run out. When his turn came for questioning, he stood firm. Name, rank and number was all he gave them as he pulled out his old dog tag; the one he could never bring himself to throw away.

'You are a resistance leader and a British spy.'

He replied once more with name, rank and number and was slapped across the face.

'Occupation?'

'I was a Protestant pastor and artist and am now an aid worker at the Camp de Rivesaltes.'

'Enough!' the officer snapped, waving his hand in dismissal. He was hustled to a cramped cell and left there without food and water, for what felt like days. If he was about to die, then he would first cleanse his conscience to a priest, any priest who would listen. When food of a sort was slipped through the hatch, he made himself clear, in both French and German. 'I want to see a priest,' he shouted, wolfing down his hard bread and thin soup. Then he lay back, trying to sleep.

There was a loose nail, good enough to scratch a portrait on the wall of Flora, with her startling eyes and flowing hair, knowing this was all he would ever have of her now. 'Flora, where are you now, my love?' he sighed. 'Sorry to leave you, but fate has not been kind to us, has it?' When he was satisfied with the likeness, he signed it KIT.

Two days later, an officer with a stoop stood in the cell doorway. 'You asked for the priest?' Kit recognised the uniform of a padre, surprised at the prompt reply to his request. He must be close to execution for this visit to be approved. 'Come in.'

'How can I help?' The padre was clutching what looked like a well-thumbed Bible. 'I have this New Testament in English if it helps...' he offered.

'I was hoping to read the Psalms of David, but thank you all the same. It's been a long time since I held one of these.'

'I'm told you were a pastor,' the priest continued.

Kit nodded. 'Many years ago... A lot of water under the bridge since then.' He wondered if the padre would understand this idiom.

'Ah yes, many storms have brought you here.'

Kit looked up in surprise. 'Your English is excellent. My German comes from a school textbook and the Great War.'

'I spent six months in Edinburgh... a fine city,' came the reply.

'I was born in Glasgow, but stationed in the Castle barracks for a while in 1914.'

There was no chair in the cell. The padre was leaning on the wall and stared at Kit's drawing. 'This is your work? Who was she? But first... I am Captain Erich Schultz.' He held out his hand. Kit pointed to his sketch.

'That's my wife, Flora. We've been apart since 1942 and I pray she's in Spain, safe with the children.'

'You have children?'

Kit began to explain about their work in the refugee camps and setting up the children's house near Montze. How an accident prevented him from joining Flora on their journey to safety out of France.

Schultz listened, appearing impressed at his story. 'How come a man doing God's work gets involved with these gangs of terrorists?'

Kit was having none of this. 'One day soon, France will be free, if the rumours I hear... It won't be long, but what we witnessed in those shameful camps was enough for us to stay on, hide and help young men forced to leave their country as slaves...' Kit broke off, anger flushing his cheeks. 'We must do as our conscience dictates, listen within to the promptings of the heart. Only then can we find peace of mind.'

'I can see you were an eloquent preacher,' Schultz replied, eyeing him with interest. 'We must talk again.'

'When will I be sentenced?' Kit asked. Better to be direct, than pretend otherwise.

'That's not up to me. Now I must go. I'll come again, if you wish?'

Kit nodded. This man meant well and his company was better than nothing. Perhaps he might even persuade him to think again about his role within the Third Reich.

Chapter 69

Béziers

Consuela O'Keeffe was waiting at the station in Béziers, waving her arms, so Flora could find her amid the crowds of passengers alighting from the Perpignan train. The journey from Barcelona had been hard with luggage and a baby on her hip so she had stayed the night in Perpignan. Since the liberation in August, the pavements were crowded with a melting pot of refugees, soldiers and people returning home, but she had found a room in a small backstreet hotel. The Tricolor was hanging from windows now that the enemy had retreated northwards. No one could miss the air of relief and excitement in the city.

'Fleur! *Ici! Ici!*' Sam's wife shouted, as Flora struggled with her bag and baby. Consuela took one look at her friend. 'You didn't tell us about this little one in your letter? Wait till Christophe sees his flame-haired son!' She opened her arms to clasp Christy.

'He's with you?' Flora's spirit rose with delight. 'Praise the Lord!'

'Sadly, no… It's been such a long time since we were all together. I'm afraid I have no news of him, but come, come. Your letter was such a surprise. We thought you were safe back in Britain, and all this time living in Barcelona?'

It was Flora's dream that somehow Kit would be waiting at his old friend's house; a silly fantasy that had helped her sleep at night, imagining their reunion. The truth was like a dousing of cold water. She shivered with disappointment.

Once back in Magret, there was so much news to share and it was wonderful to see the old farmhouse again, with its house still full of children. Later, they sat outside at dusk, sipping wine, listening to a nightingale in the tree. For a moment it was like old times. Flora recalled that first visit when she came to confront poor Kit for not meeting her as planned. How her heart melted, to find him so sick.

'I did call in at the children's house, months ago,' said Sam. 'But I must warn you, it was in a sorry state. The last I heard of Kit was that he was in the hills, with a group of young resisters. The village was garrisoned, so I didn't linger. I expect you will be heading north back home, with this little chap?'

Flora leaned back in her chair. 'Not until I know where Kit is,' she replied, having no thought of returning to Glasgow. Her long letter had received no reply, but she had left a forwarding address at the consulate, just in case. Her first priority had been reaching Montze, but Sam had no encouraging words. 'Transport is chaotic. I will take you myself, but petrol is scarce.'

'I wouldn't dream of it.' Money was the least of her problems. Thanks to the consul's office and the British Embassy in Madrid, a bank draft had been released. 'I can hire a car, but I can't believe we are free at last. There are so many friends in the village I must thank. They will have news of Kit, I'm sure. We'll wait until he returns there.'

That night, she slept deeply, waking at first light to the dawn chorus. Everything here was as it always had been. Sam's Irish status had allowed him to stay on untroubled, treating his patients around the district. They owed him so much.

From Barcelona to Perpignan and on to Béziers, her next stop would be to head back to Prades and on to Montze. Now that France had been liberated, it was only a matter of time before the Resistance would disband, before making their way home to their villages. Even now, she could picture Kit, trekking south back to where they would be waiting, back into her loving arms.

Days became weeks, and Kit sat alone in his cell, uncertain of his fate. A brief circuit of exercise in the yard brought news of battles won and a shift in the atmosphere in the prison. There was change in the air; a dangerous uncertainty, as if the enemy was preparing to leave. Worst of all, he could hear summary executions in the courtyard. It must be only a matter of time before he was marched out to face the firing squad.

The old padre appeared with a chess set and some ancient books. Sometimes he left extra bread and welcome cheese. They talked of a world without war and sometimes they prayed together. 'What is happening out there?' Kit could not resist.

Schultz shook his head. 'Better not ask.'

What did that mean? His vagueness unsettled Kit. Each day he felt was going to be his last. 'I must write a letter to my wife. Surely that would be possible, one last wish?'

'I will see that you get permission for paper,' Eric replied. 'If you let me have it unsealed, I will post it for you... I'm sorry it has come to this.'

Was this the sign Kit had been waiting for? His fate was sealed. Flora must know that his last thoughts were of her, and when the padre brought some paper, he sat down to write.

My dearest Flora,

Through the kindness of the padre here, I am allowed to write one last letter. Sadly, I was betrayed, when escaping from a battle and now find myself locked in a mighty prison, within a castle, within an ancient city, that I'm not allowed to name. I am condemned as a member of the resistance group. After my accident, I was hidden in Montze and then spirited away by friends into the woods. In happier times, I would have you laughing at their antics. They were a rabble of young louts, without much aim, other than to escape slave labour, so what could I do but shape them up into a team? We spent the winters holed up in you-know-where. The boys were unaware that it was our home, security was tight and there were frequent raids in the hills, but all that is past history.

In the time I have left, I just want you to know not a day goes by when you aren't in my thoughts. The precious years we spent together, I clutch to my chest with thanks. We made a little world of our own and

367

fulfilled a dream to give children a home and hope for a better future. That my life must be cut short fills me with sadness, but it is out of my hands now.

Be strong, my dear heart, when you hear news of me. Feel free to return to Scotland, back to the bosom of your family. They need not know anything of my own end, or the part I played in delaying your return to them.

Yours for ever

Kit

'Are you sure you want to go back so soon?' Consuela hovered anxiously, as Flora gathered the small pieces of luggage. Sam, true to his word, and despite her protestations, had managed to find enough fuel to fire up his battered Citroën for the journey to Montze.

'Kit might be waiting there, I have to go,' Flora replied.

'You'll need fresh papers to travel. Everything is up in the air, all the rules and regulations are so confusing,' Consuela warned. 'I'd hate you to be turned back, or worse.'

'She'll be fine,' Sam replied, as he opened the car door. It smelt of engine oil and leather.

'*Au revoir* and thank you for everything. One day soon, we'll meet as we did before...' Flora hugged her friend. 'Wave bye-bye, Christy.' Her baby was half asleep on her shoulder.

It was going to be a long journey. They stopped off near Prades, to eat a picnic of green beans in a dressing, bread and cheese.

'Promise us, if you find the house too much, just send word and I'll fetch you back. You will need to register for ration cards. Jerry may have left, but shortages will make life much harder, I fear.' Sam added, 'I will search for news about Kit.'

'We'll manage… if I can cross the Pyrenees on foot, I'll survive now.' Flora felt her heart thumping as they drew closer to Montze. There wasn't time to visit Lise. Sam would be anxious to return home, but the old car climbed up the track as far as it could, until the engine petered out. They made the rest of the journey on foot.

Flora stood outside her door. She could see windows broken and a sad look of neglect. It was just like it had been all those years ago, battered and unloved. She straightened her aching shoulders as Christy woke. 'Let's see the worst…'

Inside was cold and dusty, but to their relief, intact. Upstairs there were signs of occupation. Men had been living there: cigarette butts, broken chairs and tiles were scattered everywhere, but it was still liveable in.

'You can't stay here,' Sam said, 'with a baby!'

'Christy is as warm as toast. I can still feed him. We'll sleep together until I sort out all the stuff we had when the refugee children came. I'm going to stay, Sam. It's been my dream to bring our baby home to where he belongs. It's not as bad as I imagined.' Flora was trying to feel upbeat.

'Are you sure?' Sam was reluctant to leave. 'Let me at least help you draw water from the well and light the stove. It may not work.'

'Don't worry, I'm fine. You'd better get on your way. Thanks for all your help.' But Flora allowed him to bring water and test the stove before she waved him off down the track, glad to be alone at last.

Flora boiled the battered kettle, bringing out a precious

box of tea – a gift from the vice-consul's wife. It tasted wonderful, even without milk. Tomorrow she would give the place a going-over and find the cot and baby chair. Juliette and Flora may have been in a rush to leave, but they still had had time to put away all the children's stuff in the barn, covered over with sacking. Sadly, very little of their baby gear had survived. There were sticks and chopped wood, enough to light a small fire. To her relief, the vandals had not found the bedding hidden in a recess.

Tomorrow she must go down to the village for provisions and surprise Lise. She would also visit the post office, in case there were any letters for them. Tomorrow was going to be a wonderful new day.

Chapter 10

Kit could feel tension mounting in the prison. Guards were yelling and shouting orders. There was a banging of doors, with prisoners screaming and banging at their cells. Whispers went round the cells that Jerry was pulling out. Would they all be released when the jail was evacuated?

Schultz said very little when he came, but his visits, once regular, were now more erratic. Sometimes Kit saw the padre looking at him with concern. Their talks together passed the time. Erich was looking forward to returning home. His son was in the Luftwaffe, somewhere in Russia. And he had four grandchildren. He was a family man, so far from home. His wife had passed away.

Kit shared the real story of how Flora had come back into his life. The padre seemed interested in their rescue of Jewish children and asked many questions. A week later, rumours grew that the jail indeed was emptying. Furniture and equipment were being taken out, but there was still no sign of prisoners being released. Then, one night, there was a clanging of cell doors and inmates were marched out into the darkness. They did not return. Something was happening, something that did not bode well.

Next morning, the new guard shoved Kit's food through the hatch. 'Enjoy this, *Engländer*. It will be your last.'

Kit sat on his bed, winded by this news. He was condemned to die. How relieved he was that Schultz had posted his letter to Flora. At least she would know he was thinking of her to the end. All day he waited for the cell door to be opened. He took comfort from the Psalms, reading them out loud. Then the thud of boots along the gallery announced his turn was approaching. How typical of cowards, to execute men under cover of darkness. He wished he could say goodbye to the padre. How strange it had been to find a friend in such a chamber of horrors.

They were lined up, marched down the stairs. Kit tried not to shiver. His mind was racing with both fear and resignation. *This is it...* He looked out for the padre but it was a Catholic priest who was standing by as they were brought into the yard, to face the wall.

Just as Kit was about to step out into the night air, he heard a voice. 'Not that one... He's wanted, the *Engländer*. He's to come with me.' Kit turned to see the anxious face of the padre nodding, as if signalling to him. 'Come with me,' he said, grabbing Kit's arm.

What was going on? Why had he been singled out? For torture, or for more questions? One of the guards was assigned to escort them. 'Stay close by me,' the padre whispered. 'Don't speak.'

As they were walking, Kit noticed drums of what looked like explosives being shoved into empty cells all along the corridor. They reached the commandant's office. 'You can go now,' said Schultz, dismissing the guard, and he turned to Kit, reiterating, 'Say nothing.'

It was evident the officer was on the move. Inside, the shelves were empty. There were boxes scattered around as the commandant was emptying his desk. 'Yes, Padre?'

'This is the prisoner I was talking about. He will be useful when we move on. He will get the trust of other prisoners and give us vital information. I can vouch for him.'

'You better had, Padre.' The officer scanned the prisoner with suspicion. Kit was now so confused. What scheme had he been rescued for? He bowed his head in submission, as the commandant laughed. 'I don't know how you do it, Padre, bringing these awkward souls round to our side. Has the *Engländer* anything to say for himself, to save his life?' Kit stayed silent. 'Request granted, but get a move on before the fireworks light up the sky.'

'What did you mean, I must be moved on?'

'It's the only way to save your life. They'll take you north, to work in the fields with prisoners of war, to gain their confidence... or not.' Schultz gave him a piercing look. 'Don't you see... what you do there is up to you.' Kit was pushed into a waiting truck, looking down at the padre in disbelief. 'I don't understand, why are you doing this for me?' Kit whispered.

'Because you must carry on the good work,' came the reply. 'Make the most of any chances that appear and may God go with you.'

The late August heat bore down on Flora, as she hung washing on a makeshift line. Her back ached with all the scrubbing and sweeping out, to make the house clean for the baby to crawl over the floorboards.

News of the liberation of France brought relief to the area at last, lifting that dread of denunciation and a knock on the door. Was she no longer an alien? Returning to a welcome in the village was a relief, too. Lise ran to greet her, tears flowing down her cheeks. 'You have come back to us. We heard such terrible tales from Maurice that your guide was a traitor. Don't worry, he was soon dealt with.'

Christy had a clutch of adoring aunties wanting to pat his ginger curls. Lise made up little dungarees and a new coat for him to grow into.

The best news was that Sandrine's fiancé, Robert, had returned to them and that a wedding was booked soon. Lise was busy altering an old family gown to fit her slender daughter. The rest of the guests would make do with their well-worn Sunday best. During every visit to Montze, Flora would call in at the post office, to see if there were any letters for her. After each visit she came home disappointed, convincing herself that the chaos of war was delaying post, especially from her Scottish family. Had they disowned her, or did her letter never arrive? Perhaps she should write again, now that she was settled.

It was a labour of love to restore the house. Christy lay on a rug, in the shade of a tree, watching the leaves rustling above him. He was such a happy baby and now ready to be weaned. Her breasts ached, knowing they would never be filled again. More for her own comfort than his need, she suckled him each night, praying Kit would find his way home. This thought spurred her on to clear out a patch for vegetables, to collect hedge berries and nuts and kindling for their winter's stay. Whoever had left in a hurry had also left a pile of chopped logs, for which she was eternally grateful.

Friday was fish day and a little queue formed to buy whatever the fishmonger had brought from the harbour at Port Vendres. Flora waited in line, knowing she only had enough ration points left to buy the scraps. Then it was time to call in at the post office, but when Madame saw her enter, all heads turned. She shouted, 'At last, Madame Fleur, you have two letters.'

Flora grabbed them in disbelief. The first had a British stamp and was very crumpled. The second trembled in her hand. She could recognise Kit's writing anywhere. *He's alive... he's alive!*

There was no privacy to read them in the street. With Christy strapped on her back with a shawl, she hurried up the track, her heart singing with joy at this unexpected bonus. Putting Christy to bed in his makeshift cot, pouring a glass of cold water tinged with peppermint leaves, Flora sat down outside on the bench to read the first letter, to read this most important letter. The Garvies could wait a while. She could see it had been censored and stamped over. Her fingers trembled as she opened the envelope.

My dearest Flora, through the kindness of the padre here I am allowed to write...

The rest was a blur, as tears spattered the paper. This was a last letter home. Kit was in prison and waiting to die. No, no... surely not? Not now, after all this time, when things were looking good. Her head was swimming in the heat, arms slumped as the letter fell out of her hand. Flora looked at all her hard work, her back-aching toil to make a welcome home for him, and now this... He would never see his son, or even know Christy existed. All she had left of her lover was this precious note and Christy. Like so many war widows, she must face the rest of her life alone. It was just not fair. She screamed, 'Oh Kit, what shall I do next, how can I go on living here without you by my side?'

Chapter 11

It was not the first time that Kit had helped bring in the grape harvest, but this time there were guards with guns, ready to butt any slowcoach. He had been offloaded into a detention camp, guarded by the hated French Milice, ever grateful now for the padre's intervention that gave him this reprieve.

It was good to have the sun on his back, along with fresh and better grub. If you were caught stealing grapes, a severe beating would follow. News came of the blowing up of Carcassonne prison, with prisoners still alive inside. There was nothing left of it but rubble.

Kit could not believe his good luck in being out of the prison before this happened. Schultz's words still rang in his ears: *What you do there is up to you... Make the most of any chances...* At least working on farms provided a chance of better food and conditions. Each week they felt liberation here could not be far away. All the hard graft in the sun strengthened his muscles after his time in prison.

Kit woke one morning to the sound of motor engines roaring into the camp. There was cheering and gunshots. 'The Allies are here! We are free at last!' Prisoners raced to greet them, crying, 'Welcome, welcome!' A bunch of soldiers in mixed uniforms arrived to force open the gates. There was chaos as the Milice tried to put up a brief defence against the odds. And then Frenchmen were fighting each other; all that pent-up fury exploded over the Milice and few survived their beatings.

Kit turned away from such savagery. He was sick to death of all this violence. Now was his chance for freedom, but he did not want to hand himself over to the rescuers. They might force him north and into a camp for displaced people. In the chaos of that first hour of liberation, Kit just walked out of the compound unchallenged. With his jacket stuffed with a few possessions, he headed south down the first country lane where villagers were waving flags and cheering.

No one turned him away when he asked for water; instead they sat him down to share what meagre rations they had scraped together, as if he was an honoured guest. How could he go far without money? In his release from Carcassonne, all his papers were lost. Once more in his life, he was dependent on the generosity of strangers to shelter him, as he made his way down towards the south-west, towards Montze. He earned his bread picking vegetables or fruit, or whatever labour he could find, which delayed his progress. Yet, no matter what, Kit never lost sight of his determination to return and find Flora.

★

Dear Flo,

Blest was the day when your letter arrived. It was as if you came back from the dead, and with such news of your baby and Kit Carlyle. I read each sentence over and over again to Papa. He had a stroke through overworking. Virginia cares for him so lovingly. I do what I can, but with two children and Sandy's hours, it's not as much as I would like. Knowing you will be coming home to us, and bringing another grandson, will hasten his recovery.

Surely it can't be long before this war will be over and we can begin our lives again. I've passed on the good news to your friends, Maudie Wallace and the Murrays. What a story to tell of the good work you two were doing with refugee children.

We can't wait to meet young master Christian Fergus. To add our lost brother's name was so touching. All my news can wait until you are safely lodged with us again.

Passage from France should be easier as restrictions ease. What adventures you will have to share with us...

Flora reread Vera's letter through a mist of tears. It was such a relief to know her irregular life with Kit was no barrier to her return. Vera would not judge her, after all she had endured herself. Now it was time to write another letter, with the sad news that she would be coming home alone. For as much as she loved her house here, without Kit it no longer had any meaning. Hard as it would be to leave all those memories behind, she must look to Christy's future. He must have the best Scottish education and know his wider family. No one need know the exact details of his birthing. She would just be another war widow.

The train to Paris and on to Calais for a Channel crossing sounded simple in theory, but delays and difficulties must be factored in. Christy would not remember his life in France, but one day she would bring him back to show him how they crossed the mountain peaks together, and to find his father's grave. There was only Lise who would really miss her in the village. Consuela and Sam would understand this decision to return home.

Sometimes, in the silence of the evening, she heard again the clack of wooden shoes on flagstones, and saw in her mind's eye the faces of Joseph, Ruth and all the children they had harboured. There were still many displaced orphans needing a safe place, but without Kit she could not face the responsibility of another house full of needy refugees. It was time now to put her own needs first. The prospect of returning to Kildowie was exciting and yet she couldn't ignore a tinge of guilt for deserting her post.

Funny the series of places her life had spanned: from Glasgow to nursing in France, back to Scotland for her marriage to Ivo and working with Rose in the Glasgow slums, helping Vera and Sandy to settle down, then returning to work in Rivesaltes, finding Kit and building the children's house together. Then came the flight with Juliette into Spain and back here, only to be returning once more to Scotland. What a circle of places and people she had encountered on this journey, and it was not over yet. They must stay on for Sandrine's wedding. Even now, Sandrine was helping her with travel permits and all the bureaucracy needed for their journey north. After that joyful event, it would be time to leave Montze for good.

⋆

'Come, Christophe, supper is waiting,' shouted Madame from the farmhouse door. It was over a month since his escape from the camp, a month of foot-slogging from village to town, staying to find food and shelter. Two steps forward and one back, it felt now as if his progress slowed to a halt. Kit did not want to return to Montze as a tramp but respectably clad, clean-shaven, with a pocket full of francs. Until that time, he must earn where he could, and Madame was a generous widow.

'You've worked miracles today,' she said, smiling, as she passed over the tureen of thick soup. 'I don't know what I'd do without your help. It was a blessed day when Our Lady brought you to my door.'

The source of Madame's generous provisions was a mystery but Kit had never been so well fed and asked no questions.

'I hope you won't be offended, but there are a few things you may like to have,' she continued, pointing to a basket full of clothing. 'My late husband, bless his soul, always bought the best quality and you are about his size. Do try them on.'

What else could Kit do but strip to his chest to try on a shirt and jacket?

'Perfect.' The widow smiled. 'Now, when we go into town, no one will guess you are my gardener. It is good to see my cooking has not been in vain. You have a fine figure, for a man of your age.' She was eyeing him with a glint of admiration. Suddenly Kit felt his cheeks flushing with the realisation that Madame had more on her mind for him than clearing out the stables.

'Thank you, but I can't accept such a gift,' he replied.

'Poof… You have nothing on your back but rags. I have no further use for them, so I insist you take them.'

Perhaps you have another use for me? Kit thought, recalling the time all those years ago, when the pastor in the Cévennes gave him his dead son's clothing and another young widow offered herself to him. It was time to make a sharp exit. He didn't want to embarrass the poor woman, but had to admit that a set of decent clothing would be useful, now that everything was so scarce.

Early the next morning, clad in his new outfit, Kit placed a letter of gratitude through the door and resumed his trek west.

Chapter 12

Autumn 1944

The morning of Sandrine's wedding dawned warm and bright. Flora was up early to finish the last of her laundry and bathe in the little stream. On the bed lay her best frock: an extravagant purchase in Barcelona, with three-quarter sleeves, a boat-shaped neck and straight skirt, in a floral pattern. Custom meant that as a widow, she should wear black, but there was something that made her resist this, and besides which, she didn't have anything else suitable to wear.

After weeks in dungarees, it was such a pleasure to feel feminine. Christy was now the proud owner of a go-chair with straps to secure him. After years of uncertainty and worry, years of danger and deception, for once, Flora was thinking ahead. She had wept for Kit, yearned for him, but tears would not bring him back, no matter how many she shed. Christy was her life now.

Today the whole village would be celebrating the young couple's happiness. It was hard not to feel envious. That's enough, she snapped to herself, you've had your moment, so don't begrudge them theirs.

First, though, she wanted to bake bread for their coming journey and decide what she could give Sandrine as a wedding present. In this time of shortages, setting up a home was not easy. Once she left here, there would be no use for anything. The couple could come and take their pick... She paused, smiling, at a brilliant idea. What if they would like to live here? What better place for Sandrine and Robert to begin married life, to bring up children in such a beautiful spot? She could then leave, knowing the children's house would not be deserted, but full of new life. Why had she not thought of this before?

Christy's grizzling broke off her scheming. It was time for his rest. She pushed him in the little pram until he nodded off, depositing him by the cottage door in the fresh autumn air. Now she could get on with her tasks.

As Kit drew ever closer to Montze village, he felt his sore leg grumbling at the long walk. It was a relief to see no damage had been done to the pretty streets. He had passed so many wrecked houses, burnt buildings and deserted streets on his journey here. The village seemed empty, which was strange, but then he saw an old man he didn't recognise, leaning on the bridge over the ravine. 'Where is everybody?' he asked.

'At the wedding,' the man muttered, sucking his pipe and looking at Kit. 'You're not from these parts?'

Kit nodded. 'Just passing through to see my friends.'

'You won't find them at home today... at the wedding, and it'll go on all night.'

Kit knew enough about French weddings to know they were an all-day affair. He was not going to intrude on such a party, even though it was customary to be welcomed to join in the fun.

Perhaps it was a mistake, coming back to where he'd once been so happy, but tired as he was, there was one place he must see for old times' sake. He trudged up that familiar stony track, winding ever upwards, until he could see the red tile roof of their cottage. Last time, he had left in a hurry, abandoning it to the mercy of rain, storms and other men on the run. He dreaded to think what state it was in, but to his surprise there was a little vegetable plot newly dug over. He peered in through the window to see a loaf on the kitchen table and washing neatly piled by the stove, with a line of baby napkins drying on a rack above. So, it was lived in. He knocked on the door, but there was only silence. Whoever lived here now was not at home.

Kit looked up at the old barn with pride. No one would mind if he kipped down somewhere, out of sight? He felt deflated and so weary. After all these weeks of travelling towards his dream, the reality wasn't how he had imagined it to be. That cold splash of realisation washed over him. How could he expect to return to find nothing had changed, that someone would greet him? What was he thinking of? He didn't belong here anymore. Flora would be safe in Spain by now, so it was only right that the house would have new occupants. They wouldn't know who he was. Life had moved on, as it should.

He picked an apple from the tree, only to find it was just as sour as always. He filled his flask with cold water from the pump and turned to make his way towards Maurice's farm. There he would get all the news and be given a bed for the night, but his legs were reluctant to carry on up the stony path. It was no good, better to rest here for a while and pretend that he was back in the old days catching his breath, while the children were playing out by the stream.

Flora felt on edge for some reason. The wedding was a simple church affair, sadly without Father Xavier, who had been posted to a bigger parish. Sandrine looked so beautiful and happy in the wedding dress, while Lise clucked around her daughter with pride. Sebastien returned, taller, thinner, from his escapades with the resistance group. They were a family once more, so how could she not feel envious? Was that what was troubling her?

'Come on, time to take a turn.' Sebastien held out his hand for a dance.

'Thank you, but no, not yet,' she replied, not wanting to stay for the music and dancing. There was a long journey ahead of her, packing to do and a decent rest needed. No one would be offended if she slipped away. Tomorrow she would take a formal farewell of Lise and her family, suggest that the bride and groom might like to take over a cottage in the hills and gift them the furniture.

Christy was much admired, as usual, and basked in the attention, but now he was grizzly, tired and ready for bed. She whispered goodbye to Lise and the bride, who kissed her cheeks. 'You're going too soon... stay on. We're going to miss you so much.'

It was a warm autumn night with a harvest moon as she pushed Christy slowly home. Flora looked up at the leaves, already turning gold. Everywhere looked so peaceful. It was hard to believe that they'd suffered five years of war, with so much loss and grief. She was one of the lucky ones... or was she? Climbing back uphill to the house was never the same; opening the door to silence was daunting. Tomorrow they would begin the long way home, back to Scotland and the family waiting there. At least she would have a roof over her head, when thousands of others would not.

Then her attention was drawn to the shadowy outline of a man making his way towards the farm gate. Who was this stranger, someone bent on looting? Suddenly she felt stabs of alarm. What if he was an intruder? What was he doing here? She made to go back, glancing to see if he was following.

The man turned towards her, hearing the rattle of the rusty pram wheels, and raised his straw hat in greeting, '*Madame*', as she was hurrying away. '*Madame*, please, I didn't mean to scare you. I just wanted to rest.' Then he stopped short, staring down at her. 'Flora, Flora, is it really you?'

There were no words for this moment of recognition, only arms outstretched as she ran towards him. 'Kit, oh Kit... you have come home to us at last!'

Acknowledgements

The seeds of this story were sown many years ago when visiting our friends, Rhys and Kathy Davies, close to Perpignan. They introduced us to the wonderful towns and villages in the foothills of the Pyrenees. We visited what is left of the holding camp for detainees at Rivesaltes (now a museum) where the great injustices that were suffered by adults and children, held captive there between 1939 and 1945, are acknowledged.

Love and War in the Pyrenees by Rosemary Bailey inspired me to visit the Suisse Maternity Hospital at Elne and the International School founded by German dissidents, Pik and Yves Werner at La Coume, Mosset, still flourishing today.

It is from these visits that my research began.

After several books were published and much distraction caused by medical issues, the completion of this book was delayed until the lockdown of 2020–21. This gave me time to polish my story with the help of my agent, Judith Murdoch and my editor, Rosie de Courcy. They took my wayward manuscript and pulled it into shape with some excellent suggestions. I must also thank Liz Hatherell once more, for her excellent copy editing. Any mistakes are therefore my own.

During all this, I was indebted to my local friends: Jenny Hall, Kate Croll, the Northern chapter of the RNA and my 500 club friends, Trisha Ashley and Elizabeth Gill for lifting my spirits at a difficult time. As always, I rely on the loving support and encouragement of David and my family.

It was also hard finishing the text without the presence of my faithful companion, Mr Beau. He left us in March this year. The loyal friendship of a dog is one of life's treasured experiences. He is sadly missed.

Leah Fleming

For further reading

Reed, Walter W., *Children of La Hille,* (Syracuse University Press, 2015).

Bailey, Rosemary, *Love and War in the Pyrenees,* (Weidenfeld and Nicolson, 2008).

Thalheim, Werner, *Une communauté d'antifascistes allemands dans les Pyrénées orientales (1934–1937),* (L'Harmattan, 2014).

Castanier I Palau, Tristan, *Femmes en Exil, Mères des Camps: Elizabeth Eidenbenz et la Maternité Suisse d'Elne (1939–1944),* (Trabucaire, 2008).